Interior Format

DEFIANT RUIN

The Asarlaí Wars Book Three

MARIE ANDREAS

BOOKS BY MARIE ANDREAS

THE ASARLAÍ WARS
Book One: Warrior Wench
Book Two: Victorious Dead
Book Three: Defiant Ruin

THE LOST ANCIENTS
Book One: The Glass Gargoyle
Book Two: The Obsidian Chimera
Book Three: The Emerald Dragon
Book Four: The Sapphire Manticore
Book Five: The Golden Basilisk
Book Six: The Diamond Sphinx

THE ADVENTURES OF SMITH AND JONES
A Curious Invasion
The Mayhem of Mermaids

ACKNOWLEDGMENTS

Nothing about writing is easy, but it is amazing to be able to create magic. However, this creation could never happen without a lot of folks behind me.

I'd like to thank Jessa Slade for editing magic—as always, she understands my ramblings in makes sense of them. Thank you to the amazing Jill Smith for the back copy blurb. To my most awesome team of beta readers/typo hunters who plowed through the entire book and helped tighten it up: Lisa Andreas, Lynne Facer, Lynne Mayfield, and Sharon Rivest. And a special extra thank you to editor/proofreader extraordinaire Ilana Schoonover-thank you for being as fast and as good as you are. Any remaining errors are mine alone.

My cover artist, Aleta Rafton, for creating yet another awesome work of art. And to The Killion Group for their always perfect and timely formatting of the entire book and print cover.

In memory of two dedicated fans of the written word—
Tom and Libby.

CHAPTER ONE

———◆———

VAS TRACED THE LONG SCAR with the tip of her finger. It ran along Deven's ribs, crossing his olive skin almost from front to back. It was far more faded than it had been, and was one of the few still visible.

"That actually tickles," Deven said. He rolled over and wrapped her fingers in his. "Why are you still awake?" His green eyes were half closed, his thick black hair mussed from more than an attempt at sleep.

"They're fading, all of them. Soon they'll be gone." Vas pushed herself up on one elbow. "And we'll still be trapped here."

Deven pulled her closer. "That was as close to melancholy as I've heard from you without your being drunk." He peered into her eyes. "You're not still drunk, are you?"

"No. Probably, no." She swatted his arm and rolled off the cot they shared. She had hit the bottle fairly hard before coming out here to the *Warrior Wench* to work on the ship. Deven had followed her and she found more to vent her frustration on than a broken ship.

That had been almost fifteen hours ago. As if just reminded they should be sore, all of her muscles suddenly hurt. She wasn't still drunk, but this place was getting to her.

The *Warrior Wench* was mostly in shambles, as much from the final attempt at landing a crashing ship as being torn apart in the gate. Miraculously, no one had been killed in the landing, many injured; including the ship itself, but no one died.

That was the only good thing that had happened since they crashed through the gate, leaking fuel, almost six months ago. Or five months and twenty days if one was keeping count. Which she was.

"We will get out of here," Deven's voice was less sure than it had been just days ago. And the slight pause before he spoke said far more than his words.

Vas heard the cot move as he got up to join her. They were in the medical lab. Chunks of the ship were still open to space, but a few internal areas had been spared. Leaving the rest of it open to the elements saved energy as they made repairs.

The med labs were more secure than any other place on the ship and had survived with their full self-contained power. Even though Vas had been out surveying the area around them not a day before, she called up the screen to the outside as she did every morning. It helped focus her on getting out of here.

A ruin-filled landscape, devoid of life, spread out before her. The structures were far older than anyone had ever seen—and even Deven had no knowledge of the people who left them. The system they'd been flung into was so far off any charts, not even Gosta knew where they were.

The largest surprise, once the horror of being marooned in a strange galaxy had faded a bit, was that some of the buildings were still airtight. From what Mac and his team of explorers had seen so far, the air of this planet had gone bad long before the beings who lived here had vanished—or died.

That meant securing the surrounding structures for living spaces had been possible. Food still had to be created here on the *Warrior Wench*, finding only poisonous plants meant nothing to eat, and the air was deadly. They'd managed to survive…but they wouldn't be able to for much longer.

Deven reached around Vas and shut off the screen. "Are

you trying to undo all of the good I just did?" He kissed the side of her neck, but Vas knew he was doing it to distract her. The situation they were in was a romantic mood killer for anyone.

"I just don't know how we can get off this rock." She pushed away from him. "This ship might fly again, at some point. But even if we get her back up—where do we go? The gate is still sending off unstable readings and while your people might wander space aimlessly, mine don't."

He reached over and put on his pants. A good idea, but it still left his naked chest to distract her. "I didn't think you had people," he said without malice.

That had been an ongoing discussion—Deven pointing out that her crew; those here and elsewhere—were her family, her people. She kept reminding him she didn't have family and the one she did had tried to kill her. Before they unceremoniously blew up, along with her home planet, twenty years ago.

"Fine. I have people." She gathered her own clothes and put them on. "And *my* people aren't going to be roaming around some unknown galaxy in a wounded ship. Are we going to hope we can get to a system with inhabited planets and, what, beg for a way home?"

An explosive rumble knocked her to her knees before Deven could respond.

Vas scrambled up and grabbed her blaster. Then she hit her comm. "Mac? Gosta? What the hell was that?"

"Not sure, Captain," Gosta's voice responded, but she heard Mac in the background. "It came from the buildings past the perimeter."

The screen in the med room didn't have the far range that the ones on the command deck had—at least not until more repairs were made. Vas grabbed her breather and tossed one to Deven. The air within the other parts of the ship wasn't as dangerous as the outdoors, but still shouldn't be inhaled without the small breather masks.

Pretty much that meant every place except the med lab, the kitchens, the command deck, and a partitioned-off part of engineering.

She ran to the sealed door. It had taken two months to fix the damage enough for anyone to be up in the command deck without suits, but that hadn't slowed Gosta down. Mac was there most days as well. Even though there was nothing for the crack pilot to do on the deck of a dead ship, he worked on trying to scan for any other ships. There was still a chance that Ragkor and the crew on the *Victorious Dead* had survived being thrown out of the damaged gate as well and Mac might be able to find them.

The way to the command deck was far longer than before and involved climbing through access tubes. Gosta had told her the lifts worked, but Vas wasn't about to waste the energy they'd burn to use them. The emergency tunnels extended and sealed off the access tubes but she and Deven kept their breathers on.

They'd set up seals for each of the functioning areas. Once Deven and Vas came out of the access tube, she resealed the tube behind them, waited ten seconds, then unsealed the one leading to the command deck.

There was no way anyone could have thought this was the command deck of a functioning ship. Anything that hadn't been originally shattered on impact had been ripped apart by the repairs. One of the things that had survived intact, just no longer connected to any weapons or commands, was her pristine command chair. Vas hadn't sat in it since they'd crashed. She told herself the only way she'd go back in that chair was when they were lifting off this forsaken rock for good.

The larger screens were still down, but Gosta had both of the nav screens up. Unfortunately, while she could now see a growing plume of smoke, she couldn't make out what or where it was. "What's our intel on that quadrant?" When they'd first crashed, she'd made sure that scouting teams went far and wide looking for any sign of life. Deven and Mac had led the longest scouting trip—a week out and a week back going a different direction. They brought home the devastation of this world—there was no sign that anything sentient had been here for hundreds of years.

"Not much," Gosta said. "There were heavily-damaged ruins there, sunken in low. Not airtight." He paused as he read off the list. He looked up with a grimace. "It appears they could have been the remains of an abandoned mine."

Vas swore. Mines were never good and abandoned unknown ones could be catastrophic if they hadn't been closed off properly. They had no idea who had been on this world. Aside from it having been sparsely populated, dead, and abandoned a long time ago—they really knew nothing.

"We should have spent energy on scanning those areas better." She wasn't reproaching anyone but herself. They'd scouted the areas, yes. But she'd had to limit what they used. There was still a lot of power left in the *Warrior Wench*, but if they drained her too low, they would lose all chance of getting off this rock. Being stuck here was causing her to miss things.

"Should we send a team out?" Gosta asked, but Mac was already moving for the door.

"We don't have a choice," Vas said. The plume of greasy looking smoke was growing. "Deven, take Mac and Bathie, I'll meet you on the way out. I have some things to check before we go." She saw Mac slow down. The man's face was such an open book it was amazing he had survived this long. He was happy to be going, bummed about her and Deven leading. Not to mention him and Bathie were off again. But Vas wanted her out there as well. Bathshea was an engineer but like many of her crew, had been branching out to new studies. Geology was her latest. Mac could just deal with having his on-again-off-again lover along.

Deven watched the smoke for a few moments, and then

turned to follow Mac out.

Vas felt an odd tingle. "Wait, take Walvento too. He's been bored and maybe getting out will take care of his need to blow something up." The weapons master wasn't called on that often if they weren't on a job, but he got itchy if it went too long. Besides, having extra weapons along couldn't be a bad thing. Just because there hadn't been signs of life the first hundred times they looked wasn't a reason to become complacent.

She raised her hand as she marched over to her ready room. "No, it wasn't a premonition—just a good idea." She didn't look at Deven but she saw him pause before he and Mac unsealed the tunnel, then move on. Deven was sure that Vas had developed some skills of precognition. Or had them all along and was just now showing them. He mostly kept his theories to himself, but she'd noticed him and Terel dropping low-level conversations a few times when she'd come into the makeshift medical rooms in the ruins. She was going to have to nip that collaboration in the bud.

The door to her ready room was forced open—it hadn't fared well in the crash and then had been forced aside by Gon. She really should just have him take the door off completely—he'd used a little too much force on it, and at this point the door wasn't anything but a chunk of useless metal. Sort of the story of her entire ship right now.

She shook her head and went for the secret drawer in her desk. Deven was right—she was becoming melancholy. Either she needed to drink more, or go set up some more time with her mind-doc. Part of the problem was that Vas was physical, very physical. She wanted to be doing things, not tinkering around a ship. There was only so much sex could do to relieve stress. And while Deven was an extremely energetic partner—she did need more than just that.

She needed to find someone to fight. Or blow something up. The holodeck still functioned, sort of, but the energy it took was way too high to even consider it.

She holstered her extra set of snub-nosed blasters and looked at her swords. Chances were if there was anything out there, shooting it would be the better option. With a sigh, she closed the drawer on them.

Deven and the team were ready and waiting by the ramp. Since the *Warrior Wench* was designed for planet landing it had a crew-loading ramp. One that mostly survived the landing, but Gon was able to force it completely back into place. Vas was willing to overlook the new bumps it had.

A fully suited-up Walvento stood at the top of the ramp with a huge blaster in his arms and his helmeted head systematically turning to view everything around their ship. As bad as not having a ship to fly was for Mac, it was ten times worse for Walvento. They'd verified repeatedly there was no one alive left on this rock beyond their crew, but you wouldn't know that from watching him.

Walvento was mostly human but he was close to seven feet tall and made Deven look like a kid next to him. He rarely spoke nor smiled—but he was doing the latter now.

"Captain, the area is secure. But there could be hostiles in the vicinity of the explosion—we can't get a fixed reading." As he spoke, he kept scanning the horizon.

"Thank you, Walvento." Vas said. "I want you to take lead, keep your comm open the entire time." They'd been going easy on the comms due to power rationing, but with the still solid stream of smoke wafting from the area, it would be good to have him on open mic. He wasn't impulsive normally, but almost six months of enforced down time could change that.

Everyone finished getting their full airsuits on and she nodded to Mac to follow Walvento. He didn't say anything, but moved quickly. Bathshea shook her head and followed.

"I take it you and I will fight for the guard?" Deven matched Vas's steps. She'd been planning on bringing up the rear herself, but wasn't going to argue the point—not this time anyway.

"Nope. It's all yours." She patted his faceplate and followed Mac and Bathie.

The terrain hadn't changed. Vas guessed it hadn't changed in the hundreds of years it had been abandoned. The buildings were stuck in a state of slow decay. Their original designs, or what was left of them, were functional rather than beautiful, and made of stone, brick, and an odd metal. Higher doorways indicated a non-human race, but aside from this being an outpost of some sort, they still hadn't figured out who had lived here.

The area around the smoke was barren except for a single massive building. Possibly where whatever was being mined had been processed. She was going to need to send a team out to do a better study of the mine. After they resolved this current crisis.

The entire group froze as Walvento raised his right fist up in the air. Vas couldn't see what caused him to stop, but his abilities were why he was on this trip. Two fingers to the right, two to the left, and one forward. The building had an open passage, one that might have started as a door, but now went clear through the building. Vas might be the captain, but whoever had point called the shots. Walvento was going into the building; she and Deven would go around it to the left. Mac and Bathie had already split off to the right. They might be on the outs romantically right now, but that didn't stop them from working together.

Vas and Deven were almost to the opposite side when they heard crunching stone—Walvento hadn't waited for the other two teams but went out as soon as he cleared the building. Vas swore under her breath. Bored or not, that was a stupid move and reduced the impact of having the team split up. She and Deven moved faster but they still weren't around it when a new explosion flung chunks of stone in the air.

CHAPTER TWO

———— ✦ ————

V AS DIDN'T FALL THIS TIME, but both she and Deven rocked a bit then quickly moved away from the building. The explosion had come from the front of it, near the bottom. Right where Walvento was.

Bathie and Mac rounded their side at the same time but she couldn't see Walvento. She reached up to tap her comm when his tall shape rose up, shaking off debris.

"Sorry, boss, Captain," he rubbed his helmet. "I took a hit."

"Damn it," Vas said. "Next time you obey protocol or there won't be a time after that—no matter how long we're stuck here. Are you okay?"

She couldn't see his face but the head bob was chagrined. "Aye, Captain. That explosion was the crashed ship settling. Not a weapon, I don't think."

"There was a ship? Damn it, why didn't our scanners pick that up?" Vas stepped closer to the pile of metal and stone in front of Walvento. The vessel had been a small one, therefore easy to miss. Still, she'd have to get Gosta and Mac on fixing that glitch immediately. Then she held up her hand. "Move back. What's that ticking?" The sound was low and with debris raining down, she hadn't heard it at first. But there was a steady ticking coming from the pile.

Mac stepped forward and scanned the area. "It's nothing we have to worry about."

"So the ticking isn't a bomb?" Vas would have said she was certain that even her crew would overcome their extensive curiosity and run if the scanner looked like they were facing an explosive. But the gleam in Mac's eyes even through the faceplate made her question that.

"Not a bomb, that's the remains of a homing device. It's too damaged, so it's slowly dying. But something called this ship here." He held up a piece of metal. "It was a Fury."

Vas looked at the mess before them. If Mac said it was a Fury, she'd take his word for it—but there wasn't much left but a pile of twisted metal.

Deven took the piece then nodded. "It's a part of the weapons console, but I don't think there's enough metal here for a full Fury. And definitely not the missile bank. It's as if it was sheared off before it crashed through the gate."

Vas said a silent prayer to the deities at that. The missile bank of a Fury was massive and unstable. "Part of a Fury crashed here on purpose?"

Deven was gingerly shifting through the mess, but pulled back. "Mac is right. Something pulled the ship through to this planet and it's a descending autolock. The pilot was most likely dead before they even came through the gate."

Vas pointed at the mess before her. "Did the gate do that?"

Bathie had been doing her own scanning. "I think so. There's gate residue all over this thing."

Mac swore and stumbled backwards. "Damn it!"

Vas stepped over. The pilot was there, or what was left of him from the waist up. The black suit of the partial body told her who was behind it.

"The Asarlaí's henchmen had a reconstructed Fury, one that was programmed to come here, even through a shattered gate. Why?"

Deven looked at the buildings in the distance and started swearing in a few languages. "Because this piece of crap planet was *theirs*."

"This planet was an Asarlaí home world? When? When they were dying out?" Mac waved at the buildings around them. "This doesn't look like any Asarlaí work they showed us in primary vids."

Vas agreed. They had no idea who the planet belonged to, but the long-dead-but-now-coming-back homicidal Asarlaí wouldn't have been on her list of suspects.

Deven had stopped swearing but was peering into the wrecked ship. "This might have been a staging area. Something to launch their attacks from. But this is definitely not good." He pulled out a lump of metal from the wreckage.

Bathie moved forward. "A Starchaser propulsion shaft?" She looked into the mess before them, but Deven must have found the only remaining intact piece—well, mostly intact. There was no way that Vas would have known as quickly as those two that it was a Starchaser part. He handed it to Bathie.

Starchasers were deadly fighter ships that the Commonwealth had been developing in secret. At least they had been before the Commonwealth government imploded on itself.

The fighter ships were also something that Vas had found in the storage area of her new ship—the *Warrior Wench*. Or rather, a whole lot of parts were there. No intact ships unfortunately. While it was considered treason to own any part of the secret ships, she just hadn't been able to force herself to dump them. Not to mention, things had been a bit hectic when she found them.

"So they were using Starchaser parts to rebuild Furies?" Vas said. "There's no way that's a good thing. And it definitely reinforces the theory that the Commonwealth, or part of it, is working with whoever or whatever is bringing the Asarlaí back." A shudder went through her as she recalled those massive Asarlaí warships above the destroyed planet Mayhira. Right before she ordered the *Warrior Wench* and the *Victorious Dead* to flee.

Marli and her crew had also taken off—Vas assumed the Asarlaí woman joined her surviving crew on a stolen frieghter before they gated out of there. A combination of some serious hits to both ships and damage to the gate had flung both the *Warrior Wench* and the *Victorious Dead* into unknown space. At least she hoped her final command to Ragkor to get out of the gate at the first slip had saved them. Hopefully, they fared better than she and her ship had.

"But why here? It's a dead planet." Mac had grown bored after the initial excitement and was looking for something to poke through.

"It was on a homing trajectory," Bathie finished whatever she had been scanning and looked around. The pinging beep was slowing down significantly.

"Identify. Code five-two-eight. Identify."

Vas jumped, thinking the destroyed black suit had come back from the dead. But the mechanical voice was coming from the wrecked console. It then repeated in three more languages that her translators couldn't process.

From his new round of swearing, Vas knew Deven understood at least one of them.

"Identify. Code zero-two-eight. Identify."

"Okay, what is it asking for? From who? This thing doesn't realize it pulled the ship to a dead world?" Mac had picked up a thin piece of metal and looked ready to poke the wreckage. Vas snapped it out of his hand.

"Incorrect. Identify. Code zero-zero-eight. Identify."

Vas held up her hand to keep everyone quiet, then motioned to back away.

"Identify. Code zero-zero—"

"Run!" Vas yelled as she made for another building, but nothing was close enough to protect her.

The explosion behind her swallowed any replies her team made.

Silence never felt as loud as it did right after that explosion. Vas assumed the mic on her helmet and comm itself still worked, but a roar of nothing filled her head. She hadn't made it completely to the ruins, but only a few chunks of building hit her. With any luck, the explosion had been absorbed by the remainder of the building. The only pieces near her were small.

Including a shard of metal that had gone through her suit and a good few inches into her right leg. Adrenaline masked the pain, as well as the fact she was losing air. But that wouldn't last long. Removing the shard might actually make things worse; at least now there was something blocking part of the hole.

The dust and smoke dissolved quickly, but she still couldn't see her team.

"Can anyone hear me?" The roaring silence responded. Chances were she'd taken a hit to the comm mic or her ears were temporarily blown out from the explosion. Even if someone did respond, she wouldn't hear them.

Her leg was starting to burn and the air was thinning.

Vas forced herself to get up and move toward where she'd last seen the others. Movement would shorten her air supply, but having longer to breathe was useless if she couldn't get back to the ship or the habitable buildings. It had taken fifteen minutes to get here; there was no way she could limp that long while losing air.

A shape rose and slowly shook itself out of the debris. From the height, it was probably Bathie. While they were too close of a size for her to carry Vas, she'd be a perfect size to lean on.

Vas tried the comm again, but heard nothing back. Bathie turned to her anyway, so maybe it worked.

Bathie seemed fine and Vas could see her mouth move, but she couldn't hear anything.

She did see Bathie's eyes go wide as she pointed to the shard sticking out of Vas's thigh. The pain and lack of breathable air was already hitting and Vas leaned forward a bit. Bathie caught her and Vas felt vibrations as the other woman was clearly yelling.

Still couldn't hear anything.

Deven arrived first. He was covered in soot, but his suit, and body, appeared intact. Mac and Walvento were behind him. Walvento was limping a bit, but it looked like Vas had been the worst hit.

Deven tried talking to her but she shook her head and tapped the side of her helmet. The rest could obviously hear as Bathie pointed down and explained. Even with the helmet on, Deven's face went noticeably paler as he saw her leg.

Without waiting for her to suggest a plan, he picked her up and started running toward the *Warrior Wench* and their compound. He must have given a command to the others—Mac followed behind them, but Walvento and Bathie turned and went back toward the explosion site. They were out of sight before she could see more.

Even though he was being as careful as possible, there was no easy way to run with a person in your arms—especially a wounded one. Vas knew they needed to get back before the air became a problem, but each pounding step was reverberating through the shard in her thigh.

"*I've got you,*" a voice said. A voice from inside her head. She looked up to Deven's face; injured or not she was going to rip him a new one if he was using his telepathy to soothe her. They just kept fake esper bracelets on him—especially once he pointed out the real ones hadn't worked for him anyway. But they hadn't mentioned that to the crew. Most of her crew had been around Deven for years and trusted him with their lives. But they also believed his esper talents were blocked.

But his focus was on the uneven terrain ahead of them, not her.

"*You will be fine. Follow your training.*" There it went again.

"*Who is in my head? And what the hell are you doing there?*" Vas thought back.

The laugh that bounced around her skull was immediately familiar. Mother Aithnea of the Clionea nuns. "*You never were this dense when you were a child.*"

Great. Not only did she have some probably contaminated metal spearing through her upper leg and poisoned air shutting down her lungs—now she was losing her mind. Aithnea died, along with her order of warrior nuns, months ago defending the location of an ancient weapons cache and Vas.

"*And you were never a telepath. And you're dead. I saw the vid thanks to you. You died before I could come save your ass.*" Crazy or not, Vas was going to give this mental figment a piece of her mind. Aithnea had raised the young and wandering Vas when she ran away from home. Brought her in to live with her order of Clionea nuns. Then kicked her out two years later. Not having a chance to save them had pissed Vas off more than the ensuing grief had. Well, almost.

"*Surprise.*"

Vas swore as Deven missed seeing a rock and they both lurched forward.

"*I can explain later, but there is more in the air than you know. Use your healing training to slow down your heartbeat and breathing. Or you'll be joining me far too soon.*"

"*Ha! You* are *dead!*" Vas wasn't happy about that situation, but in the past few months she'd come to terms with it.

"*There are many layers beyond living—as if this man saving your life wasn't an example. No time to explain—trance. Now!*"

Vas had been young when the Clionea nuns took her in. Rebellious and homeless, she was running from people who wanted her dead—or sold off. That those people were her family hadn't sat well with Aithnea once she heard the story. Vas had never been a novice but helped around the convent for her keep. And she had to sit in on all novice classes.

When Aithnea, or whatever trick of her mind was acting like her, shouted 'trance' Vas's response was swift and automatic. Her pulse slowed as the words of the mantra spread through her. Words she would have denied recalling a moment ago if asked, but now flared to life in her mind. She no longer felt the pain from the leg injury and the burning in her lungs eased.

Deven must have felt something change in her body as he looked down with terror. She wished she could tell him she was saving herself, not dying. But her mental communication seemed to be limited to Aithnea.

He sped up and Vas felt a floating sensation fill her. She hoped this was part of the healing trance the nun novices had been taught. But since she never actually did more than watch, she wasn't sure.

"*Is this right?*" she asked, but the voice inside her head was silent.

Deven slammed his palm on the lock to open the airway into the ship. Vas imagined the sound of it sealing, but she still couldn't hear. The inner chamber opened quickly.

Deven's comm must have been working fine, as he rushed to the med labs and Terel and her assistant Pela were both there.

"—don't know what happened. She just went limp." Deven's voice was jarring as her helmet was removed and she could hear again.

"S'okay. Trance," Vas finally got out. She didn't think a religious trance should leave you feeling drunk, but it was better than the alternative. She thought she heard Aithnea's laughter but it was faint and vanished before she was certain.

"She's in a trance? Did you put her in one?" Terel quickly looked down to the false esper bracelets on Deven's wrist. But Vas knew her friend was aware they were fake.

"No. Nuns." Words were like rocks in her mouth but she was afraid if she pushed too much harder the pain was going to slam back.

Terel squinted at her. "Nope, she's not making sense. Hopefully she can hear me better than she can talk. Vas, I need to put you under. And a full breather on."

Vas really tried to fight the trance to yell no. She hated being knocked out. But the trance state had a mind of its own.

"*Seriously, when did you become so damn stubborn? Let her fix you.*" Aithnea's words were faint but clear, and the mocking tone Vas knew well came through easily.

"*But bad things happen when I'm put under—it's not good. Why can't I break free of the trance?*" It said something, although Vas wasn't sure exactly what, that she could form words and sentences in her head, they just couldn't get past her mouth.

"*Your mind knows what needs to be done—listen to it. Good night.*" The words faded as Terel placed a breather on her face. Slowly the world faded from view regardless of what Vas wanted to happen.

———◆———

"I know you're in there, I can see you twitching. The surgery was fine, your lungs are fine, and you're just being stubborn." Terel's voice was outside of Vas's head, but many of the words echoed Aithnea.

Vas preferred to think of her behavior as determined, but if others wanted to call it stubborn, so be it. Terel was correct though, she was conscious. She didn't feel anything different in her leg—most likely a numbing agent was still in place. She wanted to sort out the whole dead-person-talking-in-her-head issue before paying attention to the pushy live doctor hovering over her. But there was no reaction from the voice in her head.

"*Do you have anything else to say?*" Vas felt odd asking it in her head, but not as odd about who she was trying to talk to. Silence greeted her. Maybe the entire episode was a result of whatever weird crap was in the air outside.

She waved her hand toward Terel's voice and opened her eyes. "I'm here. You know I don't like being knocked out for this crap. You could have just numbed the leg."

"Thank you for saving my life, Terel; you are such a good friend and an amazing doctor." Terel raised her voice in a complete mockery of Vas's and put her hand on her hips.

"Fine. What you just said. But why?"

She dropped her pose. "It was more than just the leg. The particles in the air, if that's what you want to call it, outside are bad—but whatever exploded near you made it worse. I had to purge your lungs. Even you wouldn't want to have been conscious for that."

Vas had tried to roll off the med bed as Terel spoke. The stabbing in her chest confirmed Terel's words. "Damn. That hurts like—"

"Captain, we have a problem," Gosta's voice from the med lab comm cut her off. Before Vas could question his observation—they'd had many problems since they crashed here—he went on. "That ship was programmed under an ancient guidance system to return to a home base. This was obviously—well, it's obvious now with the new data, but it wasn't before, I can assure you—an Asarlaí home base. When you didn't give the coded response, it was triggered to explode."

He was talking way too fast. Even if Vas hadn't just gone through hell and a visit from the dead she'd find it hard to follow. "Okay, so they had a tracker and defense that led them to a world they'd abandoned hundreds of years ago. How is that an issue for us? We should be concerned that they didn't update their homing in the past thousand years?"

"No, no. I think the damage the ship took before it entered the gate caused it to revert to here. It had been overlaid with a new location but that information is lost. The problem is—they did it to all of their ships. Or so my calculations tell me."

Terel helped Vas finish sitting up and swing her legs over the side. The wounded thigh was stiff, but all holes had been fixed.

"Gosta, I know this is fascinating, but why does this make our lives worse than they were? Keep in mind; I've had a pretty bad day already."

"I do apologize. The problem is, this ship, our ship, was being prepped to become part of the Asarlaí fleet. You've been out for ten hours, so there was time to study it. If this ship was to be one of theirs, and it came here because of the reset…"

Vas's mind was still foggy, but even she filled in that gap quickly. "Crap. How long do we have before we explode?"

CHAPTER THREE

TEREL HADN'T BEEN FOLLOWING THE conversation closely enough and jumped. "What? Why would we explode?"

Vas heard Gosta take in a deep breath for another lightning fast explanation, but she beat him to it. "The bastards rigged their ships to return to base—any base apparently. Including this one. If the countdown is triggered and the countermand isn't given, the ship explodes—I assume through something planted along with the homing device. How long do we have, Gosta?" Vas hobbled past Terel to the door. "What's the countdown like?"

"That's just it, Captain, we've scanned everything, and we can't find it. There's not a sound on any spectrum and considering how noticeable it was on the smaller ship—they want it to be noticed."

"If we were going to explode, wouldn't it have happened five months ago?" Terel asked as she tried to block Vas from leaving.

Vas batted her away. "I'm fine. I will be fine. You had me here for over ten hours—what more could go wrong?"

"Fine. Gosta, you and Pela are witnesses. If the captain falls on her ass, leave her there because she's *fine*. Now why didn't we explode five months ago?"

"I've been working on that. My theory is that we damaged the countdown device when we crashed. It never got a chance to start counting down. The bomb with it, however, appears to be fully intact."

Vas paused on the edge of the door; her urge to get to

the deck was slowed down. "So, if we fix this damn ship, and get it to lift off, we could be releasing whatever is holding this device inactive?"

"Aye, Captain."

She sighed and nodded to Terel. "Thank you for saving me, not sure how long it will hold, but thank you." With another sigh and shake of her head she slipped on a breather and left the med lab to make her way to the deck.

There was no one else in the hall so she stopped for a moment, then paused and shut her eyes. *"You know, if you aren't just a figment of my mind, showing up and helping us find and defuse a ship destroying bomb would be a great way to prove it to me."* She cracked open an eye. Not that it mattered, but she hoped that closing them might make the voice clearer. Or just point out there really hadn't been a voice at all. She gave up and walked to the emergency tube to the deck.

If anyone other than Gosta had said he believed that the Asarlaí, or their agents, had claimed this ship as theirs before she got it, she'd have laughed them out of a space lock. But Gosta was good. And it fit with how she got it. Skrankle had taken apart her prior ship, the *Victorious Dead,* on the orders of someone much higher in the food chain than him—and he'd been retrofitting the *Warrior Wench* at the same time—also under orders of someone far bigger than him. Someone who'd blown him up when Vas took over the ship.

By the time she climbed up to the command deck, Vas was exhausted, had a headache, and still hadn't heard a peep from that voice in her head.

But there was plenty of noise coming from the command deck. She cleared the second layer of doors and removed her breather. No one noticed her for a few moments but it was mostly because the majority of her command staff, and a few non-command staff, were all up there. Even Xsit was at her station. Flarik had bumped Gosta out of his primary spot, but his secondary screen was up so he crowded next to her.

"What are you all doing?" She was shocked she hadn't heard them all when Gosta had called down before. It had taken about five minutes to get up here, but this many people couldn't have come over from the crew quarters in the nearest building in that time. Over the past few months, most of her crew had stayed in the building they'd modified unless they were doing work on the ship.

Of course her crew was nothing but helpful, so all twenty or so of them responded at once.

"I have a headache already," Vas said cutting through the din. "One of you. Flarik? You're the most rational of this bunch." She ignored Gosta's flash of hurt, but rationality fled when he was on an academic search.

"Thank you, Captain." The Wavian lawyer smoothed her pristine white feathers with a small, clawed hand. "Gosta notified us about his theory of the Asarlaí, their homing ships, and the explosions, a few hours ago. We've all needed something to work on beyond ship repairs, so many of us ended up here."

"Gosta, you were right!" Mac's voice came through the comm. "We're in engineering and these Starchaser parts have been modified. Deven says they look like Fury modifications."

Vas held up her hand to the command deck then tapped her comm. "Mac? You and Deven are exploring the Starchaser parts? The ones I had sealed into the bulkhead?" It had taken a few hours to get all of the ship parts hidden so they wouldn't be visible on any scans. Hours that those two would be taking care of after this.

"Captain, we thought…that is…Gosta suggested…" Mac floundered a bit.

"Vas, you were unconscious but recovering, and we had no idea how long it was going to take to sort this out. I authorized the search and examination of the parts and the data from the ship that exploded," Deven said.

"Fine. I would have done the same thing. And if we aren't going to blow up for the moment, it might be a good idea to find out as much as we can about those parts and their connection to the Asarlaí." She looked around the deck; she knew Deven did what he did for the crew as well as finding things out. There was an urgency to the activity that she hadn't seen in over four months. When everyone realized they weren't getting off the planet anytime soon.

"Captain? Gosta?" Xsit chirped as she looked between the two of them. "I think I found something." Xsit was a Xithinal, a small bird-like race. She was also their communications officer and it said a lot that even she was so bored she'd come out to search. She enjoyed down time.

Gosta and Vas moved to Xsit, with Gosta actually taking a step back and letting Vas go first.

"This is the launch gear on the aft side. It's showing some unusual readings." Her voice trailed off as Vas peered closer. There was a signal there. Partially dormant, like a program running in the background on an old computer but not actively engaging in anything. A string of letters crawled along the bottom of the screen.

"Deven, you guys have a working monitor down there, right?"

"Aye, Captain."

"Tell me what you see?" She sent the recordings and images from Xsit's monitor to his. He'd spent years around Marli before Vas even knew who she was—he'd seen more Asarlaí script than anyone on her crew.

"It's the device. Enough of it got damaged that it's not picking up the landing, so it thinks it's still in space."

"Damn it." Theory about the Asarlaí and this ship was one thing, and Marli had always seemed far too interested in and knowledgeable about this ship. But knowing it was something else completely.

"I'll see what I can grab from my scans before the other

ship exploded," Bathie said from one of the crowded monitor stations. "My team and I might be able to pick out codes to defuse it. When we're ready to lift off."

Vas flashed her engineer a sincere smile. Both for the work and for believing they would get off this damn rock. "Thank you. And good hunting, Xsit, on tracking it down. The footprint for that thing is tiny and would have been lost in the running of the ship. Now, did anything else happen while I was being saved by our doctor?"

"We brought in what we could from the explosion, mostly dust fragments. Aside from the two pieces Bathie brought back," Mac said.

"And I think I've broken down some of the dust. The genetic material matches what we had on file for the black suits." Terel hadn't said anything prior, but she'd probably had the comm open the entire time. She'd probably also been working on that dust the moment she'd gotten Vas stabilized.

Vas waited for her to finish; there was something else hanging there that she knew Terel was holding back from saying. "And?" she finally asked, filling in the silence.

"And the genetic markers match the ones I lifted off Marli."

"Well, didn't we already think the black suits were genetically related somehow to the Asarlaí? Since it looks like, judging by what we saw, the demise of the Asarlaí was mis-represented, this isn't too surprising."

The pause on the other end was noticeable enough that the entire command deck went silent.

"It's not just that it's Asarlaí—I'm still running the results, and I want it noted by all of you, because I know you're listening, that I won't know for sure for at least another few days—possibly much longer."

Damn it. Terel was never holding back about her finds—unless it was bad.

"I will go down there and drag out the information if I

have to."

There was a heavy sigh. "It appears that the black suits are related to one Asarlaí. Marli. Her genetic code is extremely prevalent in what I've found so far."

"She made them?" Deven cut in with a tone of disbelief. "I've known her for twenty years—she's a lot of things, but a mad woman creating a homicidal death squad isn't one of them."

Vas wasn't happy about this either—she'd trusted Marli. Within reason, but the woman had saved their asses more than a few times. But she was an Asarlaí. There was no way to know what type of person she had been before the self-imploding genocide that everyone believed had destroyed her entire race. "What if she did it before you knew her? Like long before?"

That didn't fit either. Marli had appeared genuinely upset and shocked when her people appeared. And she'd shown no sign of recognizing the black suits.

"No. Possibly. Damn it, I have no idea. I just think I'd have noticed."

"Did you ever read her?" Touchy subject, but she needed to know. And before he'd joined Vas on her crew, Deven had been far more open about using his gifts.

"I couldn't. The first time we met she'd been wearing her disguise. I followed her because I couldn't read her. Later I found out why. A much higher-level telepath might be able to read one of her people—but that would be far beyond me."

The silence on the command deck broke, as everyone had to voice their opinions.

"People, you are getting ahead of yourself," Terel cut in. "That's why I didn't want to share this with you. We have minimal information about their species. Even if this matches her completely, there could be subtle changes that affect the results. It might not be her at all."

"Captain," Xsit broke in. "Captain?"

Vas turned away from the rest of the mob. She'd deal with the implications of Marli and the black suits once they had more information.

"Yes? Did you want to weigh in on this too?"

The light-yellow feathers on the back of Xsit's head fluttered—her version of looking embarrassed.

"No, Captain. But there is a ship coming our way. A big one."

CHAPTER FOUR

—————

"A SHIP? CRAP. HOW LONG AGO did we pick it up?" She really missed the large front screens they had. Without them, Vas was stuck hovering over the smaller screens. "Is it coming through the gate?"

"No," Gosta spoke before Xsit could respond. "The scanners look like it's coming from deep space. They only showed up a few minutes ago, but they were hard to pick up."

"Want me to go out and greet them?" Mac's voice was far too excited and Vas couldn't blame him. He'd probably have already run up here except Deven would have made him secure the Starchaser parts. Most of their complement of Flits had survived the landing, but with limited remaining fuel, Vas had cut off all recon runs after the first week.

Gosta was hovering over his nav screens, ignoring the chair behind him. "Even though I repaired the scanners, I still can't get a clear reading on them, Captain. They're coming in fast but might not even be heading for the planet. They're still too far off to determine the destination."

This was a dilemma. Vas had never hidden from anything in her life and she wasn't planning on starting now. The scans when they first got here had found no habitable planets in this system. The other ship could just be passing through and couldn't use the gate. However, the *Warrior Wench* had almost no defenses left—nothing beyond the fuel-burning Flits in the hold. But if whoever was out there wasn't an enemy, they could provide some much-needed help for getting out of this hellish place. Without blowing up.

She watched the screen in front of Gosta. The ship was moving fast, he was right about that. She had a bad feeling about what was heading their way. Nothing specific, just a crawling sensation between her shoulder blades.

"Damn it, we need to get stronger eyes on them before they get here," Vas said.

Mac came running onto the deck so quickly he stumbled out of the interior door. "The Flits?"

"Hold on, fly boy." Vas turned to the communications station. "Xsit, try to hail them. Just a general call, keep the location scrambled."

Xsit sent it, but a few minutes went by and no response. At a nod from Vas, she sent it a second time.

Vas looked at the screen again, then to Deven who had followed Mac in and nodded in agreement. That the ship hadn't responded meant they weren't friendly or couldn't pick up the weaker signal. Granted, a ship from a completely different galaxy could have radically different communications. She doubted they would be that lucky.

"Yes, grab whoever you need." A chill hit her as she watched the unknown ship approach. "Actually, get all of the Flits up. Grab what intel you can send us. If things go in the shitter—you run."

Mac had been halfway to the door when her words hit. He turned, his joyful smile gone. "Captain? Don't you want us to come back? We could defend you."

She ignored Deven's raised eyebrow and Gosta's scowl and waved her hand at her pilot. "Do what I say. Just be prepared for the worst. If I tell you to scramble—your team runs and hides. We have no idea what their weapons are, but I'm not losing our only transportation and weapons at this point. Hide and come back if you can." There was no way twenty Flits could defend against a ship the size this one appeared to be. The more she watched, the more she realized it was a cruiser. Almost as big as the Asarlaí warships that chased them out of the quadrant. The only good thing was that their scanner hadn't identified it yet—and it would if it was an Asarlaí warship.

Deven and Mac left, with Bathie trailing behind. She'd looked like she had wanted to say something, she wasn't any happier about Vas's command than the other two.

The remaining shuttle had been destroyed in the landing or Vas would have sent up more people in that. This wasn't going to end well.

"Now you start listening to your intuition? After two years of me trying to train you?"

Vas grimaced. The time for the voice to pop up was when she'd been alone, not when fifteen or so crewmembers were watching her for instructions.

"Ya know—not helping. Unless you can take your out-of-body self and find out who that ship is, I'll thank you to stay quiet."

"Captain? What did you want us to do?"

Damn it. She'd lost whatever Gosta had said. The tone of his voice said that wasn't the first time he'd asked that. As the voice in her head wasn't responding, she went back to focusing on the current crisis.

"I want you, Xsit, and Flarik to keep watching that ship. I know we don't have full library access right now, but do what you can to identify that ship." Gosta had downloaded a complete, and completely illegal, copy of the Commonwealth library a few months before they got stranded here. Access to some of it had been compromised in the crash—at least temporarily. Considering the state of the Commonwealth when they'd left, this partial version might be the only version left.

"The rest of you, get over to the building, find everyone who isn't getting ready for Flit duty. Get them armed and inside the ship." She tapped her comm. "Walvento, we'll need access to all of the functioning weapons—even the secret stash. I'll be sending people down to you."

"Deven was already here. Grabbed some blasters and said you'd be calling. I'll be ready."

"Thank you," Vas said. "Now the rest of you, prepare to fight. We have no idea if that ship is good, bad, or worse than the Asarlaí—be prepared for the worst."

The rest left and she turned to her remaining three, Gosta, Flarik, and Xsit. She handed what weapons she had to them. "I need you three to keep searching. We are cutting this close—if they are friendlies we might not get another chance for help."

"And if they aren't, we are prime victims." Flarik took two of the snub blasters and secured them in her clothing. She normally didn't use weapons. It wasn't for lack of training—everyone in Vas's crews knew how to use a wide range of weapons. It was that as a non-com in the crew she wasn't called on to fight much. Plus, her claws and a few thousand years of her people being the apex predator in her home star system meant she didn't need them often.

Vas nodded. She'd have preferred to have been up with the Flits, but as captain, she needed to be the face of her crew if things went bad.

There was no way the Flits could lift off without being noticed, but she hoped that she'd sent them out early enough that the other ship wouldn't realize what they were. The way the *Warrior Wench* had landed, rolled on her side instead of her belly, had luckily spared the landing bay. However, it was still hard getting ships that were designed for space launches to take off from a planet.

Vas let out a breath of relief when she saw the first group of four take off. She hadn't given them instructions, but most likely Deven had. As soon as the first four were up, they split in different directions, becoming less noticeable than a clump of ships would.

She turned back to the screen, tracking the approaching ship when the second group also got underway.

"I'm still not pulling in any identification, Captain."

Gosta didn't even look up as his long fingers raced on the screen touchpads.

"Neither have I, but there is something odd about it." Flarik leaned closer into the screen, as it was already as magnified as it could get. "Something isn't right."

Vas had been using one of the empty stations but moved over to the one Flarik perched at.

"Not right in what way?" It looked right to her. Even if the feeling of foreboding was growing in the pit of her stomach.

"I don't know." Flarik tilted her head and peered intently at the screen. Vas was sure that back in her days as a corporate lawyer that same look had caused hardened businesspersons to crumble.

"It's having problems." Xsit had been quiet after her initial observation; Flarik was a bird of prey and even though their races hadn't come from the same galaxy, the lawyer always terrified the meek Xsit.

Flarik tapped the screen and spun with a toothy grin toward Xsit. "Excellent observation, fledgling. Yes, they are coming in fast but not completely of their own will. Gosta, switch your screen to lower level five with a thrankian filter."

Gosta looked flustered but quickly did it. "How did I miss that? Well, it is an issue that really wouldn't have been visible until just lately." He looked up with a frown. "I do apologize, Captain."

"Never mind that, how badly damaged is she? And do we have any matching intel at all?"

"Nothing on the damage. The engines appear to be malfunctioning but the movement is too deliberate for them to be completely out of control." Gosta was clearly upset about missing the damage to the approaching ship, but he had enough sense not to deal with it now.

"They are definitely heading for this planet, however." Flarik scowled at the screen.

"I have the registry…it's from the Beline system." Gosta looked over with a frown. "Isn't that your home system, Captain?"

Vas rubbed her arms at the shudder that went through her at the mention of the name. "That was where I was born, yes. But my planet is gone now. Rather, it's a drifting mass of lifeless rocks. My family died with it." She shared a look with Flarik. Her brother Borlan had survived up until a year ago when he helped a band of Rillianian pirates try to take Vas's crew and ship. Flarik ripped his throat out. With Vas's permission, of course.

Flarik met her eye but said nothing. She'd agreed that she didn't understand, nor did she want to understand, Vas's family dynamics. However, she understood when a sibling had behaved so abhorrently that death was the only option.

"That system doesn't have any ships of that size—not anymore." Long before Vas was born the Beline system was an emerging power player. Not her home world—that had always been a backwater crapstand. Nevertheless, for a brief moment in time, the other two planets fared well. Then they got into a pissing match over mining rights on her home world and destroyed themselves.

"How old is the registry on that?"

Gosta typed furiously. "Eighty years—eighty-three years and two months to be exact. It's listed as the *Defiant*."

Vas racked her brain. "*Do you have any ideas? Is this a ghost ship? Are you dead returning for good now?*" No snarky voice responded.

The last grouping of the Flits cleared the planet. Vas knew that without a doubt the one hanging closest was Deven. Giving in to her feelings for him might not have been the best thing for either of them. But she refused to change a thing. She just hoped his recent need to protect her didn't overwhelm the larger need to protect the crew.

"Captain, the *Defiant* was recorded as destroyed eighty-two years ago," Gosta added. His fingers were still flying across the pads and she had to guess gathering intel on that ship wasn't easy. He kept flipping between what was on the view screen and his monitor with the library connection.

"That looks pretty solid for a ghost ship." Vas hit her ship-to-ship comm. "Deven, the approaching ship is an eighty-year-old dead thing from my former home system. What are you all seeing up there?" Normally she'd just have the full comm open so the Flits would have heard what was happening on the command deck. Unfortunately, while they did have some comm systems functioning, that element hadn't been restored yet. Pretty much the Flits could talk to themselves, and, one at a time, could talk to the command deck—but they couldn't do both.

"Interesting. Explains the parts. Mac is closest to them and he said the readings are scrambled, as if it's made from a number of ships." Deven's response was distracted. "And it's coming in too fast. Definitely heading for the planet, but still no indication up here that it's seen you or us."

It would be too much to hope for that the *Defiant* was running blind, but it was possible. Especially if it was a monster ship. Combining ship parts wasn't uncommon in the outer rim, but most ship designers worked extremely hard to make their ships as disagreeable with other design-ers as possible. Which often led to horrible accidents.

"Captain," Walvento called up from the weapons area. "I can fire one volley of missiles. It's the only thing I have left that I can access, but we can fire."

Vas watched the ship approaching. How in the hell did a ship from her home system, reconstructed or not, end up in this unknown area of space—exactly where she was? There weren't that many of her people left anywhere, the odds of this happening were huge. Too much weird shit had happened in the last few months for her to ignore any unlikely coincidences.

Flarik and Gosta both turned to look at her in the silence. If they fired and the ship wasn't hostile, they'd have wasted their last active missile rounds. Not to mention, shooting potential assistance out of the sky wasn't a good way to get help.

Problem was, Vas wasn't good at asking for help.

"On my mark, fire." She flipped back to Deven. "Walvento has a missile cluster up—our only one, but it's up. I'm going to have him fire if that ship doesn't respond in the next minute." As she spoke she nodded to Xsit to send another round of bounced hails. The closer the ship got the harder it would be to keep their exact location hidden through the bouncing.

"Understood. There's something wrong with that ship; keeping it off world is a good idea. I'll have the rest of the squad pull back and come down." Deven's telepathy didn't usually work that well with the shielding on the Flits. That he was picking up something—even a vague something— was enough for her.

"Pull back, yes, but stay up there. I don't want those ships trapped down here if things go sideways."

Silence at first, then finally, "Yes, Captain." He wasn't happy about staying up there and, in his mind, out of harm's way. But that was tough. Lovers or not, she was the captain.

"Walvento, fire."

CHAPTER FIVE

A NUMBER OF THINGS HAPPENED AT once. The *Warrior Wench* rocked as Walvento fired the weapons. The Flits weren't as heavy in the weapons department as a Fury, but they were damn fast. They all scattered, as if choreographed, away from the approaching ship as Walvento's missiles went toward it. A bright light filled the command deck—before any impact from the missiles. And Flarik screamed.

Vas had seen Flarik go through many things—screaming in fear wasn't one of them. Xsit ducked below her console, but Vas had a feeling it was more because of Flarik than the light. Or even the series of explosions that followed, on the screens, as the missiles struck the *Defiant*.

The light was still flooding the command deck, coming from all directions and none, but by looking down, Vas made her way to Flarik. The Wavian was crouched low, almost like Xsit, and peering over the console at her screen in horror. Even with the light, Vas saw a shape emerge from the exploding ship. Huge, ethereal wings seemed to come from the sides, then they vanished, and a burning, out-of-control ship was now heading for them.

Vas touched Flarik's shoulder. "Are you okay?" Flarik's eyes were wide but she gave a tight nod. Vas tapped her comm; the glowing invasion of her command deck was fading in most areas except the command chair. "Deven, are you all okay up there? We've got some issues down here."

"W- do- ow, where th—"

The static, probably an offshoot of the explosions, cut him off finally. She took a deep breath; she'd have to count on him keeping the Flit squad safe. And himself.

"I need all personnel to report in, stay where you are, but prepare for hostiles." The *Defiant* was slowing down. The engines had most likely been Walvento's target, but it had already gotten too close. It was a toss-up right now if it would crash to the planet, or just stay tumbling around it.

"We're all here, Captain." Hrrru's calming voice through the ship comm brought relief. The small, furry Welischian had taken unofficial command of the building compound not long after they set it up. The warrens and tunnels made him feel at home.

"Thank you." Vas turned toward Gosta, who was still frantically trying to bring up something on his screens. "Any idea how this light is in here?" Now that it was fading it was even more of a mystery as to where it came from.

It still bathed her command chair.

"No, Captain. And I can't calculate why the *Defiant* is acting like it is." He tapped his screen. "It took hits, heavy ones. It had shields but they collapsed when the first missile hit. And it's coming down with more control than I'd expect."

"Xsit? I need you out from under your console. Keep trying to reach Deven or any of the Flits. You'll have to try them one at a time but keep trying. Until we know where that ship is going to crash, I want them to stay up there."

A soft, "Aye Captain," was followed by Xsit slowly climbing out. She carefully kept her eyes fixed on her screen.

Vas quickly looked to Flarik but she seemed to have recovered. At least whatever had caused her to react like that had been suppressed for now.

Vas turned to her command chair. The flare of light was gone from everywhere but there. Slowly a shape appeared within the glow. Vas drew both of her blasters. "There's someone there!"

Immediately, everyone except Gosta and Xsit drew weapons and held them on the chair. The shape was only now becoming recognizable—a biped of about six feet tall. But not solid.

"A hologram? Marli?" Vas knew one being who was an expert at holograms—their missing Asarlaí companion.

"I'm much better than her. Great to see you," the voice was masculine and familiar. "*Sister.*" It started to solidify—to change from being a hologram into something far worse. Somehow her damn brother, Borlan, had survived being killed at least twice. Vas wasn't going to let him come back a third time. She fired both weapons and was joined a moment later by Flarik.

The image had started to become opaque, but was now fading into a hologram again. "I'll return…what did you do to my ship? You bitch!" Another round of blaster fire pushed the partially solid being back but he vanished on his own a moment later.

Her command chair didn't fare as well and collapsed.

"I will find him and rip him apart slowly this time." Flarik's clawed hands clenched. Whatever had freaked her out before, having someone that she had justifiably killed come back from the dead—to threaten them again—pulled her completely out of it.

"The *Defiant* is moving off. Well, changing direction. Sort of." Gosta looked up, flustered. "It looks like the Flits are nudging it with weapons fire."

Vas spun. "What? That shouldn't be possible. Xsit—did you reach any of those maniacs yet?" The whole issue with her dead brother's repeat performance and just which ship he'd been talking about would be dealt with later. There was no way an army of Flits could push off a crashing ship, let alone only twenty—what the hell did Deven think he was doing? And a glance at the original trajectory showed it wasn't going to hit them anyway. Now it was going even further out.

"I can't reach any of them, Captain." Xsit still wouldn't look up from her console.

"*You're welcome,*" Aithnea's voice was barely more than a whisper in her head. "*Resting now.*" Then she was gone.

"Captain? You've gone pale." Flarik stood next to her and Vas wondered when she'd moved. She reached back and pulled herself into the station chair behind her.

"Yeah, I think a bit too much excitement after the hole in my leg." It was a weak excuse coming from her and she knew Flarik didn't believe it. But they both had things they weren't ready to talk about right now, so the lawyer wouldn't pry.

Vas had been ready to write off the voice in her head as just a delusion. However, one that could get twenty small fighters to push back a crashing heavy liner? No. Even she knew there wasn't a way to pass that off and she didn't even have a degree in physics like half of her crew.

"Captain, I have Deven." Xsit seemed a bit more centered now that she had a focus.

Vas nodded and took the comm. "What in the hells are you doing up there?" Reality was settling in. They still had no way off this rock and now had blown their missiles as well as the firepower of all of the Flits.

"Hey, you're the one who told me to do it. I have no idea how you knew the exact locations to hit that would push it off course, or even that you knew there was an H-ling gas mine right where it was heading, but it worked."

Vas swore under her breath. If the *Defiant* had hit an H-ling mine this close to them, the entire area would have blown up. She was glad that the comms between the entire deck and the Flits didn't work. No one else heard his end of the conversation. "What did you tell the others?"

Deven laughed. "No offense, but I just told them that was what we were doing. I'll give you full credit once we get back there. And then you can tell me how you knew that would work."

Vas's head was spinning. She couldn't tell him any such thing. At least no one else knew about it. "Excellent work on turning the ship, Deven. Come on back." She raised her voice a bit for the rest of the command deck and Deven got the hint whether he could read her at that distance or not.

"Aye, Captain. I'll bring the kids home."

Vas slid back into her borrowed chair.

"Captain? Is everyone well?" Hrrru's voice broke into her thoughts and she fought to keep from laughing hysterically.

"It looks like everyone is fine. Except for my command chair. Damn thing was too ostentatious anyway." She really fought to keep from laughing at that. Once she told Deven what was going on he might lock her up—she would if the roles were reversed.

Flarik must have heard something in the tone of her voice, as she faced Vas with a raised feather brow.

Vas gave a tight shake of her head. She and Flarik would either keep ignoring each other's secrets—or have a big showdown later.

A rumble rocked the ship. "I take it the *Defiant* has crashed?" It wasn't as loud or powerful as she'd expected.

"Yes, Captain. I'm not sure how it did this, but it didn't explode and is mostly intact. There are no signs of life however."

Vas stared at the screen even though nothing was visible at this distance. Aithnea had pushed it pretty far away. She wasn't surprised at the lack of life; she'd be more surprised if there were actual dead bodies on it. Borlan must have come from that ship, but he'd been a hologram—or at least started out that way. It appeared his image was becoming far too solid for her liking before she and Flarik fired on him.

Vas nodded to Gosta. "When the Flits have all landed

and checked in, get a crew together, and prepare to head out to the downed ship. I'll be leading. Two hours." She got up and automatically stepped toward her ready room. Then she recalled there wasn't a door on it. For the first time in the past five months, she needed it. With a shake of her head, she went for the exit instead. "Have Deven meet me in engineering." She slipped on her breather and left before Gosta could ask questions.

CHAPTER SIX

———◆———

THE LONG WINDING PATH TO engineering gave Vas time to think. Not as good as spending time in her ready room would have, but sitting in there with no door ruined the solitary effect. It wasn't lost on her that when she first took over the *Warrior Wench*, the thing she'd missed the most about her old ship had been the ready room. She couldn't even pinpoint the moment when the ready room here became as important to her—but it had.

After five months of doing nothing except mind-numbing repairs, she suddenly found way too many things to think about. In addition, she had to figure out how to tell Deven he'd been guided in an insanely impossible maneuver by the voice of her dead friend. That was going to be fun.

The passageways were empty, which was standard now. As much repair work as could be done, with what they had, on this level was finished weeks ago. They still kept the tunnels up to keep the air levels low to save energy. Same with the lighting. Skulking about the dim, tube-filled hallways of her ship was not improving her mood. But engineering was the most private and intact area she could think of.

The lights were off when she entered, but like most of the rooms on this level the door was left open. A few commands and she had resolved both issues. Full lights showed her that Deven and Mac hadn't been as good at stashing the ship parts as she'd hoped. Everyone had gotten lax being trapped here. She started to put them in a more secure spot, and then held one.

Vas loved ships and she could repair them. But she didn't have the passion for the small pieces that some of her crew did. At first glance, the dark metal looked like any other ship part. She knew it was a Starchaser part because of the design. To be honest, she couldn't tell the part was modified because, like most people outside of the secret ops side of the Commonwealth, she hadn't seen enough of them to know.

Once it was pointed out, subtle changes could be seen. It wasn't so much that she knew what they *should* look like, it was more that whatever this piece originally was, changes had been made.

At this point, they had no idea if the Commonwealth even existed anymore—or at least not as it once was. The Commonwealth controlled the Starchasers and these parts had been modified to work in ancient Asarlaí fighter ships. She had no idea where to go with that thought, but it wasn't good. She carefully laid the piece back with the others.

All her adult life, she'd been a merc. Working for herself and her crew. Fight where they were paid to fight. Simple. Clean. Understandable.

Then they fought to stop an invasion from some supposedly long dead homicidal beings who'd almost destroyed the Universe once. Not clean, nor simple, and sure as hell not something she understood the full impact of. And they failed. They'd stopped the Asarlaí from building a portal out of an exploding planet. They saved lives. The Asarlaí came through anyway. Shutting the portal might have slowed down a full invasion, but obviously massive ships had been taking the long way around for an extended time.

Now they were stranded in goddess knew where. She had no idea where her other ship was or if they had survived leaving the gate like they did. The entire Commonwealth, including the bulk of her people back on her planet, Home, could be on the shit heap for all she knew.

And the voice of her long lost, and very dead, friend was playing around with her head and the laws of physics. She leaned back and closed her eyes.

"Now that was a sigh with a story behind it," Deven's voice brought her eyes open, but didn't improve her mood as much as it should. He was another issue. She'd always lived by the rule that you never get involved with a telepath or a crewmember—and here he was an insanely powerful telepath and her second-in-command. And she was not only involved with him, she'd fallen in love.

"Bastard."

"Wait, what?" Deven looked around as he shut the door behind him. "What now?"

"I just realized that breaking my rules started this entire string of events." She held up her hand. "Okay, logic dictates that's a fallacy, but right now it works for me. None of this would have happened if I hadn't slept with you." It felt wonderful to be so illogical.

Deven laughed and pulled up a chair. "Am I supposed to run down all the shit that obviously took place long before you seduced me? Or just play along?"

Vas watched him for a moment. She still didn't even know what his real species was. The man was sharing her bed and her heart, and yet couldn't exactly answer how he came back from being blown to pieces—partly because he wasn't completely sure himself.

"You are just too complicated to deal with right now." She shook her malaise off and waved at the Starchaser parts. "You and Mac figure out anything more about these?"

Deven took the shift with a raised eyebrow. "Not really, except that Mac thinks these might have been the test parts. There are one or two there that look like they were made at the factory like the modified ones. But none of them look exactly like a Fury part—they just do a similar job."

The question he really wanted to ask—how she was able to have them move that heavy liner away from them—hung in the air. That he wasn't going to ask out loud forced Vas to do it.

"How'd pushing the *Defiant* away from us work? Find a nice safe crash zone?" There wasn't going to be an easy way to bring this up—hence privacy and isolation.

Deven narrowed his eyes and folded his arms. "It worked well, far better than I could have imagined given your original suggestion. Which, judging by the attitude right now, I'm thinking wasn't yours at all."

"No, it wasn't. It wasn't me. I've been hearing a voice in my head since I got that piece of metal stuck in my leg. I think it's Aithnea." There it was, out there. Crazy or not, the voice in her head had saved her, and possibly everyone on the *Warrior Wench* and the buildings next to it. Vas just hoped it really wasn't a sign of madness—or worse. Telepaths could get inside a person's head and while the voice had helped them so far, that by no means meant it was benign.

"That's...odd." Deven held up his hand. "Yes, the entire situation is odd, but the voice I heard over the comm was definitely your voice. It wasn't in my head. And while death might be more fluid than we thought—Aithnea *is* dead. I saw the vid. And I know she wasn't my species." The last bit was added awkwardly. He still wouldn't discuss the return-from-the-dead aspect of his existence.

A chill went through Vas. Did whoever was behind this want to make her think it was Aithnea reaching out from beyond oblivion? Breaking into a secure comm line might be harder than breaking into someone's head—except the comms were mostly down and with everything that had happened to the ship, she doubted they were that secure any more.

"We won't discuss people coming back from the dead right now, but so far there is nothing beyond a disembodied voice. It talked me into a trance when I was having trouble out there."

"You mean when you were dying?" He leaned his chair against the table that still had some Starchaser parts.

"Having *trouble*. But the larger issue is moving the *Defiant*. I'm pretty certain twenty Flits couldn't push something like that off course—even using all of their weapons."

"Agreed. That was an issue for all of us up there, but I think the others believe that I somehow helped things along." He tapped the side of his head. "Everyone seems to be happy I'm back, but I have gotten a few sideways glances."

"The Commonwealth trains them to believe telepaths are dangerous. Your coming back from death sort of emphasized there's something not normal about you—even for an esper. But since you and I know you didn't figure out how to move that ship, that means whatever is behind this voice is something other than a ghost." She winced. "Oh, and we have a second ghost." It took a few moments to explain about her brother and his third attempt at death.

"Your poor chair," Deven finally responded. "Okay, I'll continue to let folks believe I might have had something to do with helping the *Defiant* relocation—but it drained me too badly and I can never do that again. We can't have the crew believing I'm magic or something."

"Were you able to pick up anything before we shot at the *Defiant*? Life signs?" She dropped her breather over her face and moved toward the door. As much as some more time to sort things out might be welcome, she needed to get ready to take a crew out to visit the *Defiant*. She felt fine, but she knew Terel would either come with or send a medical nanny along. Unless she could get out there before Terel caught her.

"There were no signs of life, even before Walvento's excellent shots. We could scan it, could have even communicated with it had there been anyone there—we just couldn't talk to anyone down here on the surface." He frowned and slipped on his breather. "It was as if we were being blocked."

Vas didn't like where that was going. A being strong enough to move a heavy liner, with nothing but some small fighters and their mind, could have easily blocked communications had they wanted to. Which raised the question of why they would want to. Vas couldn't come up with any good reason for that.

"I assume there's no way you'd stay on the ship for this?" Deven's comment was halfhearted as he followed her through the tunnels.

"What do you think?"

She could hear the shrug even though she couldn't see him. "Oh, I knew. I just wanted to be able to be honest with Terel when she rips me apart later on."

They were both silent as they went down to the weapons section. Vas didn't know what Deven was thinking about; she was still trying to come to terms with Aithnea, or a being trying to make her think they were Aithnea.

"Did they really have to use all of the weapons? All of the Flits are drained." The complaining started in the weapons room before they even shut the doors and removed their breathers. Walvento's domain wasn't really repaired. Well, it was in his mind—things more or less worked, they were just all rigged with cables and wires crossing everywhere.

Vas was actually grateful for his terse reaction at their appearance; she wouldn't have seen him otherwise. He wasn't small by any means, but he had stuff piled all around him as he worked.

"Would you have rather that the ship landed on us?" She stepped over a pair of low hanging wires to join him.

"Or hit that mine and blown all of this to hell?" Deven added as he stayed near the door.

"There could have been another option." Walvento looked at both of them and finally shrugged. "Or not. I don't know what we'll do when we need weapons though. If we get off this rock, we're going to be dead lumps until we can find our way back Home."

Vas peered at some of his equipment—not all of it had survived the crash, nor was repairable. And there was no way he would let go of it. "Too bad there's not a similar class ship nearby that might have functioning weapons, compatible ammo, that sort of thing." Walvento was a weapons snob—he only did major repairs and refurbishments at Home.

The options weren't good right now and from the look on his face, he was figuring that out. Walvento wasn't stupid—Vas didn't bring anyone on board who was dumb—but his thought process worked a different way than hers. His face almost lit up as he followed through her thought.

"You might be right, Captain." His fingers flew over the station panel. "The *Defiant* was a Gamma class, one level higher than us, and while probably modified significantly, still should have some things we can use." He looked up with as close to a full, real smile as she'd probably ever seen on him. "I will include Gon and Marwin. We can have them bring a wagon."

Some crewmembers might get a swift kick for deciding whom else they would include on her trip—but with him, it was fine. She'd turned him from bitchy to excited and now had a chance at gathering some useful parts from the downed ship.

"Now that it's settled, I want to have way more fire power this time when we go out. What do you have down here?" Vas knew Walvento would be protective of the hand-held weapons, but getting on board with the salvage trip got him to relax a bit.

Once she and Deven were massively over-armed, they left the weapons room. Walvento was right behind as he went to go find his fellow salvagers.

"Mac is going to be disappointed if he's not included," Deven said.

"He needs to get over it. I know his job has been compromised by us not flying, but there are other things to be done besides wander this rock. He's damn good at repair too."

"Who? And why didn't you tell me you thought you saw your dead brother and that you now think you're going traipsing across the planet?" Terel was waiting for them at the top of the ramp off the ship. She only had a breather on, but she blocked the lockers for the full suits. Since the med lab currently wasn't the haven Terel knew and loved, she only came out to the *Warrior Wench* when there was an injury. Clearly she'd been on her way back to her rooms in the nearby building when she heard them.

"I did see him—Flarik can vouch," Vas said. "And he's not dead yet. Or they have clones. Or hologram replicas. You should work on seeing if there is any sort of genetic evidence at the scene of my chair." That might distract her.

Terel opened her mouth to argue but Deven got there first.

"Vas needs to go to the ship. She's fine." Deven never stepped in on Terel's turf, unless it was about his own health. That he was doing so now was shocking to both Terel and Vas.

Terel narrowed her eyes. Vas was certain she knew the exact placement of her lips, but the breather covered them. "I knew it was only a matter of time before he started defending you against even me. Fine. But I will be asking Flarik. And I need you to take this hypo." She handed a small case to Vas, then plucked it out of her hand and pressed it into Deven's hand instead. "No, you keep it. Pela and I created these—the idea being they could help deal with this air if we had to stay here longer than expected. The testing scans true, but we've haven't run any subjects yet. Vas's lungs are not fully recovered. If she starts to relapse, or anyone else has a problem—hit them with it. It's good for six pre-measured doses." She dropped her nagging and went to fully concerned medical officer. "Don't need them."

CHAPTER SEVEN

W ITH THAT OPTIMISTIC NOTE, TEREL turned and marched down the ramp and out the first set of doors.

"I can't claim that it says a lot that my medical officer doesn't trust me to carry a hypo. But I am glad she backed off. I was afraid she'd insist on joining us." Terel could be a mother hen, but after the initial injuries from the crash were taken care of, there hadn't been much for her to do in the field. It was only natural she'd be a bit concerned. Still annoying as hell though.

Deven stepped into his full airsuit; taking care he tucked the hypo securely into an outer pocket. "I think it says more about her faith in your willingness to use it on yourself. You have a track record of disregarding the good doctor's orders about yourself. This way, if need be, I can stab you."

Vas was going to argue, but he was right. She always felt Terel was too cautious. "Just make sure I'm dying before you hit me with it." The new airsuit she was using was a bit large, but there'd been no way to save her original one.

Walvento and his crew, the massive Gon and the heavy planet worlder, Marwin, joined them as she finished securing her suit. "Captain! I have two of the wagons ready for use. Might we take them both?" The tone of Walvento's voice was more like a six-year-old child on his naming day asking about his presents than a hardened weapons master.

His wagons were a collection of parts he'd salvaged from the *Warrior Wench* as well as the wrecks dotting the land outside. She knew he'd been working on a number of them, each slightly different, all designed for the awkward terrain of this world. She didn't realize he had two completed ones however. They weren't enclosed, but travelling in them, at least on the way out, would be better than walking. The *Defiant* was a good hour or more away by foot.

"Agreed. We ride out in them and if we find enough to salvage we walk back and let them haul it." It only took a few moments for the three men to get their airsuits on—Vas figured if the other two took longer than he did, Walvento would have dragged them out half dressed.

"Captain?" Mac's voice in the comms wasn't terribly unexpected. "Should I suit up? Gosta just told me you're heading out?" There was a whiney undertone to his voice that wasn't good.

"Nope. I need you to make notes on the changes to the Starchaser parts, and then find a safer and more secure place for them. It's now even more important that no one finds them if we get boarded. If they're connected to the Asarlaí in any way, we can't be caught with them."

"But there's no one here to attack us…oh. Agreed." Mac's mouth often moved faster than his brain. Once his brain caught up it pointed out what Vas would have. The *Defiant* could have attacked them. Could have had landing parties. The shields on the *Warrior Wench* were as repaired as they could be with part of her still slammed into the ground. Breaking through wouldn't be hard for any determined attackers.

"I promise you can lead a second trip out there. This is a salvage operation; we'll be stripping as much as we can off of her. It's going to take more than one trip." There was no way a ship could have survived that type of crash—controlled or not—without serious damage. However, there should be plenty of parts. Not to mention intel.

A breather-clad Gosta came barreling down the passageway, causing Walvento to quickly shut the inner doors to the clearing area for outside.

He dropped a small disk in her hand. "Captain, I put this together. I know our comms are questionable, but this mini viewer should work. If you can scan as much of the interiors as possible I can build a database of it." A second one followed. "This can record any data—if any of their systems are up well enough to search. Which they probably won't be. Nevertheless, if they are, it could help with the database. For the ship, of course."

Vas shook her head but was glad the full airsuit hid her mouth. Another excitable child. "I promise. Check on Mac to make sure he's doing what I told him." She started down the ramp. "Tell him Flarik will be checking." She had no thought of asking Flarik to babysit Mac, but the threat of it worked wonders.

She wondered if captains of stupid crews had as many issues or if it was just with all of these bright people.

Walvento had both of his wagons out in front of the main building they'd been camping in. They were odd-looking vehicles, low to the ground with six wheels. They had sides, and the back was high enough to keep things in. There were only two seats—clearly he was more concerned with stuff than people.

Vas and Deven took the slightly smaller one, with the other three climbing in the other. Gon was tall enough that he could brace himself in the back. It wouldn't be comfortable, but little seemed to disturb him. Except flights in small ships.

The vehicles were as unwieldy as they looked, but the extra set of wheels in the center of them did help them to adjust to the terrain.

The planet was nameless. They didn't even know what sector of space they were in, let alone what system. Vas refused to give it a name—when they first crashed here she'd been certain they'd be off of it in a few weeks and it wasn't worth naming. Now she refused as a matter of principle. If they weren't stuck there, Vas might call it eerily beautiful. The strange twisted plants, that struggled to survive, hung off the collapsing buildings. Well, she might have thought it had a grim beauty before finding out this had likely been a base of operations for the Asarlaí the first time they were taking over all of known space. Even though Gosta was going to be watching everything they vid-recorded for him from the *Defiant*, Vas knew he was also working on examining the evidence of this planet being Asarlaí. She wouldn't be surprised if he was also researching holograms and unpopulated ships as well. Having a lot of projects made him relaxed.

None of the structures looked like a general population had lived here—these had been military of some sort. Once the crash of the *Warrior Wench* had been dealt with, tech was the first thing Vas sent her scouting teams after. Only to find empty shells. The innards had been picked clean decades ago; either by the Asarlaí when they fled—they'd left this planet when they were still ruling Vas's galaxy—or by passing ships over the years afterwards.

Considering that long-range sensors hadn't picked up life on any of the other planets in this system, and the *Defiant* had been the first ship they'd seen since they crashed—Vas was sure everyone in this quadrant left a while ago.

"Slow down, Walvento," Deven said into the comm as he drove. "You almost lost Gon out the back."

Vas looked at the wagon ahead of them. Gon was still inside, but he did look precariously balanced in the back. "That ship isn't going anywhere."

The wagons made good time and Vas noted that as anxious as he was, Walvento did wait for she and Deven to pull up before going in.

"The ship isn't badly damaged, Captain." Walvento hadn't gone in, but he'd already scanned the outside. Not that he needed to; just a visual inspection revealed that the

Defiant looked almost as if she'd landed here, not crashed.

Vas got out of the wagon and turned on both her own scanner and the vid recorder Gosta made for her.

Like the *Warrior Wench*, the *Defiant* was designed for ground landings. The Gamma class line was the largest that could do them, and most of the ships at this level didn't do it well. There was a reason no self-respecting merc would consider a ship this size.

But for a lumbering giant that had no crew and was crashing, Vas had to admit she was impressed with the way it came down.

The ramp was partially open, but that was because the landing had managed to hit it precisely. Vas stepped back. Another advantage of Walvento and his chosen team—they were ridiculously strong. So was Deven, and between all of them they were able to get the ramp open enough for Marwin to climb inside. A soft whirl indicated that the power was still on and the ramp lowered the rest of the way.

Vas studied the boarding ramp as she made her way in. The others were ahead of her, but there was something odd about the damage. She scanned it. Gosta didn't say anything from receiving the feed, but her scanner did. Some of the damage had been exposed to space—for a long time. The angle of the ramp when they found it meant, had anyone been inside, they would have been exposed to space as well.

"Deven, keep an eye out for old damage. This ship has been salvaged and rebuilt more than once; I'd like to keep track of the changes."Vas did another sweep and closed the ramp tight behind her. Once the seals locked in place, the air was surprisingly good, so, after a second test from her suit, she let her helmet roll back into itself.

The damage inside wasn't noticeable. Items that would have blown out had an in-space explosion happened were still intact. So whatever caused the ramp to open in space hadn't left the entire ship open; they'd been able to get the shields around the ship after the ramp was damaged.

"Captain! There's someone in here, someone besides us!" Walvento's yell ended in weapons fire.

CHAPTER EIGHT

—◆—

VAS RAN TOWARD THE SOUND. Walvento's comm cut off as soon as she heard the weapons, but either he or someone else was firing back.

"Does anyone have eyes on Walvento? Check in."

"He got ahead of us, Captain," Marwin's voice was tense. "But we're closing in."

Vas slowed down and kept moving. The blaster fire had stopped, but there hadn't been any yell of all-clear.

The sound of weapons had been coming from the command deck. Deven was right outside of it, his blasters out. He nodded silently to Vas and pointed to another approach. Gon and Marwin were across from them, but there was no movement, or sound, from anyone on the deck.

At her nod, Deven crept forward and she saw Marwin do the same across the battered deck. Both she and Gon would hold back in case the attack on their man was an ambush. She positioned herself so she could see the deck as well as the corridor behind her.

The command deck was damaged, some of it recent, and there were pieces of metal and plas-steel across the ground. However, when Deven wanted to be quiet, no one heard him.

A groan came from the center of the room, but masked by an upended console. Vas hoped it was Walvento. Groaning wasn't good, but it was a hell of a lot better than silence after a blaster fight.

There was a rustle and a shape shot up from across the deck—a black suit. He took aim at Deven but Deven shot first...and blew him apart. Vas knew what these blasters could do. Even at close range, practically disintegrating a being wasn't one of the things.

"One. More. Alive." That was definitely Walvento's voice.

Marwin fired toward the doorway Vas lurked behind, and the returning fire was way too close to her. She took a quick glance down the hallway behind them, stepped out onto the command deck, and fired into the alcove next to where she'd been standing. The black suit next to her exploded into a huge mess.

That got all over her. Definitely should have left the helmet up. It missed most of her face, but managed to get the side of her head as well as her braid.

"Walvento? Are there any others that you saw?" She shook off the worst of the goo. Silence after a blaster fight was sort of pointless. If there was anyone left on this ship, they knew she and her crew were here now.

Deven was on the other side of the shattered console. "He's shaking his head no. He's pretty shot up though." He looked down at a sound and shook his head as he looked back up. "But he just mouthed that he'll live."

Vas saw the remains of a third black suit. Most likely the one who had shot Walvento. Now just a pile of goo and black fabric. She tapped her comm. "Gosta? How in the hell were there three black suits here and we didn't see them on any scanners?" She moved forward slowly, looking inside anything that could contain an enemy. They hadn't done merc work in a long time, but the training was instinct.

"Captain? I'm not seeing any other beings than you five—dead or alive. Not seeing them on the past scans either." Gosta sounded extremely annoyed—Vas knew he took this sort of technology betrayal personally.

Vas looked at the mess dripping down her. "Does anyone have a sample tube?" Terel would have come in handy after all—she always had them with her. There was a chance the black suits they were now seeing operated differently than the prior ones. In the past, they'd shown up on regular scans. The idea of fighters with their abilities and stealth tech was almost more horrifying than the Asarlaí coming back.

While she was covered in the remains of the former black suit, she knew Terel would roast her if she didn't get a clean sample. Anything on her wouldn't be clean by the time she got back.

Gon looked embarrassed, but stepped forward. "I have a few. Pela gave them to me, just in case."

Vas took one of the small packets and released the seal. "Never be upset about doing something your captain should have thought of, but didn't." She scraped as much of the goo into the tube as she could and sealed it shut.

"Can we make a stretcher for Walvento?" They needed to get him back quickly. Another crew could come out and do recon, but she'd finally been able to see him and he was hanging on just through stubbornness. The black suit had gotten in a few good shots.

"Fine. I can. Walk." Walvento could barely make those words. There was no way he was walking anywhere.

"Really, soldier? Your right leg is barely attached and your suit is shot to hell, so who knows what crap would climb into your bloodstream. Speaking of which," Vas said as she turned to Deven. "Hope you have the hypo handy. But even with that, we need to find something air tight to put him in for the trip back."

Walvento tried to speak, but Vas shut him down with a glare. "Save your energy. If you die because you are trying to disobey my orders, I'll have you resurrected so I can kill you again. You are not dying on my watch—not today. Is that clear?"

Walvento was a pain in the ass, but before joining her crew, he'd been Commonwealth military. Orders were serious to him. He gave a slight nod.

It took far longer than she'd wanted, at least twenty minutes, to find anything remotely air tight to fit Walvento. They finally found a mid-sized shipper used to protect cargo on unmanned flights. His mask still worked, so he'd get air. It was just his suit was leaking everything at this point.

They were loading him, in the shipper crate, into the back of the larger wagon when Vas's comm beeped.

"Captain? We've taken care of your orders—everyone is cleared out. We're heading toward the mine." Gosta's words stopped Vas in her tracks.

"What orders?" A chill filled her. Whoever that entity pretending to be Aithnea really was, they'd crossed the line.

"The ones you gave fifteen minutes ago—clear out the ship and the building. Make it look like we vanished long ago. We're hiding in the mine. Can you tell us what's going on yet?"

"Holy crap," Vas said, then repeated Gosta's words to Deven. A dying man wouldn't obey her to stay still, yet Gosta moved her entire crew without calling for confirmation? Or maybe he had and the voice took care of that too. Yes, the voice had saved her and her people before, but she couldn't fight the cold feeling in her gut; her ship, the only way off this place, was now wide open and unmanned.

"Gosta, I need you to all get back to the ship, now!" Vas's words were met with static and the comm went dead.

The others tapped their comms but they wouldn't even respond.

"Vas, there is something coming our way," Deven said as he lowered his scanner. He'd been looking out over the terrain, but she couldn't see anything.

"How many?" She turned to Marwin. "Can you get him out of here? Somewhere not here, and not back to our ship, or the mine." She held up her hand once she saw the scanner. She could see the vehicle heading their way. There was no way either of the wagons could get far enough away from there to be safe before that thing arrived. "Belay that order. Get him back into the *Defiant*, find the most secure place you can and hole up there. Do not come out until you hear Deven, not me, do you understand? *Not me*. And ask him what his favorite drink is. If he doesn't come get you in ten, try the comms again. Tell Gosta to ignore any contacts from me—and get back to the *Warrior Wench* immediately." She got in Marwin's face. Hard to do with the suits, but body language still worked. She didn't want to think about Aithnea, or whoever was behind the voice, mimicking others besides herself. But her hope was the first voice they'd copy would be hers. Marwin drank with Deven enough to know the correct answer.

She didn't have time to explain and using the comms wasn't safe at this point. The mysterious voice obviously had a way inside.

"Walvento's injured. You and Gon have to keep him stable and not come out. Everyone has been compromised. We're under attack and didn't even know it until now. Lock this ship as best you can once you're on board."

"Aye, Captain." Marwin wasn't happy, but he and Gon quickly maneuvered Walvento's container back up the ship's ramp. The ramp pulled up as far as it could go a few moments later.

Deven had taken out as many of the extra weapons as he could find from both wagons. "I'm only seeing the one vehicle still. It's a class three rambler, heavily modified and heavily armed."

"Do you think this was to separate us? I'm just having a hard time seeing their plan. The black suits could have been here all along, but if they were part of a trap, they'd be waiting for us—not shooting the first of us in. The voice got our crew to abandon the ship, but then sent a single vehicle after us?"

"Maybe they have more skill than bodies. The crew is gone and the ship is open. There are only five of us here and if the black suits didn't get us, there could easily be enough people in that rambler to cause problems."

Vas gave a feral grin even though she knew he couldn't see it. "Maybe for normal people. You and I, bucko, have never been normal."

"Agreed," he said. "Now, how shall we play this?"

"I say we claim to be scavengers, our stolen ship crashed here and exploded. We came to see what we could get from this ship, since the *Warrior Wench* was destroyed." At least that was plausible. The wreckage of the black suit's ship and the *Defiant* would definitely make it viable. She wanted to keep whoever was in the approaching rambler far from her ship and her crew. Who knew what ship or ships they came in.

Vas and Deven moved the wagons to block the ramp to the ship, and then disabled one of them. Gon would be able to fix it once they got out, and at this point she needed to keep whoever was in that rambler out of the *Defiant*.

The rambler stopped a healthy distance from them, a good move. Even though Vas and Deven were the only ones visible, the scanner set on high frequency would make their readings unstable—at least for now. Vas needed to get them away from here before that changed.

The rambler was designed for this terrain. Huge and hulking, it had four sets of wheels and what it didn't go over, it crushed. Vas wondered where the ship it came from was, but at the speed it moved it could be on the other side of the planet.

Two aft weapons tracked them but the other two were sweeping the area around them. Vas and Deven kept low behind their wagons. Enough to be seen—they knew they were already spotted, but if they were just scavengers they might not react that way. Defending their haul would be of first importance.

The people in the rambler waited a few moments, then

the large side door swung up and six heavily suited and armed beings came out. Their suits were big and armored, so she couldn't tell much about them. Vas let out a sigh—at least they were not black suits.

"This is our claim, bugger off." Vas pitched her voice high enough to indicate fear and slurred her words.

"We are here for a person, not a wreck." The voice sounded just condescending enough. "By order of the Garmain High Command, stand down and prepare to be scanned."

Vas had never heard of the Garmain people, high command or not. And she knew most of the sovereign states.

The stiffening of Deven told her that he had. Crap—yet another time when knowing where exactly his people came from would have been damn handy. Once they got out of this, she and he were going to have a long talk.

"We don't recognize Garmainian dogs here," Deven yelled, then fired his blaster directly over the rambler. His voice had changed; a low growly accent took over. "Go nurse off your mothers where you belong."

Vas had no idea what to add—to effectively insult people you needed to know what race they were, something to grab a hold of.

"A Drali, you bastard scum. How did you get out here?" If the speaker was upset about the close call on his vehicle he gave no indication. The people next to him stood perfectly still, weapons at the ready, but almost at a parade rest. They were far less tense than they were moments ago.

Vas glanced at Deven, whoever the Drali were, whether his people or not, the Garmainians clearly weren't threatened by them.

"We have a bounty, and you're not who we're looking for, but we have free license to kill anyone who gets in our way. There are two of you and twelve of us. I say again, stand down before we blow you and your woman up."

"There's no one here but us. If you have a bounty, go

find the poor bastard and be off."

"Not a man, and we're not leaving without fully search-ing that ship, and the other one, for an off-worlder named Vaslisha Tor Dain. Her living body is worth a lot of money to them who bring her in."

CHAPTER NINE

V AS FROZE. HOW IN THE hell could she have a bounty on her head from a system she'd never heard of until just now? She wasn't surprised about the bounty. The Commonwealth would have issued one once they knew she blew up a planet, whether or not it was run by the former government or the Asarlaí—or even if they were one and the same. She just couldn't figure out how a place this far out would have a bounty on her.

Deven glanced at her and gave a slight shake of his head. "We ain't some foreign-sounding bitch, dead or alive, go find her. But she's not on this ship."

Sometimes Vas could notice when Deven was esper projecting. He'd gotten good over the years at hiding it, but when he was stressed she could tell. She felt him send to the lead guard.

"Maybe she's not on this ship. But we know she is on this world—we received a tip. I claim this ship, the one a few clicks from here, and all inside it for the Garmainian people. Leave or we will move your corpses."

There was no way Vas was going to leave three of her people—one injured—to the tender mercies of these bastards. Not to mention, she wasn't going to let them ransack the *Warrior Wench*. But the chances of her having that control dropped as the rest of the rambler crew disembarked. Rather, eleven of the crew; the gunner was still on board judging by their continued tracking. The guns on that thing could easily destroy an unshielded ship. Might take a while, but it could happen.

"That's me," Vas said as she rose. She dropped both weapons from her gloved hands, and shook her head when Deven started to rise beside her.

Of course he ignored her and mimicked her moves. He even went so far as to lock his open fingers over his head. Not an easy feat with the bulky helmet on.

"We need to scan you, there's something coming from that ship behind you that is blocking it. Tell your man to stay in place, and move forward. The bounty is for you being alive, but it doesn't say anything about anyone stupid enough to be with you."

Vas kept her hands high. She might be worth a bounty only if alive, but she had no doubts if she pissed off the leader that rambler would be blowing a hole in Deven's head. She'd noticed a slight adjustment to where it was pointed as she identified herself. Deven had come back once—she wasn't chancing it would work again.

She slowly walked toward the rambler, halting a few feet from the leader.

He took a hand-held scanner from off his belt and slowly aimed it over her.

"What do you know, boys—this is her. The bounty said there were markers in her blood that would identify her. Seems she ran out after some interesting mayhem a year or so ago. The Prime Counsel wants to have a little chat."

Vas was grateful for the helmet on her suit—it meant he couldn't see the shock on her face. That chunk of time when she'd taken the *Victorious Dead* in to Skrankle to be fixed. She'd been gone a month with no real memories. They'd figured it was simply a grab-and-drug to keep her out of the way while the Rillianians took apart the *Victorious Dead*. How in the hell did she get out this far and get into enough trouble that they'd had a high-end bounty on her?

"Have you been looking for me out here this entire time?" She put as much condescending snark in her voice as she felt safe. She needed more information, but sure as hell couldn't ask directly for it. She also needed them focused on her, not on the two ships.

"You couldn't have gone far—and it turns out you didn't." The leader nodded to where Deven stood. "You've been hiding on Drali? There are better garbage dumps than that planet. But somehow the others missed ya, and I found you." He lifted his head to Deven. "She came without a fight, and from her documents, she's a fighter. I'm feeling generous. I can leave you here, stranded. Or I can kill you. Your call."

"Or option three," Deven said. "You can take me with you."

The laughter from the rambler crew echoed in their helmets.

"Now why would we take a Drali anywhere except to a grave?"

Vas wanted to turn around and tell Deven to knock the crap off, but she knew he wouldn't listen and it might piss off their new friends.

"Because I am not Drali." Deven's voice was suddenly no longer marked by the helmet and Vas did turn a bit to see him.

He couldn't be comfortable breathing without a mask, but he looked far too pissed to be dying of poisoned air. His scowl reminded her that the pirate version of him had come from deep inside him.

"A Kilesh? What in the hell? I should kill you where you stand." The leader and all of the rambler crew locked their weapons on Deven.

"Stupid Garmainians. Glad to see the last hundred years or so hasn't helped your gene pool. Use your scanner, you idiot. My bounty is far higher than hers." Deven's voice was even nastier than his pirate self had been.

The leader kept his blaster up but managed to scan Deven with his other hand. He swore. Then scanned him again. "Crap. Do we have an esper hood? He's right—this bastard will bring in far more than she will. Which means, if he tries anything, we find new ways to slowly torture her. Not to death, but she will wish it. Scan me—I tell the truth."

Deven's jaw clenched. Vas hadn't felt him, but he must have scanned the leader. "I am turning myself in."

The leader tapped his comm. "Tell the ship to come get us. We have a wanted fugitive," he paused and nodded to Vas, "two wanted fugitives. We need to secure them as soon as possible."

Vas had wanted to know who and what Deven's people where—but this wasn't the way. Like the other two races mentioned, she'd never even heard of the Kilesh before.

The leader motioned to two of his men; both came to Vas, patted her down for weapons, and pulled her arms tightly behind her back. The cuffs locked into place and sent a jolt when she tested them.

Another group, four this time, did the same to Deven, although they also pulled up his helmet, locked it in place, then dropped a hood over his head. The stiffening of his body told her it was sending telepathic feedback to his brain. Like the cuffs, the slightest movement would stab his mind.

"The helmet is for us, not you. This air is a killer, and like our lady friend, you do need to be alive for your bounty to count. I recommend that both of you move carefully." He paused as something went through his comm. "No, we don't need to search the rest of the planet. We have what we came for and far more. Both ships scan without signs of life—they're dead. Get down here and get us all out."

Vas slowed her heartbeat. That was the first good news they'd had since they left the ship. Her crew was safe. Deven wasn't. She wasn't. But the rest of them were, and she'd do what she needed to keep it that way. She sent a silent prayer to the spirit of Aithnea. She didn't know whether that voice was somehow her, but it had saved her crew.

The leader nodded and the two men standing next to her nudged her to move forward. Vas paused. "You said you received a tip, I don't know anyone in this quadrant other than him. Who tipped you off?"

"Not that it would help you, but he said his name was Borlan, claimed he was your brother. You have an even more messed-up family than that bastard you've been hanging with."

CHAPTER TEN

VAS KEPT HER SWEARING TO herself. The inter-action with the mutating hologram of her late, unlamented brother happened only a few hours ago. The rambler had probably been driving across the planet twice that long for their ship not to have been picked up by any of her scanners. They'd found out not long after crashing here that the far side of the world had black areas—places where no scanner could see.

So, if the rambler had been here, their ship had been here, then Borlan had been fully aware of where she was for a while. "That bastard needs to stay dead." She'd not meant to mutter that out loud, but the leader of the rambler crew was right next to her and picked it up.

"I'd agree with you on that one. He's some sort of pirate around here, but he's been telling the Counsel where to find you for months. Really determined. Your whole family hate you that much?"

"They're all dead. So was he, I thought." She shrugged; maybe talking would get her some intel. "Wouldn't think someone could come back from having a furious Wavian rip out their throat, but he found a way."

The leader's mis-step was small, and she only noticed it because she was right next to him and was watching closely.

"He's a death-walker? I have no idea what a Wavian is, but no one comes back from having their throat torn out. You're not Kilesh—you're tall, but not tall enough. And your documents would have mentioned that. How is he back?" There was a tinge of terror in his voice. She'd already guessed, but clearly Deven wasn't the first of his people to come back from the dead.

"That is a damn good question," she said. "And one I intend to ask him when I find him again."

"Eh, maybe I'll ask him myself. If you survive the inquisition, there ain't no way you'll ever see light again." He nodded to the air. "Too bad your last view of freedom is on a shithole like this. Must have been his fault that landed yas here. The Kilesh might be powerful and all, but they can't navigate worth a damn. Not to mention this rock has something in it—causes all sorts of ships to be pulled to their death. Locals know to avoid it."

Not as helpful as she'd hoped, but most likely he had no idea what it was she'd actually done during her missing month. It was interesting that a large number of ships had been pulled in recently. It reinforced that their crashing here might not have been just an outcome of the damage to their ship and a busted gate.

"Don't touch me." Deven's voice was still that low growl.

Vas turned slightly and saw that his escorts were as far away from him as they could be and still act as escorts. She really needed to get the low down on what his people were. The leader had pulled up Deven's wanted documents—but he hadn't said Deven's name, nor what he was wanted for. The rest of the rambler crew was freaked out simply because he was Kilesh.

Which raised the question of how they immediately knew that. Deven was strikingly handsome, but for the most part looked like any number of a huge group of humanoid races.

Her thoughts were cut off as she realized the rambler leader was talking to her again. She tilted her head in question.

"I said, stop watching him. I don't know how you can travel with that creature anyway. Even if you are an alien.

Makes my scales crawl." He pointed to the entrance of the rambler and Vas ducked to get in.

Inside it looked more like one of her old shuttlecraft than a ground vehicle. There were heavy straps and bars on each seat. Considering the terrain this thing was designed to go over, that might be a good thing.

He pushed her toward a chair, quickly unlocking her cuffs and relocking them to the bar next to the seat.

"You can take off your helmet once we lock the door. This will pressurize before they pull us in."

That was interesting. Their ship was able to pull in a huge rambler from a planet's surface? She'd like to see the tech behind that, but she seriously doubted they'd show it to her.

Deven made a few more snarls as he was transferred to his seat and then the door locked. Deven's guards removed the hood, lowered his helmet, and then quickly dropped the hood back in place.

"Don't think about your friend here using those powers of his. That hood was designed with Kilesh prisoners in mind. Now let's take off your helmet and see what sort of bounty we have here."

He pulled off her hood at the same time the two guards next to Deven removed theirs. His swearing accented her own gasp. The rambler crew were Saurian.

"She's a damn Kilesh!" The leader rocked back, then got a hold of himself and lifted her chin to look at her better. "No. Just one of their breeds. And a messy one at that." He'd suddenly noticed the goo crusted on her suit. It was probably more noticeable in her hair and face, which was what tipped him off.

"I'm no one's breed. I'm a human." She tried not to stare at the two crewmembers who didn't have their helmets on. It wasn't easy. There were dozens of different peoples and species in the Commonwealth—even more if you counted what remained of the rim worlds. But there hadn't been a dominant Saurian race since before the Asarlaí destroyed themselves. There had been a large and powerful race, the Lithi. The vids she'd seen as a child didn't really look that much like the two she was seeing now, but they were both a reptilian-based life form.

They had been the largest threat to the Asarlaí as they rose to power, so they were the first ones destroyed.

"Have you ever heard of the Lithi?" She really didn't intend to ask that—she needed information about her bounty and what happened to her—not a search to see if these were the Lithi's distant relatives.

The leader was still watching her cautiously; the rest of his people had found seats as far from her and Deven as possible.

"I can't say as I have, but fighters get out of primary school earlier than the academics." He watched her for a moment. While he'd been ready to shoot Deven on sight, the fact that she wasn't Kilesh, yet also was similar to them was pulling him in. Fighters might not get the same schooling the academics did in their culture, but Vas would bet this one had enough curiosity to adjust for that.

"The word sounds old—like from before time," the leader said. "We have myths of offshoots of our people who went to find a better land when the Kilesh rose to power. Perhaps they are part of them. Are they from your worlds?"

Vas really wished she'd paid better attention in school. "They were. They were destroyed when a race of horrific beings, immortal, seven feet tall, with white hair and red eyes, rose to power and tried to take over our galaxy. The Lithi were destroyed by them."

He hooked a finger over his shoulder. "Destroyers like the Kilesh? Then why are you hanging out with this one? Granted, he doesn't match what you said of the others, but you scale-less ones are all fairly ugly, regardless of color. No offense."

Vas gave a small smile. "None taken. Being honest, your people are a bit of a shock as well. As for this one," she hooked a thumb over her shoulder. "He just showed up one day. Joined my crew. I thought he was human." There might be a chance to build an ally, or at least as close as she could to someone who was going to make money off of turning her in. Personally, she'd never gone for bounty work—too much one on one. She preferred full-scale battles.

"You do look alike." He took off his helmet. He looked like the others, except his brow ridge was heavier and his face broader. Some races had genetic castes—these Garmainians could follow that. "The Kilesh are all tall, like the destroyers of your world. None of them are good, even now. However, the one you found is even worse. Can't go into details, but his wanted list is as long as your arm." He leaned forward and pitched his voice low. "And he's over three hundred years old. Tales were the Kilesh sacrificed babies from other races to stay young forever."

"Five hundred years old, we only sacrifice stupid Garmainian commanders, and we have really good hearing." Deven was toning down the snark a bit, but he still had it. Vas wasn't sure how much was an act. She shot him a sideways look but the hood blocked his face.

Either this was part of his insane plan, whatever it was, or he was just messing with the Garmainians. She did wonder about the age though. It might have been rounded a bit one way or the other, but it sounded true. Something to be said for a nice-looking older man.

"See? Even though they no longer are in control, they still act like it." The leader gave her a nod and went up to the front of the rambler.

The vehicle started moving, but not as fast as it had been coming in. "We have another ship coming in, maybe two, sit tight." The voice came over the open comm of the rambler.

"Sitting," the commander said back. He turned in his seat to face Vas. "Your brother is a right bastard. Gave you up to a bunch of teams apparently. But we found you *both* first."

Vas shook her head. How did he survive Flarik? And how did he know where they were long enough ago that multiple people had been dispatched to bring her in? Sadly, those issues would have to wait until she could rip them out of him. Before she made sure he died this time.

"Aren't you afraid of what I might do? I'm sure it listed what I'm being brought in for." She tried to keep things loose, implying more than she knew. Maybe she could get him to slip up. She'd initially turned herself in and went with them to assure the safety of her crew and ship. But she had to admit that she was interested in what happened during that missing time.

"Not much listed on that sheet. Just that you were a fighter, and to handle with caution. Also, not to trust anything you said." He grinned. "I kind of like that."

The rambler rocked and any chance for small talk was gone. Not that it appeared he knew much, but it would be good to have an idea what she did before she was brought in.

"Where is that coming from?" the leader yelled to the comm.

"The first ship is firing—from the gray line families. They won't answer our hail."

"Those bastards. This is our catch. Remind them who I am and that everything is being sent to the council." Another shot, this one close enough to make the rambler driver weave radically.

"That's the orange line ship. The two came out of space drop at the same time."

"Maybe they can destroy each other," the leader muttered more to himself than anyone else. Then he moved up front where a half partition blocked the driver. "We can't go up until those idiots stand down. Keep dodging."

"We have to back off until orders come through from the council. These idiots are refusing to stand down." The comm crackled, then went silent.

"They're still there—monitoring." This came from one of the guards hunched over some old looking equipment.

"Leader Phonial! There's another ship coming in! It's commanding all of the ships to stand down." He paused. "It came through the old gate."

"I need a visual." Phonial crowded over his subordinate.

"Who paints the name of their ship on the outside?" He turned to Vas. "This looks like something from your end of known space. Did you have a ship coming for you?"

Considering her only ship was unmoving and stuck on the ground—that was doubtful. She shook her head. "I don't have a ship. If it's from my quadrant, I can see if I can identify it." She rattled her chained hand.

"Not letting you up. The name is…the *Victorious Dead*." He was peering forward as he spoke, which was a good thing for Vas. Ragkor was alive? Her former ship was still running? She had no idea what condition they were in, and with the Warrior Wench and her crew grounded and exposed, she didn't want to take a chance finding out. Not that she figured Phonial was going to let her speak to the *Victorious Dead* anyway.

"Nope, doesn't sound familiar, but there are millions of ships in the Commonwealth. Not sure why someone would be out this far though." She really didn't know how far out they were. But Deven had always made it clear he came from a distant system.

"The orange and gray lines are going after it, and it is returning fire. There must be something it wants here. It is larger than our ships, but we have three. It will not win," the watcher said with pride.

"The enemy ship is launching small fighters…they have taken out the orange line ship!" Considering that Phonial was now hovering over the monitor, there was no reason to shout. Except for shock.

He whirled on Vas. "These are your people, maybe not your ship, but you know how they run. How did they do that? Small ships can't do that."

Vas was going to guess that small fighters were not part of the Garmainians' fleet. Interesting.

"Small fighters are common in my quadrant. Wait until the mid-sized ones come out though. Hope you like this planet, you and your crew will probably end up dying here." When in doubt, bullshit. She was surprised the Flits had taken out a larger ship, but she knew the *Victorious Dead* was probably still damaged. Ragkor would have fired with its weapons before sending out the Flits and there'd been no sign that he had.

"The foreign ship is contacting ours and saying that if we leave the area, they will back off. They are laying claim to the crashed ship twenty clicks from here. That's all they want."

Phonial glared at her, then back to his man on the monitor. "Tell our ship to stand down. We'll continue to the rendezvous point and they need to come get us. Let the gray line die out there if they want."

Vas wished there was a way to tell Ragkor where they were, but if the *Victorious Dead* could pick up the rest of the crew, that was worth giving up herself and Deven.

Phonial leaned forward. "I know you know something about that ship, but I don't have time to deal with that now. If those two other bounty hunting units came, there will be more. But I'll make sure the inquisitors know to ask you about it." He stomped back to a seat behind the driver and the rambler lurched forward.

The crew was surprisingly quiet, or maybe Vas was just used to her extremely non-quiet crew. Deven was silent. Most likely contemplating a plan of some sort.

Which left Vas in her thoughts. "*If you're still there, who-*

ever you are, you might tell me if this is some sort of plan." She hadn't heard from the voice for a number of hours, so maybe it had been a hallucination. Aside from the fact that Gosta relocated their entire crew based on it.

There was no response.

Well, not from inside her head.

"Prepare for extraction," the driver called back. The crew all checked the buckles on the seats, adding a webbing that pulled over from the side of the chair. All except two who got out of their seats. One did the same for Vas, carefully not looking her in the eye, the second reached for Deven.

Who leapt out of his seat, his hands bloody, but free from their cuffs. He ignored the hood and just started attacking. He threw the closest guard overhead toward the driver, then dropped over to Vas and broke her cuffs before whirling back and taking out three more guards.

She agreed with his actions. The appearance of the *Victorious Dead* changed the odds of being able to protect her crew, so going along with the Garmainians wasn't as necessary as it had been initially. And their best chance for escape was to not get pulled into the Garmainian ship. Vas jumped up and took out one guard running toward Deven's back. The rambler was wider than a shuttle, but there still wasn't a lot of space.

All of the guards were down; it didn't look like they were dead, but at this point Vas didn't care as long as they stayed down.

Phonial and the driver were the only two left. Phonial had a small weapon, similar to a blaster, out. He had it aimed at them but she could tell he didn't want to fire. The rambler lurched and Vas found herself floating.

Phonial and Deven were as well.

"Clamp down on that! We need artificial gravity! Now!" The driver was doing better than she or Deven but Phonial wasn't looking great. A piece of broken chair hit the driver and he crumbled.

Deven kicked against the chair back closest to him and sailed forward into Phonial. Vas joined, but not with nearly the same amount of grace. While Deven wrestled with the Garmainian, she pulled the unconscious driver out and tried to figure out the controls. The rambler was clearly being pulled up to the waiting ship; she just had to find a way to stop it and bring it back down before they got too high.

"Phonial, what is going on?" Not only was the ship calling them, it was on a live screen. "You're not Phonial. Stand down now!"

Vas nodded and tried punching buttons to at least cut visual contact. The voices on the other end weren't reassuring, though. Something about gas and taking over. Vas turned to see Deven start to move away from Phonial, when a thin dust-like substance filled the chamber. Deven was closer and it was as if he just fell asleep. Vas couldn't even get any good swear words going before it hit her as well.

CHAPTER ELEVEN

E VEN THOUGH IT APPEARED THAT Deven had been rendered unconscious by whatever the dust was, Vas was still conscious. She couldn't move, couldn't talk, and couldn't open her eyes—but she was conscious. She could still feel, however, and her body drifting around weightless and smacking into things wasn't fun.

The rambler was silent, even the ship pulling them in said nothing. She assumed that since she was still alive, and they probably wouldn't kill their entire crew, that the dust was just to immobilize, not kill.

"Seriously, if you're in my head, I need some help."

"Busy. Good luck…"

At least there was a response, but it was faint, choppy, and not helpful. Busy? Vas wasn't a prima; she wasn't the type who expected everything to be about her. But if this was Aithnea, the same person who sacrificed everything to protect Vas from being found, Vas would think she'd make time for her in this situation.

Which looped her back to rejecting the premise that the voice was Aithnea.

"Did protect you, but not from this. Protecting crew now."

Now that tone was familiar. The 'stop feeling sorry for yourself, there are more important things to worry about' tone. Maybe it was Aithnea after all.

"From what? Where are you?" Vas strained to push her thought out wherever it needed to go—she still wasn't sure that she wasn't crazy.

No response from the voice—whoever it was had vanished again.

Vas gave up on reaching out internally and switched to focusing on getting any body part to move on her command. She swore in her head when the tip of her finger moved. Then swore again at the hollow, clanking echo of being loaded into a docking bay. She'd run out of the good swear words by the time she fell to the ground after bouncing off the arm of a seat when the gravity kicked in.

She heard some groans and found she could do that too. Still no real control over her voice, body, or eyes beyond that—but a groan was a start.

"Keep them immobilized, get a new hood on the telepath, then revive our people and send them to the medical quarters. Move the bounties to lock up—but keep them apart." The speaker was the one who'd realized that she and Deven had almost liberated the rambler.

She felt hands lifting her up and new cuffs put on. They moved her to a motorized stretcher and relocked her cuffs to the side of it.

The fog began to clear over her eyes; she still couldn't move her head, so it limited what she could see, but being able to see anything was a plus. Right now it was the ceiling of the rambler—worse for wear after all the untethered and unconscious bodies and weapons had smacked into it.

The stretcher made its way onto a ship. Since it wasn't under attack that she could tell, they'd stood down, so Ragkor had backed off. Good to know her honest and true Marine was still being true to himself. Now if he and the *Victorious Dead* were able to get the rest of her people off that rock and back to Home, she'd kiss him. Twice if he found a way to fix the *Warrior Wench*.

There was little to distinguish the ceiling of this ship from any other she'd been in, but she tried. At the least it might keep her calm. In an odd way, being trapped in her own body was almost claustrophobic.

"There are two? I thought we were just here for the

woman?" The new voice was softer, a female, but with an edge—female in charge.

"Yes, Captain. But this one turned himself in." Phonial leaned over Vas as he handed his pad to someone out of her eyesight. It was hard to tell with scales, but he didn't look completely recovered from being knocked out and gassed along with everyone else.

There was silence except for a few swipes of the screen. "This is serious business. Thank you for not trusting the relay with this, especially with the two ships out here."

"You are welcome. I thought it best not to advertise our recent captive. Has the gray ship backed off from the foreign ship?"

"Initially they looked ready to stand up to them, but the survivors of the orange line must have made them an offer. The gray ship backed down and has been pulling in survivors." A chuckle. "The orange line has now lost far more than they would have gained by bringing in the bounty. They should have stood down when they saw we had beaten them here."

"Captain, the foreign ship is moving off completely. A woman contacted us this time; she says to leave the area soon."

Vas would have smiled if she could. Hopefully the two in charge were Ragkor, her newest captain, and Therlian, his second-in-command. The second voice was probably her. Vas was glad she wouldn't have to tell Therlian's daughter, Keara, that her mother had died.

"Are they your people?" The female speaker peered down into Vas's face as she spoke. Her eyes were lighter than those of the guards she'd seen in the rambler. Her brow ridges were more delicate as well. She had elaborate markings of swirls and angles on the left side of her face, and even when smiling did not look like anyone would call her friendly.

"Of course you can't talk yet." She patted Vas's cheek

and Vas almost felt it. "You and your man did well, I will give you that. Made quite a mess of my shuttle. But we were prepared for a fight from you." Her gaze darted past Vas, most likely to where Deven was. The smile dropped. "Him, I was not expecting. The bounty on him is a good one, and like the one on you, issued by our people, not his. However, to bring in the Pirate of Boagada? That's a thing of legend."

Vas really wished she could see Deven now. Hell, she wished she could move more than a finger. He was an actual pirate? She knew that pirate persona of his was supposedly a part of him—she really hoped it wasn't who he truly was. She had nothing against pirates as a people, but he'd been a true bastard.

The captain laughed. "You might not be able to move your face yet, but your eyes are very expressive. You didn't know who he was, did you? Perhaps your own people have a bounty on that name as well? You really should take better care in who you travel with." She looked up and nodded and the stretcher moved forward again.

Judging by the shape of the curved ceiling overhead, Vas was guessing this wasn't a huge ship. The small size would also help in explaining how and why the Flits were able to blow one up. The ride only lasted a few moments and she was unceremoniously rolled onto a cot.

Either whatever they had used to immobilize them was wearing off, or the jolt of being dropped helped move things along—Vas's hands moved. She waited until the ones who had brought her in left before testing it out, more on principle than anything. She had no doubts that a camera was watching her every move. Possibly more than one.

Yup, her hands worked, and she could roll herself into a seated position. The prickling that followed, along the entire surface of her skin, told her the chemical agent they used was fading fast. Too bad Terel or Gosta weren't here, either could have told her exactly what components had been used to take them down.

Of course, even if they had been here, Vas really wouldn't have cared what it was. The main thing was that she could slowly move around.

The cell was tiny. The cot she was on took up most of the room, and it was barely wide enough for her not to roll off. If Deven's cell was the same size, he was going to have a problem.

A slam came from the other side of the wall behind her, followed by swearing in a language she didn't recognize and a few heavy thuds.

"Keep the hood on him! Get the other arm!" More thuds.

"He's too strong! Grab him!"

The wall actually shook, and then the door slammed against it. "Do none of you read the depos on our claims? This one wasn't expected, but I know it was on your screen." A soft popping sound came, followed by some very Deven-like swearing…soft swearing. It faded to nothing.

"Thanks to you idiots I had to tranq him," the captain's voice pierced through the walls, "which means he'll still be out when we bring him in and I'll have to wait for the council to confirm his ident and pay us. Because six of you couldn't control him. Ignore the hood. Look at the fighting skills listed." The door slammed and then Vas's door unlocked.

"Your friend put on quite an exhibition," the captain said as she stuck her head into the cell. She turned it a bit. "Are you laughing?" She didn't sound upset, just extremely curious.

"A little. It's nice to be able to move again. You just reminded me of talking to my own crew. Mine might have been a bit brighter than yours, but they did the same boneheaded things."

The captain nodded. "What happened to them?"

Vas wasn't going to risk that this crew wouldn't go back to pick up any others they could find on the off chance they were worth money too. "The Asarlaí destroyed them." Vas was a good liar, and there was enough truth behind her words that even a low-level empath would fall for it. The Asarlaí didn't cause the planet to explode—although they'd been trying to do it in a way that would have opened a portal. But the fight around it had cost her people, and the uncontrolled crash through the gate—due to the attacks by the Asarlaí, had cost her the ship.

"Those are the beings you mentioned to Phonial. He recorded the name, but it is not one that we know. They sound very much like the Kilesh—like your...*friend.*" The captain was good. Vas had clamped down on her reactions, but the implication of the Asarlaí and the Kilesh being similar made her give away something.

The captain gave the same toothy smile, the one that was in no way friendly, nor was it intended to be so. She unlocked the cuffs. "Yes, more than friends. Interesting. Sleep well, Captain Tor Dain. Welcome to the *Terlo*, and by the way, my name is Captain Zarith." She shut the door before Vas could respond.

She almost wanted to disobey just out of spite, but she was angrier with herself for tipping her hand than anything the other captain had done. And the sedative they'd dosed her with seemed to be coming back. Except now, instead of immobilizing everything, she was just exhausted.

She fell back onto the cot, but not before she heard a faint laughter. It was a combination of Aithnea and Captain Zarith.

CHAPTER TWELVE

———◆———

VAS WOKE UP TO IMAGES of Deven—lots of images of Deven and very naked ones at that. She shook her head and they vanished. It took her a few moments to remember where she was, what was happening, and the eerie laugh that had bounced around her head as she fell into a drugged sleep.

What she couldn't figure out was why erotic images of Deven had been there as well. Not that she was by any means against those images, but they were massively out of place.

"*It got your attention, didn't it?*" That wasn't Aithnea, that was Deven. In her head—a place he had promised he would never go.

"*Damn you—what are you doing?*" She stuffed away the part of her that was glad to hear his voice, even in her mind. It *was* his voice, not that of the pirate.

"*I don't have much choice; they are not going to let me talk to you. They are seriously pissed at this pirate.*"

"*Wait, what? So you're not Kilesh? What damn game are you playing at? I could have handled this, whatever it is. You could have helped save the crew back on the planet.*"

He was silent long enough that Vas wondered if he was going to respond. He did right before she sent another thought.

"*I am Kilesh. However, we are not like the Asarlaí. The Garmainians were a primitive warlike people. My people made them stop killing each other and destroying other races.*" He paused. "*I don't think I'm the pirate they think I am. The one I made them believe I am."*

Ah, crap. A new worry hit Vas. When Deven had first come back as one person, instead of the three he split into, he'd had some memory loss. Mostly from the prior year, but in some cases further back. They'd thought all of that had cleared up—he recalled everything up to and including dying. The tone in his mental voice told her he had doubts.

"Okay, so you know who this pirate is, and you don't think it's you? Why didn't you tell me you still had missing memories? I'd think being whatever type of bastard that freaked out an entire race of people would be memorable."

"You would. One would also think doing something over a missing month outside of the Commonwealth that was inventive enough to have a bounty this strong would also be memorable. I couldn't let you go into this alone—whatever happened to you during that time had to have been connected to the Commonwealth's deal with the Asarlaí. Faking my readings to look like a person I knew would be on their wanted list was the only logical way to make sure they brought me along." He paused. *"I had missing memories before my accident. The pirate Boagada is unique—I don't think I've been him and that's all I'll say for now."*

Vas stewed in her thoughts. She was right about one thing; her crew was easily as difficult, if not more so, than that of Captain Zarith. Part of her, a very small part, was glad Deven was along. Vas was cocky in her normal activities because she knew the Commonwealth. She knew almost all of the races in it—it was her comfort zone. If she went past the rim, it was for small trips. Spending time in a non-Commonwealth jail and on trial—hopefully— for a crime she couldn't remember, wasn't high on her list of things to do. In that regard, having Deven along, especially since this was a system he was familiar with, was a good thing. She was still pissed at him for forcing the issue, though.

She waved her hand in the air even though he wasn't in the room with her. For someone who grew up with a hatred of telepaths there had been way too many in her head as of late. *"How do you know what this person's readings are? And what are readings and how can you change yours? Damn it, Deven, you shouldn't have come."*

"You're welcome," he said. The smug grin that she knew was on his face in the next cell came through in his tone. *"As for the how, it's complicated and limited. The pirate is the same race as I, so it wasn't that hard. No one has ever had an actual image of him. Or her. The myth is that it could be a woman."*

Vas put her head in her hands. At least with his voice in her head, it didn't have far to travel to give her a headache. *"Never mind. So what is your plan? I'm sure you have one."* She leaned back against the cell wall. Now that she could move, the space felt even smaller. She could still feel the ship's engines under her boots, so they were still in transit. *"Now that you know what system we're in, do you have a clue as to how far away that planet we were trapped on was?"*

"Still deciding on the plan. I figure we find out what you did, fight our way free, and then steal a ship and head for our system. As for the other, not completely. The odd thing is there is no history of the Asarlaí being out here—none. A race built on conquering others, yet they had at least one thriving outpost world no one knew about. They weren't known for being subtle or sneaky." His voice drifted off.

"How powerful were your people a thousand years ago?"

"That's a thought, we were extremely powerful. A different type than the Asarlaí, but if this wasn't their home system, they wouldn't have been able to conquer us." He gave a laugh— which sounded weird in her head.

That raised more questions about Marli. Vas wouldn't go so far as to call the Asarlaí woman a friend, but she had saved Vas and her crew—that couldn't be discounted. There was no doubt that everything Marli did was for her own gain in one fashion or another. And she *was* sneaky.

But as long as their goals were going the same direction, Vas was okay with that. It was the concern that they'd misjudged her all along that was disturbing.

Terel hadn't finished her examinations, but the fact that the genetic make-up of the black suits they'd found appeared to be an exact copy of Marli's was a huge concern. How much of what was happening with the return of her people that Marli had actually been aware of was also an issue. She'd seemed genuinely upset upon seeing the Asarlaí destroyers—even more so when she saw the beings now calling themselves Asarlaí—beings with some similarity to the Asarlaí, but almost as if they'd been diluted—weaker and smaller. However, this was a woman who had hidden who and what she was, in a system that hated her kind, for over a thousand years. Misleading others was second nature to her.

"We're approaching the council planet," the voice outside her cell was unnaturally loud and intrusive after speaking telepathically for ten minutes. She'd never admit this to anyone, but Vas could almost see the beauty and expediency of mental communication. The door flew open and a pile of fabric was thrown at her. "Change clothes now. Everything you had on gets left behind, or we'll do it for you." The door slammed shut before she could complain.

She heard the door to Deven's cell slam open but no instructions, and then it shut again.

"*Why do we have to change?*" Not that she was that upset; her clothes were ripe. But it did seem odd to worry about that with a prisoner.

"*It's their way. Anything from the old life is destroyed as we begin our life of penance.*"

It was a good thing that Vas was a fast dresser, the door flung open just as she got the tank top down over her chest. Not that it would have mattered. There was no way any of the Garmainians would be looking at her with lust—naked or not.

"Stand up with your hands out, you'll be cuffed the entire time. If you act out, speak without being spoken to, or in any way disparage the counsel, you will be gagged and blindfolded."

Vas didn't know what the plan was—she knew that even though Deven was playing it down he had something in mind—but they couldn't do anything until they found out what she'd done. She stood and kept her hands straight before her. A new set of cuffs slapped onto her wrists.

There was more noise coming from Deven's room, but no thumps, so he must not have thrown anyone. She knew that, given time, he could get out of whatever new cuffs they'd put on him if he wanted. She'd seen him do it before.

The guard who came to get her took her arm and pulled her into the hallway. Deven, still with a hood on, and his three guards had just come out as well, when klaxons exploded next to them and the entire ship shook.

"We're under attack!" The guard who had grabbed her pulled her with him toward the deck. Not what she would have suggested doing with enemy combatants in a firefight of any sort, but he looked extremely disturbed.

The ship took another hit and the klaxons wailed louder. "Get to your posts! We're under attack—small fighters!" Captain Zarith was yelling but seemed in complete control. The guard who brought her out at least had enough clarity of mind to lock her cuffs to a rail. The ones behind her did the same with Deven, only with two sets of cuffs.

The captain whirled on Vas. "You said that ship wasn't yours. Why are these little things attacking us?"

Vas squinted at the screen but they had it on wide. She couldn't imagine Ragkor having the firepower to come back after them—even if he did know Vas and Deven were on board. By now, her crew would have found the scanner she'd left behind. Hopefully, Gosta would have deciphered the message to get the crew to Home as soon as possible. Providing it was uncompromised.

"I don't think those are the same ships that attacked us before," the guard at the closest station said, as he narrowed in the view.

Good thing, too. Vas was almost about to say those couldn't be her ships. Would have been fun to explain that slip. "I don't have any ships coming after me, and certainly nothing like…that." A swarm of six of the small single fighters favored by the black suits filled the view screen. The one that had been damaged and pulled onto the planet could have been a coincidence. Six more, clearly not damaged and fighting to stop this ship, weren't anyone's coincidence.

"You do know them, however." Captain Zarith turned to Deven. "I believe they are not yours, Kilesh. Who are they and why are they here? They refuse to respond to our hails. We will be within council space in ten clicks—they will not survive. If they are friends of yours, command them to stand down."

Vas laughed at that. Deven stayed silent and she wished she could see under that damn esper hood. "They aren't our friends. They are from my system—automons of some sort. I have no idea why they are chasing this ship though."

"Code coming in, Captain. They want the prisoner. No mention of which one—just the murderer they are tracking from the planet."

Vas thought of the black suit goo all over her airsuit. But retribution didn't fit with what they'd seen so far. The black suits didn't display emotions or caring. Why would they hunt down someone who killed another one of them? Actually, killed was probably not the right word. It was more as if she'd turned off a machine. Or with the resulting action in mind, she had exploded one. The fact that they wanted her back was equally disturbing. They killed whom they were up against. Prisoners weren't an option.

The captain studied Vas then shook her head. "Not giving up either of our bounties. Not this close to council space. Make these engines get us there and fire whatever you have."

Vas watched the formation in space. They were acting abnormal, but the pattern out there was familiar. "Try to fly erratically. They can calculate patterns like you would decide to get dressed—mindlessly. But they don't handle irrational or unpredictable behavior."

Captain Zarith did a Saurian equivalent of a raised eyebrow.

"Hey, I don't want to be shot down by them either. And I sure as hell don't want to go with them. They work with the Asarlaí."

Captain Zarith spun back into her seat. "Fly as she said. Continue firing all weapons at the closest ships." Another hit rocked the ship.

Vas was impressed. The captain should have been flung out of her chair with most of her crew, but stayed through force of will.

More klaxons, but the tone was higher.

"We've taken a catastrophic hit, Captain. Three of their fighters are destroyed, but the others will reach us."

Vas leaned forward to see the screen better. There were few merc battles in space. Those were over too fast for satisfaction to either aggrieved party. But she'd done enough space fights to know a trick or two. She normally fought small ships with her own small ships, but that wasn't an option. The black suits were closing in.

"What do you have that will make a big explosion if you dump it out of your trash chute?" Vas held up her hand. "Hear me out. Get it ready, slow down, then dump and ignite. It wouldn't work if you were trying to get rid of them for good—but it should slow them down enough to let us get to safety." The irony of calling being brought in as a dangerous bounty safe wasn't lost on her. But between the two options—the Garmainians were a better shot.

Captain Zarith paused before she gave the command,

weighing Vas against the threat coming at them. "Do it. Get supplies from engineering. The fuser waste should make for a nice reaction."

If the situation wasn't what it was, Vas could see Captain Zarith as a friend. At the least, she was an intelligent fighter willing to take risks.

The explosion worked, the three black suit vessels were thrown off, and the ship made its way toward a shield. The grid of it was such that Vas hadn't been able to see it further out from the angle of their approach. One of the best things about planetary shielding, aside from the fact they made the creators of them insanely rich, was the threat from a distance. The further away you could keep your enemy, the better off you were. The grid flashed before them and Vas realized this was one that stayed up all the time. There were only a few planets in the Commonwealth that could afford such things but there were two formats. One that had a set gate or opening mechanism. With the right code a small opening would appear. The other, far more expensive option, was a permanent grid. The ships that were coded properly went through—all others were destroyed on impact. That explained Captain Zarith warning off her 'friends'.

"Captain, they are still with us. They are—" The crewmember's voice was lost as his console exploded. The black suits weren't slowing down.

CHAPTER THIRTEEN

VAS BRACED HERSELF AS ANOTHER explosion rocked the *Terlo*. Judging by the grinding and shattering sounds, the ship's shields were gone. The grid of the planetary shield was directly in front of them. Hopefully, whatever cued the grid that this was an approved ship hadn't been blown off yet. Otherwise they were going to get an up close and personal lesson on how well those planetary shields worked. Too bad she wouldn't live long enough to tell anyone.

The ship bucked again and the grid crackled as it flowed around them. The black suit ships had to have seen the grid, but stayed alongside firing. They exploded in balls of fire as soon as they hit the grid.

"Captain, we're going to crash." The voice was calm, especially considering that Vas saw at least five crewmembers injured from the hits they'd already taken. The speaker had to be the second-in-command —if not, he should be.

"Brace for impact." The captain hit a button and webbing covered her and her seat, the remaining crewmembers did the same. She turned to Vas and Deven. "I'd recommend dropping as low as you can. I apologize we can't unlock you."

Vas dropped low and she heard Deven grunt. She also knew if needed Deven would probably pull whatever trick he'd used to free himself the first time, but he stayed locked to the railing and dropped into a seated position for now.

The ship went down hard, but mostly stayed intact. It rolled a few times, and then came to a stop.

The emergency lights flickered on, revealing smoke curling into the deck. Groans also filled the area but Vas was surprised to see most of the crew getting to their feet. Deven was a few feet from her. He wasn't moving and his hood was skewed.

"Are you okay?" Vas had a massive headache from the landing and was a bit tired of communicating in her head.

"I'm fine, but that was not easy." He tilted his head and the hood dropped back down completely over him. "*I had to use my abilities to slow our descent, not unlike what I did to our ship. This one is smaller, but the angle was wrong so it took a lot out of me. There's a chance I might pass out soon.*"

He was back in her head. But for that information Vas couldn't blame him. "*What do you mean slowed this ship and ours? How can you even do that? Why didn't you tell me? Damn it, Deven…*" She let her internal tirade fade off as he slumped forward. "*That is not going to help. I'll just wait until you recover.*" No reaction and the way he was leaning would have been painful to his arms if he were awake.

He was powerful enough to slow down a crashing ship with his mind? And he'd done it with the *Warrior Wench* and not let anyone know? The last part wasn't shocking, actually. She knew there were still far too many secrets in his life. And for the most part she was fine about not knowing. But this was a major issue.

"Is he dead? We won't get the bounty if he's dead." Two of the crew came over. Both looked a bit bloody but seemed to be intact. Captain Zarith was helping a more injured crewmember get out from under rubble.

"He's not dead. He just spoke to me, but he was injured. Check his pulse." Vas hoped that Deven hadn't been seriously injured to the point where he appeared dead. Or was dead. She still wasn't completely sure how many times he'd died. But if he appeared dead, they might dump his body. Or destroy it.

The two crewmembers stared at each other for a few

moments before one finally leaned forward and held
Deven's wrist. "She's right, it's there," the first crewmember said. He'd been careful when touching him and
released Deven's wrist as if it had been on fire. "We'll need
a stretcher for this one, and more cuffs. One looks broken."
He sounded tough but Vas noticed he'd taken another step
backwards as he noticed the broken cuff. He might have
been the one Deven had flung over his head in the rambler.

"Can you walk?" The second crewmember decided
she looked properly secured so was okay to approach. Vas
fought down an urge to show that he was still within kick-
ing range and that her legs were unlocked.

"I'm fine." She winced and pulled a bit on her right
hand. She'd not noticed it before but the cuff had bit into
her wrist when they'd crashed. She really didn't like these
odd metal cuffs. Electro-mags—like the civilized world
used—were far more comfortable and harder to break out
of. And if you did break them there was a good chance
the resulting shock would kill you, which tended to keep
prisoners in line.

One crewmember held a blaster on her, while the second
un-cuffed her. He glanced at her wrist, but didn't appear
to be impressed with the injury. The cuffs were quickly
reconnected and Deven loaded onto a stretcher. Considering the way they mishandled him—mostly because it
appeared no one wanted to touch him—she knew he was
still unconscious.

They led her out of the wreckage first. By then ground
crews from the planet were coming in, trying to get everyone out and assess the likelihood of the ship exploding.
The tone of the voices as they passed told her the mirac-
ulous landing wasn't lost on them. She had no idea if this
mysterious pirate person was also an insanely powerful
telepath, but she figured the Garmainians didn't need to
know either.

Vas had been on dozens of planets in her life. So many that nothing had really surprised her for years. She found herself being pushed by the guard behind her when she stopped in her tracks as they cleared the ship.

The area around them was beautiful, but in such a completely foreign manner that it was almost disturbing. Someone less used to other worlds would probably just admire the graceful buildings that seemed to begin underground and reached high into the light sky. Vas was simply freaked out.

"What? Ya never see a capital city before? Wouldn't have taken someone like you for a country bumpkin. They must have had some sort of cities where you're from."

It was the guard who'd been too afraid to touch Deven. Vas might seriously need to show him how much damage she could do with her legs. There were too many armed guards around them for it to accomplish anything in terms of getting free. But she'd feel better.

She lifted her glance to the sky. The shield, at least that's what she assumed it was, was little more than a faint golden hue.

Except one tiny spot. If she'd hadn't spent most of her life paying attention to tiny things that might kill her, she probably wouldn't have noticed it. "Is that normal?"

The guard frowned, apparently she was supposed to have responded to his mocking, not ignore him. When she instead continued to calmly nod up with her chin, since her hands were tied down low, he eventually turned his head.

"That's just our shield; you probably have never seen something that high tech before."

"Not the shield. The black dot directly above us."

"What's the hold up? We got the other one into the wagon for transport already."

"She's shocked by our advanced technology—"

"I'm shocked by your complacent stupidity," Vas cut him

off. "There's a mark in your shield, and unless that's normal, you might want to have one of your scientists look at it. This one is a moron." She nodded to the condescending one and stomped past both of them. The transport before her was a modified rambler in appearance, although a bit less all terrain with only four wheels. Clearly, while the Garmainians were creative in building designs, they failed when it came to ground vehicles.

"That's nothing—"

"Shut up." This time the second guard cut him off. He motioned for two techs who were heading toward the downed ship. "Any idea?" He pointed up. At first, their reaction was a shrug, but Vas could tell when they both realized something was wrong.

"Control, there is a mark on the shield—right where the warship *Terlo* came through. Are you seeing this?"

Vas couldn't hear the response on the radio, but the reaction wasn't good.

"Damn it. Yes, we'll finish here; just make sure someone checks it out. Those tiny ships had to come from something larger." He clicked off his radio and turned to Vas. "You're awfully helpful for a prisoner. It's not going to make them go easy on you—not with your crimes." He turned away before she could respond.

The guard behind her nudged her forward and into the vehicle.

She really hoped that Deven wasn't underestimating how much they wanted this pirate he was impersonating. Once they found out where her missing time had gone—hopefully along with why she couldn't remember it since Deven was sure he'd broken through all of her blocks in the past year—they needed to get out of here and find a way home.

Nothing she and Deven hadn't done before. Well, except for the entire lost memories bit.

The vehicle was cramped in the back, with Deven's

still unconscious body dumped over three seats. They just needed him alive, but obviously bruising him wasn't a concern.

Vas was seated next to him. He still had that hood on, so she couldn't see his face, but it hadn't slowed him down in using his powers to slow a crashing ship. There was a chance that when the *Terlo* was attacked the hood came loose, but she had a feeling he wasn't affected by it. At least not on the level they thought he was.

She had no idea how they viewed or rated telepaths here, but she knew anyone with the kind of power Deven had would have been locked up a long time ago in the Commonwealth. Beings with that high of a ranking were all insane.

Maybe the Garmainians had good reason to fear the Kilesh.

The vehicle jerked to a halt and the back doors swung open. There were new guards this time, fancier uniforms and wearing heavy, unusual looking, blasters. They were even less gentle than the prior ones and said nothing as they hauled Vas out. Deven still didn't respond so he was silently placed on a floating stretcher.

She couldn't really see the building they were dragged into. The vehicle had pulled down a tunnel and they were going up. Beyond a lot of stairs, and swearing from the guards navigating Deven's stretcher, there wasn't much to see or hear.

"Bring Vaslisha Tor Dain this way. The council will see her first. Lock the pirate up. He was not expected so there are protocols that must be in place before he can be questioned and his death sentence carried out."

CHAPTER FOURTEEN

———◆———

V AS FOUGHT TO KEEP FROM turning toward where
Deven's body was being escorted down the hall. "*Did
you hear that? Are you conscious?*" She wasn't happy about
reaching out to him this way, but there weren't a lot of
options.

"*Yes, both. Still weak.*"

"*Then shut up and rest, we might not have much time to do
this.*" She knew how long the Commonwealth took to do
things—a long ass time. She'd been counting on that same
sort of bureaucratic crap to help them find out what they
needed and still have time to steal a ship and manage to get
back out through that shield. There was little doubt in her
mind that the shield could be made to work both ways.

"*Agreed.*"

Vas didn't respond, but she had been counting on being
able to confer with him on plans. But if he was still weak,
he needed time to recover. Luckily, she was crafty enough
on her own.

While she'd been dealing with Deven, the guards had
taken her to a pair of heavy steel doors. There was ornate
carving on them, but so tiny you didn't see it until you
were right at them. Strong from a distance, beautiful up
close. Vas filed that away. Everything a ruling power did
gave away their style—figuring out their patterns was how
you broke them.

The doors opened with no fanfare, but by the way the
people were spread out before her, there was no doubt
they'd been waiting for her. The chamber was huge, and

the dais in front of her had the only seats not pushed up against the wall. Judging by the lack of decoration, and the sternness of the people watching her—this was a courtroom.

"Captain Tor Dain, very good of you to join us. To officially mark the proceedings, I am Grand Council; you will only address me as Grand Council." As the male spoke, Vas's cuffs were removed and a collar placed around her neck.

"The collar will ensure you do not get any ideas about demonstrating either your fighting prowess or your ability to escape. Both have been well documented here." He was a bit taller than the guards were, in fact all of the nicely dressed people behind him were. Caste system or there were actually sub-races.

Vas nodded when he appeared to be waiting for an answer. The collar was heavier than it looked—an odd hot-cold feeling pulsed like a coiled snake at her neck.

"Now, how do you plead to the charges brought against you?"

That was new. She'd been dragged before a few tribunals in her time, and they always seemed to enjoy marching through the list of complaints. These people wasted no time.

"Actually, Grand Council, I have suffered memory loss and don't even recall being in your system before." She held up her hand. "I'm not denying or confirming any actions, but since I have no recollection of them, I would like to know what and when they occurred." She normally could fake her way through things—and had been hoping that maybe being on the planet would jar a memory loose. However, nothing looked familiar at all.

The Grand Council raised an eyebrow—a move that was just as effective without any actual brow. "You recall nothing of the week exactly one year and five days ago where you broke in, rampaged through the entire council chambers, stole valuable documents, defaced government art, and fled with one of our best ships? Really?"

He leaned forward and Vas wondered if she didn't move if he would still use the collar on her neck against her. He looked pissed enough to trigger it if she blinked wrong. Obviously, she'd personally invaded his space, messed up his livelihood for possibly a long time, and she didn't even remember it. His finger was twitching ever so slightly on a small knob.

"As I said, Grand Council, I know I suffered a massive memory loss recently. I would recall doing such actions. Is there vid witness of me doing them?" She took a risk and looked around the council podium and a slight shock hit her, as if ice rumbled through her neck along the collar.

"I was there." The words were spit out with such force that Vas was glad that this race didn't appear to be venomous. "You and your partners tied me up and made me watch as you took what you pleased from the archives. Irreplaceable documents that were thousands of years old. You laughed." This time there was enough force in the shock collar to cause her to flinch.

"Grand Council," A low voice cut in, "may I remind you, that you are being allowed in this case due to our respect for your service. However, if there is too much emotional impact on your side, you will be removed from this court." The speaker wheeled forward. He'd been toward the back of the dais and mostly blocked by the tapestries hanging back there. He was larger even than the rest of the upper class on the dais, but also old—extremely old. He was in a wheeled chair but was flanked by two, also large, attendants. Or rather a pair of highly trained personal bodyguards acting as attendants. It didn't matter if Vas didn't recall having ever been here before—a fighter was a fighter regardless of race or culture.

The Grand Council glared at her once more, and then turned with a stiff bow to the huge man in the chair. "Your

Grace. I ask forgiveness for my emotional outburst. I will maintain civility in this trial." The words were so tight it was clear there was more going on than just his anger and embarrassment at what Vas had done. Normally, she would try and use that to her advantage, but she'd never faced anything like this before—bluffing only worked if you knew what you were bluffing against.

"I know you will. Now, I believe the accused asked for vid confirmation of her actions. She is to be granted her requests in order to adequately defend herself. For the sake of the court, we will all watch it."

The Grand Council was not pleased, but he was also of a lower rank and couldn't protest. Vas wasn't sure whom he hated more at that point. It sounded like whatever she did; she and whomever she was working with managed to embarrass him badly. But, the fact that he still held his position after such an event had to be a good thing. The collar gave another icy twinge. Maybe it was good for him, but it probably wasn't for her.

The attendant to the Grace's right nodded to the row of people lining the walls in livery. "Get chairs for all." The words weren't all out of his mouth when the servants moved to comply. Chairs were brought forward—even one for Vas—within a minute. Once everyone was seated, the wall nearest to them opened to reveal a screen.

The visual began in what Vas assumed was somewhere deeper in this building, although it looked like the buildings were all hive shaped, something that had been unnoticeable when she came in. Part of her had been still thinking this had to be a mistake. Yes, she did have some missing time—but to do all of what was listed and not have a memory of it?

Those thoughts were dashed as she saw a familiar duster and long red braid come into view. There was no way that profile belonged to anyone other than herself. She did miss her duster though.

She was leading and motioned to two darker shapes trailing behind as they approached a door. The hallway was dim, which indicated night, but a thin line of light peeked out from under the door they approached. She went to the center and motioned for the other two to stay to the side of the door—then she kicked it open.

Based on his outburst, it wasn't shocking that the room had been the office of the Grand Council. His robes in the vid were far more ornate than currently, so maybe he did end up with some sort of demotion—or fashion changed quickly on this world.

He tried to defend himself, but Vas had him down quickly and the two men with her—she could see them better now but not their faces—had him tied and gagged in seconds. Their movements didn't look like any of her people—not surprising since her entire crew should have been on Lucky Strike during this time. They also vaguely reminded her of someone—both moved with a familiar style. They could have belonged to a merc company that she'd fought with before. Until she heard them speak, or saw their faces, there was no way to know.

They silently left the room, the two men hauling the Grand Council like a drunken sailor out of the doorway ahead of Vas. The vid Vas turned, faced the camera, smiled, and then blew it out with her blaster.

Vas shook her head and snorted at that. All that work to stay silent, no speaking, and she'd wasted that by destroying a camera? One that had already captured what she was doing?

The vid stopped. "Does the prisoner wish to add something to our viewing?"

"Yes, I'm not that stupid. There are a bunch of reasons not to have done that, and very few reasons in favor of." She took a breath and channeled Flarik as best she could. "Might I request a reviewing of the actions directly prior to the destruction of the camera? At slow motion?" There was something there. Even watching it gave her no feeling of being there; but the movements were hers, the actions were hers. All but one.

"We have seen that part, I don't see how reviewing it can be helpful," the Grand Council quickly jumped in. "Besides, clearly you took something or did something to my chambers after the others had left and you didn't wish to be seen."

Vas rolled her eyes—that would be stupid. This entire op was on camera. She'd obviously known that and didn't care. Until the moment she shot out the camera.

"I believe that is my decision." His Grace didn't even look at the Grand Council, but kept his eyes on Vas. "I am not in agreement yet that the prisoner has no memory of the events being shown, but there is confusion in her voice now." He gave Vas a short nod. "Run the segment in question again, at one quarter speed."

Vas returned his nod and turned her focus onto the screen. The version of her there did that entire bit for a reason: she was trying to tell someone something. The fact that Vas had done any sort of job without her crew was suspicious enough, and anything beyond that had to be looked at carefully.

It was easier to make out her moves in slow time, that was certain. But it still took three times of viewing the scene before she saw it. There. As her right hand lifted the blaster to the camera, her left was flashing sign language. The nuns used sign language on some of their missions to keep from giving anything away in voice. More than just noise, voices gave away a lot of information to the enemy as to where the speaker was from, and could be used in court as proof of guilt. Vas had never been good at it, but her fingers in the vid moved with a surety that surprised her.

She had to ask for two more viewings, and was told that would be the final stall. His Grace was entertaining her requests simply to make the Grand Council twitch, but that amusement had worn thin.

On the final round she figured the signed word out. Betrayal.

CHAPTER FIFTEEN

—————◆—————

DAMN. SHE REALLY WOULD LIKE more time to view the vid. All that work to attract someone's eye to a single word? And whose betrayal? Hers? Someone else's? Had she figured out that she'd been betrayed by Skrankle? Though many cultures had their own sign languages, the signals used by the nuns were used only by them.

So, she'd come to a planet she'd never been to, kidnapped a high-ranking official, and was trying to send a secret coded message to Aithnea's nuns. All she was finding were more questions. She wished she had Deven up here, he probably would have noticed a dozen clues that she was missing. Maybe they could find a way to steal the vid when they escaped.

"Did you find what you were looking for?" His Grace's words were heavy with sarcasm. Time was up.

"Actually, no. I have no idea why I was that idiotic. Maybe that's not really me at all, just a bad copy." She kept her voice neutral. His passing comment about hearing the confusion in her voice was something to watch. She didn't want him to pick up on the fact she'd seen something.

He nodded slowly. Clearly, not fully believing her, but not having enough information to press further—yet. "Then we shall continue. This does appear to be you, however. Maybe you are not as bright as you believe." He waved and the vid resumed.

The new camera angle was further down the dim hallway, Vas and her duster still following the two men and the Grand Council. He'd been squirming when they'd left his chamber but he wasn't anymore. Judging by his slack face right now, that wasn't by choice.

One of the men said something but was too far away to hear clearly. Vas looked to his Grace to see if he'd agree to another replay, only to find him staring at her. She decided not to ask.

The Vas on the image hurried up and the camera switched as they went down another side corridor. It was lined with what appeared to be valuable statues of gold, Silurian jade, and jewels. But no one, even herself, slowed down to look.

"Why'd you knock him out?" Vas glared at them. "He needs to be alive and *conscious* to unlock the bio-sensor for the lock."

"We still can use him. Just cut off his hand and run enough current from a blaster through it to appear awake. Still alive, just minus a part." The voice was low and gruff, and still not one she knew.

The Vas on screen gave him the same incredulous look she was sure was on her face now. She'd hooked up with some serious morons for this job. "No. This is my mission, and you're not taking off someone's hand because you got lazy and couldn't deal with him. Wake him up." *That* she recognized. The snarl in her voice was one she used with other merc troops—her own people only if they were being extremely stupid. Okay, and sometimes she used it with Mac. A lot with Mac, actually.

"Aye, commandant," the first man turned and started shaking the Grand Council.

Commandant was a term used by a few cultures, but his accent was off for any that she knew. Both men were taller than her by quite a bit. Could she have been working with some of Deven's people and not even have known it? Or, more upsetting, she *did* know it at the time that vid was shot.

A few shakes and the Grand Council was standing on

his own. Both men still held his bound arms but he was conscious. Both men were taller than him, something she'd not been able to discern earlier. Not that all members of a race were the exact height, but both were easily as tall as Deven.

There were some muffled sounds coming from the Grand Council and his gag was partially removed. Vas still couldn't hear what he was saying—apparently neither had her double.

"What?"

"Damn it, he's fighting. Says he won't give up the treasures."

Vas stalked to the Grand Council and forced his head down to her level. "I don't know that you've noticed, but you don't have much of a say here. We don't want your treasures. However, we need that door open. Now." She took her blaster and pointed it at his gut. "I don't know where your people keep their important internal organs, but a gut wound is a slow way to die for anyone."

Considering what she'd put him through, Vas had a new respect for the current composure of the Grand Council. Had the roles been reversed, she might have shot him on sight.

The Grand Council slowly lifted his hand and placed it on a screen next to the heavy dark wood door. He also tapped in a code.

"Did you know about that?" Vas asked the men working with her. "What would have happened if I let you cut off his hand? It's amazing your people made it as far as they did." She shoved past them and entered the room.

Vas made a note—if she ever robbed this place again; she was killing all the cameras at the source. These people obviously trusted no one, not even their own. A little paranoia was healthy, but this camera obsession was bordering on obsessive.

The new camera had been aimed at the door as she and

the three men came in. So Vas saw perfectly the faces of the two working with her. They could have been Deven's cousins.

That went a ways in explaining how the Garmainians knew what Deven was just by seeing his face—although she'd never seen such similarity before in non-family members, she really hoped these two were not in any way related to Deven. This was already weird.

"You're making that twitching move again. Is there something wrong?" The vid stopped.

"Nothing. Well, okay. I might have done whatever this was with them, but am I the only one who is disturbed that they look like clones of each other?"

"They are Kilesh. They all have similarity. The one you came in with looks like them."

Vas waved to the screen. "But those two look exactly the same." Yes, multiple births happened in the Common-wealth, so probably out here too. This was different. Maybe it was part of the repressed memory coming back, but she knew they weren't twins. A shudder went through her. She was getting some memories back—or rather, emotional memories. She seemed her usual cocky and sure self in the vid, but a wave of loathing hit her now. These two had freaked her out then.

So why in the hell was she working with them?

"Clones are illegal in all civilized worlds. Not to mention impossible."

Vas knew they weren't possible. She also knew her brother had somehow managed to come back from the dead. The bloody body left behind by Flarik was very dead before it was dumped in space after they won their battle. Was someone practicing with clones? She almost threw up as another thought hit her. Was Deven really a clone? He wasn't identical to these two, but he had died.

"*I'm not a clone.*" The voice in her head was faint. He was clearly still weak, not to mention she had no idea where in the complex he was.

"*You would say that if you were actually from a race of illegal and impossible clones.*" She fought to keep from moving as she mentally spoke to him. "*Why and how are you in my head again?*"

"*Your distress came through to me. I can't see what you are seeing but I got the idea. I'm not a clone. I'm not lying.*"

"Captain Tor Dain?" The accent on the first part of her name was odd, and it also indicated it had been asked a few times. "Do you wish to see the rest of this or simply have the charges presented?"

"I'm sorry. My people are repulsed by clones—or anything that appears to be clones. The fact I was working with two stunned me. I believe we can assume I was under extreme duress."

His Grace said nothing but the vid continued. The rest wasn't helpful however. Even though there were cameras everywhere it seemed, none of them could focus on smaller details. The two clones took the Grand Council and tied him to a chair at the far end of the room, and then they locked into parade rest on either side, waiting.

Great—not only had she been working with clones, she'd been working with former or current military clones. She fought the shudder this time.

The vid Vas went to a massive desk, and started pulling out drawers and dumping the contents on the desktop. After the third one, she pried a small silver key out of the bottom of a drawer. She waved it at the Grand Council, went to a picture on the adjacent wall, and used the key in its lower right corner.

The Grand Council had been calm since he'd been tied to the chair—that changed the moment he saw the key and got worse when she found the keyhole.

Vas was surprised that he didn't break his arm as he leapt up. Both clone guards pushed him back in his seat but he was putting up a fight.

The Vas on the vid glanced at them but paid no other heed. She turned the key and the picture went to one side. The safe wasn't as impressive as Vas would have expected.

The Vas on the vid looked up at the Grand Council. "This is it? Seriously? Just how backwards are your people?" That was one thing, Vas might not recall any of this, but at least both of her had the same levels of standards for safes.

The Grand Council fought some more, but the guards kept punching him each time.

Vas pulled out her lock picking equipment and the current Vas felt a twinge—she'd lost it after this. That explained where it went.

It only took a few seconds to pick the lock and Vas's snort on the vid matched her current one exactly. "You guys really do need to improve your security. I say that as a professional."

No one responded.

The contents of the safe were almost as unimpressive as the safe itself. A fat packet of scrolls came out, a quick look by her vid self indicated there was nothing else there.

Vas took the scrolls to the desk and slowly unrolled the first two. The Grand Council fought so hard that the guards had to knock him out again. Vas grinned as she looked at the scrolls then rolled them back up. "We have it. I believe Aithnea and your people will be happy." She tucked the scrolls inside her duster.

Then turned to the camera and shot it out.

Vas was expecting a signed word this time. She was not expecting what it was. 'Deven.' Her stomach knotted, but she knew what she'd seen. She had no idea what it meant though. She trusted Deven with her heart, but a tiny part of her mind was trying to figure out if his name was connected to the word she signed before—betrayal.

The council room was silent as the vid went blank.

"I will fill in the rest since, as you have seen, the Grand

Council has an emotional vesting in this. You and your companions left as quickly as you came. Your ability to avoid all of our security was impressive. You then broke into a secure ship factory, one that was designing a prototype starship. Five times our current size, with better gate travel and weapons. You stole that and fled." He held up his hand. "Oh, and you fired upon the hangar, destroying the rest of the prototypes and all studies on the ship. You wouldn't happen to know what happened to that ship? My people scanned the planet where you were found, and neither ship was ours."

"I lose a lot of ships, so I wouldn't really know. But which was worse, whatever papers I took or the ship?" A shock went through her collar. Not enough to hurt, just enough bite to reminder her she was a prisoner. The focus seemed to be on those papers, but having seen their current versions of ships, she'd say that ship was the bigger issue. She really wished she could recall any of this. The bigger issue was what in the hell her signing had been. Betrayal of Deven? By Deven? Maybe the two words weren't related and part of a code she'd sent back to Aithnea.

She had been in contact with Aithnea and was working for her? What was in those papers? And the fact they were working with the Kilesh? And for some reason she'd signed Deven's name… *Did you know any of this? About Aithnea?*" She tamped down on the confusion about seeing herself sign his name a year ago in a vid. It needed to be dealt with, but not now. She knew he was still recovering, but he felt it was okay to pop in her head—she could return the favor.

"*No. I was able to see through your eyes briefly and I recognize the people you were with, though not specifically. They are part of a black ops group. A very black ops group. I'd never heard of the nuns before I came to the Commonwealth, but I had been there for over twenty years. Things could have changed back home.*"

Vas let him go. She wasn't used to communicating that

way and was sure she'd get shocked again, or worse, if someone realized what she was doing.

"They are both crucial. Tell us where they both are and we will spare your life. The life of your companion can't be spared—he has too many crimes against him. But we can make his death less painful."

"I am not trying to be obtuse, I really have no memory. I left my real ship at a repair yard in the Lotin system—in the Commonwealth. I was meeting someone on another planet and was supposed to be gone two weeks. I was gone a month and only had scattered, false memories of that time. My ship was stolen so I assumed the mind block was done by whoever took my ship." She held up her hands. "That is the truth. Scan me." Okay, she hadn't meant to say that, she didn't know if they had that ability, but she sure as hell wouldn't want to have anyone else in her head. Unless they could give her answers. Damn it, she had to do something to find out what had really happened—the more she found out, the more mysteries came up.

"We do have ways," his Grace said. "Some of us are sensitive, I am one. I can tell that you believe what you say. Moreover, you do have an empty location in your being… we can find those missing spots. No one can hide all thoughts from our machine. You might not be the same person you are now—but you will give up your secrets."

The Grand Council leaned forward with a grin. "You will wish you had simply confessed."

CHAPTER SIXTEEN

———————

VAS KNEW THAT WASN'T A good thing. For one thing, he looked far too happy. At the same time, if there was a chance for them to actually see what happened, what she was missing, she had to take it.

"Do it. I won't fight." She felt a twinge but blocked whatever Deven was going to say. *"No. I have to do this. Even you couldn't see what had been lost. If they can, we need to know. Block yourself."* Deven had somehow been able to hide the extent of his abilities for over twenty years in an esper-paranoid Commonwealth—he could hide himself now.

He didn't say anything but she felt the equivalent of a mental hug. Once they got out of this, she was going to tell him that sort of mind contact was okay. It was surprisingly comforting.

"Call forth the confessors. I would normally say we will try to be gentle, but in your case, and concerning the items you took, that will not be possible." His Grace nodded to the guards in the back.

Two guards came closer, one on each arm.

"Can I at least ask what the hell was in that safe? The ship I get, and I'd like to get it back too—whatever it was. But what were those papers? I'm not going to remember much after this, am I?" Considering her history with telepaths, Vas was shocked at how calm she was. Maybe all the people who kept plowing through her mind were making her immune. Or her need to know what happened had seriously overwhelmed her common sense.

"You are correct, you won't recall much. The documents were old, ancient scrolls from thousands of years ago. Before the Kilesh even came forth to this quadrant. The scrolls held the secrets to power far beyond our current levels."

Vas waited for the rest, then shrugged. "And you haven't used them why? It would seem to me that a lot of power could have saved you from the Kilesh." Most likely the papers were useless mumbo jumbo that had no real meaning but kept being mindlessly protected for generations. Her people had had things like that, precious documents that couldn't save them as their world grew weaker and finally was destroyed.

"The scrolls couldn't have been read by you, or any outsider, although you obviously knew what you were looking for. They are in a code lost to all. One favored by a mystic race of powerful nuns who passed through here eons ago. But we will find a way to read them and use them against our enemies." The Grand Council had an unhealthy gleam in his eyes—she had a feeling his relationship to the scrolls was more personal than professional.

"Once you get them back," Vas said. She winced a moment later as a shock went through her neck—it was worth it.

"We will not listen—" The rest of the Grand Council's taunt was lost as an explosion shook the walls. Plaster drifted down and a second later the sirens started.

"Go, find out what that was." His Grace waved at half of the guards.

A second explosion, one that sounded closer to Vas's trained ear, brought more rubble crashing down.

"Get the prisoner to a cell and make sure the second one has doubled guards," His Grace yelled. "Whoever is trying to rescue you and your companion will not succeed. We will kill you both before I let that happen."

Vas couldn't think of a snappy comeback before the two guards grabbed her and half dragged her out of the room.

She would have told him to look to his own enemies since she had no one in this section of space with the ability to mount this kind of offensive. Not to mention her people weren't stupid enough to attack an entire shielded planet. At least she hoped not.

"How did they get through your shield?" She yelled it back over her shoulder but wasn't sure if he'd heard her. She had warned them about that spot in the shield already. There was a bad feeling in her gut that she knew who was attacking.

The corridor was filled with heavily armed guards running in all directions. While the people in the council room had seemed surprised, it was reassuring to not see shock or surprise on the faces of their military. Good fighters never completely let their guard down, even when home.

Surveillance screens mounted along the corridor filled with images as she was rushed by, but a bottleneck of guards let her finally get a glance at one. The shield was gone, or at least whatever gave it the yellow tinge was. The sky was a bright blue. Three large ships hovered in the air and from their aggressive positions she figured they didn't belong to this planet.

Her gut clenched as a closer view clearly showed what they were—the gray ships. Not the massive Asarlaí ones that appeared at the end of the battle of Mayhira. But the ones that had terrorized and destroyed the outer rim worlds.

Smaller ships were coming down from the larger ships in waves, some being destroyed by canons on the planet. It didn't look like the people of this world had a chance to get any of their own ships up, but it was good to know they hadn't counted on the shield as their only planetary protection.

The smaller ships were trying to land, and rows of black suits attacking the Garmainians on the ground indicated they'd already had some success.

Vas swore as the hallway cleared up and her guards dragged her forward. There was no way that those black suits would go through this much to find her, or Deven for that matter. They were after something else. That was reassuring. It did also mean that their reach was farther than expected. That was not reassuring.

The guards got her to a small corridor and pushed her through. The first guard was unlocking the cell when the corridor they'd just left exploded in a ball of fire and flying stone.

Vas was flung free of both guards and slammed into a wall. She got up almost faster than she went down and ran for the closest guard. She was no longer cuffed, and the collar seemed to need to have a controller behind it. One that was back in the council room if she was lucky. If she wasn't, she was probably going to die anyway. Might as well bring it on her own time.

The first guard went down but grabbed her leg and tried to push her off balance. She was expecting that and kicked him in the head with her free leg, then continued on to the second guard.

They'd been running with small blaster-like weapons in their hands and she'd hit the first one before he could raise it. The second one got his up and was tracking her mid-body when a shape tackled him from behind. The shot went over her shoulder, blasting a massive hole in the wall.

The two forms fought briefly, and then the guard was out cold. Deven grabbed his weapon and nodded to Vas. She grinned and held up the one she'd taken off her guard.

"Excellent timing," she said, then briefly looked for anything like a weapons locker. A small desk had two more small blasters, but that was all. "I'm assuming there's a way out?"

Deven shook his head and laughed. "It's good to see you too."

A brief image of her signing the words 'betrayal' and

'Deven' hit her as she looked at him. Her gut knew it wasn't that he had betrayed her. No way to prove it, nor to know what the words did refer to—but he wouldn't betray her. She stepped up to him, pulled his head down for a quick but memorable kiss, and rocked back. "Very good. Now, our way out?" She briefly filled him in on what she'd seen in the hallways.

"I don't know what all you could pick up, but one of the things I stole when I was here before was a very nice warship prototype. Hopefully, we can find something along those lines."

They both peered down the damaged hallway; there were few people in it now and no sound of troops. Blowing it up had been a side effect of some other action. Deven pulled Vas back quickly and then she heard steps. They were marching; so, it was someone's military—she just wasn't sure whose.

They passed without looking into the darkened hallway where she and Deven were hiding.

Black suits. Only five, but they seemed to know exactly where they were heading. Toward the council chambers.

There was a tiny part of Vas that wanted to find out what in the hell a technologically inferior race like the Garmainians could have that the Asarlaí and their sidekicks would be here for. Luckily, her sense of survival stomped that thought into the ground.

The hall dropped back into silence. Well, as much as it could with groans coming from both injured fighters and the building they were in alike. Vas nodded to Deven and stepped out.

The hall was damaged but it held up better than Vas would have expected from the force of the hit it took.

Deven looked over and at her nod, he took the lead. Yes, Vas was the captain, even in this situation. However, when there was someone with better eyesight, hearing, and who was a telepath around, they led.

They both kept their weapons out, so were ready when a pair of Garmainian guards rounded the corner.

"We don't want to hurt you. Your people are going to need all the fighters they have to defend against these black suits. But we are getting out of here."

The guards paused, and then both lifted their weapons. Vas and Deven shot first.

"Damn it, I'd rather not have to do that. Aside from grabbing us and putting me on trial, they didn't do anything. And from the vid I saw, they might have been justified." She swore. "I wanted to get a copy of that and see what Gosta could pull out of it. Can't go back now."

Deven's grin was a smug one. "You mean a copy like this?" He pulled a small, flat disk out of his pocket. "I went to the chamber first. I didn't know they'd moved you. The vid was running again, but no one else was in there so I stole it."

Vas kept her laugh low. "You are the best second-in-command a woman could ever want."

Weapons fire was coming from behind them now, so they both started running for the way out. From the surveillance screens, she could see that two of the gray ships were still in orbit. Vas wondered if the third had gone to another part of the planet, and then saw a wide column of smoke and the remains of a gray ship protruding on the edge of the city. She nudged Deven. "At least we know the Garmainians have some serious ground to air weapons. It might not be enough to save them though. We have to keep that in mind when we find a way off this rock."

"Agreed. And we need to get out of here before those black suits find what they were looking for. I seriously doubt they will let this world survive."

Vas looked at the beautiful structures, half of which were already demolished. "Is this their only world?" There had been a lot of changes to her psyche in the last year— she wasn't sure if they were good or not. In the past, she wouldn't have thought about the beauty of a world, nor cared about their people.

Deven kept watching the area around them. There were one or two ground skirmishes in the distance, but the target clearly had been something inside this building. "No, it's their capital, but they are wily enough to have a fully functioning back-up government on another world." He pointed to a group of ships on the ground. More the size of a large shuttle, they were trying to load civilians into them. Two were in the air with the ground canons keeping the gray ships at bay. Actually, Vas had seen those gray ships fire. Had they wanted to, they could have gone after the smaller vessels outside of cannon range. They were focused on the planet.

They were probably pissed about their ship going down as well. Vas didn't know if they were manned by the wanna-be Asarlaí or the black suits, but neither group seemed terribly good at adapting quickly. They were used to overwhelming their prey, not outthinking them.

"What about that one?" Vas pointed to a slightly smaller shuttle further out from the others. "Can you disguise us long enough to get on board?"

Deven could use his abilities to change appearance—that of Vas too as long as she stayed near him. However, it took a lot of effort and Vas wasn't sure if he'd recovered enough yet from that whole 'keeping a crashing ship from exploding as it crashed' event.

His pause told her she was right, he was not fully recovered. Then he nodded. "It won't be long, but yes. We need to move now though." He pointed to a group of black suits making their way toward the building—judging where they were coming from, they were survivors of the downed gray ship.

"Do it," Vas said. She always held still when he cast these glamours, he used to tell her she didn't have to—she noticed he didn't this time.

The familiar tingling ran over her skin. Deven now looked like a bulky Garmainian guard, and judging from what she could see, so did she. With a nod, Deven ran out into the open and started jogging toward the ship.

"We need you on this one!" A voice came out from behind them. It was from a guard in the middle of a clump of larger ships. One ship they might overwhelm but something larger and with more ships and people around it would be too risky.

Vas lowered her voice, trying to mimic Captain Zarith as best she could. "Orders. We're assigned this one—more of the invaders are coming in."

The guard opened his mouth to argue when weapons fire from the approaching black suits cut him off.

"See to your own ships." Deven had also lowered his voice, but his tone was full pissy commander. Vas shook her head. He probably gave himself a higher rank on his uniform than her. Something he used to do often.

"Aye. Good luck." The guard ran back toward the clump of ships.

Vas and Deven got to the smaller ship just as the ramp was starting to rise.

Deven jumped on it. "Hold! We've been assigned to this ship."

The ramp didn't go back down, it was only a foot off the ground, but it did stop moving.

"We've already got guards. You two go back to the fighting." The voice was familiar—Phonial, the rambler leader. Made sense that someone who went on retrieval missions was also a guard. However, he'd come across as a bounty hunter, not someone who worked for the military.

Deven went up with Vas right behind him. Yup, Captain Zarith, Phonial, the rambler driver, and what looked like most of their crew were all on board—trying to look like prosperous citizens.

"Sorry about this," Deven said, and then turned to Vas.

"To you too." A stabbing blackness invaded Vas's mind and she lost consciousness.

CHAPTER SEVENTEEN

V AS WOKE WITH A HEADACHE and no idea of where she was, or why. The confusion lasted only a few moments as the entire series of recent events slammed into her. The headache remained and became worse.

She forced her eyes open, wincing as the glare from the ship's lights stabbed into her skull. "Damn it, what did you do?"

Deven was looking like himself again, so she assumed her glamour was gone as well. She was sitting in the co-pilot's seat and a nice empty star field was before them. She looked back and saw about twenty Garmainians, only a few looking awake, tied and gagged in the seats behind them.

"If you knocked them out, you could have just left them on the planet. What are we going to do with them?" She waved her finger at him. "And don't think we're not talking about what you just did—we will. Later." She had no idea he could pull that kind of crap, but in front of twenty enemies was not the place to bring it up. Let them think he'd used some sort of weapon. This trip was just letting her in on an entire slew of new Deven tricks.

"The black suits were coming. If I'd left them behind they would have been slaughtered." Deven kept his gaze ahead, but there was no defense in his voice. He'd do the same thing again.

"You're a softie." Vas turned in her seat, fighting against the headache still bouncing in her brain. If it was a side effect of Deven's trick then everyone who was conscious had the same issue. "I know some of you are awake. I also know that you're a bunch of bounty hunters, and most likely weren't on your planet's evac list." Two winces that faced her were confirmation. Probably of the headache as well. "We needed your ship. However, I promise, we'll find a place to drop you off. Maybe that nice cheery planet you grabbed us from. So just sit tight." The winces turned to glares, so Vas shrugged and turned forward in her seat. They might be upset, but at least they were still alive.

"You're a softie now too. The old Vas would have spaced them anyway."

Vas took a deep breath and shook her head. "Not unless someone was paying me. Were we followed?"

Deven's grin dropped. "Yes, and we still are. It's one of the black suit short-range fighters. Jumped behind us right after I cleared the gray ships. There was some confusion when the Garmainian vessels tried to verify who was on here, but a volley from the gray ships cut that off."

Vas pulled up the monitors. It didn't matter that she'd never even heard of Garmainians before—shuttles all seemed to be designed the same. After a few tries she was able to find the long-range scanners. Yup, there it was, just hanging on the edge of scanner range.

"Does this thing have any real weapons?" She hadn't been that impressed with the weapons on the ship that had brought them in. This one looked even less combat centered. Probably a transport between planets.

"Some, not a lot though. But I think we can lose that ship."

"I think we need to not underestimate them. Their entire focus was on the council building back on that planet; yet one ship breaks off to follow an escaping shuttle? And is holding back and not engaging?" She leaned over and pulled his face toward her. "Are you feeling okay?" The dark circles under his eyes told her the answer.

"No. Because of the Commonwealth, I haven't tried

anything on the edge of my abilities for decades. To do so many in a short time is hitting me."

Vas stood. "Get out of the seat. You take this one. I have a plan." She pulled on his arm.

"I can do this. Tell me what your plan is."

"No. Look, you've saved us more than once. I need you to rest in case our asses need saving again. I assume you're heading back toward our crew?" At his nod she finally got him out of the pilot's seat. "I'd rather our tail didn't report back. They might not have realized how many of us were down there—and by now the *Victorious Dead* would be there as well."

She pushed him into the co-pilot's seat. "I learned this from the nuns back in the day. The simple classics are always the best. Watch and learn." She reached under the console, smiling as her fingers found the wires she wanted.

Deven had secured his seat and Vas killed the engines. Everything except emergency lights and the bio-filter that would keep them breathing a little longer.

And the long-range scanner, the shields, and one very active but appearing dead, weapons system.

Vas watched as the ship following them slowed almost immediately. She cut the emergency stabilizers and the ship slowly started drifting. "This works better with a few minor explosions, but I don't want to chance something tricky in an unknown ship. Ignoring my current actions, of course."

The black suit fighter moved forward with caution, closing the gap between them. Their shuttle just kept spinning slowly. "Are our passengers belted in? At the rate this guy is moving we might roll over a few times before he gets close enough." She knew what those little fighters could do; she'd have one shot and that was only with the element of surprise. If she didn't destroy them on that first round, there wouldn't be another chance.

"I got them tied up, gagged, and got us off the planet—

belting in wasn't high on my list." His words were accented
by a few thumps as they rotated a bit more. Vas looked back
at their unwilling passengers as they started slowly tumbling from their seats.

"Sorry. On the plus side, this might keep you from being
blown apart." She ignored the glares; more of them were
conscious now, and went back to watching the screen.

The black suit fighter was close enough that she could
use the short-range scanner. It was within weapons range
now, but still enough distance between them that it might
be able to evade her shots. She needed to wait.

A little more turning and the thumps behind her continued. So did an odd muttering sound. Most likely people
swearing at her with gags on. She'd had that happen
enough that she was used to it.

The black suit fighter continued to move closer. It was
definitely close enough to have fired with a fair chance of
success had its goal been to destroy them.

Which meant it was time to bid their tail goodbye. Vas
counted down the seconds with her hand so Deven could
see. She would have said them out loud, but she didn't
know how sound masking these shields were. Thanks to
Gosta they'd gained the advantage more than once by listening in on parts of conversations on nearby ships. Not to
mention, saying them out loud wouldn't help the people
in the back—even prepared there was no way they could
have braced against anything.

Vas fired. She knew without the stabilizers the ship would
rock, Deven knew, the people in the back now knew. As
she fired she kicked on all the power, but there would be
some serious bruises back there.

The black suit fighter blew up, sending debris dangerously close to their shields. Vas punched the engines and
they engaged. Sort of.

"What happened to our power?" Deven had been
watching the monitors on his side and tapped one screen

for emphasis. "We're losing it, something is draining it."

Vas kept the ship moving at full power but she felt the drain on the engines. Deven had fed in a flight plan, but she wasn't sure they'd make it before the engines died completely.

"That ship didn't fire. I would have seen it if it had. The shields are still intact...crap." She pointed to a scanner. "There. The shield was modified. Someone was working with the black suits. Had I not killed the engines when I did they would have died anyway." She turned to the back. "Did you all hear that? One of your own people, maybe even someone on this ship, was working with those bastards."

Deven was running calculations but his swearing was growing louder. "And there's another ship approaching. These scanners are worse than one of our shuttles, but it's big. We can't escape. It'll be on us in a few minutes. Unless it isn't after us, in which case it will fly past us, leaving us limping until we're stranded."

Vas was doing her own calculations but pulled back and looked at him. "What the hell is up with you? I've never heard that from you—you sound like Mac." That was something she never thought she'd say to Deven. He was a lot of things, but defeatist and pessimistic he'd never been.

"I'm sorry," he said. "I've not been this wiped out in twenty years. I'm not as young as I used to be." He ran a hand over his eyes.

The approaching ship was now on both scanners and it was slowing down.

"Stand down your weapons, and prepare to be boarded. You have two of our people on there. We will get them back, or blow up your ship."

Vas had never been so happy to hear Ragkor's voice.

"Ragkor, it's me. Deven and I are flying this thing. But it's been compromised. I don't know how long it can stay airtight and moving."

"Captain! We heard you'd been taken. Should have known that wouldn't last. We can send a shuttle over."

Vas looked at the twenty people behind her. Even if she let them go, this ship wasn't going to last too much longer. Besides, there was a good chance the gray ships had found what they wanted and destroyed the planet they came from.

"Do you still have two shuttles on that ship?"

"Aye, both have been repaired, but it's just you and Deven, right?"

Vas sighed and swatted at the hair that flew up. "No. We liberated this ship and Deven kept the original users on it since their planet was about to be blown up." Captain Zarith was watching her and her eyes widened. "Oh yeah, those gray ships are killers—that world is probably astro-rubble by now."

"What was that, Captain? I missed the last part."

"Nothing important. But we need to get our prisoners off this ship. Something is latched on near the engine."

This time Ragkor started swearing. "It's a leech mine. I haven't seen one since the service. I'm sending one shuttle, all we have time for. Get everyone in—we need to be out of range in five minutes."

Crap. Vas had heard of leech mines, nasty little buggers not really in use by the Commonwealth military anymore—not officially anyway. They pulled energy from a vessel and used it to blow up the ship. Where a black suit had gotten one, she didn't have to guess.

She set the shuttle to stay in place and locked the stabilizers. Then she unbuckled herself as Deven did the same. Both ran to the back and started hauling up Garmainians and pushing them toward the door. "You all have a choice. Come with us, where, as I said, we'll find somewhere to drop you. Or stay here, knowing this ship is going to blow."

Captain Zarith nodded and moved to the door. The rest of her crew followed.

"And you will be locked up until we can figure out what to do with you. There's a chance one of you was a saboteur. And even if not, you did handcuff me." She held up her injured wrist. "I really don't like being cuffed."

The ship rocked and the familiar sound of the boarding channel from the shuttle echoed in the small space. The ramp from the ship suddenly developed a hole, but the metal cooled immediately. "Sorry, this was the fastest way." Therlian was first in with a huge blaster rifle in her hands. Once she was sure things were legit, she stepped aside, and three crewmembers started hauling in the Garmainians.

"Captain, another black suit single fighter is heading this way. It's loaded with explosives if the readings are right."

CHAPTER EIGHTEEN

———————

V AS STARTED A STEADY STREAM of swearing. Why in the hell go through this much effort for one ship? If someone on here was that important to kill, wouldn't sending more than one fighter from the start have made more sense? Or not let them off the planet? The fact that the ship was triggered to blow, not just limp in space, could be an indication that the saboteur wasn't on board—or not. Zealots were known to kill themselves to make sure their statement was made. Although, if things had happened naturally, the shuttle would have slowed down long enough for that black suit fighter ship to have taken someone or something off of here before it blew up. The second ship must have been a backup if the leech mine hadn't destroyed them. She'd have to really check all of the Garmainians.

Deven started picking up Garmainians and throwing them into the shuttle. Therlian kept her gun on everyone but the other crewmembers helped drag them all in.

Vas was the last one. She looked around for anything that might be important, and then followed Therlian into the crowded shuttle. She let out a sigh of relief when she saw who was flying it.

"Mac! I am damn glad to see you—get us the hell out of here." Normally the shuttle would re-board the *Victorious Dead* then they'd get out of here. They didn't have that time.

"Aye, Captain," he grinned and did what he did best: got the hell out of there.

The *Victorious Dead* let the shuttle go ahead of them, Ragkor counting on the bulk of his ship to help protect the shuttle from the exploding debris.

There was no way that Vas could get through the bodies to the front. "Mac, has the second ship changed course?"

"Not yet, Captain. It's hell bent on that ship you were on. And Walvento is going to cry at the loss of all those explosives on the second ship. It's got enough to take down a cruiser level at least."

Damn it. That was massive overkill. For a group who had been planning their attacks extremely well, an over use of force like this could be very bad.

"Keep us away from them," Vas said and automatically went to tap her comm...that of course wasn't on this prisoner's outfit. She glanced down—she was incinerating this when she got back to real clothing.

"Ask Ragkor to get as many scans of the approaching ship as possible. I want Flarik to look for anything that will help us." She was going to add more but the screens in the front flared to a blinding light and a concussion wave hit the shuttle. Had the *Victorious Dead* not been between them and it, everyone in this shuttle would be sucking stardust now.

Klaxons rang through the shuttle and there were a few more bumps where things got through, but it stayed intact.

"Captain, I recommend we get you all on board as soon as possible. There are three more fighters heading our way."

"Agreed."

Mac spun the shuttle back to the massive ship that had been protecting it and worked his way into the shuttle bay.

Once it was in, and the airlocks reestablished, Vas punched open the ramp. She wasn't normally a claustrophobic person—hard to be that when you'd spent most of your time on a ship—but this shuttle had gotten to her.

"Captain!" Ragkor was the first she saw and he broke all semblance of decorum by picking her up in a huge hug. He gently put her down with an embarrassed grin. "Sorry about that. It's just, we really thought all of you were gone, then to find the rest but discover that you and Deven had been captured?" He glared at the Garmainians being brought down the ramp. "These are the people who did that?"

"Ironically, they are the exact people who did that. But they're like us, just doing a job. My brother told an entire planet who had a bounty on me where I was."

Ragkor raised an eyebrow. The bit with her brother and the Rillianian monks happened before he came on board the *Warrior Wench*, but she knew he'd studied everything about that battle. "I thought he was dead?"

She sighed. "So did we all. Appearantly, that bastard is still around somewhere." She was standing near Captain Zarith so she reached over and removed her gag. "How long ago did the bounty listing come through?"

Captain Zarith worked her jaw a bit. The gag could not be comfortable, but considering that Deven had used their own equipment against them, none of them could complain. "About five months ago. He gave us some indication where you were, but it still wasn't easy to find you. Not to mention, he didn't give it to the council. He gave it to one of the back planets far from here. Most mercs don't feel right hanging out in the capital."

Vas nodded. She and her people felt the same. The issues of her non-staying-dead brother, Borlan, and why he set a bunch of bounty hunters on her tail when he was himself heading for her in the *Defiant* would be dealt with later. "Un-gag all of our guests. They will need to be housed in secure locations, but they are to be treated fairly."

Ragkor nodded and got his crew moving the still bound Garmainians out of the shuttle bay. He followed behind and Vas knew her orders would be followed exactly. Another advantage of a former Marine on her crew.

Vas waited until they'd cleared out, and then turned to

Mac. "How is everyone back on our planet? Walvento?" He'd taken worse hits before but they always had better resources on hand.

"He's fine. We found them after a few hours—they were hiding really well. We still don't have the *Warrior Wench* up and fully running, but we're way closer thanks to Ragkor's people." He glanced around, even though it was clear that there were just the three of them. "I was saving this as a surprise, but I have to tell you both—a bunch of us have been working on repairing the *Defiant*. It's weird, for a crashing ship, it didn't take a lot of damage from landing." He shrugged. "Maybe there's something odd about that planet. Anyway, we're hoping we can get it in good enough shape to leave with us once the *Warrior Wench* is ready." With his pale coloring, big light blue eyes, and red hair, Mac was the poster child for innocence—especially when he was excited like right now. It was such a misdirection of genetics.

Vas wasn't sure what she thought about that. But the bottom line was that another ship could come in damn handy. "Okay, but it stays under me. I know you want your own empire one day, but we need to have a unified front. We've no idea what is going on back at Home or even in the Commonwealth at all."

Mac's eyes got rounder. "Oh no, it was meant to be all yours. I sure as hell am not crazy enough to want to captain something." His mouth slammed shut right after the last word fled. "That came out wrong. What I meant was—"

"That you respect me so much that all you wanted to do was add another ship to my fleet." Vas ruffled his hair. They might have only been gone a short while, but she found she'd missed him. "And that we need to get my second-in-command into bed."

She laughed as Mac's eyes went wide again. "A bed, he needs to rest." Deven had been listening to her and Mac, but was only nodding vaguely. He was also listing to one side.

"I'll be fine," he said. But he was still listing. Vas had seen
Deven so exhausted during battles that he'd fallen asleep
standing up. She couldn't figure out why he wasn't doing
that now. His face was drawn and pale and the circles under
his eyes looked carved in stone.

"Who is the medical officer on this fine ship?" She knew
she'd seen the crew manifest but that had been a hell of a
long time ago. Beyond a few folks who'd left the *Warrior
Wench* she really hadn't paid much attention. She had hundreds of crewmembers stashed back on her secret planet,
Home.

"Actually, Pela is here, she came along with me, and a few
others to make sure you got back okay. The doc is Delthin,
but he's letting Pela have full run. I think she'd agree with
you, Captain. He looks awful." He leaned toward her as he
spoke but shrugged his shoulders at Deven. He and Deven
were close, but Vas was his captain after all.

"Fine," Deven yawned. "Don't send Terel's evil sidekick
after me. Find me an empty room and I'll crash in it."

Vas had expected him to fight more, that he didn't definitely pointed out how tired he was. Regardless of how
long he rested, she was ordering a full examination by
Terel when they got back to the *Warrior Wench*.

They left the shuttle bay and Vas was hit with the fact
that this ship really wasn't hers anymore. Oh, it had been
put back as close to original specs as possible—even if
Marli had added a few extras. But it still had the new ship
feel. When it had been taken from her almost two years
ago, she'd known she would stop at nothing to get it back.
Now she welcomed it, but her ship was the *Warrior Wench*.

Mac led them down to the crew quarters and pushed
open a door. "This row is open, but this room is the biggest. I was planning on claiming it if it took a while to find
you."

Vas pushed Deven into the room and aimed him at the

bed. It said a lot about her own condition that she thought about joining him. Only to sleep. She shook her head and forced herself to let the door slide closed.

"How long ago did you come looking for us?" It had been a while since she'd been here, but she still knew the way to the command deck. Mac stayed with her down the corridors to the lift.

"Ragkor showed up before we realized you were missing. That was four days ago. It took Gosta this long to track down what planet probably had you." Mac laughed. "He found the wanted bounty electronic flyer and that it had been cancelled as bounty apprehended. He was pissed that it had been that simple, but grateful to find you. Why'd they grab Deven, though?"

Vas entered the lift and punched the level of the command deck. "Near as I can figure, he played himself off as being an even bigger bounty than me. The Garmainians aren't on friendly terms with Deven's people and there's a pirate out there that Deven knew enough about that he could make them think he was him." Vas wasn't going to get into the entire possibility that Deven was this pirate, or had been at some point. Part of the reason this pirate had been impossible to catch was that no one was sure who it was. It seemed to change.

Which told Vas there was probably more than one. Deven not being sure himself was disturbing though.

"Oh, and Wilthuny escaped," Mac said just as the lift doors opened on the command deck.

Vas's response came out louder than intended. "What? How? You and Walvento assured me her room was secure." Empress Wilthuny had power in the Commonwealth, but had turned to success by whatever means necessary when that power started being taken away. They'd finally captured her right before they had to flee from an armada of massive planet-killer-sized Asarlaí ships.

Vas had them secure a cell in the building they'd housed

most of the entire crew in, she'd tested it herself, and it was foolproof. Or so they thought.

Mac flashed red as Ragkor, Therlian, and the rest of the *Victorious Dead* command crew turned to them. "Well, she managed to get away when we were evacuating per the orders that might not have been you...we thought maybe she died, since she only took a single airsuit. Two days ago, another ship showed up in orbit. Wilthuny reappeared, stole a Flit, and joined the other ship."

Ragkor was turning red now. "That was my fault, Captain. The other ship was unmarked, and in stealth mode. But she must have communicated with it somehow. She landed the Flit in its landing bay and it took off."

Damn it. Wilthuny still had enough resources to be dangerous, and obviously not just in the Commonwealth. "Was Gosta able to find out anything about the ship that picked her up?"

Therlian shook her head. "Not a thing."

"Okay, well, we add it to our current list. Three gray ships showed up about fifteen hours ago on the Garmainian capital planet. They didn't destroy it initially; they were after something on the planet and sent down their black suits. By the time we left, the fighting was still going on but the planet's canons had managed to ground one of the gray ships. She could have been working with the Asarlaí on this and been picked up by one of them." If Vas was lucky, Wilthuny had been on the ship that crashed.

She looked around the command deck, so like and yet unlike that of her former ship. "Anything else I need to know about before we get back? And if not, is there an empty quarter where I can go take a shower and borrow some clothes?" She really needed a long one at this point. And they'd had to seriously ration showers on the *Warrior Wench* since they'd crashed. It was a good excuse to share shower time with Deven, but right now she needed real water and lots of it.

There hadn't been anything crucial and after a few low-level bits of information that could be read in a report later, Vas cut them off and asked Therlian to walk with her to an unoccupied crew quarter.

Vas waited until they were in the lift, and then turned to the tall, former nun. "This might sound strange, but did you ever hear of any of the order living on after death—on this plane? Being able to communicate telepathically?" Vas wouldn't have had this discussion with anyone else, including Deven. But Therlian was the only known surviving member of the Clionea order. She'd left them when she'd fallen in love and gotten pregnant. Vas knew she could trust her not to say anything.

Therlian raised one thin eyebrow, assessed that Vas was serious, then frowned. "Theoretically a practitioner of the arts could force their way into this plane after death, but I never read of it happening. Aithnea always insisted it was impossible. Do you want to share why?"

Vas took a deep breath, hit pause on the lift, and explained about the voice that had so far sounded like Aithnea to her, and like Vas to both Deven and Gosta.

Therlian probably wasn't even aware of the way her body and face automatically assumed the nun's listening position. It was a way of presenting oneself to the speaker and any watchers to be completely open. Absorbing both what was said as well as what was not said.

She remained silent for a few moments after Vas finished.

"That is unlike anything I read in the scrolls. And I read all of them. Could it be a telepathic being that is somehow connected to the planet where you crashed? Perhaps one able to tap into your emotions?"

"I thought of aliens as well. But the voice knew the meditating technique. It saved me when my suit was punctured, and saved all of us when the *Defiant* was crashing. And it saved the rest of the crew and let the Garmainians take us." She laughed.

"That does sound like Aithnea, especially if she felt there was a lesson in there for you."

Vas nodded. That did sound like Aithnea and matched what the voice said when it left Vas to the bounty hunters. "Oh, and I know you had already left the order by then, but I think a little over a year ago Aithnea worked with a local race—Deven's race as it turns out—to steal something from the Garmainians. Do you recall her mentioning any dealings with them or the Kilesh?" She still had the hold on the lift. She had no idea how many people, if any, knew of Therlian's past. Vas wasn't going to let that information be public if she didn't want it put out there. No one aside from Deven, Terel, and Therlian knew that Vas had spent two years with the nuns. Not as a novitiate, but as a working houseguest.

Therlian shook her head. "Neither of those names sound familiar. I take it that was somehow messed up with that bounty situation?"

"Aye. I mentioned it on the vid they caught of me stealing some scrolls. The problem is, I hadn't seen or talked to Aithnea in years before she sent me the Last Rites ritual vid link. I don't have any memory of the entire event around the theft, and the items I stole were gone by the time I woke up and headed to pick up my crew on Lucky Strike. One of the items was a nice, state-of-the-art warship prototype that the Garmainians would really like back. The rest was a pack of historical scrolls. My theory is the ship went to the Kilesh and the scrolls to Aithnea. I just wish I knew why and whose fault it is that I have no memory."

"Aithnea." Both Vas and Therlian said at the same time.

"Yeah, I kind of guessed that—I just wish I knew why." Vas released the pause on the lift and they got out at the next floor. The first room was empty.

"Help yourself to the bath and the bed. Ragkor keeps all of the guest rooms stocked. I'm not sure if he realizes we're not a luxury cruise ship. I'll bring down something to wear, and then I'll send someone to wake you before we reach the planet. You look like crap."

Vas laughed and hit the light. Therlian was right. When this had been her ship the unused rooms were stripped down. This looked like a modest guest room in a hotel. "Thanks on all counts. A sleep in a bed that isn't in a jail would be nice."

Therlian nodded and shut the door.

———◆———

Vas's dreams were violent and disturbing. Every time she tried to reach for a vague box, one that she really needed, pain slammed into her and visions of people she knew dying slowly shattered her mind.

Finally she made it to the box, close enough that she could see it. The red Gathian rustwood box she'd found on Therlian's planet—the one the Commonwealth, the Asar-laí, and possibly others had been killing to get. It was still hidden behind the wall of weapons in her quarters on the *Warrior Wench*. So why was it invading her dreams now?

A pounding on the door brought her out of the dream. Of course her first thought was to reach for the blaster she normally kept under her pillow. It took a few seconds to remember where she was and that there was no weapon under her pillow. She'd have to mention that as an idea to Ragkor—firearms for guests.

She rolled to her feet. The long pants and shirt that Therlian had left for her were too big, but they worked. She kept the boots the Garmainians had given her though.

"Sorry to wake you, but we're at the planet," Therlian said. "Mac wants to name it Planet Mac by the way."

"It was just a suggestion," Mac said further behind her.

"A bad one," Vas said as she sat back down to put on her boots. "I don't think that place deserves a name—not as long as we can get off of it anyway."

"Deven is putting the Garmainians onto two shuttles,"

Therlian said as she punched the lift for the shuttle. "It will be less painful to transport all of you down that way."

The shuttle bay was controlled chaos. Along with Mac and Pela, Marwin, and Gon had also apparently come along on this trip. They were all acting as escorts for their prisoners. Vas really didn't think of them that way—unless one of them was actually working for the Asarlaí. The sooner they could get the ship off the planet and leave the entire bunch there, the better. She had no doubt that Captain Zarith could find out all by herself if they were betrayed by one of their own.

Deven looked better as he nodded to her from over Marwin's head, though there was still too much fatigue in his eyes. She'd have Terel go after him once they got back to the *Warrior Wench*. But she needed his skills, so real rest would have to wait until they found a way back to Home.

Once the Garmainians were secure, things settled a bit and Ragkor walked to the far shuttle with Vas.

"I don't think I need an escort."

"I'm going with you, as long as you don't mind. I can fly the first shuttle. Gosta has the *Warrior Wench* almost ready to lift off but there are still some issues with the core, and I can handle that type of engineering. He contacted me while you were asleep."

"As long as you can get us up in the air and out of here," Vas said, "I don't care who comes with us." Not to mention she knew Deven would probably try and fly down. He looked better, but she didn't want to push things if she didn't have to. Ragkor nodded and went up to the pilot's seat. Mac would be taking the second shuttle down.

The ride back to the planet would be short but still give Vas time to really study the Garmainians as she sat in the back of the shuttle. Studying them when she had been their prisoner hadn't been an option.

They were calm, especially for a group of fighters who had been taken prisoner. All but one. Phonial. He was two rows ahead of her, and while his movements wouldn't have been noticeable in a twitchy group like her crew, they were when compared to the rest of his people.

"Captain Zarith, how long has Phonial been part of your crew?" Vas had sat the Captain next to her in the back. Since the Garmainian crew was split, there was a chance if there was someone with an issue within them they'd be on the other shuttle, but at the least she could ask the captain some questions. She kept her voice low—luckily this shuttle was quite noisy.

"Two years. He came on as a grunt and moved up quickly." There was no question in her voice as she spoke, and she was watching him now as well.

"Is he always that twitchy?"

"Never." Saurian faces weren't as mobile as some races, but her scowl was evident.

Gon was up front with Ragkor but was keeping a watchful eye on their guests. Vas saw him look her way and she nodded toward Phonial. He nodded as well and made sure he faced him.

Phonial grew a little twitchier, but Vas wasn't sure what he could do if he was planning something. He was bound, and they'd all been frisked a second time on the *Victorious Dead* in case anything was missed when Deven had knocked them out.

They were preparing to begin final descent when Phonial jumped to his feet. "I did it! It was me, and they have a bomb on me, too! They threatened my family..." He stumbled back into his seat, sobbing.

"Ragkor get this ship down now, I don't care where, we need to land." Yes, breathing the air of that world would be bad, but so would blowing up in the atmosphere.

"Aye, Captain—it will still be a few minutes." Everyone around Phonial tried to twist away, but the shuttle was too small. If he was implanted with a bomb, and it went off, no one here would survive.

Captain Zarith raised her bound wrists and pointed ahead. "May I question him? These can stay on." There was fury in her eyes, but compassion as well.

"Aye." Vas moved so Zarith could go to her crewmember.

"I'm sorry," Phonial said. "I'm sorry. It was the only way. I have littles; they were going to kill them. I'm so sorry."

Captain Zarith stood next to him and calmly backhanded him with her bound hands. "Stop blubbering and tell me what happened. You betrayed us? You let them put a mine on our shuttle?"

"Yes. I was instructed which shuttle to liberate. To make sure the whole crew got on—but I was supposed to take it back to the planet we found them on. The explosive device was already in place. They wanted to kill all of us, didn't tell me why. The one in my chest was a backup and should go off any minute now."

"You know what this means."

"Kill me before it does, please. But if you get back to Garmain, see to my family, don't tell them what I did?"

Captain Zarith looked to Vas.

"Wait. Gon have you been recording all of this? We need sensors. If he has a body explosive, the *Victorious Dead* should have picked up on it."

"Aye, Captain." he looked down at his scanner.

Deven had been silent, but turned his focus on Phonial. "There is a device, near his heart. It was blocked very well."

The shuttle was lower now; a semblance of atmosphere would be there.

Vas nodded to Captain Zarith.

Captain Zarith pulled Phonial to his feet and led him to the doorway. It would have been hard for her, with her bound hands, if he fought, but he was leading the way.

"My notes on what they did, and information is in my bag. I am sorry."

"Everyone, when I yell, hold your breath as long as you

can. Ragkor, you open the door on my count then fly as high as you can get this thing."

"Ready."

"Now!" Vas held her breath and braced herself.

The door slid open in emergency speed. Zarith went to shove Phonial out but he ran out on his own. Ragkor gunned the shuttle's engines and shot straight up as the shuttle door shut.

CHAPTER NINETEEN

———◆———

T HE SILENT EXPLOSION BEHIND THEM a moment
later chilled Vas. They had almost all died. Phonial had
fallen quickly but the explosion had been enough to buffet the shuttle. The engines coughed, but Ragkor leveled
it out.

"Captain Tor Dain, I apologize formally for my crewman," Captain Zarith said and bowed awkwardly.

Vas nodded. She would have pointed out that it appeared
that Captain Zarith had no knowledge, but the formal
apology and bowing was similar enough to some of the
cultures in the Commonwealth that she knew excuses
would not be given.

"I accept your apology." Vas gave a small nod. "Ragkor?
Are you going to be able to land us in one piece now?"

"Aye, Captain. Gosta wants to know just what in the
heck we were doing dropping weapons that close to his
ship. Those were his words, not mine."

Vas shook her head. Gosta was getting a little proprietary
about the grounded *Warrior Wench* and the adjacent building. Granted, he'd been instrumental in finding ways to
make everything work, but *his* ship?

Ragkor laughed. "He said to belay that."

"Too late, we all heard. Now get us down before someone else blows up."

The landing was far less exciting than the arrival. They
didn't have enough airsuits but Ragkor had gotten them
close enough to the compound that they could make it
with breathers. Gosta sent an airsuit-wearing Bathie to

hand them out. It took a while to get them on everyone in both shuttles—Vas still didn't feel ready to unlock the Garmainians just yet.

Vas left them all in the building, with Ragkor helping Bathie find secure places to put them. She dragged Deven along with her into the *Warrior Wench*.

"You need to see Terel. Now." Deven had been far too silent and distant the entire way back. He was hiding it, but something was still wrong.

"I'll be—"

"If you say fine, I will punch you." Vas stopped in the tunnel that connected to the ship and spun him to face her. "You're not fine. You've been getting worse since we left that planet. I assume that telepathically knocking out myself and twenty Garmainians would be hard on an esper. But I'm not one, and as far as I know there are none in the Commonwealth who could have done that. However, you have been declining rapidly since then. You're letting Terel see you."

He peered down at her, his green eyes looked sad, and then he crumbled.

"Damn it!" Vas struggled to hold him up. She was a strong woman, but he was a lot bigger than her and a dead drop wasn't easy to move. Again, she automatically reached for a comm that wasn't there. She resorted to yelling.

Gosta was surprisingly the first to respond and he came from the ship end of the tunnel. He was taller than Deven, but about half his weight. They'd still have a problem getting him all the way to the med labs themselves.

"He just collapsed; I need a stretcher to get him to the med labs."

"Aye, Captain." He tapped his comm and issued orders.

Vas was impressed. When Deven had died before, she'd tried to make Gosta and Flarik her team second-in-command. Gosta hadn't felt comfortable ordering others around during that failed experiment. Being trapped here for all these months had made some good changes.

When he was satisfied that help was coming he turned back. "You do realize that I hadn't meant to say *my* ship to Ragkor, right? It's our ship. I was just caught up in the moment."

"I know," Vas said. "And for the record, although all of you believe otherwise, this is technically my ship."

Pela came from the direction of the building just as Terel and Gon came from the *Warrior Wench*. Pela got there first and checked Deven's pulse and under his eyelids.

Terel directed them to get him rolled onto an anti-grav stretcher.

"His breathing is short and shallow, pulse slow, and his gums and eyelids are pale." Pela paced alongside Terel and Vas as the anti-grav stretcher moved down the tunnel.

"What happened to him?" Terel was all business as she took in the readings the stretcher was feeding back.

"He massively over taxed himself. I'll give you a full briefing later, but he's been pushing his esper abilities far—he took over the ship the Garmainians had. Twenty of them and me. On top of other things." She wanted to keep most of his recent abilities on the down low, but Terel would have to know.

Terel shook her head. "I'm not an expert in telepaths. No one outside of the mind op reserves are and their expertise is mostly how to turn insane ones into weapons. But he's in shock. Let's get him back to the lab and I should be able to tell more."

They were crossing into the ship itself when the alarms started.

"What the hell?"

"There's something on Deven. It's setting off the alarms…it's an explosive device?" Gosta's voice went up a few octaves at that.

"Okay, we have to get far away. Help me roll him back to the shuttle." Vas was already pulling him backwards. Hopefully they could find and defuse the bomb, and live long enough to hunt down whoever put it there. She wasn't going to let it take out the entire crew. Not even for Deven. But he wasn't going without her.

"I need to go with you." Terel was helping her push the stretcher back.

"You need to stay here. It could blow."

"Hell yes, it could. But while you're good at cutting things open, you usually don't do it with the goal of people surviving." The look she gave Vas said she wasn't going to back down.

Vas gave in. "Gosta, get everyone locked down and have the building and ship secured. We'll return when we can."

Everyone with her looked ready to argue and more of her crew were coming down the tunnel. "No. Everyone stay away. I'm serious. Ragkor and Gosta are in charge until we're back."

She turned the stretcher and they raced down the tunnel. Who had put a bomb in Deven? The when had to have been when they were both prisoners. She stopped. "Keep going to the first shuttle, get him secured, I need to check something." She ran back down the tunnel, bypassing her confused crewmates, and crossed into the ship.

No alarms. At least only one of them had been given it. Hopefully the *Warrior Wench*'s sensors were working better that the *Victorious Dead*'s.

"Keep going!" She waved to Gosta who had slowed down, then spun back to follow Terel. They were already on the shuttle and Terel had secured Deven's stretcher as best she could. A simple emergency surgery kit that came with the shuttle was going to have to be enough. She waved a small scanner over Deven twice before it finally went off.

"Damn it. It's not that deep, but it's near a major artery. You're going to fly like an angel to keep me from killing him or exploding all of us."

"I can do that," Vas said as she ran to the cockpit. And Ragkor. "Get out; you need to keep everyone else safe."

The big man shook his head and finished prepping for liftoff. The ramp was up and the shuttle was hovering. "The biggest threat in this shuttle is Deven. Your crew will be fine, and so will mine. But I am a damn good pilot and Terel is probably going to need someone to help her."

Vas ran her fingers through her hair. One advantage of it being unbraided—that move worked better. "Damn you. I hate it when you're logical. Keep us steady, and we'll live long enough for a long discussion on insubordination." She stepped back to Terel. "I'm yours. Thanks for warning me Ragkor was on board by the way."

Terel shrugged but didn't look up from her patient. "He was right. Unlike you, I don't argue with right. This will be fast. I have him as sedated as I can." She had bared his chest and had straps around his torso and both shoulders to keep him on the stretcher. "I have to cut here. I need you to stand next to me and hand me equipment."

"Okay," Vas said as she stepped close and took the small tray. There seemed to be way too few pieces for something this detailed.

Terel immediately placed a knife over his chest. A free-floating scanner showed the bomb, and it was damn tiny. No larger than a fingernail, it glowed an eerie red on the scanner. The scanner not only showed Terel where to cut, it was taking in as much information about the bomb as possible. If they survived this, they'd have a better idea what was going on.

Terel's knife was sure and she quickly got down to the red part. Deven moaned a bit and his hand twitched, but he didn't regain consciousness. Terel swore as he responded, but Vas knew there was no stopping now. Another twitch from Deven and Terel's knife almost slipped. He muttered something that Vas couldn't understand.

Then Terel held up her bloody blade with a small glowing scrap on it. Vas sat down the tray and took the knife and bomb from Terel and ran for the ramp. "Drop door, now!"

A small weapons drop side door opened to the left of the ramp. It had a shield to keep the air inside the shuttle but a rotating compartment. Vas gently placed the knife with its exploding passenger into the compartment then hit the door closed. It would rotate out and release the bomb.

"Is he stable?"

Terel peered into the scanner. "Yes."

Vas ran to Ragkor. "Get us the hell out of here."

He didn't answer, but the shuttle veered away and accelerated.

Vas turned back to Deven. He was still far paler than he should be, but he seemed to be breathing better. Or it could be wishful thinking on her part. She turned to the view screen, but at this distance there was no way to see the tiny bomb. Maybe it wasn't going to go off.

Then the shuttle took an impact hit as she was proven wrong.

The alarms went off but Ragkor was able to stabilize the shuttle.

"Damn it! Who are these Garmainians and what is their obsession with tiny bombs?" Vas stayed out of Terel's way but came closer to Deven. The suture device was closing his wound, not that the incision had been large; it would be gone probably within a few days.

"My question would be why? They put it in one of their own and then directed him to steal a ship and get his crewmates on it? How quickly are they getting them into people?"

Vas knew where Terel was going with this and she was thinking it herself. The Garmainians had plenty of time to plant that thing in Deven. Whether it was set to go off at a certain time, or when he was a distance away from them, hopefully the scans could tell them. But Phonial would have been a rush job. There was no way whoever planted it knew they were going to be invaded by the gray ships. Unless they were already working with them. She needed to find those notes he said he'd left, all of the Garmainians belongings had gone with them.

"What if they knew the gray ships were coming? We've got enough evidence that points to a portion of the Commonwealth actually working with the Asarlaí, or whoever has been on those gray ships." Vas couldn't pin down why, but she just felt that the Asarlaí she'd seen, the ones Marli mocked, hadn't been on the first runs of those gray ships.

"They set him up knowing the invasion was coming? But that was their capital planet, right?"

Vas nodded. "And we have no way of knowing if any of the people who should be there, were. The ones trying me were high ranking, but his Grace was old. There might have been a thought to gain power. Tragic if the majority of their current rulers were destroyed in an outside attack."

"Gosta has uploaded the scans we got from the shuttle's sensor from the prior explosion and is running a comparison with the one from Deven. He also asks when we're coming back down." Ragkor had been keeping the shuttle heading out.

"Sorry, I think we can turn back now." Vas was still trying to put together the why of blowing up a shuttle of mercs. Or getting something from one of them before the shuttle had been destroyed. If they just wanted to kill them, there would have been no real reason for the leech mine. Whoever was behind this wanted something, and set up a bunch of exploding fail-safes to make sure everything else was destroyed. She looked down at Deven as if he could give her answers. His color was a little better. The mercs weren't in positions of power, and Phonial had said whoever was behind it threatened his family if he didn't go on the suicide run.

Terel was punching things into the small scanner and

swearing.

"Do you want to share?"

"Sorry. I sent the scans to Gosta. We're limited in comparing to the bomb on the shuttle you escaped on and that man, but the bomb in Deven wasn't from the Garmainians." She looked up. "It was Asarlaí. And it looks like it had been inside him for months."

CHAPTER TWENTY

———◆———

V AS FROZE. "MONTHS? LIKE SINCE we've been here?" That would be horrifying. That the Asarlaí had somehow gotten a hold of Deven with none of them noticing.

Terel adjusted a few things on the scanner, and then shook her head. "There's no way to know for sure. If it hadn't blown up, I could maybe tell. I can do a deeper scan of the tissue around the area when we get back to the *Warrior Wench*. But, to be honest, I'd say it's been more like six or seven months."

That was almost worse than the idea of stealth Asarlaí. "You mean when Deven was put back together? Could it have been in the body of one of the others?" There had been three Devens for a bit, until Marli reunified them. One was a bastard of a pirate. Just dealing with him briefly made Vas think many people would want to blow him up.

"I'm still not sure what she did to get them back into one. But it seemed like more of a mental transfer than physical one." Terel looked up. "His body changed a lot when it was blown up—so it must've been after that."

"Crap. So you think Marli planted a bomb in him when she saved him? For what purpose? She could have let him die." There wasn't a lot of room to pace in the shuttle, especially with a stretcher in the middle. But Vas managed. "And why didn't it go off earlier? What triggered it now?"

Terel closed the scanner and covered Deven's chest with a sheet. "I have no idea, but it was in him and it was so dormant and hidden that none of the bomb scanners caught it. That's a bit out of my medical expertise. But I would bet that she was the one who put it in him. I'd say have some of your gizmo lovers try and find out what they can about all three bombs. She could be sneaking around this quadrant—and not on our side."

Terel had never been fond of Marli, but it was mostly because of Marli's irreverent attitude. Unlike some of the people on Vas's ship, Terel wasn't really that bothered that Marli was an Asarlaí. Her dislike was on a personal basis.

But Vas had to agree that Marli worked on her own agendas and didn't feel the need to share them with anyone else. "Did you find out more about the black suits?" Terel had been studying the genetic matter of a few of them—they'd been like Marli's, but she had been wary of jumping to a conclusion.

"Some," she said. "Okay, yes. I finished the study while you were gone. There is no difference between the genetic makeup of the black suits and Marli. It's as if it all came from the same person."

Vas looked at Deven, willing him to regain consciousness. She needed to talk to him about this—he knew Marli better and longer than anyone. Yet she'd planted a bomb in him. Or Vas was jumping to conclusions because Marli was about as trustworthy as an Ilerian in a bank vault.

"Don't bother," Terel said. "I slipped him a nice cocktail to keep him under. Along with potentially blowing him up—that thing was tapping his energy." She tilted her head. "Has he done any more difficult and unusual telekinetic tricks recently?"

Ragkor was on approach for the small landing strip near the *Warrior Wench* but Vas noticed he was carefully not engaging in their conversation.

"Like I said, he mentally knocked out all twenty Garmainians and myself so we could steal their transport."

"Which happened to have a bomb—no, two—already on it." Terel shook her head. "The only expert we know on Asarlaí weapons might be behind all of this—not to mention, she might not be alive."

Vas thought of the way Marli ran across the command deck at the end of the battle, determined to join her crew. She'd vanished on the way to the transporter and so had the ship her crew was on.

"I think she's too stubborn to die." Vas steadied herself as they landed. "And I agree that she works on her own agenda—but saving Deven's life, just so she could put a delayed bomb in him, seems extreme even for a socio-pathic Asarlaí."

Terel just shrugged.

They both put their breathers back on and slipped one over Deven's face. Then Ragkor dropped the ramp. Gosta, Pela, and at least six other crewmembers were waiting.

"Med labs?" Pela asked.

"Aye, and keep him in the secure tube bed." Terel held up her hand as Vas opened her mouth. "No, I do not think there is another explosive in him. But I need him to get more rest, and more oxygen. I can control both if he's inside one of those. Plus, if we did miss anything the scans in the tube bed will notify me of it."

Vas nodded and stepped aside as they wheeled him out. She had some bounty hunters to question.

They'd found a series of rooms that could be locked well enough that the Garmainians were secure. The center room had been Wilthuny's. Glazlie, one of the triplets, was the first guard she saw.

"How are they?"

"Not a noise been made. They were polite as far as pris-oners go."

"Is Flarik on the deck?" Flarik was good at intimidation, but she was also a savvy negotiator. Vas didn't want to haul the Garmainians along with her on the trip back to the Commonwealth. However, she also needed to know what they knew. Flarik's presence could make that possible.

"She's in a short hibernation right now, should be out soon though." Glazlie winced, then added, "It was an unplanned one—happened right after you vanished."

That wasn't good. Flarik's people, the Wavians, were extremely advanced birds who didn't like space. They'd evolved to go into hibernation on longer trips, but it had become such a part of their biology that they needed it whether they were on a ship or not. Unplanned meant she'd almost passed out.

Vas decided to wait—having Flarik involved would be worth it, not to mention the down time might help the Garmainians loosen up a bit. She went to the command deck instead.

Mac practically jumped on her when she got there. "Captain! The new ship is ready—the *Defiant* is space worthy."

Vas looked around. She'd only been up in the shuttle an hour, maybe less. He'd said before it was a work in progress.

"You finished it that quickly?" The *Warrior Wench* was also looking more like its old self. The interior tunnels were all gone and everything looked normal.

Except her command chair.

For a moment, Vas had forgotten she'd blown her chair apart when the hologram of her late brother tried to invade her ship.

"Sorry, Captain," Gosta said from his station. "We haven't been able to fix that yet."

Vas hadn't even seen him look up, so he must have been expecting her reaction. At least they'd cleared up the mess. But it was still a sad sight to have a hole there.

"I set up another station for you until we can get to Home and fix your chair." Gosta did look up at that, as he pointed to the nav station nearest the command chair.

Vas had taken a while getting used to the ostentatious chair when she'd first taken this ship, but now she found she missed it. "Thank you. Now, about the *Defiant*?"

Mac bounced a bit more, and then flipped an image to

the now working main screen. It was of the outside and a lump of metal. "We were almost done a few days ago, but I wanted to wait until you got back to make the final touch. I present your newest ship member, the *Defiant*." Fathers of newborn infants didn't have as much pride as Mac's voice did right now.

Vas looked at the ship on the screen. It hadn't been the most graceful of designs to begin with. The *Victorious Dead* had clean, compact lines. *Warrior Wench* was more embellished, yet still graceful and sleek. She'd even gotten used to the tats—once they'd made sure none of the remaining ones had any interdimensional rips in them.

However, the *Defiant* really was an ugly lump. At least now. "I swear it didn't look like this when we first went to investigate." The more she looked at the image, the more she realized how oddly it had been cobbled together. "What in the hells did you people use for spare parts?"

"The ruins of the ships around the area. Had to go a full day out for some. It's amazing that the *Defiant* didn't explode when it crashed, but it did still take some heavy damage. I think it looks very good considering." The tone in Mac's voice was pure pride. The fact was, that was an ugly ship.

"*Defiant's* ruin, more like," she said as she looked at the mismatched parts blended together. "Actually, that name fits for many reasons—you did repair it out of junk. The more important reason is my unlamented brother—Ruin was his nickname for me. It's our ship, no Commonwealth around. I say we rename it *Defiant Ruin*. What of it, Gosta? That thing needs a new name if it's going out into the worlds with us. Can you update its registry?"

Updating a Commonwealth registry was pretty close to impossible, even for a hacker like Gosta. But this ship had already had its registry tampered with and this far out of Commonwealth airspace, many of the already damaged safeguards around it would be too weak to function.

Gosta was still focusing on something at his station—since he'd seen the *Defiant* reassembled, it wasn't new like it was to Vas. He pulled up some code. "I'd say yes, and it won't even be a challenge. You don't have to keep it *Defiant* anything you know, we could change it completely."

She shook her head. The name was odd for a ship, but it fit. And if her brother was still out there, the name would bug the crap out of him. "Nope, that works."

Gosta nodded, his long neck bobbing as he worked things out in his mind. "I think I can give it a fictitious history and registry going back at least a dozen years. It will need to be done before we get into Commonwealth airspace, but I can make it appear secure." The rest of his words were lost in muttering to himself.

"Make it happen," Vas said. She went through the scans on the new ship. She'd want to go see it in person, to appease a still extremely animated Mac if nothing else. It was larger than both the *Warrior Wench* and the *Victorious Dead*. But it had good weapons, or would once they could restock them. It still had some, but it had obviously been low on them when it crashed.

"Captain, if it's okay with you, I'm going to take one of the shuttles and go back to the *Victorious Dead*. I did a scan, and the core just needed a small tweak. I'll leave the second shuttle for your ship." She hadn't even noticed that Ragkor came up behind her and was standing at parade rest until he spoke.

"Good idea on both counts. Can you come back and drop off about ten or so crew from your ship? I'd like to operate *Defiant Ruin,* and if we take from both ships we won't deplete either. We can re-crew when we get to Home."

"Aye, Captain," he paused. "Who will be leading her until then?"

Good question. And her answer could make a difference as to who they both selected to serve on her for now.

"Hopefully, Deven. If not, Gosta."

Ragkor didn't say anything, but she'd been facing him and saw his eyes widen. Gosta, however, did say something.

"Captain, that is very kind, but I don't know that I could…needed here…um." He kept looking between the ship on the main screen and whatever information he'd been pouring through on his own monitor.

Vas kept her grin to herself. Six months ago, Gosta wouldn't have even thought about commanding any-thing—just being second-in-command had been too much for him. Now she could tell he was seriously think-ing about it. And trying not to show that he was.

"Captain? I would like to serve with Master Gosta." Hrrru had mostly spent the past almost six months orga-nizing the building most of the crew called home, but he was back at his station and had been quietly watching.

"Agreed," she said. Deven was in no condition right now, and she had a feeling even if he were, he'd want Gosta to have his chance. "Obviously, Mac should pilot." The grin he gave her could have blinded an army. He didn't even appear hurt at not being asked to temporarily captain.

Vas still hadn't changed into her own clothes, but some-one, most likely Gosta, had thoughtfully put a comm on her station. She pinned it on and tapped it. "Terel? How is our star patient, and when can medical be ready to get off this rock?" Considering that the med labs had been one of the first repaired, asking was simply a courtesy.

"He's out for at least another twelve hours—I wanted to give him time to recover. And I want him to take things easy for a few days afterwards. The rest of us are ready whenever you are."

Vas smiled and opened the shipwide comm, something she hadn't been able to do for almost six months. It felt good to have her ship back. She'd feel whole again once they got back into space. "Gosta, Mac, and Hrrru will be running our newest ship, *Defiant Ruin,* as we make our way back into the Commonwealth. My plan is to head for Home and see what's been happening since we've been gone. I'd like six or seven more volunteers for *Defiant Ruin*. Let Gosta know if you're interested." She clicked off.

Gosta bobbed his head. "I will need to go gather things. I shall return immediately." He was like a kid with a new toy, but one he needed to gloat about in private first. Vas nodded for him to leave the deck.

She looked down at her borrowed clothing. It was better than the prison garb, but she'd like to be in her own clothes. "Hrrru, I want you and Gosta to run final check on all departments here, then start running them on the *Defiant Ruin*. I'll be by in three hours for an inspection." She nodded toward Mac. "Take him with you when you go over there. I'll be in my quarters for a few hours, and unless there is an emergency that Ragkor, Terel, Gosta, and the rest can't handle—please don't disturb me." She looked around, but the faces were all happy. They were almost as glad to be off here as she was.

CHAPTER TWENTY-ONE

———◆———

V AS SCREAMED AS THE WINDS bore down on her. She couldn't see, couldn't hear, nothing but the sand and wind filled her existence. Then a buzzing sound of an alarm cut through the dull roar. It broke her free of the wind storm, made her realize she was actually in her own bed on her own ship.

That shot of reality pushed the sand storm clear of her mind. "Lights." The thin lines of the perimeter lights in her quarters came to life first, followed by a single spot near the door. Once she moved the full lights would come up, but right now she needed to clear her head. Her first sleep in her old bed in almost six months and she had a nightmare about her home world. Most likely triggered by thinking about her damn brother.

She rolled out of bed and checked the time. She'd come back to her quarters three hours ago, long enough to take another shower and grab a nap. It was a power nap and would have been more refreshing if she hadn't woken up in that nightmare.

"*You know, it's all in your head. Our minds are our worst enemies. There was no storm.*" There was that voice again. She'd almost missed it the past few days—almost.

"*Therlian and I still don't know who or what you are. Why don't you go poke in her head a bit.*" She slid on her normal black ensemble and started braiding her hair.

"*Therlian. I am glad you found her. She is a strong person. There is much she can teach you, and vice versa.*" Unlike the prior times, the voice seemed very casual, almost chatty.

Vas tried to block her emotions and thoughts as best she could. "*Yes, she is. She and her husband have a wonderful boy, too.*"

The laugh that echoed in her head certainly sounded like Aithnea. "*When she left us, she was pregnant with a girl child—named her Keara. Her husband died a number of years ago and she has not claimed a new mate. She is fond of your young captain, Ragkor, however.*"

Vas tugged on her braid, both to finish it and in annoyance. "*So, if you're you, Aithnea, how in the hell are you doing this? Why are you doing this?*" Another thought hit her. "*Just what did you have me steal on the Garmainian council planet over a year ago? Were those two men with me Kilesh? And who was I warning about a betrayal? What did Deven have to do with it?*"

The voice was silent. It was odd, Vas knew she was still there, but she was silent.

"*There is much I can't tell you now. You were correct, the ones working with you were Kilesh. The sisters and I were working with a fringe element of their government—one who was concerned about a rapid tech increase from the Garmainians. I don't think that attack from the Asarlaí was the first time the two races had run into each other. The Kilesh wanted the ship and to destroy the tech behind it. I felt their argument was sound, so I contacted you to help them.*" Again a pause.

"*And I went?*" Vas shook her braid, ripped it out, and started over.

"*Obviously. There was something for the sisters as well, a collection of scrolls that were rumored to have been part of our history.*"

Vas wished she could recall any of this. "*When did I go? Was I there the entire month?*" Might as well try and figure the timeline if the details were still going to be foggy.

"*No. You had done what you'd intended. Dropped off your ship and crew and started a recon for new jobs and a possible second stash planet—your words on that. I found you toward the end of your second week. I presented my proposal, and you accepted. I can't stay now; I have other things to attend to."*

It sounded so simple. Just two old friends setting up a job. That she couldn't recall, even after viewing it. She finally tightened her braid and flung it over her shoulder.

"Just tell me why you took my memories." Vas no longer had her duster, but she slid a black jacket on over her tank top and went for the door.

"You wanted me to."

Vas stopped with one foot into the hall. *"Wait, you can't leave on that."* Silence greeted her and this time she knew the voice was gone. Damn it—*she* requested it? When things were back to normal, or as close as they ever got, she needed to review that vid again and find out what in the hell she'd missed.

The deck was calmer than before. Xsit was quietly running something on her communications console and Bathie was sitting at Gosta's console.

"Are we on schedule and is Flarik functioning yet?" She wanted to get away from this place so bad she could taste it, but she also wanted to question the Garmainians before they left. And she really wanted Flarik with her.

Bathie looked up with a grin. "More or less. Gosta and Hrrru made too much noise checking engineering and it echoed to her chamber. She wasn't happy, and Hrrru has been over at the *Defiant Ruin* since then." She held up a small chip. "As for the schedule, I think everything has been given the all clear here. Gosta and Mac joined Hrrru an hour ago—they took Ragkor's people over as well. Ragkor gave me this. It's the scans they made of the gate when they came through. It appears stable. Well, more stable than it was when we crashed through it. But the flow appears steady enough to let us get out."

That was concern number five hundred running through Vas's mind. That they would have three ships in the air and no gate to get through. Space travel was possible without gates, but it was slow. Very slow. Not to mention they still had no clear idea where they were in relation to the Commonwealth, let alone any place inside of it she wanted to go to.

"Keep working on that. Make sure that gate won't give us any problems. We won't be leaking fuel on the way out, but I'd rather not have a repeat of the trip in." She went to her temporary chair and pulled up the specs herself. She wasn't checking her crew; she just wanted to see it. "Did he say where they'd been stranded?"

"A world similar to this one, also abandoned. Two systems over. They didn't know what they were looking for, but I don't think the homing-and-explode device was on the *Victorious Dead*. They didn't crash, but the gate they came in on was also damaged. He recorded everything he could. Everything." Bathie rolled her eyes at that one. Like many of the crew, she liked new data. However, if someone had recorded five plus months of it, that would be enough to even drive a hard-core data junkie crazy.

"So we're not sure where this gate will get us," Vas said. It was a statement, not a question. "But it's not here. I say stay on our timeline and let's leave this place."

Xsit looked up from her console with a chirp. "I am trying to see what I can scan, not that we have full power, but there are more frequencies."

"Thank you, Xsit. Keep it up. And record any readings you get through the gate." Always a good idea to make a note of where you've been. She had no intention of ever coming back, but she knew that might not be her choice. She closed her console and grabbed a breather. "I'm going to check out *Defiant Ruin*. Ping me when Flarik is ready to be social." Vas could just contact her directly, but if Flarik was short on sleep and already bitchy, giving her a little more time was a good idea.

Vas wanted Flarik to help get answers out of the Garmainians; she didn't want her to scare them into silence.

Bathie nodded. "Oh, warning, Mac decorated that thing."

Vas shook her head. That couldn't be good.

Walking through the *Warrior Wench* brought a smile to her face—it was good to see everything up and running, no tunnels, and no breathers. They had worked damn hard for the past five months trying to repair this thing, but she knew how far away they'd gotten when she and Deven had been captured. They wouldn't have been ready to leave for a few months, if that soon, without the help from Ragkor and his crew.

She was heading for the ramp when her comm pinged. "I know you're not thinking of more exposure to that air without a suit."

Vas shook her head. There were way too many times that she wondered if Terel was some sort of esper, despite her protestations to the contrary. She claimed she was simply very good at knowing what stupid moves her patients would make.

Vas wasn't up to a fight right now. "Fine." She handed her breather to a passing crewmember and grabbed an airsuit off the rack. It wasn't smart from an economical point—and these emergency suits had saved their lives after all—but Vas found she wanted to burn them all when they got back to Home.

Airsuit secured, and nagging held off, she went down the ramp. Sometimes when they'd been wrapping up a long campaign, Vas almost felt a sadness for leaving. And this had been a hell of a long campaign. Against a busted ship and a dead planet, but still a campaign. Worst of all, no pay for it. She'd never wanted to leave a place so bad.

She grabbed one of Walvento's wagons to get over there quickly. The *Defiant Ruin* looked even more mashed together the closer she got. It definitely hadn't looked this bad when she saw it before. There must have been a lot more damage done to it than she initially thought.

The ramp lowered as she approached, and she entered and removed her airsuit once the locks reengaged. This area looked pretty much the same. Aside from the ramp, not a lot had to be repaired. The corridor beyond it was another thing.

Vas wasn't vain about her ships. There were people, like the prior owner of the *Warrior Wench*, who spent more on making the inside look extravagant than on the weapons and engines. However, she had to admit this was at the other end of the spectrum. She understood Bathie's comment.

Like the outside, parts were just slapped up wherever. No real care was made as to how they looked, or if they had been modified to fit. Just that they did what was needed. It was like a small kid with their first tree house.

Vas shook her head and kept walking. She never thought she'd build a fleet. She'd always been content with a fast, strong ship and one campaign after another. But now it looked like a fleet was being built for her. Sadly, she had a feeling they were going to need it. As long as this beast could fight, and keep its crew from being shot out into space, she didn't care what it looked like.

The path to the command deck veered more than she recalled but she also wasn't trying to pin down black suits while having a man under fire.

The deck was smaller than either of the other two ships but looked more functional and less awkward than the rest of the ship. "I see you've really worked on aesthetics with this one, Mac."

He'd been in the pilot's console, probably a major letdown after flying in the *Warrior Wench*'s pilot sling for over a year. But right now this was his baby and he seemed happy.

"Isn't it wonderful?" Mac wasn't always the best at picking up sarcasm—love for his creation made that even worse. "It's got even more weapons than the *Victorious Dead*—we just need more ammo. Someone really modified it a while ago. Most weren't working, but Gon and I fixed that."

Vas held up her hand as more was about to come out. "You have done an excellent job. Now, if our Captain Gosta could provide me with a tour? I still have plenty to deal with before we leave this rock."

"Interim, I'm just the *interim* captain, right?" Gosta had been studying charts, most likely ones he'd been studying for an hour, when she came in, but his head popped up at her words.

Clearly, while he'd been intrigued by being a captain, he still wasn't ready for a job change. Vas was actually glad. There were plenty of people in her extended crew who could captain a ship—there was only one Gosta.

"Agreed. And I appreciate your stepping in like this. Mac needs to be kept in line." Vas moved toward the doorway, ignoring Mac's worried looks.

The tour Gosta led her on was brief—it really wasn't a complicated ship—and aside from the unique repair options, and heavier than normal weaponry, there wasn't anything unique about it.

But her brother had been here.

"Did you scan for any Asarlaí items?" Vas asked as she looked in one of the crew quarters. Small, more like a monk's chamber, but doable.

Gosta had been walking behind her but stopped. "I had meant to, but then one thing pushed out another. The black suits could have left any number of explosive, mind-destroying, soul stealing devices on board." Embarrassment and shock at his own lapse crossed his face. He rubbed his hands nervously and looked ready to run back to the command deck.

Vas covered his hands with one of her own. "You have had a lot on your mind, but as captain, missing something could cause your ship to explode. When you get back on deck, order a full sweep. You, better than anyone, will know what to look for. Who is running weapons?"

Gosta went from worried back to embarrassed, although

on him it mostly meant his thin cheeks went from a yel-
lowish red to an orange-red. "Walvento? Unless you want
him to stay on your ship. I wouldn't want to steal everyone
for this ship…"

"Terel cleared him?" He'd been bad when they'd left
and that hadn't been that long ago. At Gosta's wide-eyed
nod, she smiled. "I think that's a brilliant idea. This ship has
weapons the other two don't and he needs to get a feel for
what they can do. Excellent thinking."

Gosta's neck bob wiggled a bit, but he smiled and completed the tour.

Vas left Gosta running scans for Asarlaí markers or mate-
rials on every section or part of the ship. Nothing had
appeared yet, but he was going to keep running them for
a while. She was putting on her airsuit when her comm
went off.

"I heard you were in need of my assistance? Glad to have
you back by the way, Captain." Flarik sounded her usual
terse self, but not any worse than that.

"Thank you. Yes, I would like you to help me question
the Garmainians who captured Deven and me. We ended
up kidnapping them to get off their world when the gray
ships attacked, and I want to find out more about what
they know before I let them go."

There was a pause. "Did you hit your head? You want to
let your attackers go? And how long was I out that the gray
ships are back? Where are they now?"

"My head is fine." Vas drove the wagon across the desolate
landscape to the building. "There's no reason to kill them
as they were just doing a job like we do. You were out a
week, and the gray ships are hopefully far from here—they
were taking their time blowing up the planet, as there was
something they wanted on it. The Garmainians are in the
building—I expanded Wilthuny's old cell."

"You heard about her leaving us. I will meet you at her
old cell. The Garmainians will talk to me." There was a

growl in Flarik's voice that didn't bode well for Wilthuny
if they ever caught up to her. Flarik had wanted to kill her
immediately for the crimes she'd committed. Vas wanted
to hold onto her until they got back to Commonwealth
space. As often the case, Flarik had been right.

Vas signed off and went into the building. Her airsuit
joined the others on the wall hooks; the building was airtight enough that not even a breather was needed. Those
first few weeks of doing everything with at least a breather
on were horribly etched into her mind.

A different guard was standing at ease in front of the
main door for the chambers.

"Good to see you, Divee. Flarik will be along shortly.
Please send her in as well." The dark-haired former navi-
gator nodded. He'd been deck crew but had cross-trained
into engineering and liked that better. But he still did a few
rotations on the deck and security. Having crew trained
in multiple disciplines was going to be important if she
expanded her fleet.

The rooms in this section all led into each other. Wilthuny had been confined to just one of them, but Vas and
her crew had kept a wide distance from her so converting
them to accommodate twenty people wasn't hard.

Zarith was in the front room, looking out one of the
heavily plasteel-covered windows. You could almost see
out, but little more than light and shapes. Not that there
was much to see out there anyway.

"I'm sorry I didn't come see you sooner. There were
other things to take care of."

"I understand," Captain Zarith said. "At what point will
my crew and I be executed?" She was extremely relaxed
and composed. Vas admired that. There was bravado, which
a lot of captains and leaders had. Then there was this kind
of bravery. Aithnea had that and would have liked Zarith.

Vas took a seat across from her. "I said you and your crew
wouldn't be killed. I honor my words."

Zarith gave a sharp laugh. "That was before one of my crew tried to blow you up. I had a feeling that might change the game."

"Did he do it at your command? Were you holding his family prisoner? I didn't think so," Vas said. "I don't even hold him completely responsible so I certainly don't hold you or the rest of your crew. I just want to ask you some questions, then we'll work out what to do with you—but I won't kill any of you."

Captain Zarith looked up and a real smile filled her face. Small, Vas was sure it didn't get much use, but it was there.

A door opened behind her.

"I take it these are the people we are interviewing?" Flarik had her professional lawyer voice on, and when Vas turned she was dressed perfectly.

"Yes. Please sit." Vas motioned to one of the empty chairs. "Captain Zarith, this is my legal advisor Flarik. I just thought she might be helpful in looking into all of the… what?" Zarith's eyes had gone round when Flarik came in. Vas thought the good captain was going to try and bust through the plasteel window when Flarik sat.

"I have never seen…I mean, I have heard of you."

Vas looked from one to the other but Flarik just scowled. "You've heard of Wavians?" It could be possible, she still wasn't sure how far they were from the Commonwealth, but if Deven could make it from here to there, maybe some Wavians made it from there to here. They had been a brutal race before they joined the Commonwealth.

"No. Yes. Well, that one." Captain Zarith was upset. And from what Vas had seen of her that wasn't common at all.

"I assure you I have never been anywhere near your worlds." Flarik looked down at Zarith, who seemed to be shrinking in her seat.

Vas leaned forward. "What do you know of her?"

The captain shook her head, forcing herself to look at Vas instead of Flarik. "It was at least ten years ago, maybe longer. We had a merc job out of the system. We do bounty hunting now, not enough other work. Then we did merc jobs. I was the third-in-command. We faced an equally out-of-system band. On a planet Cabst. Their captain, Flarik, ate our second-in-command. We fled."

Flarik didn't laugh much and it was disturbing when she did. The sound was a cross between a dying Ilerian and a broken wheel converter. Horrifying and could destroy glass if let run too long.

Vas dropped her face into her hand. She recalled that battle. She didn't recall the Garmainians but they could have been wearing suits. Flarik had to take over when Vas fell ill to food poisoning and Deven pushed her into the captain spot.

"That was a stupid battle," Flarik said. "Your people were ridiculously out-matched, and the people who hired you had no intention of paying you. I bit him so you'd run."

Captain Zarith blinked and shook her head. "No, our captain said you ate him, that the enemy were all vicious bird people. He justified our leaving."

"He was a coward," Vas said. "Flarik wasn't the captain then—I was. I was too ill to stand, so my second officer field promoted Flarik. I did mention she's a lawyer, right? They usually don't eat people literally."

"We haven't eaten sentient beings in hundreds of years," Flarik said. She wasn't laughing anymore. "Vas is quite correct. Your captain at the time was a coward. After I bit your second-in-command, he ran off into the jungle of the world we were fighting on. He might still be there."

Zarith rocked back in her seat and looked between Vas and Flarik. "You do seem more like a lawyer than a flesh-eating monster. I am sorry I reacted that way." She gave a nod to Flarik.

"Okay, now that that's established, what can you tell us about your government and who might have sold you out to the Asarlaí?"

"I thought you wanted to know about who hired us to bring you in? And is your second-in-command really the Pirate of Boagada?" She gave a slight grin. "His fighting seemed awfully staged when we brought you in."

"He will be disappointed that he got caught. No, he's not who he was pretending to be. He is a low-level telepath and was able to convince your sensors who he was. He was determined to stick with me." Vas saw Flarik's feathers above her eye flicker up—she caught all the lies in those words. Zarith didn't need to know anything more than she already did about them. "As for who hired you, I'm assuming it was the Grand Council? And my brother let them know where to find me."

Zarith nodded slowly. "I'm willing to tell you anything. Especially if it will lead you to the bastards who destroyed the capital and might have tried to blow us up."

An hour later, Vas knew way more about the workings of the Garmainian government than anyone, ever, should know. She couldn't think of a viable reason to escape, but she'd checked out after fifteen minutes.

Flarik loved it. That was another reason Vas had wanted the history-loving lawyer involved—she ate this stuff up. Vas had been hoping for a clearer, shorter line. Just something that would tie in to why the Asarlaí were there and maybe figure out what they had been up to. There wasn't much of that, but things did get interesting when the planetary cannons and shield came up. Those were things Vas understood.

"I don't know how the shield fell, unless they did have an inside person who was able to drop it. I'm not surprised that our cannons brought their ship down though. The Kilesh have much larger ships than ours so we can't beat them in space, but they leave our planets alone."

"You have both systems on all of your planets?" Vas couldn't imagine the Commonwealth even considering such expenses. At least not beyond their capital planets.

"Yes, but they won't work if they can be taken out that easily."

"I think the black suits that followed us in and exploded on the shield weakened your shield. When you get home, you might want to tell whoever is in charge."

"If we get home," Zarith said and looked from one to the other. She'd gotten less nervous about Flarik, but still wasn't comfortable around her. "You haven't figured out what to do with us."

"How far is this planet from the rest of your system?"

"A few hops. It's a dead planet, so our ships stay clear. There are many in this system."

"So, if we leave you here, with some slightly disassembled radio equipment, and maybe a weeks' worth of food and water?" Vas tilted her head.

Zarith smiled. "We'd be fine. Thank you."

"Did you get what you were hoping? Aside from proof of my fearsome reputation?" Flarik said once they'd gotten back to the *Warrior Wench*.

"I'm not sure what I was hoping for, but there wasn't much there. I just wish I'd gotten more insight as to what the Asarlaí ships were after. Not destroying a planet outright isn't normal for them, although they might have finished it off once they got what they wanted. And I was hoping she might know something about what it was I supposedly stole a year ago."

Flarik's laugh was less shocking this time. "I thought you'd mentioned they had you on vid? That's not an alleged action at that point."

"I know, but I just wished they had more information about what was in those papers." She almost mentioned asking Aithnea about the job, but there hadn't been any information on that end yet, and she wasn't ready to explain the disembodied voice in her head to the extremely pragmatic Flarik.

"Captain? We have a ship coming in from the gate,"

Bathie had gone back on the deck and was taking Gosta's spot. "It has live weapons, raised shields, and is definitely heading for us."

CHAPTER TWENTY-TWO

V AS WAS IMPRESSED. THERE WAS absolutely no tension in her voice. "We're on our way." She tapped her comm again. "Terel? Is Deven still out?"

"Yes, Captain," Pela answered.

Vas and Flarik ran to the lift and to the command deck. Bathie and Xsit had been joined by three other crewmembers and were all focusing on the screens, both the large one and the ones on their stations.

"No contact from the ship yet, Captain," Xsit said.

"Damn it. What stats do we have on it and how long until it reaches us?" There was no doubt that it was coming to them, but the image right now was too vague for Vas to determine the type of ship. But anything armed and shielded couldn't be good. Five months with no ships within hailing distance, and now they were the most popular port in the system.

"I'd say less than ten minutes. She came out of the gate fast and hot. She might be damaged as her exit wasn't stable." Bathie was a whirl as she flipped between screens at Gosta's station.

"Damn it, it's an Asarlaí ship." Flarik had taken up one of the unoccupied stations as was her usual practice. Vas had offered her an assigned station of her own, especially since the *Warrior Wench* had way more than was needed, but Flarik liked being station nomadic.

"That's too small for a warship." Not that there weren't small fighters, but this was the size of a supply ship, not small and sleek like a small fighter, nor big and bulky like a cruiser.

"It's not," Bathie said, but she was flipping screens even faster. "It's a modified shuttle. From the *Scurrilous Monk*."

"The ship that was destroyed almost six months ago?" Vas tried to get a closer look at the approaching ship. Yup. It was a modified shuttle. She'd have to take Bathie's word for where it was from.

"Yes, I didn't think they got anything off before it blew up." Flarik was running scans as well. "I recommend we raise our shields and tell *Defiant Ruin* to do the same. *Victorious Dead* already has theirs up. The approaching ship still hasn't powered down weapons."

Vas whirled to Xsit. "Any chance they are listening to us?" She'd scanned the shuttle's weapons, and while the smaller ship had a far more than standard array, it was facing three warships. Even if they thought both ships on the planet were helpless, it would be hard to miss the *Victorious Dead* in orbit.

"No, Captain, no response…wait." Xsit turned her head as something came through her earpiece. She flicked a switch to put the audio open to the deck.

"Please shoot this ship down, I can't control it. I'm as safe as can be, please shoot this ship down." It seemed to be in a loop. And the voice was Marli's.

"What in the hell?"

"Captain, we just started receiving a recorded loop from the approaching ship. Am I to blow her out of the air?" Ragkor didn't sound like that would upset him much at all.

Within a few minutes that thing would be within firing range of the grounded ships. Even with shields up the damage could be significant.

Marli had saved their asses a number of times. She also might have been the creator of the black suits. And possibly planted a bomb in Deven.

"Blow it up. I don't want debris hitting the planet."

Deven wouldn't be happy, but she was obeying what Marli said—and the Asarlaí woman had shown herself to be damn hard to kill.

A moment later, weapons from the *Victorious Dead* tracked the incoming ship and it exploded. Vas wasn't too surprised when a small pod ejected from the wreckage.

"Pull in that pod. After a full scan, keep it in quarantine. If she is on it and still alive—she stays locked up."

"Aye, Captain."

Vas looked around the deck. "Crisis averted. Now let's get us the hell off this rock. Gosta? What's your status?"

"Relieved, Captain." He paused. "Er, we are nearing ready. Estimated time to completion is three hours."

That was ahead of schedule, and she'd take it. This unexpected addition of the attacking shuttle made her shoulder blades twitch. "Let's get out of here in two. And Gon and Walvento, please get together rations and water for a week for twenty people as well as a deconstructed radio."

"I don't have any deconstructed ones around—"

She cut Walvento off. "Then take one apart. Get everything together and take it to Divee for the Garmainians. Also leave their weapons in a timed lock box—open in seven hours." She didn't want to leave them defenseless in case the first ship to answer their hail wasn't on their side, but at the same time she didn't want them doing anything stupid before she and her crew got off planet.

"Aye, Captain."

Vas looked around the deck. "I assume there is no problem getting this ship off here in two hours?"

"We're ready when you are. Definitely ready before the *Defiant Ruin*," Bathie said with a grin. She and Mac being on the outs again meant the level of competition between them would increase.

"I'm assuming you'll be taking the pilot sling?"

"Yup. Divee is coming up here after we secure the Garmainians. I'll make Mac work for it."

A little competition was a good thing, but she'd keep an eye on them.

"Captain, we have the pod in a secure bay," Therlian said. Most likely Ragkor was scanning for any other ships. "There is a life sign but it's weak."

"Keep it in lockup until we're out. I don't want more complications." She cut off and turned to Xsit. "Record everything we receive from that shuttle—even dead air can sometimes leave clues."

Xsit nodded and went back to her screen.

What was Marli up to? When Marli had vanished, she'd been going toward a troop ship of Wilthuny's that had been taken over by the survivors of the *Scurrilous Monk*. Walvento had seen her vanish as she was running toward him, and the ship took off right after.

So why was Marli now floating around in an exploding shuttle? One that shouldn't exist.

Both ships were getting ready to take off, Deven was still out, and everything was in place for the Garmainians—she could run a few quick studies.

"Gosta…sorry, Bathie. Can you pull up the final vids we have of the battle with the gray ships? Take it about fifteen minutes out before the *Scurrilous Monk* exploded." She might need to go back further—there had been a lot of work trying to stay alive during that time, things could have been missed. "Send it to my ready room." Vas was already halfway there when she noticed the door was back. Good thing too.

She shut it and pulled up the vid Bathie sent her.

The recording wasn't any less painful to watch now than when it had happened. The *Scurrilous Monk* was in a dominant position, having destroyed the smaller gray ships—her gut still clenched as the massive grays came out from the weird space mist.

Nothing came off of the *Scurrilous Monk*—even after three watchings and going back a bit. But that shuttle came from somewhere. She'd checked the readings Bathie had—that shuttle had been definitely registered to the *Scurrilous Monk.*

"Bathie, can you get the audio? To when we were communicating with them?"

The files were immediately in her system. It was tricky trying to listen to the background conversation between Marli and her second-in-command, Savan. But one phrase stood out after the fifth listen: "The shuttles are gone."

Vas knew Marli's people hadn't been able to escape using them; they'd transported themselves over to Wilthuny's former ship. Vas had missed that the shuttles were gone unexpectedly.

So their shuttles went missing or were destroyed, and now, six months later, Marli shows up trapped in one. Vas shut down her screen. Right now she needed to get them back into Commonwealth space. But she'd be picking Marli's brain on this one later.

"Captain, we're ready to lift off." Bathie was smug. As she should be with how early they were.

"Call in everyone who is staying on our ship, make sure the *Victorious Dead*'s shuttle is secure in our hold. I need both you and Gosta to make a quadruple check on the crew list—we can't leave anyone and we're not coming back."

She went to the deck and found Deven sitting at his station. He looked groggy but better than he had.

"Terel knows you're here?"

"Terel is watching him like a hawk, actually." Terel had taken over another empty station, one that Vas had walked right by, and one that had a great view of Deven.

Vas held up both hands. "I am not getting between you two, but Deven, since you're here, get us ready for launch once the crew is secure."

It took a little longer than hoped. There were a few complications over at the *Defiant Ruin*—which Mac loudly claimed were not his fault. However, they engaged the engines without a problem. Divee came running up and took Bathie's spot.

Warrior Wench would go up first. Having two ships lift off at the same time wasn't an issue, but lifting off a planet took a lot of fuel—if they couldn't get this one airborne, they didn't want to waste it.

There was a pause after the engines engaged, and Vas knew she held her breath, but then the ship gracefully launched itself into the air.

"Excellent work, Bathie. Mac could take lessons."

"I heard that!" Mac yelled back through the comm but didn't move his ship yet.

The *Warrior Wench* cleared the planet's atmosphere and smoothly took its place alongside the *Victorious Dead*.

"Everything seems okay. Are we good?" Vas waited for all of her sections to check in before giving Mac the okay to lift off.

It wasn't near as smooth at Bathie's, but Mac did get his ship up and in line with the other two faster.

"Excellent work." She turned to Flarik who'd been analyzing the data from the *Victorious Dead*. "So, do we think this gate will get us out of here?" She figured they'd have to do a few jumps, but jumping blind wasn't fun or safe in an unknown system.

"Yes and no," Flarik answered without looking up. "I think we can get through, but all three ships need to be close together. The gate has become more unstable from when Ragkor arrived." She looked up with a frown. "And Marli's shuttle was sparking when it came through. We need to move fast and everyone needs to be close."

"Send the specs to the other two ships. You both heard that? No competition, no games. Fly tight and we move now."

CHAPTER TWENTY-THREE

———◆———

THEY STAYED AS CLOSE TOGETHER as possible, but there was still a fair amount of space between them. *Victorious Dead* would go first, then *Defiant Ruin*, then *Warrior Wench*. Mac got a little pissy about "his" ship being in the center, but Vas didn't want an untested and heavily repaired ship bringing up their rear.

The gate wasn't as stable as she'd like, but it was a serious improvement over the way they'd come in.

The ship started shaking as they entered the gate, but the readings all held. The hop was short, and Ragkor said he'd go to the first system just to keep things easier.

A binary star far from the gate and no close planets— another gate abandoned a long time ago. Once all three ships checked out okay, they went through another. By the fifth gate, they'd made it back to Commonwealth space and Vas recognized the system.

"Where is the traffic though?" She scanned the area slowly. This was an outer rim system, but hadn't been hit by the gray ships yet before they'd left. It was a busy ship lane due to being a connecting system with non-Commonwealth worlds.

There was nothing on any scan she could find.

"Xsit, use every frequency you have and see what you can pick up." There were two nearby commerce worlds. Not as high-end as the planets closer to the center of the Commonwealth, but the very pinnacle for rim worlds.

Vas picked up faint radio noise, but nothing near what it should be. But she knew her station wasn't as strong as

Xsit's.

Unhappy chirping was not what she wanted to hear.

"Nothing. There is nothing. The first planet, Softwi, has an auto-distress." She clicked it to loud speaker.

"We are under attack. Please answer. Anyone, this is the Glod Empire, we are under attack and taking heavy losses. Please respond." On the third loop she cut it off.

Vas turned to her deck crew. "Who attacked them? Both planets are still there, so that's not the gray ships."

"I think we can assume they've changed their behavior," Deven said as he flicked an image to the front screen. "This is a remote satellite, the one the distress call is being bounced off of."

An image far too familiar to everyone on all three ships came to life. Four giant gray warships coming into orbit around the planet. But they weren't destroying it. Large shuttles were sent down and major cities were destroyed from orbit. Deven advanced the time lapse—two hours after it began, every urban center on both planets was gone. The shuttles and their fighter escorts rejoined the gray ships and left orbit.

"Wait, why did they send down shuttles?" Vas had been watching things closely, but there was only so much a distance satellite could pick up.

Deven ran it back and forwarded it a bit. "At least five massive shuttles went down to the surface halfway through their attack, they were bringing back people. They came back in the same formation with the fighters."

"Are there any signs of life on either world?" Vas watched the vid run through again with the same actions taking place on Softwi's sister world, Bastl.

"No. The auto-distress is the only sign of anything," Deven said. "And before you ask, it does have a time signature. Five months ago. It happened right after we were lost."

Vas found that she'd risen out of her seat as the attack

played out again. She was a merc, but anyone observing such a slaughter would be driven to act. Finding out that it had taken place months ago, that the corpses below were nothing but bone now made her physically ill.

She shook herself. The gray ships had been stealthier in their attacks before that final battle she'd had with them. They must have gotten enough ships into Commonwealth space—even with Vas and her crew destroying the portal they'd planned to create—to launch a full offensive. She wasn't sure what she'd been expecting on their return, but this was definitely not it.

She opened a comm to her ship and the other two. "Change of plans. It appears that the Asarlaí have grown far more aggressive than previously. They are no longer destroying planets to incite fear, just killing and possibly enslaving the populations." That would fit with historical Asarlaí behavior and explain the shuttles. "I want all communications silent. Regular bounce backs to Commonwealth buoys need to be cut. No connections to anything outside of us three." She paused as Deven started pulling in images from every world he could get on the local relay system in a way that would allow him to see what was there, but not disclose who was watching or where they were. Granted, it was just this sector of space, but not a single world showed life signs large enough to be sentient.

She took a deep breath, forcing herself to stay calm as a wave of horror tried to engulf her. "It appears that while we were gone, the Asarlaí had their war. And they won. We will try and make it to Home, if it's still standing, but I don't want to risk communication until we are closer. We are on our own, people. Let's make sure we can survive." She cut the comm and fell back into her seat. She prided herself on being tough. On knowing the next course of action quickly and accurately.

She had no idea beyond trying to see if her base was still

intact and if the majority of her extended crew were even alive. Or if, like the planets below them, there was nothing but rubble and a distress call that was never going to be answered.

She was still staring ahead, looking, and yet not looking at the screen, when a pair of hands came and squeezed her shoulders.

Deven was still pale, but the concern in his eyes was what tore her up.

"I look that bad?" She laughed and put her hand on one of his.

He tapped her head. "You feel that bad up here. And I'm not much better. No one on any of these ships is. Part of me thought we'd come back to fight the war—but it went on without us and our side lost." He gave her shoulders another squeeze, and then returned to his station.

Vas stared at the desolate planets before them. Fighting was one thing. But being out of the fight, never having the chance to fight, that was what was going to haunt her nightmares. Aithnea had sacrificed herself and her entire order to protect Vas and her crew. There was something big Vas was supposed to do. Fighting to defend hundreds of worlds would have been big.

"Why did you die to save us if this was going to happen? There's a chance that we wouldn't have been here to fight if you hadn't shielded our location months ago, but we weren't here anyway. Everyone is gone." She had no idea whether the voice was in fact a manifestation of Aithnea or if it was somehow tied to the planet they'd been on. But Vas really needed some answers. To say this made no sense was an understatement.

"You can't save everyone."

Vas clenched her fists. She needed to yell at someone right now, get some of this pain out of her system. Yelling at a voice inside her head wasn't going to be reassuring to her crew. She rose to her feet.

"I need to work something out. I'll be in my ready room. Deven is in charge. All ships maintain radio silence and continue to Home. Gosta, plan out a quick but non-direct path. If we are seen, I want all three ships to have a scatter plan. Separate, fight back, do what you have to, but don't lead them to Home." She swallowed the words, "if it's still there". With a nod from Deven, she left the bridge.

"Can't save everyone?" Vas mentally yelled before the door was even shut. *"How about no one? If you had gotten us out of there sooner—or even better, helped us during the attack so we didn't end up stranded—we might have stopped this."* Even as she said the words she knew they couldn't have done a thing except maybe take a few grays down with them when they died. She didn't care. She was mad and scared. Being scared was still novel enough that she needed something to lash out at and logic wasn't going to stop that.

"You would have made a hell of a nun. That is one of my few regrets, that you never chose the path."

Vas stomped around her ready room, grateful for the privacy. Explaining why she was waving her hands around but not saying anything would have just confused her crew more.

"That's not the point. We should have been here. We needed to be here."

"You needed not to die in vain. Our order has no problem dying for a noble cause—it's one of our first tenets. Had your crew been here and fought in that battle, your deaths would have been meaningless. There is still a chance you can die with honor."

Vas threw herself into her chair and rubbed her hands across her face. "So what do we do?"

If no other actions of that voice made her believe it could be Aithnea, that laugh would do it. *"I have no idea. I am powerful, but not strong enough to pierce the veil of time. But I know there is more for you to do. I didn't cause anything that happened to your ship or crew before you left the Commonwealth—I couldn't. And my ability since I was able to make contact has been far more ethereal than brute strength."*

Vas was ready to argue that. Yes, Deven had done some of the heavy lifting when the *Defiant* was coming in, but that wasn't all of it. But even just this bit was helping her clear her head. After five plus months of inaction, then fighting to get free of that damn planet—she'd been looking for a nice battle with someone who needed their asses clocked. Finding grave planets was a shock.

"Okay, can you give any information that would be helpful at all? I mean about right now."

"Sadly, no. I don't even know how much contact I can have with you. Time is different here. And no, I can't tell you where here is. Just listen to your gut and your heart—and your crew. I think—"

Damn it. Her mental voice had started getting fainter toward the end, then cut off. But the brief conversation had helped Vas pull herself together.

The deck was mostly silent when she came out.

"Any updates?"

Deven had been watching the main screen. He'd moved the view to the star field they were going through, but she could tell by some of the faces before her, that some of the command crew—and possibly the rest of the crew—still were watching the dead worlds around them.

Vas sighed and tapped her comm. This hadn't been easy for her; she couldn't expect it to be for them either. "I know everyone has had a shock. This wasn't what we were expecting—we're fighters and right now we've missed the battle. However, we have not missed the war. The Asarlaí might think they've won, but I have the smartest, craftiest, and bravest crew in any Universe. We will find a way to take back the Commonwealth. It might take a while—but we will do it." This felt odd and awkward. She wasn't one for cheering-up speeches. If she gave any, which was rare, it was more of, 'this is what we're paid to do, let's go kill something'. Telling them what they already knew—

namely how damn good they were—wasn't her style.

"Actually, you know what? This is just like any other job. We're going to strategize, regroup, and plan the hell out of our opponent. Then we do what we're paid for. We take them down."

"Who's paying us?" Mac cut in from the *Defiant Ruin*.

"I am." Vas and Deven said it at the same time. Followed by Ragkor, Therlian, Gosta, even Flarik. Soon the entire crew on all three ships was yelling it.

Vas looked around. This was what they needed—a reminder of who they were. It was up to her to find a way for them to do what they were best at. Even if the best case was simply, as Aithnea put it, dying with honor.

She slid back into her temporary command chair. "I want reports on anything we see, even the tiniest item, sent to me immediately. Flarik, see what you can find on the dark lanes. If the Commonwealth went under, those would be more active. The mainstream worlds might have fallen, but the criminals, villains, and thieves will have survived. Find them. Ragkor and Gosta, I want hourly updates, even if it's just to tell me what you ate."

She closed the open comm, and then tapped over to the *Defiant Ruin* only. "Get me Hrrru."

A moment later the Welischian came on. "Captain?"

"Hrrru, I need you to mask our ships. Your people hid from everyone with a skill unmatched until now. I need you to work with Gosta on hiding us."

"They won't last long, nor be as thorough as on a planet, but some of our techniques could be converted…yes…yes. It will make us a little harder to see on scanners. And when we go to ground I will have plans in place as well." He was talking more to himself than her, but then he paused. "My people should be contacted once we reach Home."

Vas dropped her head. This is where it would get hard for some of her crew. Many of them didn't have any real ties to their people or where they grew up. Some, like the handful of Welischians she had, were fiercely devoted to their clans. "They might not have been spared, you realize that."

"I know. However, I also know they are alive." His voice held far more confidence than Vas felt. "I can't explain, but they are there. We will get Home, and we will find them."

She shook her head and wished she felt like he did. "Very well, then you have your orders, go forth."

She had no idea how the Welischians could have survived, but they'd managed to overthrow hundreds of years of slavery armed with little more than their claws and their brains—she was not going to go against that.

Their travels were slow and a bit convoluted. They took her seriously when she said take a non-direct way home. Staying away from major systems took a bit more planning but was worth it. They hadn't seen any recent signs of the Asarlaí, but since they also didn't know where they had gone, avoiding everything was a good idea.

Even though she'd assigned searching the dark lanes to Flarik, Vas found herself looking as well. The Commonwealth controlled all communication within its planets. Not so much that it cared what the worlds were saying or doing, it just wanted to make sure it made the commerce off of it. With that system compromised—everything Vas saw made it appear to still be in place; there was just no activity—the dark lanes were the only option.

Usually she avoided them. It was never clear who was on there and they were usually only used by the underside of society. Vas and her people weren't the cream of society, but until it had imploded, she'd been a legally registered merc through the Commonwealth.

But that time was gone. So, the underbelly of society would be their new home.

"It works better if you enter the search to the left," Deven said as he sat down in the station next to her.

"Why do I think you have far more exposure to this than I? Or most of the crew?"

He grinned and shrugged. "A man has to keep his secrets; you might get bored with me otherwise." His smile dropped. "I heard Marli showed up while I was out?"

"More or less. She was in an out-of-control shuttle but locked in a pod. As far as we can tell she hadn't been conscious and had set up the autoresponder on the shuttle weeks ago. Ragkor has her and the pod secured." She played the recording of the auto-call.

"That's not very Marli-like," he finally said after the third listen. "Nor is locking herself in a pod. She has a death wish; I'd think if the shuttle was out of control, she'd want to go with it. Especially since her crew obviously wasn't with her."

Vas hadn't thought of that. Marli had been around for hundreds of years. She'd made herself immortal and distanced herself from the Asarlaí long before they managed to destroy themselves. She'd mentioned being tired and wanting a way out a number of times, but Vas had mostly thought it was just talk. The look on Deven's face said it wasn't.

"So, what? Her crew was killed, and she managed to escape in a pod from her previously destroyed ship? Then tried to kill herself but jumped into a pod at the last minute to avoid death? Your friend is a crazy ass megalomaniac and that behavior doesn't fit." But she had seen how Marli felt about Savan and the rest of her small crew. If they'd been taken out by the Asarlaí she wouldn't have handled it well.

"No, she would have charged them, not retreated," she said finishing her thought out loud.

Deven tilted his head in question.

"Just thinking about her actions and there's got to be something else behind them. She might have a death wish as you say, but she's not going to go out alone. And unlike that ore cruiser from a year ago, her shuttle wasn't on a collision course."

"Okay, then where did the shuttle come from? Why was she coming through that gate? Where are—" Deven's words were swallowed as the alarm went off. He went to his console.

"Report." Vas pulled up the star field but couldn't see anything

"Three Asarlaí short-range fighters," Deven said. "They haven't scanned us yet because I pushed out our sensors to their limits so we'd see them first. Appear to be in a standard search pattern, no indication of anything else."

Vas wanted nothing more than to blow them out of the sky. But she also knew that would just tip off their location and more importantly let the Asarlaí know that there were ships that could still do that out here. She drummed her right hand on the console to keep it from pushing the weapons button.

"Orders? Captain? Can we destroy them?" Mac got there first but she knew Ragkor would be right behind.

"Sorry," she said and looked around her deck. "We can't. Trust me, I want to personally go out there and blow those bastards to hell. But we have much larger targets and we need to stay unseen and intact to go after them. Stand down and maintain silence and distance." She looked at the screen again. "In fact, pick up our speed and slowly start veering toward the Dsilan system."

Bathie sighed but got the ship moving.

Vas walked over to Deven's station. "Are they the same type that came out from our weird ship portal?" Those shadow fighters had freaked her out and not just because they came from a space rip that had been created in the side of her ship.

Deven pulled up closer shots of the ships. "Not that it looks like. I'll compare these scans to the prior ones, but these just look like normal Asarlaí fighters—still deadly though."

Vas watched the fighters as she led her ships further away.

They were on a standard recon, something that might have been done by a Commonwealth military team. They looped around the planet near where they came into the system then moved toward the gate. They spent some time around the gate. Then they went through it.

She hit her comm. "Gosta? Is there any way we can find out where they just went?" Call her paranoid but that was too close for comfort. They showed up not an hour after she and her other two ships came in? Then gated out? This wasn't a popular gate—or it hadn't been.

"Not sure, Captain—the last coordinates were the only thing I could read."

"And?"

"The coordinates were of our jump here—but not of the first jump. I could have read them wrong, or there could be other locations with similar numbers."

This wasn't good. But there was no way she could take the time to track them. None of her three ships were in great shape.

"Thank you, look through the footage later and tell me if anything stands out." The fighters obviously hadn't come in the same way they did—or if they did it was long before them.

Vas spent their travel time studying the information they'd pulled from the satellites of the planets as they passed. All had the same imagery—and on all of them shuttles had been dispatched from the gray ships and the planets not destroyed. Just this sector of space had taken a week. Some planets clearly got their own ships off before they were invaded, but they were crew movers and fled away from the approaching gray ship armada. Most of them made it out of the range of the satellites so they might have found freedom somewhere. But there were some destroyed ships in the space lanes as well.

"Captain? Ragkor here," the voice crackled across her comm. "We might have a problem."

Vas saved the vid she'd been watching. "Just one? Which one?" It as an old campaigners joke, but neither of them laughed.

"Marli is out of her pod and demanding to speak to you. Marko wants to know if he can blow her out an airlock if she gets out of the quarantine area." There was a pause. "I have told him, no." He left the question off the last line. But she knew he was thinking it.

"Kindly inform our guest, that I am not on that ship, that right now she needs to simmer down and be quiet, and we'll deal with her when we're safe." Vas shook her head. That damn woman was a pain in the ass. She'd tell Ragkor to shove her and her pod out one of the missile ports and fire her at a passing gray ship, but she was afraid the Asarlaí would send her back.

Vas looked at the *Victorious Dead's* path and noticed they were veering off. Not a lot, but definitely not the formation they'd been following. If they'd seen something following them they would have notified her and taken off. But this was just a causal drifting.

"Ragkor, what the hell are you doing? You're off course."

"No, I'm not captain, I'm right… How did that happen?" Ragkor cut off but his ship still veered.

Vas tried her comm to get back to him but it didn't go through. "Xsit, patch me through to them directly." She had no idea what Ragkor was pulling, but headstrong and rebellious wasn't a good idea in their current situation. Nor did it fit his personality type

"Captain, we're not doing it," Ragkor said. "My pilot assures me he is trying to follow the original flight plan."

"I said, let me talk to her," A voice cut in, one Vas knew well. Followed by an awkward security cam takeover. Marli was in her human disguise and looked far worse than Vas had ever seen her, but she was smiling. "Hello, Vas! Thank you for picking me up and all, but there's a small item I need to get along the way. Won't be but a moment."

Vas watched as the screen split. Marli on one side calmly telling her she needed to make a stop and the *Victorious Dead's* trajectory.

"You can't just take over that ship. I have no idea how long you were in that damn pod, or where your shuttle came from, but your people kicked the crap out of the Commonwealth and are all over the place out here. Unless you've suddenly decided that you want to run into some old family members, you need to release control of that ship and let us get to safety."

Marli's laugh had no mirth. "There is no such thing as safety—not from them. I was here during part of it, you weren't. But what I have to pick up will help. If Deven is still with you, I know he'll agree."

Vas shrugged to Deven.

"I'm here, Marli—what is so important?" Deven and Marli had been friends for over twenty years, longer than he had known Vas, but the tone of his voice said things were wearing thin with him as well.

"Furies. A forgotten hauler of Furies. Crashed not too far from here. Actually, gently landed and under guard but appearing to be a crashed massive hauler. I led the bastards off in my shuttle when they got too close. We get the Furies; we change the tide of war."

CHAPTER TWENTY-FOUR

V AS LOOKED AT DEVEN. HE shrugged and cut the
comm. "If anyone could manage to get her hands on
a bunch of dangerous and exploding ships, it would be
her." There was a tiny bit of admiration in his voice. However, he'd also been a big fan of the Furies—even after he
recovered from dying in one.

Vas put the comm back on. "Where did you find a hauler
filled with them? No offense, but that seems a bit suspicious."

Marli's laugh filled the command deck. "I have so missed
you, Vaslisha. I'm glad you made it back here. You will have
to sit down and have a drink with me when things have
settled and tell me of your adventures and how you rescued
me. But for now, I have them because I built them. Well, I
oversaw building them. A very long time ago. When I left
my people, I loaded up a hauler and hid it. It has taken me
a while to remember where it was. But once Savan and I
found it and blew up the small moon I'd hidden it in, we
thought we were clear. Those gray bastards showed up just
as we were about to jump, so we hid the hauler as an old
crash, and I took off in the shuttle." She paused. "Now can
we go get my ship?"

Vas started to respond, then shook her head. Of course
Marli would have a bunch of lethal old fighters that she
couldn't find. "I don't suppose they are fully functional?"
If she was building a fleet it would be nice to have some
firepower—of course Furies were almost as unstable as the
people who made them, so they wouldn't be the top of

her list.

"Well, some are, not all though. Even back then there were people in the command who didn't completely trust me. But the ones that aren't intact yet are mostly assembled. I have every faith in this crew, plus mine, to be able to get them up in no time. They're in much better shape than those three Deven took on."

Vas hit the mute button on the comm again. "Okay, so yes or no?" She looked around her command deck. Yes, she should ask the other ships as well, but the final choice was hers and she didn't want to have an hour-long debate each time something came up. In this case, she was mostly asking Deven, but it would be rude to exclude input from Flarik and the others.

"I think we should," Deven said. "If we can get the Furies running they could help us out. But also, having another larger ship on our side wouldn't be a bad idea."

"I can help with Fury rebuilds," Bathie said. "Mac used to show me his work on the other ones."

"I would vote for dropping her off on her planet and leaving her there, but that is an emotional response." Flarik smoothed down the feathers on the back of her head. "However, on a logical level, I don't think we have the luxury of not retrieving anything that might help us. Weapons, ships, even a murderous Asarlaí. We don't know what other things she might remember about her people that we could use against them."

Terel had been listening to the conversation. She wasn't usually on the command deck, but since she didn't trust Deven and his health right now, she was up here and she was going to give her thoughts. "I'd also like to do more studies on Marli. But we have to be careful. If she was actually the creator of the black suits, and is playing some sort of internal struggle with her returning people—she isn't going to react well to us finding that out. And we still don't know if she was behind our other issues." The pointed look she gave to Vas indicated she hadn't told Deven about whom they suspected was behind the bombs. Including the one inside him.

"She's not going to be happy if she wasn't the creator and these creatures somehow have her genetic material either," Deven said. He had slightly narrowed his eyes at Terel's obviously vague comment, but Vas knew he'd wait until they weren't surrounded by the deck crew to find out what they were talking about.

Marli hadn't acted as if the black suits were hers and she'd killed as many as she could find. But it was impossible to tell with her.

"Fine, we do it. In part for the ships, but also her crew. There can't be too many people left in the Commonwealth who haven't been taken or killed by the Asarlaí, and we did fight together before." Vas believed in honoring prior alliances. Granted, the one with Marli's crew was an odd one, but they'd still lost crewmates fighting alongside Vas and her people.

She flicked the mute off. "Agreed. But you *tell* Ragkor where to go—no more taking over ships. And you and your crew report to me now. We're getting too many ships and there needs to be a cohesive leadership."

"Very well," Marli said. "Should we call you Admiral Vas?"

The *Victorious Dead* stopped pulling to one side.

"I have control, Captain." Ragkor came through on the comms.

"I really like admiral, gives you an air of authority," Marli said.

"Captain is fine. Give Ragkor the coordinates and he'll transmit them to both our other ships. I don't suppose this hauler of yours has any weapons itself?" Hopefully, if Home was still intact, they could weaponize it there. Walvento could weaponize a child's pony if he was given a chance.

"Oh, it's extremely weaponized. I call it a hauler because that's what I disguised it as. Be assured, the *Scurrilous Monk* is a full Asarlaí warship cruiser. It was one of the best when I stole it. That was a prime reason I had to hide it for a while."

"But your other ship was named that—I saw it blow up."

"I've liked that name for a long time."

That didn't change Vas's feelings about getting Marli's ship. They were going to need as many fighting ships as possible. If Marli thought she could get a cruiser and fighters that were a few hundred years old in full fighting condition, it was good enough for her. She was a bit concerned at how easily Marli agreed to follow commands, but that wasn't something she had the luxury of worrying about now.

Vas opened the shipwide comm to the other two vessels. "We're making a detour. *Victorious Dead* will be lead on this, but we will gain a new warship which we need." She didn't want to mention the Furies—there was no way to know how much work they needed.

"Aye, Captain," Ragkor said. She knew he'd agree without question. He'd been showing more willingness to buck the system before they were separated, but he was still someone who followed orders without questioning each and every one. Unlike the rest of her crew.

"We're on our way, Captain." The confidence in Gosta's voice was good to hear as well.

Vas nodded to Bathie and the *Warrior Wench* moved out after the other two.

Deven came back to the station next to her. "I know she's agreeable now…"

"But I don't trust her," Vas laughed. "Agreed. But we don't have many options. The majority of the ships back at Home are low-armed troop movers and replacement Flits. We need more ships to fight with."

"It still won't be enough. The Asarlaí hit hard. It doesn't

look like all of the Commonwealth was working with them—enough ships that fought back and lost had Commonwealth insignias."

Vas looked at the screen that tabulated worlds still with life—the number didn't look good.

"So, from what I'm seeing here, they grabbed some entire populations, destroyed more, and then retreated to the core worlds?" She tapped the screen. Deven hadn't been able to get satellite information from any planets more than a day's flight from the rim, but the core would be the logical destination. "What in the hell are they up to?"

The Asarlaí of the past had conquered Universes slowly, over a period of four hundred years. There was nothing unified or large like the Commonwealth to band worlds together. The only thing that made this attack similar to their original campaign was the viciousness.

"Captain, I'm picking up long-range signals," Xsit called out. "Two heavy cruisers coming from the core. Heading to the sector we're going toward."

Damn it. Marli might not have hidden her ship well enough. "How close? Can we get there before they can?" It was risky. Thanks to Bathie and some bored engineers, the extremely boosted sensors now on the *Warrior Wench* meant they'd probably picked up ships before they themselves were picked up—but that would only work for a short time if the ships were closing in on them.

"If they stay on trajectory, we might be seen." Divee looked up from his screen. "It's too close to tell for sure."

Vas nodded. "Send the intel to Gosta. Nothing against your abilities, Divee, but that's his type of problem. Gosta and Ragkor, we've got ships coming in that you can't see yet. I need to determine if we can get Marli's ship and get out of here, preferably without being spotted. Keep in mind that we really need that ship."

They'd keep moving toward it unless there was absolutely no option. But she didn't want to be seen. The longer the

Asarlaí didn't know she and her ships were out here, the better chance they had to survive to fight back. But they needed Marli's ships and they sure as hell didn't want the Asarlaí to get those Furies

"Understood," Gosta said. Ragkor didn't respond, but she knew he and Therlian were probably hashing out the risks. Therlian had the nun's mindset—get the ship and the weapons. Ragkor would be more cautious and not want to risk wasting troops.

"Ragkor, have your pilot increase speed. Everyone else, keep up with them," Vas said.

Xsit had sent the image from the long-range scanners to the large front screen along with an estimated level of protection. It was all speculated on what Vas knew of the farthest range screens and then she added another fifteen percent more distance. At the rate they were going they should be clear, from what she could tell. Right up to the planet. If Marli's ship was ready to jump when they got there, they might pull it off.

But they couldn't risk a distance radio call to let Marli's crew know they were coming in fast.

"*Can you mimic other people besides me?*" Vas called to the voice. She did have two telepaths—Deven and Marli. Even though Marli wouldn't admit to it, too many things she did indicated she was. But at this distance it wouldn't be wise to risk them.

"*I can, within reason. What are you trying to do?*"

The voice was stronger than it had been before, so hopefully that was a good thing. Vas quickly outlined her plan.

"*You want me to impersonate an Asarlaí to her own troops? Just where did I go wrong raising you?*"

"*We need this one in order to fight the rest. I can't risk the comms or the telepaths—I take it your communication is a bit less detectable.*"

There was silence, just as Vas was about to try and reach out again, the voice came back.

"It's done. I had to keep it short. They have telepaths there also and too long a communication would tip them off. They believe Marli sent them a one-way message to ready the ship and that she was coming."

"Thank you," Vas sent, but there was no more response. Marli would probably be pissed as hell, but there weren't any options.

"Captain? Marli is demanding to speak—"

Ragkor's voice was cut off. "What are you up to, Vaslisha?" There was mostly curiosity but that could change in an instant.

"Trying to save all of our asses—is that okay with you?"

Marli laughed, then cut the comm.

"The cruisers have their shields up," Bathie said.

"I would too if I was cruising through a quadrant that I'd just kicked the crap out of."

Divee shook his head. "They didn't have them up when Xsit first noticed them."

"Either they have better sensing equipment than we thought, the fighters actually did notice something and reported back, or we're leaving a trail of some kind." Deven was working his way through a bunch of screens at once.

"Captain?" The high-pitched chirp at the end of her word wasn't a good sign. Xsit was freaked out. "There are three more fighters, maybe the same as before, I'm not sure. They are coming our way. Well, heading toward the planet we're going toward."

Vas looked to Bathie, but she shook her head. They were moving as fast as they could. The *Warrior Wench* was faster than the other two, but it wouldn't help if they had to leave them behind.

"Could we lead them off?" She was tossing the question out there.

Flarik had adapted her current chosen console and tilted her head as she ran figures.

"I think so, but, and I hate to say this, we need your Asarlaí friend. She is the only one familiar with these ships."

"I agree on both counts," Deven said.

Vas got up and paced. Usually in a brainstorming session she'd get her main command crew in the ready room and shout out the issue—but there wasn't enough time. She tapped her comm for the *Victorious Dead*. "Ragkor, I need Marli to get back in that pod and for you to jettison her. Marli, I know you've highjacked the *Victorious Dead*'s internal comms somehow, but we're being hunted by two cruisers and three fighters—I want to use the *Warrior Wench* to lead them off, while our other two ships go get your crew. I need you with us on this ship."

"My people won't listen to you—well, they might, Savan likes both you and Deven, but the other two ships are filled with strangers. I could help you if I switch ships, but how can we get my ship if they will fire at the remaining two?"

Vas took a deep breath and shut her eyes. She'd been avoiding telling people about the voice in her head. Deven and Therlian knew but that was it. "Okay, you're not going to believe this," she nodded to the command crew currently watching her, "none of you will. Somehow, for the last two weeks or so, I've had a voice talking to me. Aithnea. Yes, she's dead. But that voice saved me more than once and saved all of us when the *Defiant* was going to crash into the *Warrior Wench*. I'm not sure I completely believe it, but I trust it. It can communicate with Savan and your crew, but you need to give me something to tell them." She hoped Aithnea agreed.

"I'm getting in the pod. Have your people shove me out. We need to talk." Marli's humor was gone.

Within a few minutes the small gray pod was floating in space. They got her on board and out of the pod. Vas briefly thought about locking her up, but they needed her too much at this point. Those ships would all be in scanning range in minutes.

Marwin escorted Marli up to the deck, his hand resting

on his blaster. Vas wasn't going to tell him that it was completely useless.

"Tell the other two ships that there's a concealment screen here." Marli went to an unoccupied console and pulled up an image. "There, off to the far side of that moon. When we head the other direction, they should go there. It won't hide them for long—that's why I didn't suggest it earlier. But if we suddenly cross the cruisers' sight line, it should be long enough."

Vas relayed it to Gosta and Ragkor, along with admonishment to wait to move until the *Warrior Wench* took off. All three ships were already heading toward the moon, but Vas had Bathie slow down.

She turned to Marli. "Now, what do we say to your people?"

"I want to talk to her, it, whomever is in your head." Marli's arms were folded and even though she still wore the human disguise of a petite brunette woman, the Asarlaí presence was clear.

"It's not that easy. It's not like she speaks out of me." Vas sighed and turned her thoughts inward. "*I'm sure you've heard. We need her and we need you to communicate with her crew again. If you want us to fight, then we need the tools.*"

"*I truly hate Asarlaí, even tame ones. You molded the Universe to suit your needs, never caring what magic you destroyed along the way.*"

Vas didn't realize that hadn't just been in her head until she noticed that everyone was staring at her. Actually, they were staring at her comm badge where the voice was coming from.

Vas gave Marli a shrug.

"*Asarlaí—I will help them, and in doing so, help you. But if you betray this trust, know that there is nowhere, not even death, that you can flee to be free of me.*"

Marli's eyes went wide and her usually animated face froze. For the first time in her dealings with Marli, Vas actually felt like she might have the upper hand. Of course she had no real idea what the voice could do—even if it was Aithnea.

Marli apparently felt differently. She wasn't scared. Vas didn't know if Asarlaí's felt that, but there was a level of respect there now.

"I ask forgiveness, not for my people—they should all rot in hell. But for anything I did long ago. I will not betray the trust of those you watch over. But I do ask a boon."

Even Deven raised an eyebrow at that.

"*What.*"

Vas was impressed. In a thousand years she wouldn't be able to get that much scorn into a single word.

"It will be one easy for you to keep, I promise. When this battle is over—help me die. I have been here far too long and want to leave, but I will wait for this final battle." The longing in her voice was almost human.

"*Kill a deathless Asarlaí? That is a boon I will gladly honor. Agreed. Tell me what I must tell your crew to get them to work with the others.*"

Marli came closer to the comm and whispered some words that even Vas couldn't hear. When she finished she smiled and backed away. "You have some serious power packed inside you, my friend. I hope it is for the good." She spun on her heel and marched to the lift.

"Come along, escort. Show me to my rooms."

Marwin looked like the entire command crew did—dazed.

"Marwin, take her to the empty guest rooms on the second level."

"*It is done. The crew of the Asarlaí woman understand and will be waiting until the other two ships get to them.*"

"*This doesn't absolve you for whatever it was you caused a year ago.*" Vas smiled at her crew. The voice was only talking to her now and she was responding internally, but she probably looked a bit odd. "*We'll deal with it later.*" She thought she heard laughter as the voice faded, but wasn't sure.

"Okay, folks, yes, you heard a disembodied voice come from my comm. Yes, it is disturbing enough to overshadow an Asarlaí. But right now we need to get our asses out of here." She flipped the comm open to the other two ships. They were to approach the planet and simply identify themselves by name. Aithnea and her code words would have done their work. Then they would head for Home.

The *Warrior Wench* was going on a hide and seek mission.

CHAPTER TWENTY-FIVE

—◆—

V AS WAITED A FEW MORE moments, just to make sure all of the players were in place.

"On my command, Bathie, you punch us out of here at full speed." She flipped her plan up on the large screen and focused on a section of space. "We'll cross their flight path within a few seconds once we go through here. The fighters will be within scanner range first, then the cruisers. We'll have enough time to get into the Szan Nebula before they can catch us. The cruisers can't maneuver in there—too big. We can pick off the fighters and any more they throw at us. Then out through the Web and to Home."

Silence.

"Vas? The Web?" The concern in Deven's voice was more disturbing than the silence.

"People have made it through. I made it through."

"You made it through in a four-seat fighter. That place has destroyed more ships than any sector."

"I can try, Captain." That was not good—Bathie actually sounding hesitant. The woman normally had enough confidence that she made Vas look humble.

Unfortunately, they didn't have a lot of options, nor time. The cruisers couldn't enter the Szan Nebula and hope to get out but they could wait for them on the border. The Web was a massive space anomaly filled with dead zones that could destroy a ship's power. Maneuvering within it made the nebula seem like a smooth ocean trip.

"You get us through the nebula; I'll worry about the Web. We don't have a choice, folks. We have to keep those cruisers watching us, so the others can leave unseen. We can't win a fight against them with only one ship."

Her command crew nodded, but no one looked happy.

"Good. On my mark." She waited until the other two ships were close to the concealment screen Marli had set up. "Now."

They'd been slowing down, but Bathie got them to full power in two seconds. Mac would be jealous.

The other two ships were hidden by the time Xsit called out. "The fighters see us, they are adjusting course." A minute later. "And the cruisers are doing the same."

"*I hope you know what you're doing, I can't help with this.*" The voice was faint again.

"*So do I, and good to know.*"

The Asarlaí ships were closing in but still not within firing range—but that wouldn't be for long.

They weren't going to make it to the nebula in time. The fighters couldn't take the *Warrior Wench* down, not as long as she had shields, but they could slow her down so the cruisers could get there before they could get into the nebula.

"Evasive maneuvers, Bathie," Vas yelled as the fighters hit firing range. "Gon, fire at the lead fighter, pulse missile only." They were still limited in weapons. The *Victorious Dead* had shared what they had but that meant neither ship was well armed.

The missile sped toward the smaller ships as the *Warrior Wench* zagged away from them. It still amazed Vas how a ship this big could move so well. But she was eternally grateful for it.

Gon's aim was true. The pulse missile exploded directly in front of the lead fighter, pushing it back with enough force to blow off its nose. The explosion also caused the second fighter to have to pull back and dodge away to avoid exploding debris.

It still got in a few shots as it followed the *Warrior Wench* into the nebula. "Shields took more of a hit than expected," Deven called out. "Recalibrating levels."

"Record that data. A fighter shouldn't have done anything to us." They might have limited weapons, but Vas had made sure their shields were up to snuff.

"Aye, Captain."

Another shot from the second fighter went wide as it also crossed into the nebula. "Use a lazon missile, Gon. We don't want to take another hit."

Like the pulse missile, this shot hit, but not before the fighter got in another strike at their shields. The fighter shattered behind them.

"Shields at fifty percent," Deven said.

"The cruisers are entering the nebula," Divee yelled. "They are firing."

The ship rocked but stayed true. Flying at full speed in the nebula was almost impossible, but Bathie was keeping up a good clip.

"How in the hell did those fighters drop our shields that fast?" One more hit like that and they would have been shieldless.

"I'm not sure, Captain." Divee was running navigation but that type of question would have been Gosta's.

"Focus on navigating through this, Divee. But if anyone else has ideas, shout out now."

Deven started swearing. "It's worse than taking a hit. The shields are still losing power. We're down to forty-eight percent and falling. They have new weapons that are targeting the shields."

"Try ascending your shield modulation," Marli cut in on the comms. Obviously, along with giving her a room, Marwin had given her a comm. "I'm coming back up. I didn't think you'd get into trouble this quickly."

Vas rolled her eyes, but she wasn't going to say no. The cruisers were creeping into the nebula. Most likely waiting for whatever damage those fighters did to their shields to destroy them completely. Along with superior firepower and number of ships, a weapon like that would have gone far in decimating the Commonwealth defenders. Fighters could get in quickly, set up a destruct sequence on a larger ship's shields, and then the cruisers followed to easily finish them off.

Marli made it to the command deck in seconds, and took over the remaining unused console. Her fingers flew over the touchpad and she shook her head a few times. "Damn it, they've got a stealth bot in their weapons. Sneaky bastards." She was really talking more to herself than anyone on the deck, so Vas just let her work.

"Shields back up to fifty-five percent and climbing," Deven said. "Good job, Marli."

"Great job more like it. We didn't get back to Commonwealth space until the battle was almost over, but damn, they have seriously increased their game." She cracked her fingers for effect. "But I'm better."

They were moving through the nebula at as fast a pace as before and the cruisers were still slowly forcing their way through. Vas wasn't sure how far in they could go. The Szan Nebula messed with frequencies both within and outside a ship. Traditionally, the larger the ship, the greater the effects due to some odd specifics of this particular nebula.

"We need to get further away before they release their fighters," Vas said but her words were too late. A bunch of smaller ships were descending out of the first cruiser. The second was hanging back; most likely they felt one ship could take out the *Warrior Wench.*

"Not on my watch," Marli snarled, then started making calculations in the air. That they left a blue trail that anyone could see was a little disturbing. With a vicious grin she nodded to Vas. "Can all weapons be transferred to you and me? Nothing against your man down there, but I have a plan." As she spoke she sent the odd and ethereal notes in the air to Vas.

The plans were simple, but played off the fighters own power and the forces of the nebula. "I like it. Gon, shift all weapon controls to the second nav station and my temporary one." The lights for full weapons—such as they had left—came on her panel.

Vas had seen something similar in some of the studies she'd done when she'd first taken command of the *Victorious Dead*. The *Warrior Wench* was similar enough in size and weapons to make the cross fire happen.

"Now you take your side, I'll cover mine. Timing has to be perfect."

Vas shot a scowl at Marli. "Please, I was not born yesterday. You watch your end, I have mine. Deven? Check the set up?"

They didn't have time to link the two stations, and both would have to fire exactly in order. Marli was handling a rack of pulse missiles, and Vas had the remaining lazon missiles. If they made it through, they'd have no weapons left.

Vas's would need to go a second before Marli's. This also counted on the position of the fighters: they needed to be close enough to the cruiser that they became added missiles against it. If they got too much distance from it, the trick wouldn't work.

"You're good to go!" Deven yelled.

Vas hit her launch and a yell from Marli indicated she did the same. The missiles flew toward their targets, half to the fighters, and half to the cruiser. The fighters tried to evade, but it was too late and they exploded and were slammed back into the cruiser. Its shields weren't enough to handle their entire fighter fleet being slammed back at them and started buckling.

"Their shields are falling—and they are down. Their engines are collapsing as well." Flarik changed the view on the main screen. The cruiser had explosions all along its bow, but the rest of its power was going out. Soon the explosions were the only sign of activity.

"Unfortunately, we don't have anything to finish them off with. Bathie, get us into the Web as quickly as possible."

"The second cruiser is moving forward," Xsit said unnecessarily. With the image on the screen they could all see it.

"I can go over there and delay them. Your mover is up, right?" Marli was already almost to the lift.

"Nope, it was too damaged during our crash landing. Not to mention, seriously? You would try that inside a nebula?" Vas was going to have to watch her. Marli implied she would help get them through this before she killed herself, but that was debatable.

"You should have told me immediately." Marli continued on to the lift. "That needs to be fixed."

She was gone before Vas could respond. Deven got up to follow her but Vas waved him off.

"Don't bother. She's done what she can. Let's just get out of here."

The Asarlaí cruiser had to go wide to avoid its still exploding companion and Bathie got more out of the engines than Vas could have hoped for.

The brightness of the nebula made the Web before them even darker.

"We're in." Bathie's voice sounded hollow as all the light left the ship.

CHAPTER TWENTY-SIX

——◆——

THE ENGINES STILL APPEARED TO be on, the air was still running, and the lift opened and closed, but there was no light from any of the consoles or the deck itself.

Vas turned toward Bathie's spot. "Cut engines now. We can't see crap and there's a lot of bad things in here." Then she hit her comm to the rest of the ship. "Does anyone have power?" The comm system was separate from the main ship systems so hopefully if they were down it wouldn't be.

"Medical here, Captain," Pela responded. "We have no lights, but the rest of the systems are working. Life support, doors, I can even hear the keys on the monitor when I type things in, I just can't see anything."

One by one the other sectors all checked in the same. Things were working, just no lights.

She'd always said Deven had eyes like a feline, and he demonstrated that now by walking to her console without swearing once. "I'd almost say it's us and not the ship, but I can see outlines and I'm sure if Hrrru were here he could as well."

"Okay, that might have been me," Marli said over the comms. "I thought I'd fixed this…damn thing…nope." She cut off again.

"Marli, if you're responsible for our lights going out, you need to fix it now. We're in the Web and are blind."

"But I can fix this, really."

"Stop it. You said you'd follow my commands—I am ordering you to un-do whatever it was you did."

Silence followed, but one by one the light systems came back on. They'd been right; everything was still working, there was just nothing to illuminate it. How in the hell did trying to fix that twice-cursed people mover end up removing every bit of light?

Vas was going to ask then shook her head. Better not to know. "Get back up on deck, Marli."

"I can go see what she did," Deven said, but Vas shook him off.

"As long as everything is back, let's just leave it alone. I'm going to need you to help get us through the Web."

He laughed and went back to his station. "I thought you had the Web figured out?"

"More people working on it the better," Vas said and turned back to her console.

Nebulas were messy, odd things. Each one seemed to have different aspects designed to mess up ships trying to cross them. Had they gone through the Szan Nebula the long way, Vas was certain they would have seen far more of these aspects—and she was really hoping that second cruiser was going through them now. But the Web was unique. There were rumors that it was the residue of the final battle against the Asarlaí. Aside from the rumor, no one knew how it was formed; it had just appeared. Mystics stated it was the remains of the great deity who created all. Of course, the most devoted of them felt the need for pilgrimages. These usually ended up being one-way, which did cut down on the religions that worshipped it.

She'd made it through once, before she took command of the *Victorious Dead*. She'd been in a small cruiser, one that was more fighter than cruiser but held four people. They were running a recon for a larger mission, got trapped in the Szan Nebula, and took some serious damage. Then they got stuck in the Web. The Web shifted regularly, so there was no way to predict what would happen there— Vas and the ship made it out, two of her crewmates didn't.

"Captain, we're nearing an anomaly." Divee sounded calmer than usual—one of the reasons he didn't spend a lot of time on deck was his tendency to get excited.

Anomaly could mean anything, especially here.

"Can you be more specific?"

"No. I'm sorry; I have no idea what it is."

The front screen changed and Vas had to agree with him. She had no idea what that was either. It was an anomaly because there was no way that was normal.

A deep black pit with thinning gray spirals whirling out of it hung just minutes from their ship.

"Evasive maneuvers, Bathie, just stay clear of it."

The ship changed course but then the thing appeared again.

"Crap, is it sentient? Why is it following us?"

The lift doors opened and Marli came back on deck. "Oh no. Get away from that. Do whatever you have to do, but get away from it." She shivered and started rubbing her arms.

Again, for the second time in just a few hours, Vas heard what almost sounded like fear in Marli's voice. Which meant any normal person who knew what she did would be screaming in terror.

"Try it again, Bathie, hard to port."

The ship moved again, much sharper this time. It took almost a full minute, but the thing came back. By now the tendrils were reaching for the *Warrior Wench*. Vas had never missed Gosta and his mass of knowledge as much as she did right now.

"Marli, what the hell is that thing?" Vas looked away from the screen when Marli didn't answer.

She was still standing near the lift, her brow furrowed and her hands were now covering her mouth. "Do you have any of the Furies left? Wait, I know you don't. What about those little fighters you have?" Her voice was too neutral.

"None of our Flits have weapons. We're stripped." Deven was watching Marli almost as if he expected her to attack.

"That's okay; I can just go out and…do something." Her eyes were unnaturally wide as she watched the image on the screen.

Deven, Vas, and Flarik all shared the same look. That was less Marli-like than her initial disturbance of the thing. Much less. She sounded confused.

"It's a techno-biological entity, Captain." Terel usually used her name, that she didn't told Vas a lot. "It's reading as multiple beings, like a hive."

"Yes, yes. I will go greet it." Marli headed for the lift, but Deven got to her first.

"Fight it. Whatever those things are doing, fight them." He held onto Marli but didn't seem to be needing much force.

"Bathie, keep trying to move us away from it." Vas had no idea what was going on, but Deven was starting to shake his head as if something was swirling around it. He kept hanging on to Marli though. She wasn't putting up a fight but seemed focused on getting to the lift.

"They are…using…telepathy." Deven gritted his teeth and held on tighter to Marli. "And they hate Asarlaí."

Great, she admired their taste, but as she'd told Aithnea, they needed this one. Each move Bathie made, the swarm followed. They were making slow progress through the Web—the swarm wasn't fast and seemed to have to regroup with each movement—but it would overcome them eventually.

"It calls to me. I must follow." Marli was seriously freaking Vas out now.

"We have to kill Marli." Deven seemed more in control again, except for his words. "No, not for good. But we need something to stop her from existing on their level. They are an ancient weapon, and right now they are going to tear this ship apart until they get her. They are sentient of a sort, but mostly focused on one goal. Destroy all Asarlaí."

Vas had no idea how to kill an immortal Asarlaí in the first place, let alone how to make her dead but not dead.

"I might have something that will work," Terel said. She left the station she'd been at and ran past Deven and Marli locked in their strange tableau. "Hold on."

Vas looked around as she left. Deven was really the only one who could restrain Marli, and Vas doubted even he could if she really fought back.

Terel came back to the deck, hypo in hand, and stabbed Marli in the shoulder with it.

Marli had been almost in a dream-like daze, focused on getting to the lift and out into space. But she arched back and screamed when the hypo emptied into her shoulder.

Deven caught her as she crumpled to the floor.

The swarm held in place, but after another location change from Bathie, it didn't follow.

"What the hell did you just use, and can we weaponize it?" Vas was grateful the swarm was moving off, and that they still had Marli, but any advantage against her people had to be looked at. Something that dropped her that quickly was something Vas needed in her life.

"I've been conducting tests on her blood. I noticed there was a chemical compound that literally made the cells move away. Figured it probably wouldn't be great for the rest of the body—and if she hadn't somehow made herself immortal, might have killed her for good." She looked down at Marli and felt her pulse. "Not back yet." Then back to Vas. "As for weaponizing it, I don't know. If we were fighting an army of her, it might slow them down? The other Asarlaí won't have the exact reaction she did; adjustments would need to be made." She shrugged. "But I'm seeing what can be done. A genetically targeted weapon might at least make a dent in them."

Terel looked down at the unconscious woman that Deven was still holding and nodded to him. "Do you feel okay after whatever that thing did to your head? If so, can you bring her down to the med labs?"

"I thought you wanted Deven to rest for at least a few days?" Vas kept her smirk to herself, but Terel's glare told her she heard it regardless.

"That's obviously pointless. He's clearly fine, and no one listens to me anyway." She stalked off to the lift. Deven picked up Marli and followed.

"Bathie, slide out and I'll pilot us out of the Web." Bathie usually loved the times she could pilot, but it appeared that dealing with the swarm had chased that feeling away for a bit. She was already out of the pilot sling and on her way to kick Divee out of navigation by the time Vas was out of her chair.

Vas made it a point to fly her ships at least every few months—maneuvering a cruiser like the *Warrior Wench* was different from a Flit or Fury. But being grounded for almost six months meant it had been a while since she'd been in the sling.

The ship felt sluggish, but whether it had to do with the time it spent on the ground, the rough repairs, or the Web was unclear. But Vas would have to work around it to get out of the Web.

Although the ship had a navigation station, navigation was obviously built into the pilot's sling as well. Vas looked out on the screen and followed her intended route. They had avoided three minor space ripples—distortion waves that could numb a ship's sensors—and two black sections that were so dense, nothing would come back from them.

Then an Asarlaí cruiser appeared from behind the third ripple. Vas hit the ship wide alarm and immediately went into evasive maneuvers.

CHAPTER TWENTY-SEVEN

——◆——

THE ASARLAÍ VESSEL STAYED IN place. Actually, it appeared to be drifting a bit.

Deven came back on deck without Marli. "Terel said it might be a few hours before Marli recovers, so we need to get out of here before that." His eyes went wide as he saw the Asarlaí ship. "But there's no one in there?"

Vas knew he'd scanned them telepathically, something he shouldn't have been able to do if their shields were up.

"Their shields are down, Captain," Bathie said and confirmed that thought. "Stabilizers are mostly holding the ship in place, but they're almost done. And there are bodies outside the ship."

Vas pulled up a closer visual. Yup, possibly a few hundred tiny forms drifting around the ship. She hit her comm. "Terel, can you scan those? I'm assuming Asarlaí?" She ran some numbers, and then shook her head. The pilot's sling was too limited. "Deven? Can you tell how long that ship has been like that? How in the hell did it get through the nebula?" It was eerie. It wasn't dead in space, but it was dying. Its crew left everything on and in place. The fact that the stabilizers were slipping probably indicated it had been out here for a while. But Deven would have a better idea.

Terel was first. "You are correct. Those are the frozen remains of two hundred and twenty-three Asarlaí."

Vas kept them at a distance but wanted to gather as much information as she could. Gosta and Hrrru would find some way to use it later.

"That ship stopped in space five months ago," Deven said. "There is no atmosphere inside the ship and there are bodies inside it as well—can't get a good scan on what they are, but I'd guess not Asarlaí. I have no idea how it got into the Web. Nothing that size should have made it through the nebula."

Damn it. Now it went from something to avoid to something to investigate. Towing the dying ship with them out of the Web and taking all of the systems apart would be ideal, but Vas knew the *Warrior Wench* didn't have that kind of power. Getting through the barrier between the Web and normal space was going to take almost everything they had.

"Bathie, get back over here and take the sling, Divee, get back on navigation. Deven, Terel, and I are going to investigate the cruiser." She waved down the looks before they got too far. "We have to move fast. There's no way of knowing when Marli will recover and we don't want to be here when she does. Pretty much guarantee this was the work of that creature—but unlike us it didn't have to rip apart the ship to destroy the Asarlaí." She hit the ship wide comm. "We've got a chance to see an Asarlaí cruiser up close, but we're not going to have much time. Terel, Deven, and I will be flying over there in Flits. Flarik is in charge until we get back." She nodded at Flarik. She didn't look happy, but she nodded back.

Deven didn't say a thing but pulled as many data storage pods as he could find. "I wouldn't spend more than an hour there. The Flits have no weapons left and there's no way of knowing what else is out here."

"Agreed," Vas said as she followed him to the lift. "We'll need full decon suits as well. We have no idea what killed the others on that ship." She paused the lift. "Now answer me honestly, or I will lock you up in Terel's med lab for the next week. I want you along on this because you catch things I don't. But Terel and I can do this without you. Are you sure you're all right?"

He tried laughing it off, and then saw her face. He rested his hand on her cheek. "I am fine. I just overdid it; I was doing a lot of things I'd never tried before."

Vas pulled his head down and gave him a fierce kiss then rocked back. "Don't you ever scare me like that. You ask me before any stupid stunts. I'm not losing you again." She kissed him softer. "You got that?"

"Aye, Captain, loud and clear."

Vas released the lift button and they got out at med level. Terel was in her decon suit and had two more suits and full scanners ready.

"I've got Pela watching Marli's monitors carefully. If it looks like she is recovering I told her to shoot her again with the serum. I'll be honest, I'm not sure what this is doing to her, but we know what that thing will do to us if it knows she's here. And since you won't let me space her…"

Vas took a suit. "We need her."

Terel sighed but didn't say anything. After Deven and Vas got their suits on they went down to the shuttle bay.

Marwin had readied three Flits. "I could go as well, in case you need back up."

"And do what? You'd ram any enemies? No weapons, remember?"

"Oh. Yeah. Offer still stands." Like Mac, Marwin loved flying the smaller ships, but having another unarmed ship out there wouldn't help. They needed to get over, download as much data as they could, find out whom the other bodies were, and get back as soon as possible. It wasn't just the return of the swarm that had Vas worried—there were other far more sentient things in the Web.

The bodies went by too fast to see clearly on the way to the Asarlaí ship, but they still made Vas feel like she was flying through a graveyard. Her onboard camera recorded what it could and when Vas captured an image the beings weren't even wearing space suits. It was as if they'd just walked into open space.

Considering that had she been allowed, Marli would have probably done the same thing, Vas found herself admiring the strange swarm. And it was a damn good thing they didn't care about anything other than the Asarlaí.

The flight bay doors to the ship were open, so all three flew inside. The doors to the ship, ones that would have kept breathable air inside, were also cracked open.

They could shut everything up and see if life-support would still work, but they didn't have the time. She also had no idea what killed the other beings on the ship.

A quick survey of the flight bay gave no information, not even much in the data port inside the bay command console. It had been damaged by debris, most likely when the swarm attacked the ship.

Vas scanned for the bodies. She really hoped they were Asarlaí, and it just didn't show up that way. Otherwise they might have been prisoners from one of the conquered worlds. This ship had fallen right as the war was ramping up and might have already had Commonwealth people on it.

There were forty-four bodies and the closest one was a few feet down the hall. Vas sped up. A familiar looking black suit covered the form, but its head was blown off.

"That wasn't expected," Deven said.

Terel shook her head, her expression unclear in the hooded faceplate of the decon suit. "That's not any less disgusting knowing what died."

They found five more of the headless bodies on the way to the command deck.

"All single slices to the neck, no other wounds." Terel didn't even slow down as she scanned the sixth one.

"And no weapons near any of them," Deven added. "They were massacred." He'd ducked into a few rooms along the way, but they held nothing of interest.

"So that swarm made the Asarlaí kill their companions before they stepped out into space?"

Deven shook his head. "I don't think so. The telepathic force I felt was simple and extremely targeted. It was calling them to come out."

The entrance to the command deck had a pile of bodies, all stacked as if they'd been blocking the doorway when killed.

"Maybe they tried to stop their Asarlaí masters from leaving the ship?" Terel looked up. "There is a connection between the black suits and Marli—I still haven't been able to narrow it down, but there is something. Maybe the swarm can pick up the difference between them."

"Interesting," Vas said. "Keep recording everything. Take any samples you can safely transport off the bodies." Like the ones in space, exposure to space had left them frozen. But Terel already had a small blade and sample container out.

Deven went to the command console and slid in the data pod. He jumped back a second later, shaking his hand. "Damn it, it shocked me."

Vas pulled out her blaster. "Like it was alarmed?"

"No. More just like a shock. Honestly, it looks like they left everything running five months ago. The system is collapsing on itself."

Vas went to another station—weapons, it looked like—and put a data pod in. While it pulled information she tapped the screen. It was still running what it had seen before it shut down. A swarm, about five times larger than the one they'd seen, surrounded the ship. That bit of recording just kept looping.

Vas and Deven moved around the stations, putting data pods in each. Gosta had found a way around the type of security that the core of a ship would have: hit the individual stations with data retrievers designed to mimic the system they were stealing from.

"Captain? There's something large coming our way," Bathie's voice was tense.

"Large? A ship? The swarm?" Vas popped out the pod she just filled.

"More like a storm."

"There aren't storms in space." Terel was still in the corridor trying to gather enough goo or parts from the black suits to help in her studies.

"They exist, just not here." Deven pulled his data pods and slipped them into pockets.

"She's right, it's a storm." That was Flarik. "I know I am not an astrophysicist, but it is a storm. Clouds, lightning, measurable disturbances, and it is going to be here in less than fifteen minutes. You might want to come back. Immediately."

Vas had no idea what was coming their way—storms did exist in space, but she'd take Deven's word about this not being the right area for them. Of course this was the Web, so who knew what in the hell was coming for them.

"Grab your pods, data ports, body samples—whatever. We're out of here now." Vas grabbed her last data pod and ran for the doorway. Terel looked up but was fighting with something on the black suit in front of her.

"Just a minute. There's an odd logo on this one. I need to get it off." She was pulling on the fabric, but it wasn't moving.

"We're going now. We'll work with an image of it."

"No, I think there is something in the fabric of it. I almost have it."

Deven moved Terel aside, broke the arm off the corpse, cut the rest of the limb off with his blade, and dropped it in a sample bag. He turned to her. "I can pick you up and carry you to the Flit it you'd like."

Terel looked from him to Vas. "You wouldn't."

"Grab her," Vas said as she started to run. She ignored Terel's yell.

"Vas, this isn't...oof...tell him to stop." Terel's yelling stopped when they got to the flight bay.

Since the docking bay doors were open, Vas had a great view of the storm—and that's what it was—that was heading for them.

"We need to get off this thing," she yelled and flung open the first Flit for Deven to drop Terel in. Terel was pissed as hell, but she wasn't stupid. She started the flight sequence and closed the hatch before Vas even got to the next Flit. Whatever was out there, it was already starting to chew through some of the furthest bodies.

Terel got off first. "Go, damn it!" Vas yelled at Deven as she finished her sequence. He was too damn honorable, but he sometimes forgot she was the captain.

Deven followed Terel. Vas got her Flit out but the storm was pushing her back toward the ship. She engaged the afterburners, Flits had a short burn that could be used for emergency speed but went through too much fuel to really use in battle. She hit them now.

"Hit your afterburners!" The winds were pushing her Flit sideways but she got around it. Then a frozen Asarlaí body slammed into the canopy. The crack was the last thing she wanted to hear.

CHAPTER TWENTY-EIGHT

"VAS! YOU'RE SPINNING!"

Vas had noticed that—it happened right after the Asarlaí body missile. "And the canopy is cracked. One of the Asarlaí slammed into me." Leave it to them to cause problems even when they were dead.

She fought to keep flying for the *Warrior Wench*, but the fact that the Flit was still spinning meant that more than the canopy was screwed. Had she not been in a decon suit with her own air, she'd have died at impact.

"I can't level out."

They were getting closer to the *Warrior Wench* but there was no way she could land like this. If she went in spinning, she'd end up being crushed by the ship.

She watched as Terel made it into the flight bay and Deven right behind.

"Cut your engine when I tell you," Deven said.

"What? Damn it, if I cut it I'll keep spinning." The *Warrior Wench* was coming up fast.

"I'll grab you. I have the arm up."

Crap. Crap. Crap. That thing was to help with repairs. They'd had to use it once to pull in a damaged shuttle and it almost crushed the thing. It would smash this Flit.

"There has to be another way."

"Do you trust me?" There was a calmness in his voice that filled Vas. Damn him to hell. She did trust him, but she knew he had to be using his abilities to keep her calm.

"Yes."

"Now."

She cut the engines and held her breath.

The grating as the arm grabbed the nose of the Flit was a nasty sound but not as bad as she feared. It was more like grabbing the nose of a wayward animal. The arm slowly pulled her in.

The flight bay doors slammed shut behind her.

"Go!" Deven yelled into his comm and not at her.

Vas waited until he came over and helped remove the broken canopy. She felt the *Warrior Wench* engines straining. Noises coming from the bay doors indicated that they were still being overtaken by the storm.

Deven helped her out. "You're shaking."

Vas waited until she was on the floor and had her helmet off before she started smacking him. "You bastard—stay out of my head."

"Did you need it?" Those green eyes tore right through her.

"Yes." She smacked him once more for good measure. "And that's not the point. If your captain says stay out of her head, you stay out of her head. You've been way too—"

Deven picked her up and kissed her. "You're welcome." He didn't put her down.

"I will kick you, I swear to the goddess, I—" He kissed her again and this time she really wished they weren't in such a public section of the ship.

"Damn you. Put me down. I needed it." There was only one person she'd surrender to and it was this smug, green-eyed demon man.

"Captain, the storm has shredded the Asarlaí ship like it was made of paper. It's still behind us."

Deven gently lowered her so her feet touched the ground again.

"We're on our way. Keep up speed and try changing direction, not too far off my plan though." If they went too far off there was a chance they'd be lost or trapped in the Web when Marli recovered. They dumped their decon suits in the bin and ran to the closest lift. Terel ran to a second one to go to the med lab.

The deck was more hectic than when they left, and Bathie looked up with hope when Vas ran toward the pilot sling.

"Thank god, this is nasty." She didn't remove her hands from the guidance until Vas had hers almost on top of them.

"I tried to stick to your plan, but avoid the storm as well. We can't outrun it."

Vas slid into the sling, Bathie reclaimed navigation, and Deven took care of some calculations. Vas didn't even need to ask. If there were a way out of this, he'd find it. She and Bathie just needed to keep them flying and intact.

She veered as far as she felt comfortable and the buffering from the storm weakened, but it was still working on overtaking them. "Are we sure that's not like the swarm? It's behaving too smart and really seems to hate ships." She'd glanced at the images. Bathie was wrong about the huge Asarlaí ship being shredded like paper. It was more like a pile of paper had been exploded by a blaster at point blank range. And that ship was at least twice the size of the *Warrior Wench*.

"No signs of life of any sort from the storm, but it is stronger than anything I've ever heard of," Deven said.

Waves of energy proceeded the storm, throwing bits of space debris out in front of it, striking the *Warrior Wench* repeatedly. Vas almost tumbled out of the pilot sling as the front of the storm actually touched them. The energy it contained within was far worse.

Vas drove the engines as hard as she could and made another course adjustment. They were within minutes of where she calculated the way out was, but they might not have that long. There were only a few places where the Web was thin enough to breach. If they missed this one, it was likely they'd be destroyed by the storm or the swarm before they could reach another.

"Captain, Marli is breathing." Terel's voice on the comm was not what Vas needed right now.

"Damn it," she said but kept her eyes and hands on flying. "Do we see the swarm yet?"

"No, Captain," Xsit said. Not having anything to communicate with she was helping in any way she could. The more eyes watching for problems right now, the better.

"Wait, I see it," Deven said. "The swarm is on a collision course for us."

Vas took a deep breath. There was no more power from the engines; they were straining as it was. But great piloting could always add a bit to speed. She needed to relax, shut everything around her out, and get into the zone. That was how she'd managed to get out of the Web before. She ignored the fact that she'd not run into the swarm nor any type of storm then—and it had still almost been impossible to get out.

"*I know you can't help in here, and you might not even hear me, but I'm going to try some of your tricks.*"

"*They aren't tricks—it's meditation.*" The voice was faint and for all Vas knew she might have just been talking to herself.

"*Tricks, meditation, if it works, it works. Any ideas?*"

"*Focus.*" The voice faded away.

Vas took another breath, more controlled this time, and let her thoughts focus on one thing, outrunning both the swarm and the storm. She immediately realized she was looking at it wrong.

"Vas! Why are you charging the storm?" Deven sounded ready to come over.

Vas shook her head and finished her change in direction. They could still get out. The exact location where they could escape the Web was firmly fixed in her mind—even if it was now behind her. It was mere moments away, but the storm would have overrun them before they could hit it. Unless the storm was slowed down by another force.

She agreed with the swarm's hatred of the Asarlaí, but not enough to sacrifice her ship and crew.

The swarm followed her into the path of the storm. The two collided, slowing down the momentum of both and Vas turned the *Warrior Wench* out of the way and back to the barrier and escape. Because of the angle she was coming at, she didn't hit the thinnest part directly. The barrier fought back, slowing the engines to almost nothing. She punched the engines again, moving more toward the center of the weakest part. The ship groaned and shuddered, but then they were free.

"All departments check in." Vas felt calm, but when she lifted her hand she was surprised to see it shake.

Aside from a few bumps and a cranky Asarlaí, they seemed to be fine. Well, they had no weapons, three of their remaining Flits had no fuel, and the engines were now making an odd grinding noise. But beyond that they were good.

"Does anyone know where we are?" Vas looked up as stars filled the front screen. A brief feeling of being in this situation before hit her, but then passed. But unlike when they crashed through the gate almost six months ago, she knew what system they were in. They just needed to do some adjustments.

"I have us," Bathie said. "We're actually less than ten hours from Home. That Web thing kicked us out a few days' travel ahead from where we should have been."

"And we didn't lose time?" Vas knew anomalies could mess with time and distance.

"Not that it appears," Deven responded. "We were in there a total of six point two hours and that's the same time lapsed out here. We just took one hell of a short cut."

"One I won't be recommending to anyone." Vas shuddered.

"Divee, map us a way to Home. Bathie? You want the sling back?" Vas gratefully got out of the sling. "Go as quickly as the engines will allow, but they took some damage coming out of there and I don't want to strain them further. Let's go home."

Once everything was secure, and Marli was assured no one was trying to kill her—at the moment—Vas went into her ready room. Her first thought was to call Gosta, but while close range communications could be masked, longer range ones would be a lot harder. And even if the second Asarlaí cruiser hadn't made it back out of the Nebula, it would have contacted its people about seeing the *Warrior Wench*.

Hopefully they had enough data to find a weakness in the Asarlaí. The fact that whatever that swarm had been it could control such strong people and make them fight to kill themselves was impressive. Flinging a storm at it hadn't been the best idea but the force of the two meeting slowed them both down enough to let the *Warrior Wench* escape, so Vas would do it again if she needed to.

The shaking came back in force once she closed the door to her ready room behind her. First in the Flit and then in the sling. Vas never shook—well, not unless it was related to a hangover or physical illness.

She sat behind her desk and willed her body to comply.

"*It's a natural reaction to excessive stressors.*" The voice was back, faint as before but back.

"*I've been under excessive stressors, as you called them, for most all of my life. I don't shake.*" Vas held up her hand to demonstrate, but the shaking did seem to be less.

"*Hmmm, what's changed? Maybe you've broken through and finally realized you have a human heart and care about people?*"

"*I've never—*" Her thought argument was cut off by a knock at the door. "Come in." She dropped her hand into her lap.

Deven came in, then shut the door behind him. "I can now hear whoever it is you're talking to, and I agree about the stressors. But you've always cared about people." He dropped into the chair across from her desk.

"Wait, you can hear us?" She wanted to ask the voice, Aithnea, whoever it was, but he did know what they'd just said.

"*He can. Not sure when that happened, but it's probably for the best.*"

Vas dropped her head in her hands. On the plus side, the shaking had stopped. Maybe annoyance and general confusion wiped out stress.

"Like that, yup, heard it. And since I know she can hear me, I'll repeat—you have always cared about people. You were just blocked from tapping those emotions for years."

The same moment he said the last line, the voice said almost the exact same thing.

"Seriously? In unison now? I know there's not a lot left, but I need a drink." Vas held up her hand to motion Deven to stay in his chair then made it to her bar. It was a former small safe, but Vas converted it to a hidden bar. When they had been trapped on that planet, there had been no way to restock the alcohol and Vas had finished off most of her supply—what she hadn't made available to her crew. But that left her with one bottle of Xylint. A smooth, aged alcohol that slid down then burst into flames in your gut. She needed that right now.

She took a long swig, and then poured it into a glass. Then poured a second glass and handed it to Deven.

"Now that all people with bodies have had something to drink, how about both of you stay out of my emotions? Did either of you think maybe I'm exhausted and that has led to the shaking?"

Deven took a sip of the liquor and stayed silent.

"*Well?*" Vas added the mental emphasis.

"*Are you shaking anymore?*"

"No, I'm not." She took a long sip of the drink. "But since running around drunk all the time isn't going to work, I think I'll just continue ignoring it. We all almost died—a number of times. And there's a hell of a lot more where that came from." She'd spoken out loud since the talking in her head was getting annoying and it didn't matter since Deven heard Aithnea anyway. "But, that being the case, I'd really appreciate if both of you would stay out of my head as much as possible."

"*Agreed. But I will be back. There is much to prepare. Watch over her, Deven.*" The voice vanished before waiting for a response. The half-smile on Deven's lips told Vas he'd heard it.

"Sorry, but a dead leader of a mythical order of warrior nuns outranks you." He set his empty glass down on her desk. "Get some rest. You look exhausted, and we've no idea what's waiting at Home." He leaned over and kissed her forehead, then left the ready room.

CHAPTER TWENTY-NINE

VAS WAITED A FEW MOMENTS, warring with herself over having more to drink and finally conceding that she could use a rest. She put away the bottle, and then went out through the deck.

Given the madness of less than an hour ago, the current calm was almost disturbing. Had Gosta and Mac been in their regular positions she'd almost think things were normal.

No one acted odd, so Deven must not have said anything when he came out. "I'm going to my quarters. Deven has the deck. We have no idea what Home will be like, or if it's even there. Therefore, I'm actually going to order a rest for the entire deck crew, except Deven and Flarik. The rest of you—get some shut eye."

She tipped her head to Deven and Flarik. They could easily manage the ship right now and Deven had been knocked out for almost twenty hours and Flarik only slept when hibernating.

Vas meant to shower, get undressed, and get into bed. What happened was her stumbling into her room, leaving the lights on long enough to fall onto her bed, then commanding them off.

She woke up a few hours later twisted in her sheets, fully dressed, and confused as hell. At least there had been no horrific dreams. Maybe if someone was too tired nightmares couldn't attack.

It took at least three minutes of sitting bolt upright on her bed before she recalled what had happened in the few hours prior. She hit her chron. Well, a few hours prior to the few hours that she just spent passed out.

"*Are you there?*" She did a test, but nothing answered. "*Deven? Can you hear me?*" No response. They either didn't hear her or were actually respecting her wishes. She rolled off the bed, showered, dressed, and re-braided her hair. Instead of heading for the deck, she went to the small desk she had in her quarters.

She'd not used it much. It was small and delicate, and she preferred large and sturdy. But having a place that was away from the deck to just work things out was handy sometimes.

If being marooned for months had any upside, she come to reluctantly appreciate the value of calm and quiet. She was a woman of action, and she liked being in the thick of things. But she also knew the importance of stepping back, resting, and making an assessment. She'd point out to Aithnea that obviously some of her teaching had rubbed off, except that she didn't want to invite the dead nun back in her head—not yet anyway.

She pulled out a pad and stylus. That was another teaching: keep things simple when trying to focus. Aithnea made the nuns use charcoal sticks and paper, but the closest Vas had was the electronic pad and a stylus. At least she could write her thoughts instead of typing them.

How the hell did the Asarlaí come back? She made a note to talk to Marli for theories. When they'd shown themselves at the battle of Mayhira they hadn't looked like Marli, nor of the vids she'd seen of them growing up. They'd been similar but…diluted. For a race that came back from being destroyed, diluted wasn't bad as long as that dilution extended to their powers and skills as well—but who brought them back? How?

Marli would be the first on that list, but she really hated her people. Who would benefit from their return? People like Wilthuny had been benefitting, at least until they turned on her. And it appeared that a portion of the Commonwealth had been working with them as well. Someone found a way to bring them back, and those same someones pulled in unscrupulous power players in the Commonwealth to help. It would be interesting to know if any of them had survived the takeover. Wilthuny had been cut loose; Vas had a feeling many of the rest of the Commonwealth elite who had sided with them had been as well. Most permanently.

Without thinking, she added her brother's name to the list. He'd been working with the Rillianian monks—a group working with the gray ships that turned out to be the Asarlaí. So, yes, the undying bastard was a big part of this. She wrote *Clone?* next to his name. Marli had made herself immortal. Deven was some sort of that. But as far as Vas knew her family wasn't. So how did the bastard keep coming back? The Rillianian monk who had attacked them had tried to get her back to his rulers. Alive. Vas and her crew destroyed him and his people, but had that plan changed?

She really wished she hadn't left the Xylint in her ready room. She made a few more odd connections and notes to study the attack on the destroyed Asarlaí ship, then sent a copy to both Gosta's and Flarik's files and went back on deck.

Deven and Flarik were still the only ones there and both seemed lost in their own projects.

"Nothing changed?"

Deven looked up from whatever he was reading. Had her command chair still been intact, he normally would have sat there while taking command. Apparently, her modified station wasn't interesting so he'd stayed in his own seat. "Not a single thing. The engines definitely took some damage getting out of the Web, so we can't outrun anything. Since we also have no weapons, we can't fight back either. I wouldn't recommend running into anything larger than an escape pod."

"Has he been like this the entire time I've been gone?"

Flarik looked up and blinked her eyes. Vas could see she had three screens up and all were loaded with text. "I apologize; I was doing some research on the Commonwealth." She peered at Deven. "He looks the same to me."

Vas laughed and went to her chair. She checked piloting and nav. Both could be routed to other stations during slow times. The reactions wouldn't be as good as flying in the pilot sling, but it helped keep a skeleton crew when needed. They were within a few hours of Home. There was no way of knowing if the Asarlaí had found her secret planet until they got within range. There were no habitable planets within a full day's travel of Home, so there was nothing nearby to gauge how far the Asarlaí had come this direction. Home was an aberration in its system and hopefully the gray ships wouldn't have gone out this far if there were no signs of worlds for them to conquer.

"Any chatter on the dark lanes?"

"Very little," Deven said. "It's harder to get information, but there is some. I do think there are free survivors of the Asarlaí attacks out there. Finding them might be more difficult than expected. They've gone to ground deep."

Vas's comm beeped. "Vas, thank gods you're finally awake. That monster Deven wouldn't let me disturb you." Marli was in fine form, and the grin on Deven's face showed he appreciated being called a monster.

"What do you want, Marli?" Vas checked through updates, but there really wasn't anything new. Quiet travel for a few hours was a nice change.

"I need to speak to you. Immediately. Now. Your attack doctor has chained me to a bed."

Vas looked up at Deven but he just shrugged. It was very Terel sounding though. Especially if she was still trying to find out what that swarm did to Marli.

"I'm on my way," Vas said. She needed to talk to Marli

anyway—find out more of what had happened when she vanished. She just had wanted to wake up more before beginning battle.

The corridors and lift were empty, and she noticed the lighting was at nighttime settings. Made sense. Most of the crew had been up since they'd left that damn planet.

The med lab was dark with the low lights clicking on when she crossed the doorway. There was a light coming from under the doorway of one of the smaller rooms inside.

Vas knocked as she opened the door. If Marli was literally chained to the bed, she couldn't offer to open it anyway.

She was sort of chained. Terel had hooked her up to enough bio-monitors to effectively trap her in bed.

"Wow, that is…impressive. How long have you been that way?" She pulled up the only other chair in the room and brought it closer. Not close enough that Marli could hit her, but close enough for comfortable conversation. If Marli had wanted, she could easily have gotten up, left the room—hell, left the ship if no one was watching. So, while she didn't do that, she also didn't look happy.

"Since I woke up, or came back to life if what that doctor said is true." She narrowed her eyes. "She tried to claim I died? That I'd been trying to follow some mystical creatures, then suddenly collapsed? All I recall is coming up to the command deck, the doors opening, then I was down here and everything hurt like hell." She glared. "It still hurts by the way."

Vas kept her face neutral. She'd wondered how Terel was planning on explaining that she had a way to kill Marli—albeit temporarily. Just bypassing that part entirely worked. There were too many things about Marli and whatever involvement she had or didn't have in the creation of the black suits—they had to watch how much information she was given.

"I'd think dying and coming back would be painful.

Have you died before?"

"No. I've managed to avoid it even when I've been wishing for death. Perhaps she can share some of her results—just in case your warrior nun fails to honor her deal."

"I think she'll be more than happy to kill you, my warrior nun friend that is. Terel might be up for it also, both sharing the information and killing you." She leaned forward. "So you can't recall anything about the swarm?"

Marli rubbed her forehead. "No. I had her send me the images, but they look like so much space junk. I do know most of what you call the Web was formed after my people were already declining. No one knew where it came from, even then."

Vas filled her in about the Asarlaí ship they'd found, and the results of the storm on it.

"I'd like to see your data. First the swarm, then a massive space storm? I'd say the Web was created to go after my people."

Vas didn't hide her grin. "It's the only thing good about it really. I'll send you what we have. But I was wondering just what happened to you when you left our ship after the battle at Mayhira. You found your crew, obviously."

Marli sighed and fussed with one of the cords connected to her hand. "Barely. Thanks to the bitch Wilthuny, I also ended up drifting around in open space. Even an immortal wouldn't like that." Her face fell. "The shuttle of hers was in bad shape. I lost a quarter of my crew through a gas leak within the first day." She stared at the blanket on her bed for a moment, and then shook her head.

That was the one thing Vas admired about her; even if they weren't sure how far they could trust her, she honestly cared about her crew.

"When I did get to the shuttle, Savan got us out of there immediately. We had almost no control and the gates were unstable. We ended up a few systems over with a busted shuttle. We liberated a few ships and worked our way back here. I recalled where I put that cruiser and I wanted it back."

"So you saw nothing of the battle? The war?"

"I saw the final rim world fall. Clagan. We were still far enough away not to be picked up as a threat. They decimated a few large cities, brought up a ton of prisoners, and moved out. All in less than two days. We went down to do a recon, but there wasn't anyone left. Disgusting."

"The destruction of an entire world? Yeah, most people would say so." Vas had really been hoping that Marli had seen more of the power of the enemy.

Marli waved her hand. "That too, I don't agree with that behavior. No, the taking of prisoners. That was never done by the Asarlaí." The undercurrent of bitter self-loathing that was often there when she mentioned her race surfaced again. "Kill, conquer, and leave behind broken. They left people on their home worlds; just destroyed their ability to function on their own—contact with the lesser races was minimal."

That made Vas think of the other thing she wanted to bring up. "They didn't look like you." She nodded toward Marli's face. "The real you, not that façade. You even called them on it."

Marli's scowl was back. "I don't know what those things are, but they aren't real Asarlaí. The real ones were bastards, but they weren't sloppy. Everything about those others has been sloppy."

"Could they be clones?" Vas still wasn't sure how her brother kept coming back, or why the black suits all seemed to have the same genetic code.

"No." A shudder rippled through her perfect features. "That was one thing I agreed with the rest of my people on—clones were vile. They would never use clones."

That was a final statement. Even if she knew anything about cloning, clearly Marli wasn't going to talk about it.

"What do you know about a race called the Garmainians?" She doubted Marli would have a clue as to why the gray ships had attacked one of their worlds, but maybe some past context would help.

Marli laughed. "Now that is a name I've not heard in a long time. You mean those cute lizard people in quadrant Za, right? They were so charming. Of course, that was over eight hundred years ago...no, longer than that. I went to Jain about a hundred years before my change and we swung by their home planet. Very simple beings, but charming. We left them alone—orders from above that were never clarified."

"Not so simple now. We crashed on a planet near their system, one of the Asarlaí's former support worlds, we believe, and they came hunting a bounty on me. The Asarlaí attacked their capital world, but they were after something." She briefly explained what she felt safe telling Marli. Marli was infuriated about the attack on the Garmainians, and seemed to know the world Vas and her crew crashed on.

"It sounds like Jain, a war supply station. The tracker in this ship was an old, albeit nasty, trick. Yes, our older ships did have those devices, but it was stopped as a practice before I changed myself. It caused the destruction of at least a dozen ships that could have been fine, but instead were destroyed along with their crew."

Vas nodded. All interesting, but not directly helpful. "What do you know about Deven's people?"

CHAPTER THIRTY

—————◆—————

"THE KILESH? NOT MUCH. HE'S the only one I've ever met. They come from far enough out of known Asarlaí space that we never ran into them."

"They have been antagonizing neighbors of the Garmainians for centuries, it sounded like."

"Hmmm, did you see any of them? I would so like to study them. Deven isn't normal, did you know that? Not just that trick with coming back in three people. His genetics had been modifed sometime between after I first met him and when he came to ask me about your blood."

Xsit cut off that conversation with a comm call. "Captain, we're nearing hailing range of Home. No other ships detected yet, but Divee says the others should still be a few days behind us." Xsit and Divee had obviously come back on deck.

Vas got to her feet. "I'll see if Terel can release you at some point. I'm going to go see if we have someplace to stay for a bit."

Marli nodded and slumped back in her bed.

The daytime lights lit the corridors now and Vas ran into a few crew this time as she made her way back to the command deck.

Flarik and Deven were still there along with Xsit, Divee, and Bathie.

"Any signs of activity yet?" She settled into her temporary command chair.

"Nothing so far," Deven said. "How's Marli?"

"Cranky. She doesn't recall what happened to her on the

bridge and wants to examine your people." Vas looked at the scans for the last hour—not a ship within range. "She also claims you're abnormal for your people."

Deven shrugged. "I think the entire reason she and I became friends was that she wanted to know more about my people."

"Captain, I'm picking up ships."

"There's some fragmented ship chatter on the channels."

Divee and Xsit echoed each other as Vas hit the wide search on the main screen.

"They're hovering around Home. No signs of planetary destruction though." Divee was staying calm at least. Maybe there was hope for him.

"Should we turn back?" Bathie asked.

Fully armed, and with an armed flight of Flits, the *Warrior Wench* could hold her own in most fights—but not against the massive gray ships and definitely not as weak as they were. Vas hated slinking away, but without the *Victorious Dead*, *Defiant Ruin,* and Marli's *Scurrilous Monk*, they couldn't fight off an unarmed garbage scow.

"We don't have much choice, Vas." The tone in Deven's voice was too kind, but a quick look told her he wasn't prying into her thoughts—at least not obviously.

"Scan the ships. Bathie, slow us to half impulse. Don't retreat, but keep movement slow and be ready to run if need be." Vas watched the screen. Damn it. She might not spend much time there—it had been almost two years since she was last there—but she liked having Home as a secure option. A place in her mind where she could have down time if she ever got to the point where she fell into something a few drinks wouldn't distance her from. And it was one of the reasons she was able to recruit the best mercs in the business. Having a safe home for their families was worth more than all the platinum in the universe.

"There is some sort of distortion on the ships, almost as if they are there and not there...at the same time. I can't get any solid readings on them." Divee was trying every-thing on his console, but Vas watched as the distant ships seemed to fade in and out.

Then they and the planet vanished.

"What in the hell?"Vas started trying different combina-tions on her console, but all readings came back negative. The ships and Home were completely gone.

"I have nothing. But I know they were there moments ago." Flarik's voice was calm but the short feathers on the back of her head were standing upright. Impossible events did not make her happy.

Deven was trying both the console he was on and the one next to him, but he shook his head when he looked up at Vas. "Nothing."

"I have something," Xsit's voice was softer than usual, and Vas just barely heard it.

"Wait, what?" Vas got out of her chair and ran to Xsit's station.

"There is some fragmented chatter. Even choppier than before." Xsit took off her earphones—usually she didn't need them, but obviously whatever she was hearing was faint.

Vas put them on. There it was. She was watching the nothing but stars screen ahead of her, but chatter, more like everyday life than commands, could be heard. "Too soft to hear what they're saying though." She handed the earphones back to Xsit.

"I know, and I almost didn't hear them—it might not look like it, but someone *is* out there."

Vas watched the screen for another few seconds. "Try hailing them."

"Captain? Is that wise?" Flarik might have been the only one to say it, but everyone on deck, including even Deven, looked like they agreed.

"We don't have a choice. We're flying dead, anyone can pick us off, and it could be days before the other three ships can join us."

"And the fact that they were visible, then suddenly not indicates they do know someone is out here." Deven nodded in agreement but still looked concerned.

"So why haven't they attacked? If it is the gray ships, they should have attacked. And as far as we know, they don't have cloaking technology." Flarik scowled at the screen as if she could make them show themselves by sheer willpower.

"They hid their ships near planet Mayhira," Bathie weighed in. She was in the pilot sling, her hands on the controls but her eyes were on the star field on the main screen.

"That was more a misdirect than true cloaking, regardless of Marli's assertions," Deven said. "And they weren't hiding an entire planet."

"We can debate this for weeks—but the fact is, again, we're in bad shape. And this is my call." Vas nodded to Xsit. "Try hailing them. Divert the call as best you can, but we're the only thing besides them out here—they probably know something is here even if they don't know what."

Xsit nodded and gave the standard, "we see you, who are you" call. But she didn't identify the *Warrior Wench*.

Vas was hoping that at this distance, whoever was out there couldn't get a good lock on identifying them anymore than they had been able to identify the five or six ships circling the planet.

"Identify yourself, or be prepared to be blown out of the sky. This is your only warning." The voice was clipped, vicious, and one that brought a smile to Vas's face.

She leaned into Xsit's console and tapped the button. "Grosslyn, you old bastard, how are you hiding my damn planet?" Grosslyn managed Home—supposedly when Vas was gone, but even on the few times she was in residence, she let him maintain control.

"Please repeat that?" The tough edge had fallen from the

voice.

"It's me—us—you green-skinned, used-ship-selling shark."

"Captain Tor Dain? We thought you'd all been blown up with the—never mind. Get down here quickly before someone sees you. Is it just your ship?"

"For now. We have more coming in a bit. It's going to be hard to come in if we can't see you." As she spoke, Home and the six heavily armed ships around it came into view.

"That better? Don't worry, those ships are yours. I'll explain when you get down here. Grosslyn out."

Vas really wanted more explanations—but she knew Grosslyn. He wouldn't say anything until she and the ship were down there. She turned to Bathie. "You heard the man—land this ship immediately." The other ships were a different design; obviously they were in orbit both as protection of the planet and because they had been modified to no longer be good at landing.

Heavily modified. Once they started moving closer for a landing, Vas went back to her station and scanned the new ships. They weren't new at all, but radically adapted people-moving cruisers. At least the first three were. He wasn't kidding that they were hers; those were her three largest troop movers now converted into heavily armed cruisers.

Two of the others were Syngarian cruisers, also adapted, most likely due to damage. The last was completely unidentifiable. It was the biggest of the group—about twice the size of the *Warrior Wench*, and so grossly overarmed that Vas really hoped she hadn't paid for it.

"I think Grosslyn has a lot of explaining to do."

"There is more than money, you know," Deven said.

Vas looked up from her scanning. "I didn't say anything about money. I just want to make sure we have documentation for all of those ships. Just in case the Commonwealth isn't completely… Yeah, it's the money. But getting our galaxy back takes precedent."

Flarik perked up. "If we track all expenditures, we could probably bill the surviving government for at least partial recompense." She held up one clawed hand as she typed out some comments with the other. "This is a good idea. I will establish a file and make Grosslyn share his expense information."

Vas shook her head but didn't say anything. It honestly never dawned on Flarik she should ask for permission on things from her captain. In her mind, she was right; therefore permission was a foregone conclusion.

Because she was right ninety-nine percent of the time—and Vas really wasn't going to fight with a Wavian lawyer for that tiny one percent—Vas let it slide.

Bathie brought the ship into the landing field on the edge of Luck's Ride. It used to be the only town on Home, and Vas had thought it amusing that a destroyed dive bar in a forgotten galaxy had provided the name for it. Now, after almost a year of bringing in refugees, there were a number of cities and towns popping up. It was night on the side they lived right now, and clusters of lights could be seen clumping down the primary continent. With their minor population explosion, Vas was having serious thoughts about Luck's Ride's name.

The field was emptier than usual since it was missing three giant former crew transports that were now filling the night sky.

Vas made her way to the crew ramp as Bathie brought the ship down. She didn't visit Home often but drew an odd sense of peace from that first moment when she stepped on the planet.

She'd managed to get to the ramp before the rest of her crew had and hit the ramp drop as soon as the engines died down. She'd also beat the ground crew.

The ramp lowered and the nearly empty landing field was before her. The night sky was filled with stars and the lights of the six ships circling the planet. If Vas hadn't been looking up at that moment, she wouldn't have noticed the slight fading of the stars. The cloaking shield. The lights of the ships looked the same however, so most likely whatever was generating the cloaking shield was covering the ships within it.

The idea that it was one massively powerful shield instead of seven separate ones made Vas feel a little better. Not a lot though. Cloaking technology was tricky and too easily abused.

"Captain Tor Dain!" Grosslyn yelled as he came running up and lifted her in the air. He was an Ilerian-Syngarian breed. About six and a half feet tall, and three feet wide—but the wide was all muscle unlike his Ilerian relatives who trended toward soft and flabby or his Syngarian ones who were thin. "We feared you and both ships were lost at the battle of Mayhira. I am sorry the *Victorious Dead* did not survive—they were a good crew." He set her back down again with an embarrassed nod. He was definitely not one for that type of demonstrative behavior. But he had thought she'd been dead these past few months, so it wasn't completely out of character.

Flarik, Bathie, and the others started coming down the ramp. Everyone had packs, as they would all stay at their small and rarely used homes near the landing field. Vas had a larger home, further out, but would be staying at the smaller one Deven had. At least if the look on his face combined with the fact he had both of their packs was an indication.

Of course it was for professional reasons—after all, her home was a good half a day's ride from Luck's Ride—Deven's was five minutes from the landing field. It had nothing to do with the fact they'd had no real time alone together in almost a week. She realized she'd lost focus when Grosslyn asked her the same question twice—in a tone that said it was actually three times.

"I said where is the rest of the crew? Were they lost along

with the *Dead*?"

Vas shook her head; she'd picked a bad moment to let her libido take a detour. "The *Victorious Dead* wasn't lost. Well, like us, it was actually lost in a distant galaxy, but we found each other and made it back. They are on their way here, but we took a short cut. There will be two more ships with them, a cruiser called the *Defiant Ruin* that is being staffed by the other half of this crew, and the *Scurrilous Monk*—Marli's ship."

Vas turned as the crew finished coming out. "Terel? You did unhook her, right?" Yes, Marli could have freed herself, but Vas knew it would be the principle of bugging Terel that would make her stay.

Terel shifted her pack on her back. "Yes, and she said she needed to make herself ready. Did you know she has a lavish home a few streets over from the landing field?"

"I did not, but she was here for a while fixing the *Victorious Dead*, and they had to put her somewhere."

Grosslyn's face lit up at the first mention of Marli's name. If he caught on to the annoyance in Terel's voice about her, he willfully ignored it. "I am not sure why Lady Marli is not at the helm of her ship, but we will welcome her. Both of you are proud of what we did in the ships above, yes?"

Just Marli's name had dropped Grosslyn from a cranky curmudgeon to a schoolboy with an inferiority complex and a soul-stealing crush. Vas wasn't sure she could handle what would happen when he saw Marli.

"I'm surprised at the ships above, but given the current circumstances, they are a good thing. How did you know to put them together though?" The time it would have taken would have been problematic, except she had a few thousand extended crew here and they'd been idle for a long time. But Grosslyn wasn't the type to come up with ideas like that on his own—especially ones that cost money.

"You did. You talked to me, via the comm, right before

we lost contact. And Lady Marli confirmed it a few minutes later. Six months. We put them all together in less than
six months."

CHAPTER THIRTY-ONE

——◆——

V AS WAS ONLY HALF LISTENING. *"You spoke to my people here as well? Six months before you talked to me?"* She was pissed, but since Grosslyn would think it was at him, she tried to keep it off her face.

"It was her—*not me. I am most definitely not that woman."* The way the voice spoke, Vas turned around just in time to see Marli come down the ramp.

Vas watched as Grosslyn and most of the other ground crew immediately stopped what they were doing and stared at Marli. Her human guise was attractive, but this was far more than that. They'd been clustered around the crew of the *Warrior Wench*, but that was because these were their friends and family. But the way they were watching Marli superseded all of that.

It was the same way the Gahan had watched Savan when he'd controlled them on the planet Mayhira.

"Hell, no." Vas marched up to meet Marli as she descended the ramp. She lowered her voice. "Whatever you've done to my people—undo it now. And then you can explain whatever you did faking a call from me to them."

Marli smiled and waved at the ground crew, then dropped the smile and turned back to face Vas. "It was a simple glamour. I needed them to help me help you. That *Victorious Dead* ship of yours was no easy fix." She tried a winsome smile. Then dropped it when Vas just glared. "Fine. It was a simple mind trick, one I didn't think would last this long." She closed her eyes, and then opened them a moment later. "It's done."

Vas turned to her ground crew, while they were still looking on and smiling; they seemed to be slowly turning back to the ship's crew. A few gave Marli a shy smile or wave before turning away.

"Don't ever do that to my people again. Now, what did you do when you faked my voice six months ago? And how? Your ship was being destroyed at the time."

Marli finished her walk to the ground. "I did it before everything went to hell. Well, things were still going to hell, but I thought I had the upper hand. Anyway, your crew had been so happy when they were repairing the other ship, I thought this would keep them busy and couldn't hurt. By the way, I just suggested adding heavier weapons to some of your troop transports and maybe adding a cruiser or two. I figured you might want to expand."

"They did far more than that," Vas said. "That's another thing: no more pretending to be me."

"They really outdid themselves, and you have to admit having more ships right now is a good idea. Did you know that final huge monster was made from scratch? I did a full scan of all of them as we came down. I think I'll have to incorporate some of Grosslyn's ideas into the *Scurrilous Monk*."

Vas did have some pride for her people—they did an amazing job in a short time. And that final ship was impressive as hell. "But that's not the point. You tricked them—don't do it again."

Marli's grin was pure imp. "Deal."

Vas shook her head and joined Deven as he waited for her. The crew was dispersing, a few heading to their homes, but probably most going off with the ground crew for drinks.

"That look has to be more than just Marli getting to you," Deven said. "She does that to everyone, by the way. There's a reason I've been avoiding her this round."

"I just wonder what we're doing. What we're going

to do. It took over a hundred years to finally eradicate the Asarlaí, and that was only after they'd been destroying themselves for a few decades. And yet, in less than six months, they have conquered the Commonwealth." She looked up at him. "And they are in your home galaxy now as well. Although, I still don't understand how they were on those planets, yet never ran into your people."

Deven started walking and used the packs to point toward his home then toward the bar district. Vas nudged him toward his home. They could go to the bar later if they wanted.

"Actually, my people didn't relocate to that galaxy until after the Asarlaí had left. When I first met Marli I tried to figure a timeline. They'd only been gone a few years when we migrated. My people knew of them, but didn't really care as long as they stayed away—I honestly think a battle between both could have destroyed entire galaxies."

Vas knew almost nothing about his people, and Deven liked to keep it that way. But if he was willing to talk about them now… "So what do you think their reaction will be at the Asarlaí incursion into their space now? The Garmainian planet we were on was definitely destroyed. Who knows how many others they went after."

Their boots crunched on the gravel leading up to his door. The rest of the front was a well-tended garden that would be impossible to cut through. Even on Home, he made it hard for people to catch him unaware.

"That's something I've been thinking about." He turned off the alarm on the front porch. "The original Asarlaí had a respect for my people in that they didn't want to see who would win. According to Marli, they also were under orders to leave the Garmainians alone. These current ones have disregarded both."

Vas took a moment to look out over the lights of the city spread out before her. The growth to other areas of the planet was a weakness, in that more people, meant more chances to be noticed. The long dead Asarlaí were back, but just as Home had changed for her, the Asarlaí had changed. They seemed as strong and homicidal as the history vids said, but there was always a chance for weakness where there was change.

"Do you think your people would help the Commonwealth?" She turned back as he opened the door and hit the lights.

He shook his head. "They will defend their planets, and possibly the remaining Garmainian ones as well. Our peoples have never been close, but my people won't let the Garmainians be slaughtered. But they won't defend people they don't know. Not to mention, while my people aren't as insane as the Asarlaí, they wouldn't be great rulers for something as massive as the Commonwealth. They'd only help if they were planning on taking over. There's a reason I don't live on their worlds anymore."

"We don't have a lot of options," Vas said as he held the door open for her. She'd been in his place once before, not long after they'd built the first quarters. It looked far more Deven-like now. Graceful art from a dozen different worlds filled the space. The massive sofa and matching dark chairs were luxurious and soft, just begging tired people to collapse on them. "Sometimes I forget this side of you."

Deven dropped both packs and came closer. He freed her hair from the wrap around the end of the braid and slowly separated the plaits. "What? That I like beautiful things and being comfortable?" He kissed the side of her neck. "There is nothing wrong with that—contrary to what you think, a home doesn't have to be harsh and spare."

Vas turned and caught him in a kiss. She needed the warmth that flowed through her at their touch. She broke the kiss and pulled back. "You almost died again. I was holding it together, but you almost died. Again." She punched his arm. "I can't take that. I can't. And my house isn't spare, it's simple."

"I think you can handle anything. When the Universe ends, there will be Vas, saying, 'is that all you have'?" His smile didn't reach his eyes. "But I will try not to die again on you. At least not without a damn good reason." His arms pulled her close for another kiss, and this one ended with them falling into the giant sofa. "And I've been to your house—that thing is ugly. No wonder you never want to come back."

Vas pushed him deeper into the sofa. "I come back plenty...at least once in the last...two years?" She shrugged. "I was a bit busy. Which I think I need to be again." She pulled his shirt off over his head and started laying down a serious collection of kisses down his torso.

Only to be cut off by her comm. "Captain? We have a problem." Flarik's voice was more tense than usual.

Vas sat up but put her hand on Deven's chest when he tried to do the same. Flarik wasn't one to call without reason, but her reasons weren't always ones Vas felt were crucial. There was still a chance to save this evening. "What is it, Flarik?" Vas turned up the volume so Deven could hear it as well.

"Marli has stolen the ships."

Vas released her hand from Deven and flicked his shirt back at him. "Can you clarify that, please?"

"Grosslyn gave her access to the ships in orbit. She grabbed all except the *Warrior Wench* and that monster ship and took off. I am currently getting more information out of Grosslyn. Permission to torture?"

Vas tried to stay calm. What was Marli up to? Had this been her plan all along? Get Vas's people to build her a fleet and then steal it? Damn it, what if going to rescue the *Scurrilous Monk* had been part of the trap as well? "No torturing, yet. The crews all went along willingly?"

"She sent a vid of you telling them to do so. I can show you it when you get here."

Vas climbed off the sofa, Deven was a second behind her,

dressed, and heading for the door. "We're on our way. Have Xsit call back the crew."

"I know Marli does a lot of stupid things, but I can't see her being behind this for no reason." Deven grabbed their packs and locked the house up behind them.

"Oh, I'm sure she has a reason. Just not a reason any of us will like." There were two main options—it was a spur of the moment reaction to something that had recently happened. Or it was a planned action. One that she'd been waiting six months or longer to execute. If Marli were a normal person, Vas would say there was no way she could have set things in motion that would involve Vas and her crew rescuing Marli in that pod. But Vas had no doubt that Marli could have made it happen.

The office of the landing field wasn't large to begin with and as it started filling with her crew it got progressively smaller. But a nice neat circle was cleared around Flarik and her prey. Wavians had a long and violent history before they 'civilized' and joined the Commonwealth. Flarik was channeling that now. Grosslyn was easily twice her size, but he was trying to see if he could burrow through the solid rock floor.

"Grosslyn, do you want to tell me why you gave away five of our ships?" Vas's use of her calm voice caused the crewmembers closest to her to take another step back. Yelling and screaming Vas was bad. Calm and cold Vas was worse.

"She…she…" He kept trying to talk but the words wouldn't come out. He wasn't injured—well, nothing more than Flarik roughing him up, nothing worse than what he probably got into at the bar. But he looked in extreme pain.

"She put a block on him," Deven said and stepped forward. "I have to have your permission for this or it won't work." He stood next to Grosslyn, hands out but not touching him.

"She…" Grosslyn gritted his teeth and finally nodded. "Yes. Do. It."

Deven put his hand on Grosslyn's forehead. Deven didn't need touch to read a mind, but whatever this was it was something deeper.

Grosslyn whimpered and tried to curl up tighter, but didn't move away from Deven. A thin trickle of sweat appeared down his neck. Finally, Grosslyn collapsed and Deven stepped back.

"He'll be okay. It just took a lot to break that thing," Deven said. "Marli placed a command block in his head when she was here helping with the *Victorious Dead*. He didn't have a choice on obeying her, but the only commands I could see involved her recent heist." He stretched his fingers as if they'd cramped. "There are more people involved however."

Flarik had moved aside as Deven stepped forward but she came back now with a holocube. "This is what was sent to the ships. The monster one isn't fully staffed, so I assume that's why she left it. The other five were, and many of the attending crew would have been involved in the rebuild for the *Victorious Dead*." She flicked on the cube. A tiny Vas appeared telling the viewer to obey Marli like they would her, and she and the rest of the fleet would join them later. Vas's blood went cold when she heard her own voice wishing them good luck in battle.

"Do we have an idea where they were heading?" Marli's death wish might have finally pushed her over the edge, but she wasn't taking Vas's people down with her.

"It looks like they are on a trajectory to meet the other three ships." Bathie had taken over one of the control consoles in the office. "At least they are heading toward where we thought they would be coming from."

"Grosslyn, do you know who else was under Marli's control?"

He was recovering but still sitting in a dazed pile on the

floor. "No. You know I didn't do this because I wanted to, right?" Grosslyn was a big, curmudgeonly being; seeing him like this wasn't good—nor was it good for the people he was still going to need to lead.

Vas raised her voice. "Grosslyn was not doing this of his own volition, nor were any of the other people Marli is controlling. Marli is stronger than anyone can imagine. But we have to go after her. I will be leading the *Warrior Wench* and the...what is that damn thing called anyway?" No name had popped up for the huge ship when they passed coming in.

"It doesn't have a name, Captain." Koan, Grosslyn's second-in-command, said as he stepped forward. "They were going to name it after you. We thought you'd perished."

Vas sighed, it was a nice thought, but she wasn't going to be leading a ship named after her. "Deven? You have something you'd like to name that beast? We need it to have a name, just on principle if nothing else."

Deven studied her for a second, and then a small smile appeared. "*Aoenyth*. It's a word from my people."

Vas tried it in her head a few times. A far prettier sounding word than any warship, especially one like the giant out there, would warrant. But it sounded right.

"What does it mean?" Not that it mattered really, no one in the Commonwealth spoke Deven's native tongue, but it was a good idea to know just in case.

"Beautiful friend or something similar. There's no direct translation."

"We're calling a massive warship that?" Grosslyn was starting to return to normal based on the snarky tone.

Vas looked around. "Yup, we are. Get it in the registry, Xsit. Now we need to finish crewing the *Aoenyth* as well as fortifying the *Warrior Wench* crew." There was no way to alert the crew on the stolen ships that they'd been tricked, not without taking a risk on Home's location. Not to mention if Marli had brainwashed them, telling them wouldn't have mattered. She didn't want any people who had been controlled by Marli on either ship—at least not until the control had been broken. A way of finding who else might be under Marli's control came to mind.

"Grosslyn, do you have a list of who helped rebuild the *Victorious Dead*?"

He nodded as Deven helped him to his feet. "I can get that."

"Excellent. Deven, you, Flarik, and Terel will go over the list. If you find someone, Deven can break down whatever Marli did." She paused. That could be a lot of people. "Do we have any higher level telepaths in town?"

"Yes," Grosslyn said as he went to a console. "At least five: three level fours, and two level threes. Not as high as Deven, but they might help?"

Deven nodded. "I can clear them first. Their esper levels should allow them to break down the block. Marli would have only done the harshest level block on the leader." He nodded to Grosslyn.

"Okay, let's get this moving, people." Vas looked at the time. "Marli has an hour lead on us as of now. I want to be trailing her ass in less than two."

CHAPTER THIRTY-TWO

D EVEN, FLARIK, AND TEREL STARTING checking the ground crew. Deven scanned their minds, Terel reviewed their physical health, and Flarik matched up skills with what was needed on each of the two ships. The *Warrior Wench* hadn't been fully crewed before it split the crew in two to staff the *Defiant Ruin*, so another seventy-five people would be needed. It had been years since Vas had run with a full crew on her command ship.

The *Aoenyth* could take a crew of over five hundred, but only had eighty-two on board. That was going to be harder to crew, but considering the under-crewed status most likely made Marli leave it behind, Vas was fine with the extra time it would take to staff it.

While they worked on getting the crew up to par, Vas commandeered a swarm of techs to go over the *Warrior Wench* and fix everything. She also had them replace and re-supply weapons, fuel, and any other supply she could think of. Not only was the Flit she'd crashed needing to be replaced, but at least two others—the ones Terel and Deven had flown—showed enough damage to pull them. They also were able to get three replacement shuttles.

After just over an hour and a half, they had restocked and repaired the *Warrior Wench* and added enough crew to both ships to make them battle worthy. Deven and the other telepaths had found eight more people with the Marli touch and cleared them.

Grosslyn had avoided Vas as much as possible, only coming up as she was getting ready to board the *Warrior Wench*.

"I will file for a replacement once you have left, but… might I still remain on the planet? I don't know that there is anywhere to go at this point."

Vas had been squatting down and double-checking the weapons locker near the ramp and rocked back on her feet to look at him. "What are you talking about? You lost a battle against an opponent none of us could hold our own against. I don't punish people for being outmatched. You know what she really is." Only a few of the people on Home knew what Marli really was—that would need to change if Vas was now going to have to defend them against a rogue Asarlaí as well as her resurrected people. But Grosslyn knew.

"I know, but—"

Vas stood. "No buts. Right now we are facing an unimaginable foe, and I don't just mean her. I saw what the Asarlaí did to those planets. I need to have Home guarded by the best." She poked him in the chest. "And you're the best. Keep things hidden and don't trust anything that seems to come from me unless there is this code attached." She wrote down a code. Her birthdate and the date she ran away from her home world. Marli might have access to the numbers, but she wouldn't know they were needed. "We're going out there and getting our damn ships back. Marli can rot in hell for all I care. I can't do what I need to do without knowing this place is safe. I need you for that."

He was silent for a few moments, his head tipped down. Finally he looked up and nodded. "I won't let you down again, Captain."

She patted his cheek. "You haven't yet. Now let's get these people loaded."

The two remaining troop transports had taken the crew up to the *Aoenyth*. Vas had thought maybe Deven might like to captain it; he'd named it after all. But he declined.

Grosslyn started shouting orders to the ground crews to finish last minute work and clear the area.

Vas finished checking the weapons and moved up to the command deck. To find a duplicate of her former command chair locked in place where the old one had been. She walked up to it. Yup, all the same commands, all the same comfort.

"They had less than two hours—how is this even possible?" She was glad she could go hunt down that damn Asarlaí woman in comfort, but not if something else got overlooked.

"Grosslyn motivated some of the furniture designers from town. The techs made sure it was completely functional." Bathie swung into her pilot sling. There were going to be some fights about ownership of that once Mac got back on board. Yes, he couldn't pilot all the time, but he tried. And Bathie was showing herself to be an excellent pilot.

Vas slid into the seat and gave a sigh. Now she could go kick some Asarlaí ass. Well, kick it once it was out of her ships.

"Take us up and out, Bathie. We'll lead, and the *Aoenyth* will follow far enough behind to break free if we get trapped." She wasn't going to risk both ships—Marli had far more firepower than Vas, but hopefully this wasn't a complete takeover.

The lift off was perfect, and the massive *Aoenyth* dropped in behind. Vas hated leaving no ships with the planet, but she needed the support. Grosslyn had insisted he could keep Home safe, and if he couldn't, one ship wouldn't make a difference anyway.

Once they got back, Vas was going to demand a full report on everything they'd done to Home.

They were a few minutes out when Xsit chirped and flipped the front screens to view behind them—nothing was visible but stars.

"Even though I know that's a shield, it's still disturbing," Vas said.

"Agreed. I got Grosslyn to send me the specs, and just on the surface, they are using a similar misdirect to what the Asarlaí had on their ships. I think we know who laid the groundwork on that." Deven wasn't happy.

Vas nodded, she wasn't happy about Marli's help either—but if it worked she'd use it. "Okay, everyone keep an eye out on any frequency you can. We can't risk hailing, but we know the *Victorious Dead* and the others wouldn't have been that far out." She really hoped this was just part of some misguided plan from Marli—one she could talk her down from. And not something more sinister.

They were an hour into the flight when Xsit chirped again. "I'm picking up chatter. Between ships and too soft to pick out words—but there are a few ships ahead just out of viewing range."

Vas swore as she automatically turned to Gosta's station. She needed the rest of her command crew back on this ship. "See what you can find, Flarik. The signatures should be familiar so we should be able to pick them out."

"I have them," Flarik said a few minutes later and the front left panel changed. There they were: her five missing ships, plus the *Victorious Dead*, the *Defiant Ruin*, and a monster one almost as large as the *Aoenyth* that she assumed was the new *Scurrilous Monk*. Or actually, the original one.

"Scan for any other ships. I don't want to comm this far out if there are enemies nearby." Well, enemies beyond the damn Asarlaí woman leading the pack in front of her. The ships were moving slowly, at half impulse if she'd have to guess.

"Nothing else out there that I can tell," Xsit said. "And the *Victorious Dead* is hailing us."

Vas nodded. "Transfer it to my chair. This is Captain Tor Dain. Who am I speaking to?"

"Captain? It's Ragkor. We've been waiting for you. Marli said you wanted us to launch an attack on an Asarlaí outpost. But Gosta has been refusing to budge."

Deven hit the comm mute switch. "Vas, Ragkor and most of his crew were part of the *Victorious Dead* reconstruction, the tail end of it but still."

"Damn it, you're right, they could all be compromised. Can we open a tight communication to the *Defiant Ruin*?"

"I've got them, Captain," Xsit said.

Vas flicked open the other comm line. Ragkor's was still flashing but she could ignore it.

"Gosta? This is Vas—what the hell is going on?"

"I'm sorry, Captain. We should have obeyed your orders. But there was just something wrong with them. I didn't like that Marli was representing you. It just felt wrong… in my gut."

Vas laughed. Gosta was all science and research, relying on his gut was new for him. "Actually, your gut was right. I didn't issue those orders and the command crew on board the *Victorious Dead* has most likely been compromised. What orders did Marli give you, specifically?"

"She said that you ordered us to follow her and the rest of your new fleet to a secret base. We were to blow it up, and then you'd meet up with us." He paused. "I'll send over the coordinates of where she was sending us."

Vas briefly skimmed them. It was a system nearby, but she wasn't ready to start picking off Asarlaí targets until she had a better understanding of the situation. Yes, they now had ten heavily armed ships, but the Asarlaí were better armed and there were more of them. She'd go after them when there was a better chance of winning. Or at least taking down a hell of a lot of them before they went down.

"Okay, we need to handle this carefully. Obviously Marli knows we're out here and she'll have figured out I'm not happy. Ideas on what to do?" She'd thought it would be harder to find the missing ships but now that they were almost upon them, she was at a loss. She wasn't going to fire on her own people, but she also wasn't going to let Marli lead them into an ambush they weren't ready for.

Deven looked up from his screen. "I think we can—"

Vas still had her comm to Gosta open and she heard the alarms. She opened the one to Ragkor as well. Same alarms. "What in the hell is going on?"

"That." Deven sent the distance scan to the front screen. Two massive Asarlaí war ships were racing toward the waiting ships. Their course didn't indicate they'd come from the nearby gate, so they must have been local.

"Damn it, how fast can we get to our ships?" There was a slim chance the Asarlaí hadn't noticed the *Warrior Wench* and the *Aoenyth*. Or they did, but just didn't care.

"Open a comm to the *Scurrilous Monk*." Yes, that wasn't how Marli got out here, but Vas knew she'd jump to her flagship as soon as she could. "Marli—what in the hell do you think you're doing?"

"Admiral Vas! You joined us. As it turns out, I'm grateful. Our friends seem to have come calling before I was ready." If Marli was at all concerned about stealing Vas's ships and crew, she didn't give notice.

"We can't fight them off."

"Oh yes we can. It's just a little more work than expected." Marli cut the comm and Ragkor's vanished a moment later.

"Gosta, I want you to be ready to run. We can't win this fight."

"I know, Captain, but we don't have a choice. Another cruiser just came out of the gate," Gosta yelled.

The *Defiant Ruin* went from a slow crawl to engaging speed and spun to face the new ship. The *Warrior Wench* kicked up speed as well.

"Captain Rost, I need you and the *Aoenyth* to stay close to us, but try to get between the *Defiant Ruin* and that cruiser." Rost was a good man, one she'd had on her command crew for a few years until he decided to settle down. She hoped she made the right choice in giving him the *Aoenyth*.

The *Scurrilous Monk* started firing at the lead Asarlaí vessel and got in a few strikes, but the next shots bounced off without affecting them.

"They have modulating shields. We can't keep up with them." Ragkor opened his comm again as he also moved his ship to protect the *Defiant Ruin*.

"Captain, I think they are trying to call for backup," Xsit's voice went higher. "I captured their transmission and sent it back at them." She bounced in the air. That was a seriously talented feat and hard as hell to complete. It caused the attempted transmission to act as a weapon against the system it came from.

"Good work," Vas responded. That would be something to brag about later—if they survived.

All of the ships were firing as the *Warrior Wench* and the *Aoenyth* got into the fray. Rost moved his ship toward the *Defiant Ruin* and Bathie charged into the fight. One of the revamped Syngerin ships was taking a pounding and Vas directed her there. Their weapons didn't seem to be impacting the Asarlaí vessel but they kept firing.

Then the Syngerin ship's shields failed and their shuttle bay took a direct hit. The resulting explosion rocked the ship back.

Vas had no idea who was on that ship, but they were her people. "*Sythin Garlin*, abandon ship now, get to your life pods. We'll cover you."

Bathie swung the *Warrior Wench* into a blocking position, as more explosions rocked the damaged ship.

There were pods coming off of it, but not enough for a ship that size and some were being destroyed by the Asarlaí ship. "You bastards. Rush them, all weapons on my command." The rest of her fleet, such as it was, were engaging the other two Asarlaí ships—this one was hers.

Bathie didn't question and Vas saw all of the weapons light up on her console. Vas was counting on sheer strength of firing everything at once to overwhelm them. If it didn't work they were dead.

She kept her hand over the weapons console.

"Shields down to sixty-two percent." Deven's voice was a soothing calm in the madness even if his words weren't.

"Fifty-eight percent."

Vas still held off. One shot. They had one. She was going to ram this ship down their throats if she had to.

"Forty-three percent."

Vas took a deep breath and fired everything.

CHAPTER THIRTY-THREE

BATHIE HAD KNOWN WHAT THEY were doing, but still had a hard time pulling the ship free of the resulting fireball. Vas hadn't known if it would work, but they needed to do something to give time to get the survivors off the dead Syngerin ship.

Bathie pulled them around in time to see the rest of their ships, the *Defiant Ruin* included, finish off the other two Asarlaí ships.

"Everyone make sure to grab all of the pods." The downed ship was still being rocked by explosions, but smaller escape pods and at least two shuttles were still coming out. There was no way they could save it, nor the people who had already died. But Vas would make sure no one was left behind.

"Vas, we can still go after them," Marli's voice cut in, but for the first time since Vas had met her a bit of uncertainty crept into her voice.

"Go to hell, Marli. Help rescue the survivors and get my ships back to Home without being trailed. You and your crew can go do what you want afterwards." Vas continued to monitor the escaping pods. They were being picked up quickly and the two shuttles were already on board the *Aoenyth*. Minutes passed and no new escape pods appeared.

"There are no further signs of life on the *Sythin Garlin*," Deven said.

"And cross-checked. No life left on board." Flarik wasn't double-checking Deven's work to be difficult; Vas always ordered double or triple scans anytime they had to leave something behind.

She ran the final herself. No life signs and now all pods were inside ships.

"Gosta, we don't have anything left. Will you put our companions at rest and do the final honors?" There was no way to salvage the ship and Vas didn't like leaving things behind for their enemy to examine. Destroying the ship ensured that wouldn't happen.

"Aye, Captain," Gosta said. Vas knew this would be hard for him. No matter how many scans you did there was always the fear that someone could be saved, that the ship could be saved. But that wasn't always the case.

The fact that it only took two shots from the *Defiant Ruin* to shatter the Syngerin ship into fiery pieces told Vas that was the right thing. It would have broken apart on its own eventually, but she needed to make sure.

"Scanning all frequencies for chatter," Xsit said.

Deven also had an earpiece in and was carefully watching his screens. "No traces of any ship activity between here and Home, nor any ships within contact range.

That wouldn't last for long. "All ships, we move now. If we're spotted, scatter and do not take the same route back to Home. All comms on tight range only." Vas switched her comm back from wide.

Although she could almost feel everyone in the ship holding their breath on the way back, there were no calls from either Xsit or Deven that any other ships were in the area. They made it back to Home without further incident.

Home popped back into existence right before Vas was going to send a hail.

"Good to see you, Captain." Grosslyn paused. "The *Sythin Garlin* isn't with you." It wasn't a question.

"No, it is not. I'm not sure how many people we lost. Right now the surviving crew is spread over the rest of the ships. I'm sure many need medical attention. That will be your first task." She knew Grosslyn was already beating himself up for his responsibility in the losses they'd taken. But they didn't have the luxury for that now.

"Aye, we will be ready."

Vas called to the fleet. "If you have anyone from the *Sythin Garlin*, send them down to the planet immediately—obviously injured first. Use your shuttles. Once they are down, leave a working crew on each ship, but everyone else go in the transports. Meeting with all command crews in one hour in the main hangar. Vas out."

The *Warrior Wench* and the *Defiant Ruin* were the only two ships designed to land, so they went down. They were also the only two ships Vas completely trusted at this point. Well, they and the *Aoenyth*. At Deven's suggestion, Vas had sent the telepaths he'd worked with in screening the crew along with the extra five-hundred crew people. They'd not found any sign of Marli's tampering. Probably another reason she didn't try to take that ship.

Vas was alone, waiting in the hangar when Marli arrived.

"Admiral Vas, I do admit that was an ill-placed plan on my part—"

Vas hit her in the jaw so hard that she dropped to the ground.

"What the hell gave you the right to take my people, against their will? Oh, that's right, I forgot, you're a damn Asarlaí—you do whatever you want."

Marli didn't immediately get up but she rubbed her jaw. "I'm not like them."

"You say that. Repeatedly. You left them because you couldn't stand what they had become. But you are just like them. You cover it with witty charm and an attractive façade—but you are just like them. Take what you want, sure that you are right." Vas stepped back. Her fists were still clenched and part of her really wanted Marli to get up again. Another dozen punches would feel good. "You were wrong this time. And it cost good people their lives. People who were so much better than you."

"I didn't...I thought we could..." Marli shook her head and let it fall to the floor.

Deven walked in. "Did you finally kill her?" He peered down at Marli as he walked by. "I would have thought she'd return to her natural form upon death."

"I'm not dead," Marli said as she flung one arm over her eyes. "I am, however, admitting I made a mistake. A big one."

Vas leaned down closer. "Are you crying?"

"No, my people can't cry." She dropped her hand and rolled to her feet. "We also can't feel sorrow, yet somehow here I am doing that. Too many years of being around you people has done that. Might I address the command crews once they are gathered? Deven can stand right next to me armed to the teeth if you'd like."

Vas looked to Deven. He watched Marli, and then nodded.

"I can keep an eye on her too. Not a lot I can do where I currently am, but I would love to try to fry an Asarlaí brain."

Vas smiled at the voice. She'd actually missed it while it was gone. Whether it was Aithnea, just her own thoughts bouncing back at her, or some weird new alien threat—Vas found it oddly comforting.

"Agreed." Vas had no idea what she was going to do with Marli. At this point she was torn between needing her and her ship and taking her up in a shuttle and seeing how long she could survive in space without a suit. She imagined that an immortal would just keep dying and coming back.

The logical thing to do was to wait and see what her actions were with the command crews. Vas had planned on having Deven and the other higher telepaths clear all of the command crews—but she hadn't told Marli she knew what had been done to them.

If Marli addressed that, removed the blocks and admitted what she'd done—Vas might see if there was a way to work together. She watched Marli as she smiled and welcomed the command crews into the hangar. Vas wasn't going to hold her breath for that to happen.

Grosslyn stood off to the side, away from Vas, Deven, and Marli, but the rest of the crews as well. Vas made a note to have the local mind-doc meet with him. Whether he wanted it or not. Those crew deaths were on Marli's head, not his, but Vas knew he wouldn't accept that for a long time. If ever.

Deven nodded to her when everyone was inside. Vas stood on top of a heavy metal crate, then pulled Marli up next to her. "Before I address our situation, there are some things Marli wished to say."

Marli looked surprised at being pulled up on the crate, but the crowd filled the hangar. Vas wanted everyone to see both of them. Deven moved closer so he was almost touching Marli's leg with his shoulder.

"Thank you, Captain Tor Dain." Marli was as serious as Vas had only seen her once before—when her ship was being destroyed and she feared for the lives of her crew. "I first want to apologize to the crew standing before me. Captain Vas never instructed you to follow me. I did that on my own. I did it for what I thought was a worthy cause: a chance to launch a sneak attack on an Asarlaí base. I was wrong and I failed you all. Most importantly I failed the crew of the *Sythin Garlin*." She shifted on her feet. "I did it because my fear and hatred of the Asarlaí was stronger than my concern for those I was dragging into battle."

Vas watched her carefully. Marli's hands clenched and unclenched—almost as if she was actually nervous.

"I have another confession, two, actually. The first is that I used telepathic trickery to make many of you compliant to my wishes. I am going to release all of you now." She raised one hand, dipped her head down, and an almost visible wave went through the room. Not everyone was affected, but enough to be disturbing. All of them froze a bit, and then shook their heads.

Vas leaned forward and looked to Deven. He turned toward the crowd and then nodded. Marli had released them.

"Now, the second part of my confession, and my demonstration to Captain Tor Dain that I have released you. The reason I hate the Asarlaí with such irrational power, is that I am one." Without warning, Marli dropped her glamour. At seven feet tall with impossibly pale skin and hair, and red eyes, there was no mistaking what she was. A hangar full of blasters immediately pointed at her. Vas was impressed—that verified that she'd lifted the block off of the command crews. She would still have Deven and the others go through anyone who'd worked on the *Victorious Dead* with Marli, but this was a start.

Vas held up her hands. "Please, lower your weapons. Yes, Marli is an Asarlaí, but up until this last event she's helped our cause and us. She saved the entire crew of the *Warrior Wench*. She was estranged from the Asarlaí long before they were destroyed. And it is the belief of myself and my second-in-command, that she can help us defend against them. If we have to face them in battle, I want someone who knows them on our side."

The muttering that followed wasn't good, but blasters were lowered if not completely holstered.

Deven didn't stand on the metal crate, but his voice reached the furthest corner of the hangar. "I know her better than anyone. That being said, I don't trust her not to do what is in her best interests. But I also know how much she hates her people. Right now, her best interests are the same as ours."

The muttering was dying down and Vas nodded to Terel. "If you don't mind, I think Marli might need a quiet place to rest." Marli was sagging to one side, but mostly Vas just wanted to get her out of there and give folks a chance to settle down.

Terel nodded and reached out to help Marli off the crates. Marli was over a thousand years old, and maybe it was just because she wasn't wearing her glamour anymore but she looked it.

Vas turned to the command crew. "You all know what she is now, and the rest of our people will as well. But I don't know that having her walk around in her glamour would be a bad thing—it might be less disruptive. What say you?"

A lot of 'ayes' were heard and everyone else nodded.

Marli flashed Vas a grateful smile and slipped her glamour back on as she and Terel walked away. It was in part for her—Vas needed her functioning well if she was going to be of any help. An already suicidal immortal could cause a lot more damage than she already had if things got mentally worse for her.

But she mostly did it for her crew. Yes, they were all aware of what Marli really was, but this would make it easier for them to work with her.

Vas waited until Terel and Marli were out of the hangar. "I want to remember the crew we just lost." She glanced at her scanner. Gosta was sorting the crewmembers of the destroyed ship and the crew death total was in. "Fifty-one people lost their lives today." She let the words sink in. "Fifty-one of our friends, shipmates, family. Whether they were related to any of us by blood or not, they were still family." They were an extended crew of mercs, losing people in battle was one of the drawbacks. But Vas never wanted herself or them to become hardened to it.

"There will be more, of that we know. The Asarlaí have come back and have retaken the Commonwealth. They took over the entire thing—hundreds of planets destroyed or under their control or frozen in hiding—in a few months." She started to pace then recalled the crates weren't that big. "We will be up against horrific odds. Terrifying odds. Many of us will die. All of us in this hangar could die fighting this fight." She paused and watched them all. "Do we do it? Ride forth into a possibly unwinnable battle? Or do we hide and run until they find us, and they will."

"Fight!" The yell was universal and quick. No thinking. Just reacting.

"I can't hear you," Vas yelled back.

"FIGHT to the death! Theirs or ours!"

Vas smiled and nodded. This wasn't a campaign they'd been paid to fight, this was war. Ugly, nasty, war. Her people needed to be completely involved or they might as well give up now. "Go to your homes, your bars, wherever you feel you need to be. Mark my words; it's only a matter of time until they find us. We don't have long to get prepared and fully re-armed before we take the fight to them. Today remember those we have lost. Get some rest. Then tomorrow, prepare your ships and your crew. For war."

CHAPTER THIRTY-FOUR

DEVEN STAYED SILENT UNTIL ALL of the command crews had left. Flarik and the rest of their own command crew had gone as well. She was going to work on crew reassignments. Vas wanted the *Defiant Ruin* to be manned by the survivors of the *Sythin Garlin*. They would need to be supplemented, but Flarik would find the best fits.

It would be a good focus for them and she wanted her command crew back. Gosta had already communicated that he was thankful for the opportunity to captain the *Defiant Ruin*, but he was fine if he never had to do it again.

"You did well," Deven said, then helped her down from the crate.

"You don't think we have a chance."

"I don't think we have a choice." He shrugged. "The Asarlaí aren't the same as they were, something has changed. If we can find that and exploit it, we might have a chance. It's going to be brains, not brawn, that win this fight." He slipped his arm around her shoulders as they left the hangar.

"Ah, but without brawn to distract, taunt, and hopefully weaken the enemy, brains can't have the time to come up with a solution." Her smile dropped. "I don't agree with Marli's rash attack—it was stupid, ill-planned, and gave us away before we were ready. However, I do agree with taking an offensive stance. We can't face them and survive in a full battle, but in smaller ones we can."

"We did take out three Asarlaí cruisers. Your 'fire everything' technique was a bit questionable though—not a lot of repeated use with that one."

Vas squeezed his side. "I didn't have a choice. And it worked."

"You made a guess."

"I did. But, yeah, that won't work as a strategy. I already have Gosta studying the vids of the battle for anything that might help though. I'd rather not lose one ship and strip another of all its weapons each time we meet them."

Deven stopped at the edge of the landing field. "My place? Or breakfast first?"

As much as Vas really wanted to pick up where they'd left off hours ago, her stomach was pointedly reminding her she hadn't eaten in almost twenty hours. "Breakfast first, then your place."

"Deal." He turned them down a side street. "I think Delilah's place is still here." The street broadened a bit—Home was mostly put together by fighters so not a lot of planning went into the city. Things popped up where they popped up. Delilah was a former merc who was gray and weathered when she joined Vas's crew twenty years ago. She was one of the original crewmembers and her retirement ten years ago had been hard for Vas. Delilah was still the best weapons expert Vas had ever known. She was also a serious cook.

The morning was still early enough that the restaurant wasn't crowded. The buildings on Home reflected the lifestyle of their owners. Deven's was gorgeous and full of comfort, Vas's was simple and spare. Delilah's restaurant was the home everyone wished they grew up in. Just one with a massively huge dining room.

"Damn time you got back here." The voice was heard before the tiny pale woman came around the corner. Delilah came up to Vas's chest, but there was no way anyone would try to stand against her. Vas was never sure what species she was; it wasn't polite to ask, and Delilah never told. She was fierce, feisty, and at over two hundred years old, she still looked seventy. "You have been away from Home for far too long." She stopped and slowly studied them. "And thank the goddess you finally got together." She pushed Deven in the chest. "You were pining for her so hard you used to hurt my head."

Deven opened his mouth, then just shut it and nodded.

"Now, come this way. I saved you the best seats." Delilah's attitude dropped as she spun around and hugged them both fiercely. Finally, she stepped back and wiped her eyes. "Don't you two ever do that again, you hear me? Damn you both, I thought I'd never see you again." She wiped the last tears away and shoved them toward a table set apart from the others. "Sit and I'll bring food."

"I think she worried about you." Deven held the chair out for Vas.

"I think she worried about both of us. Not to mention, you did actually die. I was just missing and presumed dead." She let out a breath she didn't know she'd been holding. She'd had an orderly life before all of this, but she'd also had a mental block impacting her emotions and reactions. She hadn't been emotionally dead, just numb. Now she felt everything just in time for the world to go to hell on her. She missed her old life.

"If you keep sighing like that people are going to think you're getting soft in your old age." Delilah came out with the first course. Soup and bread. It was breakfast time, but she liked to stick to a pattern and her soups were always the best so Vas wasn't going to argue.

The soup was an odd conglomeration of egg broth, vegetables, and thin strips of meat. Weird, but it worked. Kind of like Delilah herself.

The next two courses were meat and gravy on toast, and an omelet of some kind. All served with steaming hot solie to drink and more bread.

Delilah waited until Vas was pushing away her last

half-finished roll before pulling up a chair. "Now that that's taken care of, just who is this?" She stared at Vas and tilted her head.

"That's Vas," Deven said. "You already forgot her?"

"Daft boy." Delilah hit his arm. "Inside there. Someone is bobbling about in our fair captain's redheaded skull. I'd like to know if I need to bring in an exorcist or not. You don't seem too disturbed, so that's a good sign, I suppose."

Vas smiled and waited for the voice to react to being called out by an old lady. "*I'm an old lady too—it's not a bad thing. It means we survived being a young lady.*" Vas knew Deven had been able to hear Aithnea when she talked in Vas's head. Judging by the widened eyes on both he and Delilah's faces, they both heard her now.

"Seriously? You're a telepath too? And in all those years you never told me?" Vas couldn't believe it. She'd mistrusted telepaths her entire life and now they were popping up everywhere.

"Yup. I knew you didn't like them, so I stayed mum. Then this little biscuit came on board and I really went numb. Those Kilesh can be the worst sort of snobs." She flashed Deven a grin. "By the time I realized he wasn't like the rest of his people, and that he was hiding his true teke power, it seemed odd to come out and mention what I was." She shrugged. "So I didn't."

Vas started to respond then held out a hand. "Wait, you knew what race Deven was? You were a telepath and you knew what he was, and you never told me?" She glanced from one to the other.

"He didn't want you to know, and it had been a long time since I'd been in Kilesh space—I might have been wrong. Now, back to your friend?" She peered disturbingly into Vas's eyes.

"*I am Aithnea, and I am pleased to meet you. Unfortunately, my body had a bit of an accident, so I can't be there in person.*"

"Oh, the nuns. I am so sorry all of you died. But I really

admired you. I thought of joining your order when I was young—but I like the males too much."

Vas cringed as laughter echoed in her head. "That's really disturbing you know."

"A little voyeuristic, isn't it? Hanging around in some-one's head?" Delilah was still staring into her eyes oddly.

"A bit, but I only appear when called."

"What? I have almost never called you. I certainly didn't start this." Vas looked to Deven for confirmation but he just shrugged. "Seriously, you started coming into my head uncalled for."

"You were dying. Your mind wasn't fully accepting of the fact, but your body was. It called me."

Vas closed her eyes and pinched the bridge of her nose. Life had been so much easier before.

"Well, however you got there, whatever you are actually doing, I am glad someone is going to be there to keep an eye on our girl." Delilah shook her head. "I was going to have to force my way on board that new fancy ship of hers. Thank you for saving me from that." She reached over and patted Vas's hand. "No offense child. That ship is a tart and I just don't like flying the way I used to."

Vas opened her eyes and smiled. "Hopefully we can keep Home hidden, but if we can't I want you to run as far as you can. You still have the *Gilly*, right?"

"Aye, that I do. I don't take as many side trips as I used to. Space was getting weird even before those bastards invaded. But the *Gilly* is primed and ready with enough room for my staff and neighbors."

Many of the residents of Home kept their own ships, and as many as possible kept them in their own landing areas. It wasn't that they didn't like the larger official landing field; it was that as mercs they'd destroyed more than their share of entire fleets by a single strike on a communal landing field. Mercs who lived long enough stayed that way by a healthy dose of paranoia.

"Good," Vas said. "If you could also check on Grosslyn that might be a good idea. He's holding himself responsible for the loss of the *Sythin Garlin.*"

Delilah sighed and shot a stray white hair flying off her forehead. "I have told him and told him—he needs to relax. All of that tension and lack of emotion was going to come out in some negative way." Her smile lit up the room. "Have no fear. I'll make sure to keep him right—especially if we have to bug out."

Deven got up and gently kissed Delilah on the forehead. "Thank you for keeping my secrets." He pulled back Vas's chair. "Shall we?"

"How soon will you be heading out? Time for one more meal before you go?"

"I'd say we have a day. Maybe two?" Vas snatched the half-eaten roll; it was too good to let it go to waste. "I don't want to linger too long; those Asarlaí ships were blocked from sending their distress signals, but who knows what went out before that. At the very least it will be noticed that they're drifting around their last known space life-lessly."

"And you also want to make sure you're ready for a long battle." Delilah nodded. "I never envied you the balancing. Come by before you leave and I'll make a bunch of rolls to take on your ship." Her face crinkled with a wide grin.

Vas also kissed her on the forehead. "Thank you."

She and Deven made their way out of the restaurant, nodding hello and waving to people as they went out. They stayed silent all the way back to his place. The problem was, along with no food, neither of them had had any sleep in almost a full day. For Deven it had been even longer, but he needed less sleep than others.

Vas kissed him slowly on the lips, lingering there. It was good to be with him and not to be on that damn crappy planet.

"You're thinking of sleep," Deven said. He laughed. "I

hate to say it, but so am I."

"Here Delilah was all excited that we are finally together and all we want to do is sleep. Sad people we are." Vas fought a yawn.

Deven took her to the back of the house. His master bedroom was just as lush and inviting as the living room—and his bed was massive.

"Rest first." He yawned and looked ready to fall over. "I wasn't this tired before."

Vas started laughing. "Damn that woman. When I'd be too tired but felt too busy to sleep on the ship, she'd drug me to sleep. She got us both." She poked him in the chest. "Not unlike a certain second-in-command I know."

"I only did it once, and we both know how damn stubborn you are." He slipped off his shirt and fell into the bed on his back. "But it wasn't fair that she got me too."

Vas fell down next to him and lay her head on his chest. "She knows how stubborn you are, too."

Vas's dreams were chaotic and vicious. A storm was coming, but unlike the ones she'd dreamed of before it wasn't a sand or wind storm. Thunder, lightning, earthquakes, the entire fabric of the Universe was shattering before her. Everyone she loved or knew was dead or dying. And she couldn't do anything.

"Vas. Vas, you're screaming." Deven's voice cut through the horror and made her fight back. Finally, she opened her eyes.

"Damn it. The dreams are worse." She snuggled as close to him as she could.

"You're freezing." Deven rubbed her arms. "What was it this time?"

Vas told him, but the words didn't seem as terrifying as the images had.

"I lost everything."

Deven held her close. "I won't let that happen. Didn't I come back from the dead for you?"

Vas pushed the nightmare aside and smiled. "Damn right that you did as well. Leaving me to go die when I was telling you I was in love with you. That was bad form." She tilted her head, holding her mouth over his. "How long had you pined for me by the way? You didn't dispute Delilah's observation."

He studied her face, finally settling on her mouth. "From the moment I saw you." He rolled her over and kissed her before trailing kisses down her neck.

"There are too many clothes," He looked down at his own pants. "On both of us."

He pulled her shirt off and they both helped each other with the pants. Thank goodness they'd both left their boots in the front room.

He traced her body with his hand, and then applied more kisses.

"I normally love our foreplay, you know I do. But right now, I need you. All of you. And we don't have much time." Vas slid her hand down and found that he was not going to have a problem with that. She rolled him back over and straddled him. A sigh escaped her as she slid on top of him.

All of the fear, tension, and sorrow that had filled her life the last few months vanished. They'd had sex while trapped on the planet, and it was always amazing. But not like this. This was a true sharing; mind, body, and soul of all she was—of all he was. She reached out to the mental connection they'd had on the Garmainian planet. "*This, I need you.*"

"*All I am is yours.*"

The sharing through their minds at the same time as their bodies was almost too much. Vas collapsed on his chest two hours later. "Is it always like that for tekes having sex together? I'm not a teke, but damn." She kissed his sweat-covered chest, but beyond that she seriously couldn't move.

"I've been with telepaths and it's never been like that.

Ever." He wrapped his arm around her.

"So how long do you think we can hide out here?"

He kissed the top of her head. "Not long enough."

They stayed there wrapped in each other's arms for a good half hour before one of their comms went off.

"If I give you a direct order to ignore it, would that work?" Vas was more relaxed and comfortable than she'd been in as long as she could remember.

"No, because I know you wouldn't mean it. I do think it's your comm anyway." He eased his arm from around her and Vas rolled to the edge of the bed.

"There better be a damn good reason." She held up her hand as she sat up. "Belay that. We've had too many damn good reasons. I'd rather it was a mistake and they don't need us." She fumbled over to her shirt and grabbed the comm. "Vas."

"Captain? I think you need to see this," Gosta said in his, "I found something really exciting but you might not think so" voice.

Vas hated that voice. She was always afraid there was something important, but then found out it was something that was important only to him.

"What? I'm tired, and you should be tired too." Deven had darkening coverings on his bedroom window, and Vas honestly had no idea what time it was.

"You need to see the vid that I've studied of the attack on the Asarlaí."

Vas held the comm toward Deven but he put up both hands and went into the shower.

"What is on the vid, Gosta? I'm tired and cranky—fill me in. I can see it later."

He paused. "Very well, if you are willing to trust my observations. However, Hrrru does confirm that it is what I believe it was. And he—"

"What. What did you observe?"

"It wasn't just the weapons from the *Warrior Wench* that

destroyed it. Oh, to be sure, if less than a full barrage had been fired, it wouldn't have been destroyed. It was more than that. There is some sort of space dust coating the Wench's entire hull. Some of the dust particles were suctioned into the cannons and magnetized in the blaster fire. The particles seemed to enhance the effect of the weapons on the Asarlaí vessel. Where did you get the dust, Captain?"

Dust? Vas pushed herself up but the sound of running water told her Deven was still showering. "Can you be more specific?"

"We're analyzing it, but it would help if we had an idea what we're looking at. Did you run into any problems?"

The damn Web. "Yes, in the Web there was a swarm of some odd creatures. They managed to disable an Asarlaí cruiser by convincing the crew to try flying without the ship. There were also some violent winds. We ended up kind of running one into the other on our way out."

"Living creatures? That could be. This dust might be their remains. Thank you." Gosta cut out but then a second later the comm pinged again. "You don't need to come down to the hangar then. Not yet anyway."

"Thank you Gosta. Vas, out." Vas tossed the comm over in the direction of her clothes. It wasn't that she was anti-science or research. It was just that she liked to see things further down the line than people like Gosta. She usually had one or two of her own projects going on, but mostly she liked seeing the results—not always the process.

She couldn't help speculating while waiting for Deven to come out of the shower. So, the storm smashed some of the swarm into her ship and particles from them got caught up in her weapons fire.

And led to an exploding Asarlaí ship. Right.

"What did Gosta want?" Deven was out of the shower and watching him move made Vas want to drag him back into bed again.

She shook her head and reminded her libido that there

was a war on. Then she explained Gosta's theory.

Unlike her, Deven nodded. "It could happen. The Web doesn't operate like normal space, and the swarm was anything but normal. I don't think they were biological though, probably nanotech."

Vas stayed on the bed enjoying watching him dress but that got her attention. "Nanotech? So you think that swarm was created."

"It makes sense. They were almost robotic about what they wanted—the Asarlaí. If we hadn't had Marli on board they probably would have ignored us. Someone created them to go after the Asarlaí on a mental level. Maybe other components were added as well."

"I'll leave that to you to figure out with Gosta and Hrrru. If we can weaponize space dust, or get that swarm to come out and play outside of the Web, I'm all for it." She grabbed some fresh clothes out of her pack and headed for the shower.

They needed all the help they could get.

CHAPTER THIRTY-FIVE

AN HOUR AND A HALF later Vas and Deven were heading toward the hangar. They'd grabbed a quick meal at Delilah's and come away with a delivery of fresh baked goods that would last a week or more.

They'd been in mid-meal when an extremely excited Gosta, calling on Deven's comm this time, had begged them to come down to the hangar.

Even Vas had given in at the tone of his voice. So Delilah loaded a truck with her goods and sent them all off.

"Gon, unload the truck and get it all stowed in the galley of the *Warrior Wench*." Vas nodded to the big man as the truck stopped.

"Aye, Captain. Oh, and Gosta has moved all of his work back to our ship. He said you'd know where to find him."

Vas was honestly surprised he hadn't done that before-hand, but he must have still been gathering samples when he first called and being outside the ship was important. Of course he could be in his quarters or on the command deck since he had an installation of the Commonwealth library in both locations.

They went on board, heading to the crew quarters first. Vas wanted to drop off her pack before hunting down Gosta.

"You know the crew knows that we're sleeping together, right?" Vas asked as Deven turned to go toward his quarters.

"I hadn't thought about it, but probably, yes."

"Why don't you move into my quarters? They're big

enough for two easily, and that way we don't have to go scurrying through the hallways." It hadn't been an issue before. Vas wouldn't consider a sexual relationship with Deven until she knew he was completely back to himself. When he'd first recovered from being in three bodies, he'd had gaps of memory—including the months prior to his death.

But he had gotten them back, and then they'd been trapped on that planet. Merging their quarters there had been easy. On the ship, they were quite a distance apart.

"Do you fear scurrying?" He retraced his steps to the main corridor.

"No, but I'd prefer to keep my second-in-command handy at all times."

A third voice cut in. "Oh man, please, move into her room? I seriously…it's like seeing your parents being romantic." Mac had been coming down an adjacent aisle and appeared before them shaking his head.

"You heard that, we have to move in together for the sake of the kids."Vas nodded to Mac."How was your ship?"

He shrugged."It was okay, but it didn't feel right. Besides, I think it was good you moved the survivors there—let it become theirs." He nodded to both of them and turned for the lift. "But seriously? Stay in one room, please. The crew will thank you." He shut the lift doors before Vas could retaliate.

"I really don't get enough respect from my people," she said. They walked side by side to her quarters.

"And you like it that way." Deven opened the door, tossed both of the packs on the bed, and shut it.

"I suppose so. I am just not going to admit it. Especially to Mac."

They went to the command deck first, Gosta's quarters being closer to the engineering section than the regular crew quarters.

"There you are! Captain, Deven. I think you will be

surprised by what we found." Since the *Warrior Wench* wasn't in the air, Gosta had projected his research onto the main front screen. "The swarm are nanotech. Not from the Commonwealth and very, very old."

Vas nodded. "We figured they might be nano, but we didn't know the age."

The scowl on Gosta's face said he'd expected a more surprised response. "Well, did you two know that the entire Web is a weapon? It has the same stuff the swarm is made of. One is an extension of the other."

Vas stepped forward to get a better look at the big screen. The information was now massive, but there was so much up there she still felt she couldn't take it all in.

"Now that we didn't know." She turned to a beaming Gosta and smiled. "And it was worth bringing us back early for. Can you tell anything at all about who made it? Can the swarm be brought out of the Web?" Even though Marli had come back to life while they were trying to flee the Web, the swarm hadn't followed them past the edge of it. Vas presumed it had to do with the storm buffeting them about, but maybe not.

Gosta's smile crashed. "Not yet on either. It does appear, hypothetically, that if the swarm is a separate component of the Web, it could function on its own—away from the base." But the tone of his voice indicated he really wasn't sure—which meant at this time, no.

"As for who created it," Hrrru said from his station. The short furry Welischian always looked startled but it was just the dark fur around his eyes. "Like Master Gosta said no one from the Commonwealth." He tapped a long claw and one of the sub-screens on the front changed. "It would be better if we could gather direct data from the source, but using the information recorded from your trip there, it appears the Web is far older than the Commonwealth. Not much data is available from the library because once ships started vanishing into it the Commonwealth put it off limits. There were actually warning buoys stationed around it. Until they were all stolen a few years ago and the Commonwealth didn't replace them."

Deven went to his station and started pulling up data. "Have you tried looking into the Kilesh? Nanotech wasn't unheard of in the early days of my people."

He gave an almost indiscernible pause before saying, 'my people'. Vas knew it was going to be a while before he was comfortable with the crew all knowing about it. Considering that she'd been the only one there when his race was disclosed, she'd told him she would keep his secret if he wanted. After about a two-minute think he'd shaken his head. It wasn't time for secrets.

Most of the crew hadn't really reacted. Since the Kilesh weren't part of the Commonwealth, nor even a people who traded with them, the vast majority hadn't even heard of them. Deven had always been from some far-away system, and that hadn't changed in their minds.

But it did in Deven's. The plus side was that now they could access information about his people—and maybe find a way to use that for their battle.

Gosta and Hrrru were furiously working away on their stations. Vas wandered over. "You split the library again?" The Commonwealth library, a supposedly uncopyable and unduplicatable storage system of all the knowledge amassed in the entire history of the Commonwealth, had been copied, and taken by Gosta a little over a year ago. That he'd managed to create and steal a copy, as well as install it on two different stations, was both a testament to his skills and how seriously obsessed he was with knowledge. Now, if Vas was seeing correctly, he'd duplicated it to Hrrru's station as well.

"I might have…extended the reach of its parameters. Captain." Gosta pulled himself up to his full almost seven-foot height, something he rarely did since his natural stature was hunched over. He looked like he expected a court marshaling.

"Can you extend it further?" Vas watched as Hrrru sped through his search. The amount of data was terrifying. "I know when you first retrieved it we agreed that it needed to stay on a secure server in your room to make sure the Commonwealth couldn't trace it. But I don't think we need to worry about them right now, and clearly you've found a way to keep the system secured in multiple locations."

Syngerin didn't really have a blushing ability, but Gosta was only part Syngerin. The other part was mostly human and an odd green-red blush crept up his gaunt cheeks. "I have and I probably could. I am sorry, Captain. I thought I'd found a way I could keep the data and our connection to it secure from observation when we were shipwrecked. I just didn't want to mention it until I was sure. I tested it on the *Defiant Ruin*—it worked."

"Gosta, I am never going to get upset at you for finding new ways to help this crew, this ship, or me. I'm glad that you waited to verify it before telling me. Now, can you get it securely into all of the ships in our fleet?"

"Even the *Scurrilous Monk*?" Hrrru didn't look up as he spoke.

Vas turned to Deven. "Well? What do you think? She's marginally part of this fleet. But none of us trust her, and she probably has even more data she won't share with us in that ship." Especially if it was actually taken out and hidden when the Asarlaí were still alive. The first time. Now if they could just make them dead again as well.

"I'd say no," he said. "This is Gosta's baby, so it is his choice, but unless she's willing to do a full exchange—meaning Gosta, Hrrru, and I go over and download all of her databanks—she can't have the library."

"Gosta?" Vas agreed with Deven, but he was also right in that it was Gosta's project. She'd support him either way. To be honest, with Marli's tech from her prior ship she probably could have lifted the library without asking. Vas had no idea what the current ship's abilities were aside from a lot of weapons and supposedly a storage bay full of Furies.

"I agree with Deven." He shook his head. "I don't think she should have access to it unless she gives us her data."

Vas nodded. "Agreed then. Please make a secure connection to all of the ships in the fleet, except the *Scurrilous Monk*. Make each ship have two dedicated users, along with their captain and second-in-command. I'll discuss the trade of information with Marli later."

"What have you been able to tell about the Asarlaí locations? Anything that might still hide non-Asarlaí?" Getting away from Home and hopefully trying to find more survivors to band with was about the only option. Unless she just wanted to take all of her people and flee. But seeing the Asarlaí making inroads against the Garmainians, made her think that wasn't a real option. Running for the rest of her life as their ships got picked off one by one wasn't a choice.

Plus, even though she'd be hard pressed to admit it, Vas found she actually cared about the Commonwealth. It had its issues, and all politicians were crooked as hell—but overall it had kept its people alive. She could respect that.

Gosta switched the screen upfront. The Web, the swarm, and any other ways of stopping or disabling the Asarlaí would be a constant search. Even if they found other people to join them, they wouldn't have enough firepower to face the full might of the Asarlaí head on—they would have to strike where they could and develop indirect ways to bring them down.

"It looks like after we were lost, they wasted no time in regrouping and attacking the Commonwealth," Gosta said. "Marli's little trick with her exploding dead ship has rendered the entire system around Mayhira unapproachable. Luckily, Mayhira had been the only inhabited planet and it did take out a few Asarlaí ships as well as ruining that attempt at a dimensional portal the Asarlaí were trying to create." He looked up. "There have been no other signs of a portal, but they are still coming in using the gates—just hopefully in lesser numbers."

Vas looked at the details on the screen. "Still enough to take over the Commonwealth in a matter of months. Anything in the dark lanes?"

Hrrru perked up at that. "I was helping Master Gosta search and there is chatter. Not a lot, but there are people out there. Once the Asarlaí had destroyed or disabled the powerful worlds, they only did a brief visit to the others. If the world lacked space travel, they ignored them completely aside from destroying communications satellites."

Which made sense. Those worlds would have no way to fight back and the Asarlaí might want to save them for later. Vas made note of the ones that were marked. All were rim planets.

Originally they'd thought the worlds that had been destroyed were in the Asarlaí's way, and could interfere with their invasion. But the planets destroyed didn't all match that scenario, and if their invasion had been counting on the dimensional portals—both those embedded on ships in the decorative tattoos, and the massive one that was planet Mayhira, then they wouldn't have to be worried about planets that might be near the distance gates.

Vas was looking at the screens with the Commonwealth worlds and their known statuses spread out. There really wasn't a pattern. She knew the Asarlaí that had come back were not the same creatures Marli was, but there would be no reason for such a random massive waste of resources.

Deven rose and was watching the screen. He started swearing. "Can you find data from right before the worlds were destroyed? Preferably on the Hailon scale?" The Hailon scale was a level of high frequency resonance imagining. It was used by the mining companies for their digs.

Gosta tried a few passes, then after a few minutes shook

his head. "We can keep searching but there isn't a lot of recordings for the destroyed worlds."

"What about Lantaria?" Deven stood back a few steps to see Gosta's screen for the searches and the larger front one.

Lantaria was a good idea; they'd actually been there when that one was blown to hell. Rather, they took off right before it had been destroyed.

Gosta thought so to by the way he started nodding enthusiastically. "I can see what we have. I also retrieved all of the information our troop transports had pulled in." Another few minutes and he looked up. "Yes, there is major activity on the Hailon scale. It was directed at the planet's center. They didn't find whatever they were looking for so they blew up the planet."

Vas shook her head. "That makes no sense. There's no sign they even scanned the planets they left behind. At least not these." She waved toward the far left of the screen.

"Maybe it wasn't that they didn't find what they were looking for, but they did." Deven went to Gosta's station and entered a command. The front screen changed.

"They were destroying planets high in Loxian, an ore known to be used in building ship cores."

Vas shook her head. "I know what Loxian is. It and sand were the only two exports of my home world."

"A world that was destroyed over twenty years ago." Gosta had no inflection in his voice, but Vas knew where he was going.

"They said it was a natural disaster. The Asarlaí wouldn't have been cruising around, destroying worlds twenty years ago. Someone would have noticed."

"Like they noticed when Lantaria was destroyed?" Flarik had come on the deck silently, but she'd obviously taken things in quickly. "The Commonwealth commanded you to ignore it. Your home world was a distant rock not even noticed by its neighbors until it exploded. How hard would it have been for the Commonwealth to have covered that up?"

"So they are destroying the ability to build ship cores. They blew up my home planet twenty years ago because of that, and the Commonwealth ignored it all." Vas looked between all of them. Everyone looked serious. "Why would that make sense? Twenty years? They destroyed my home world and then, what, took a nap for twenty years?"

Flarik paced then settled down into an empty console. "How long before its destruction did you leave?"

"That doesn't matter," Vas said and stalked to her new command chair.

"It does. Rather it could." Flarik was being almost gentle. And that was something that made Vas nervous.

The other three were just watching them, but Deven looked concerned, almost sad.

"My brother had tried to kill me, yet again, and my parents wouldn't stop him, I kept having nightmares about a storm, so I left. The planet had the accident that destroyed it right after I left." She started swearing as her own words struck her. "I never remembered those nightmares until now. And Borlan had been even more aggressive than any time aside from turning me over to the rogue telepaths—he'd truly almost killed me." She was talking more to herself than anyone else as images and feelings that she'd held at bay for her entire adult life started tumbling into her head.

"*Control them, don't let them control you. I wondered what was chasing you all those years.*" The voice held the same sorrow that Deven's and Flarik's faces did.

"*So you couldn't tell? Was this the same block that made me hate telepaths?*" Something had happened to her when she was nine and her brother had sold her to a band of rogue telepaths. Her parents had cared about her then and managed to get her back. They'd refused to believe it was Borlan though. That block had been broken by Deven over a year ago. But she hadn't really tried to think about her home world since then.

"*I believe it was. Those who placed it in your mind did such a good job at hiding we never guessed. But while most of us higher nuns have some unique abilities, true telepathy is not one of them.*"

Vas figured three of the others on the deck probably thought she'd lost her mind. She was sitting there reacting to a voice in her head. Hopefully Deven could stop them before they called Terel. "*How can you not have telepathy and be talking to me like this?*"

"*It's complicated. I have to go, I am sorry. And sorry that your brother destroyed his home world to kill you. Deven sees it too—he can explain.*" With that bit of cryptic mumbo, the voice vanished.

"What?!" Vas shouted that outloud, startling Flarik, Gosta, and Hrrru but not Deven.

Deven came to her chair and nodded to the others. "The captain and I need to talk. Keep searching what you can find. The world destroyed in the Beline system twenty years ago, the Rillianian monks, the worlds left now, everything." He took Vas's elbow and propelled her toward her ready room.

Vas shook her head. "I have every right to be pissed—he destroyed an entire planet to kill me? I thought he'd been on it when it exploded." She started for her desk, and then went for her booze safe instead. She poured half the bottle in a glass, waved the bottle at Deven, and then put it back when he shook his head. A huge portion of the glass vanished in a single gulp before she walked over to her desk.

"Pissed is one thing, drunk is one thing; shouting to yourself in front of the crew is another thing entirely." He took her glass and took a long pull off of it then handed it back.

Vas shook her head. Yes, yelling like that was a stupid thing to do, and she had little love for her parents when they died—she felt they'd abandoned her to Borlan's attacks.

"So he was working for the Asarlaí then? To wipe out an entire planet to destroy a little girl?" She finished her drink.

"I don't think it was the Asarlaí who did it—but we know he worked for the Rillianians, and they were working for the Asarlaí. If the Asarlaí couldn't get through to this dimension back then, they could still send orders."

Vas thought of the holographic Asarlaí she'd seen when the Rillianian monk and his crew had hijacked her ship. "It is interesting though—the image they sent to the Rillianians was of true Asarlaí. That thing looked like a male version of Marli. But we now know they don't look like that anymore."

"Easier to control people with an image that looks like the vids. Are you going to be okay?"

Vas nodded. "Yes. I have to be, don't I?" She pulled out one of the snub blasters from her desk and slipped it in the holster. She nodded at Deven's look. "Just thinking about that entire thing makes me want to be armed. All the time. Hope you don't mind blasters in the bedroom."

CHAPTER THIRTY-SIX

THEY CAME BACK OUT ON the command deck to find the rest of their crew trickling in. Vas knew most of them had looked forward to spending at least a few days on Home, but with Marli's impetuous attack, they didn't have that option anymore.

While the rest of the crew, and crews, got sorted. Grosslyn came on board, dragged Vas back to her ready room, and went over his defense plan for Home. The shield had been based off some of Marli's tech, and at first he'd wanted to destroy it. Vas convinced him that using what they could from Marli, while continuing to watch her, was a valid idea.

He did point out that the strain of hiding the ships that couldn't land took its toll, so that was one more vote for getting them all out of the area. They had enough troop transports that were rigged for speed and could bug out immediately if any of his newest invention—long distance sensors—were triggered.

"And then we have this," Grosslyn looked happier than he had for the past day but for a normal person, it was still not a happy look. He'd taken over her desk and proudly pulled up a live feed. Six live feeds to be exact. Each showing a pair of massive guns. Really massive. Each one was pointed to the sky and was easily three stories high.

"You have twelve huge guns stationed on the outskirts of the towns?" She zoomed in to get a better look at the pair just outside of Luck's Ride. "They look like battlement guns—but those are only found in the Commonwealth core planets." Yup. Definitely what these two started out as, but they had modifications. "I hate to tell you this, and I have no idea where you got them, but they didn't stop the Asarlaí from conquering the Commonwealth. How are they going to stop them here?"

Grosslyn beamed which was a terrifying sight. Some people should not smile. "Well, it appears that the Commonwealth core planets didn't fight back—at least not the capital. But, had they tried and had they had our modifications, they could have at least given some serious action."

He hit a key combination and a demo popped up. It was of the two guns she was looking at firing at three large ships. The first fire was an odd green line, and then standard lasers cut into the ships. All three ships exploded. Vas played it back four times.

"What is that first one?"

"It's a short circuit laser. Very short lived, and they burn out extremely fast, but they can shut down an entire ship's systems for at least thirty seconds. Including shields. If we have a full invasion, the guns we have won't be enough to save the planet, but we should be able to buy enough time to get most of our ships off and out of here."

Vas watched the demo and the schematics a few more times.

"Where did you get these again?" He hadn't answered her the first time, which meant she might not want to know.

"Marli stole them," Grosslyn finally said. "It was when we'd found out that the *Warrior Wench* and the *Victorious Dead* were missing and assumed destroyed—I had to do something and she showed up with these."

A closer inspection revealed the guns weren't new—they were intact, but older models. Knowing the spending ways of the Commonwealth government, they'd never been fired and had been scuttled for junk so new prettier ones could be installed.

"You did well," Vas said. "Like I said, Marli has to be watched, and we can't trust her completely, but she can also get us things we'd never have. And you made them better." She flashed him a smile. The extra laser was brilliant. Even if it didn't last long, it would drop their opponent's shields.

"Thank you, Captain. I will protect these people with my life." He nodded and bowed his way out the door.

Vas waited until she figured he'd left the command deck then came out as well. She'd only been in there maybe fifteen minutes, but the command crew was settled in as if they'd been ready for hours.

"Xsit, open a comm to all ships and the hangar," she paused, "including the *Scurrilous Monk*." She'd have to watch what information was shared with Marli, but at least for now they were on the same team.

Normally, Vas would have a full workup and conduct a shipwide meeting as to who they were working for and what the end goal was. Now she had nine ships with her, instead of one. And they were working for themselves and pretty much all of the Commonwealth. The end goal was just to stay alive long enough to find a way to destroy the Asarlaí.

"It's open, Captain." Xsit bobbed her head. The yellow feathers on the sides of her face, normally flat and smooth, were ruffled. But she had a fierce grin. Xsit wasn't violent, not by a long shot. However, she was more than ready to fight back.

"This is Captain Tor Dain. Yes, even with this many ships, I'm keeping the term captain. I still outrank all of you though, so don't get ideas. We're going out this time not for glory, or riches, or because we're paid to. We're going out to save our people. To avenge every world that was destroyed or taken. We know these Asarlaí are different than they used to be and we are working to find a way to exploit that. But until then, we have to save as many people as we can and destroy as many enemy ships and outposts as we can. Make them regret they came back here." She paused and looked out over her command crew. "If any of you do not feel that you can be a part of this—no one will judge you. You can leave now and help with the defense of Home. We leave in ten minutes. Vas out." Her command crew looked at her briefly, and then each of them went back to work.

Vas hadn't thought that her immediate crew would leave, but she wanted to put it out there. This was a different undertaking than what her people had signed on for.

"Call from the *Scurrilous Monk*," Xsit said.

Vas's eyebrow rose. That was interesting. Most of the time Marli just took over the comm.

"Got it." She hit the comm on her chair. "Vas here."

"Captain Vas, I just wanted to report that we are ready, and none of my crew has wanted to jump ship. Also, that we have two Furies that are mostly intact and two more that are close but need work if you would like them. We can send them over once you're in the air."

Vas would love a fleet of them, but aside from their tendency to blow up, she only had three people on any of her ships who could fly them. Herself, Deven, and Mac.

"Thank you. How many more do you have?"

"Seven and I have seven trained pilots for them. Pilots who are looking forward to shoving them down the Asarlaí's throats."

Sometimes Marli's seeming disconnect with her people—she was an Asarlaí, but they were *Asarlaí*—was perplexing. But Vas was beginning to understand. Marli hated all Asarlaí, especially herself. But she wasn't going to lump herself in the same boat as them.

"Excellent. We'll come close enough to bring them over." Vas felt as if she wanted to add something, Marli had actually been as close to apologetic as Vas had ever seen. Then she thought better of it. Marli did screw up, and it cost the lives of good people. And if it wasn't that they needed her knowledge and her ship, Vas would dump Marli's ass as fast as she'd punched her. Instead, she cut the comm.

"You heard her, we will have some Furies. Let's not get into a situation where we have to explode them." She nodded to Mac. "Unless we take a hell of a lot of them with us."

Mac gave a small smile. He loved ships and had been training a little on the last Fury before Vas destroyed it. But it had been his best friend, Jakiin, who had died in one. He'd sacrificed himself to destroy an interdimensional gate to save hundreds of refugees. Deven had also died in that fight—but he'd come back. Jakiin wasn't so lucky and Vas knew Mac still missed his friend.

"I would like to take the third ship. I can handle it." He sounded like a small child.

Vas smiled. "I thought you might."

Bathie was no longer needed on nav or pilot, but she was operating an engineering console. "I've not flown one, but I've done many Sims. I would like the fourth if we can make it work. Actually, with those extra Starchaser parts I know I can make them work." Her grin was fierce.

"Deal. You get all four up to flying level and you can be the fourth." Vas turned to lift off prep, but then turned back. "Oh, and no one mention to Marli or her people about the cross over between Starchaser parts and Furies—she might not know yet." It wasn't to be vengeful for all the things Marli never told her. Well, not completely. It was also a security measure. Marli couldn't steal what she didn't know about.

The rest of the prep for lift off went according to plan. The two ships on the ground, the *Victorious Dead* and the *Warrior Wench*, lifted off without problems. The troop transports had taken up the remaining crews to the other ships.

As they approached the *Scurrilous Monk*, Vas got her first good look at it. It was massive, almost as large as the *Aoenyth*, but far more primitive. Marli said it was a ship from the distant past and Vas didn't doubt it. A quick scan revealed weapons not seen in hundreds of years, but all looked to be live.

"How did she keep it hidden and keep everything running for a thousand years?" Vas muttered to herself, but no question went unanswered if Gosta heard it.

"I have started looking into that, Captain. Prior to her hiding it on this recent planet, I believe the ship had been concealed for all of these centuries in a massive stasis chamber secreted within a planet. She somehow constructed the planet around the ship." He shook his head. "I have no idea how she did that, but I will establish how such a feat was completed."

Vas had no doubt he would. Every time Vas thought she'd seen all of Marli's tricks, the woman did something new. A stasis chamber in a planet holding a massive warship in perfect working order for a thousand years. More or less. Just mind-boggling that all of that knowledge and skill was trapped in the head of a semi-polite sociopath. Vas sighed.

"I'm impressed, but don't tell Marli. Does it have holo projection ability or a transporter?" Both of those had driven Vas mad on Marli's prior ship. Marli popped over whenever she wanted and used her transporter to steal what she wasn't offered. They had a transporter on this ship as well, but it had taken heavy damage in the crash and Vas wasn't sure of its safety enough to order it repaired.

"No on the transporter—at least from what I can tell. And probably no on the holo projector." Gosta shrugged and looked embarrassed. "I couldn't scan some areas, so she might have things we are not seeing—but I think she would have used both already if she had them."

Deven was running his own scans on the ship they were approaching but looked up. "Excellent observation, Gosta. They still have some areas blocked from any scan we have. But we know her—she would have used those things if she had them. The tech for both wouldn't have been around a thousand years ago—hell, it's barely around now."

Vas and Deven went down below to see to the transfer of the Furies. Vas didn't think Marli would see to the transfer herself, but it was a big enough deal that she wanted to be involved directly.

A shuttle from the *Scurrilous Monk* waited outside of their second shuttle bay doors with the four ships in tow behind it. Like the main ship that it came from, the shuttle was huge. Unlike the main ship though, the shuttle was new.

"Where did that come from?"

Deven looked at the console in the shuttle bay, then back up to the ship coming in beyond the shuttle bay shield. "It's registered to a ship called the *Song of Life*, a Xithinal exploration vessel. The ship itself was disabled and all hands taken or killed five months ago."

"So, she salvaged from the dead." Vas shrugged. The Xithinals couldn't use it anymore. Times of battle meant nothing could be wasted—nothing could afford to be.

The large shuttle barely fit in the doors, but there was just enough room for it and its four tows to fit. The Furies were released and the shuttle left.

Vas and Deven entered the bay once the air balanced again. Furies were old, possibly older than Marli. They were single or two seater fighters, twice the size of a Flit and with more firepower than ten Flits combined. Unfortunately, that firepower came at a cost. When all missiles were fired at once, they were able to take down ships hundreds of times larger than they were—that form of attack was what gave Vas the idea to fire everything at the Asarlaí cruiser. But that ability also lead to the Furies' high explosion rate. They'd been abandoned as a viable form hundreds of years ago, with only die-hard collectors or mad men still using them.

The first two were pretty much intact. Vas would have Deven and Mac work with Bathie on going over them. The second two were little more than piles of parts and Vas was surprised they'd stayed together long enough to make the trip to her ship. If anyone could make them work—those three would do it.

"So? We have Furies again." Vas rubbed her arms and stood back a bit from the ships as Deven looked them over.

Something must have caught in her voice, or he was cheating again and looking around in her head—he looked up sharply.

"Are you going to be okay?"

"Yes. We can't afford to ignore any advantage that comes our way—we're too outmatched for that luxury." She dropped her hands when she noticed she was still rubbing her arms. "But if you die in one of those—again—I will find a way to bring you back so I can kill you myself." That made no sense, but it fit her current emotions. They needed these damn things, but she would be happy if she never saw one again in her life.

Deven finished his inspection, made sure the ships were secure, and came to her side. "I promise that I will only die if there is positively no other option." He said it with such a studiously serious face that Vas laughed.

"You bastard. I will hold you to that." She slipped her arm around his waist and they left the shuttle bay.

All ships had checked in as ready, now they just needed to know where to go.

"Gosta? I believe you had found a suggestion for our first target?" At his nod, she turned to Xsit. "Please open the all ships comm with a feed to our main screen." Vas wasn't exactly sure how this was going to work. Occasionally she found herself with multiple ships—mostly backup troop transports. However, she'd never had to strategize nine warships before.

When Xsit also nodded, Vas hit the comm. "Thanks to Gosta, we have our first target. The goal is to find an outlying ship or station and destroy it, but we want to start as far from Home as possible. I will leave the details to

Gosta. Please give him your full attention and make sure to record the screens for reference." She held out her hand to Gosta and settled back in her seat.

The plan was simple: he'd found a target, two of the standard gray ships protecting a small moon with a research station. The station had been Commonwealth, but the wrecks of ships still in orbit around it testified that it wasn't one that went down without a fight.

It was far enough away from Home that it shouldn't lead anyone investigating the attack to them, and through some gate switching it would appear that Vas and her fleet were actually coming from outside of the Commonwealth.

That had been Hrrru's idea and a good one. None of the ships in the fleet would show as active in the Commonwealth systems, so the hope was that the Asarlaí would view them as spoils of war—once they realized it wasn't their side flying them, it would be too late.

Gosta took longer to explain things than she would have, but this was his plan, and Vas knew it was important to him. He and Deven had worked out a strategy to hit as many outlying ships and posts as they could, then vanish. Then they would travel to the other side of the Commonwealth perimeters and do the same. All the while, Terel and any scientist she could tap into would be trying to find a way to use the chemical she'd killed Marli with against the rest of the Asarlaí. And Hrrru would be trying to find a way to use the Web and get the swarm to come out of it. There wasn't enough dust remaining on the Warrior Wench to use, and they hadn't been able to synthesize it.

There was another hour where all of the ships, except the *Scurrilous Monk*, lobbed in questions and comments. Vas let Gosta field them until it was clear he was getting overwhelmed then nodded for Deven to step in.

After another round with Deven, Vas called an end. They would be closing in on the final gate to take them to their target.

"That's enough for now. I'm sure there are plenty more questions, but seriously, you hit all of the big ones in the first half hour. We will be entering the final gate in a half hour. You know the drill, so follow your orders. Do not engage the enemy out of order. The *Aoenyth* and the *Defiant Ruin* will hang back on this one. Everyone else, stay in order." That had been one of Vas's contributions—staging the fleet. Yes, all of them at once would be more impressive—it was also overkill and she saw no reason to reveal all of their firepower to any recording devices until they had to. Marli's first job was to take a Fury and destroy all forms of communication she could find. She'd already left the *Scurrilous Monk* and would be approaching the station and the accompanying ships from the opposite side as the fleet.

The station wasn't small, but it was clear that it was the only thing on the planet. "Gosta, what was the research here?" There had been too many things going on, but now that she looked at the station and the ships as something more than a good first target, she started asking questions.

Gosta tilted his head. "The last it was recorded by the Commonwealth it was a research facility for the outer flocks of the Xithinal home world."

The Asarlaí had shown to have a policy of either destroying planets, or taking what they wanted and leaving the rest. From what they'd been able to tell, most of the Asarlaí action, the places they stayed at, were the core worlds.

So why did they have two ships obviously staying here? And scans revealed a lot of life signs on the station. Vas was waiting for them to get close enough to determine what those life signs were. She'd bet they weren't Xithinals.

CHAPTER THIRTY-SEVEN

A S IF SHE WAS READING Vas's mind, Terel pinged her comm. "I have a scan—there are either a few hundred Marlis over on the station, or it's swarming with black suits. The ships have about thirty crew each, and their scans are similar, but not the same as the black suits. I'd say the Asarlaí are guarding whatever their gelatinous black-suited creatures are doing down there."

Gosta had been silent, but judging by the fury of his typing it was because he hadn't had the answer to her question. "They were looking at fertility. What?" He looked down again at his screen. "Why would they be guarding that? No offense, Xsit."

Xsit chirped and tipped her head. "I don't know why that would be of interest to anyone other than our people either. Also if that is the Flecking station—it was shut down over two years ago."

Deven had been pulling up his own data. "Vas, I have a feeling the Asarlaí were here all of that time. The two ships are the smaller versions, the first ones to come through to our space—but they are heavily armed. There is something big going on there. If we're going to abort we need to do it before Marli gets into position."

Vas turned to Xsit, "What exactly where they studying there?"

Xsit shrugged her shoulders. "It wasn't a secret. Like the Wavians, my people lay eggs. We were having trouble with egg walls being too thin and destroying viable embryos. This was a facility looking at artificial egg shells."

She seemed to notice that everyone was looking at her and ducked a bit into herself. "They couldn't make them small enough to work for our people. So the facility was abandoned."

"Crap," Mac said. That even he got the implication wasn't good. "So they're using them to grow black suits."

"It's not a large enough facility to be the only one—not to mention I have a feeling the black suits have been around longer than the time the Xithinal abandoned it." Terel called through the comm. "But growing them in enclosed pods would be the best way for whatever they are."

"Okay, people, what do we do? Do we hold back and hope we can get some data? Or continue as planned?" Vas wanted those ships and that station destroyed but not if there was something they could use to take them out for good.

"We're out of options, Vas. I'm picking up Marli's Fury on an attack." Deven flicked his screen to the main screen. Marli's Fury was nothing but a blip but judging by the explosions as it made its run she found things to blow up.

"We have to go with the original plan. I want those ships down before they can get out their own small fighters. Or shoot down Marli." As much as she would love to have Marli out of her life, letting her be taken out by the Asarlaí wasn't going to be a real option—not yet. "Move us in, Mac."

The *Warrior Wench* and the *Golaig*, one of the refitted troop transports, were the first two in. The second troop transport and the *Victorious Dead* would be hiding behind them, and then drop down next.

The closest Asarlaí ship picked them up at that moment and turned their way. They were close enough to fire but Vas waited. She didn't want a prolonged firefight—the closer she got the better. "Walvento, fire when we're twenty clicks out. Deven, how is Marli doing?" The screen had changed to the star field so it was almost impossible to see her destruction of the communications systems. The second Asarlaí ship fired first but wasn't close enough to get through their shields. Which wasn't their plan.

"Captain, we have another attack on our shields—we're holding them off but it would have been a short fight if we hadn't known to modify our shields." Bathie swore. "Damn it, they are mutating on the fly. I don't think so, you bastards." Her hands flew over the console as she adapted their changing shield rotation to stay one-step in front of the Asarlaí's shield breaker.

"Fire now, Walvento. *Golaig*, you too." Vas wasn't in the mood to play tech heads with the Asarlaí. They fired a full barrage of missiles at the first ship with the *Golaig* hitting the second, then they moved and her second two ships dropped into place. The *Warrior Wench* and the *Golaig* had blocked the second ships from the Asarlaí sensors and another volley slammed into the Asarlaí ships before they would have realized they were there. Then all four ships separated, engulfing the Asarlaí vessels.

"Keep adjusting all shields constantly, they can adapt to us." Bathie was shouting to the other ships now. Sweat was flying as she moved over and was running two consoles at once, but her lips were peeled back in a feral grin.

"Fire again, Walvento." They got off another round of missiles. This time many got through the shields. All four ships let loose a controlled attack while Bathie and the people on Vas's other three ships fought to stay ahead of the Asarlaí's shield-destroying weapon.

"The second Asarlaí ship got off a dozen fighters. The *Victorious Dead* destroyed their bay, but those ships are out and going for Marli." Gosta looked up. "They aren't Furies though; they look like the shadow ships we saw before, but smaller."

Vas wasn't sure if that was a good thing or a bad thing. The Furies were a known element—the shadow ships not so much. Marli had freaked when they'd seen the first of them come out of a dimensional rift but whether it was because of their firepower, or the fact they were strictly an Asarlaí ship, Vas wasn't sure.

"Scramble ten of the Flits and have the *Victorious Dead* do the same." She looked at her screen. The rest of their ships were holding back, out of range of the Asarlaí for the moment. But they were so close to the edge it wouldn't take much forward movement for the Asarlaí to scan them. "Push the Asarlaí back away from the planet. I don't want them knowing there are more than four ships out here." Hopefully, Marli had managed to destroy all communications arrays for the ships and the station, but Vas didn't believe in hope. She believed in making sure.

There'd been no response from the planet, as far as Vas could tell. There were smaller guns outside the station, but they would only help when the enemy got close. Most ships could do their damage from a further distance out.

"Xsit? Did your people arm your stations?" Vas asked as the specs from the weapons came back.

"No, Captain. Why would they? Anything of value was kept on the capital planet."

"Then why are there four Xithinal heavy artillery guns surrounding the station? And I'm no expert, but they look to be far older than two years old." The Xithinal were Commonwealth members, so if a section of the Commonwealth had been corrupt, it was possible there were some Xithinals involved with that corruption as well. Vas had just always thought of the meek bird race as, well, meek.

Xsit chirped as she verified for herself what Vas said. "I have no idea, Captain. I will strongly discuss this…when we have removed the Asarlaí." The steam went out of her fight as she realized that her world and most of its people were probably killed or prisoners of the Asarlaí. It was one thing to know it logically; another to have the reality hit you in the gut.

"Walvento, target those ground guns, but try not to destroy the station. *Golaig*, keep firing on your Asarlaí ship." Vas didn't want to stop the attack on the Asarlaí vessels, but hopefully the *Victorious Dead*'s firepower could do some work while they detoured to study the station. The original plan had been to destroy the station, but this outpost was becoming too interesting to waste.

"The guns are moving, Captain." Walvento sent an image from the weapons station down below. The guns on the planet were slowly moving, and judging by the way the dirt was crumbled around the base of each one, they'd been doing it for a while, just too subtly to be noticed.

"They're changing aim—they are going to fire on their own station," Deven said.

"Damn it—Walvento, destroy the guns now." If whatever was going on in there was more important destroyed than trying to defend and save, she needed to see what was in there.

The *Victorious Dead's* pulse guns sent a lancing beam to each station gun. Three exploded immediately, but the final one had a chance to get off a round before it was hit.

The station went up in a ball of flame.

Vas slammed the arm of her chair. "They got it anyway." She had a feeling she was really going to regret not seeing what was in that facility. She could send one of the ships down and try to suppress the fire, but she needed all four—especially since the Asarlaí were using heavier artillery. The Asarlaí had figured out their shield breaker wasn't working, so were throwing everything at them. "We've lost it, people. Back to the Asarlaí and those fighters."

"Aye, Captain." Walvento sent a fresh attack, an inspired combination of pulse and lazon missiles, at the engines of the nearest Asarlaí ship. Vas knew he wouldn't take not being able to stop all of the ground guns well. Good—let him vent that frustration on the Asarlaí.

"The *Golaig's* been hit," Gosta cried out. "The Asarlaí

cracked the *Golaig*'s shielding."

Vas looked as the *Golaig* took a hit in in the aft. The explosion was large, but the ship stabilized. "Captain Lhati, can you still fight?"

"Negative, Captain. They got our weapons port. We were modulating as fast as we could, but they got one in."

"Thank you. Now pull back." Vas debated calling down one of the other ships, but she just didn't want that information getting out. In case there was still any recording or communications device, let them just see four ships.

The Flits were fighting the Asarlaí fighters, and three had already been destroyed. Then she saw two of them attack a Flit and it exploded. They went after another but Marli intervened and destroyed the enemy fighters.

However, the Fury was wobbling in space.

"Deven?" Vas called and pointed to the screen.

He paled and punched the all-ship emergency comm. "She's going to blow. Her weapons got hit or she over stressed them. Everyone get away from Marli!"

CHAPTER THIRTY-EIGHT

T HE FLITS WERE FASTEST, AND all broke off, but two of the Asarlaí fighters tore after them. The larger ships had a wider arc to get around and Vas was impressed at Mac being able to change direction as fast as he did.

"Someone go after those two shadow fighters, damn it," Vas yelled right before Marli's ship exploded.

The blinding light wiped out all of the monitors on the command deck and the main screen as well. They came back after a moment.

Both of the Asarlaí cruisers had already been damaged by Vas's ships. The Fury destroyed the one farthest from Vas. The second one was tilted and had explosions all along the side that Marli had been closest to but still showed active weapons.

"Walvento, can we get something up to blow that bastard apart?"

"Aye, Captain."

"Good. Fire." The rest of the Flits were far enough away, and most of the remaining Asarlaí fighters were close to the listing ship.

The weapons went through the Asarlaí ship and launched a new round of explosions before it finally broke in half.

The two fighters that had been chasing her Flits found themselves facing eight more Flits. They were shot down as well as two stragglers trying to escape.

Vas looked at the data coming in. The station was still burning, so she sent the *Victorious Dead* to go drop suppressant on it. Maybe there was something salvageable.

Both of the Asarlaí cruisers and all of their shadow fighters were destroyed, along with all the communication satellites that three sweeps could find—or not find.

Marli was gone.

Vas looked at the screen—that Fury went fast and hard—it took the ships down, but at the cost of the pilot. A coldness crept into her gut as losing Deven and Jakiin hit her all over again. She didn't feel anywhere near the way she had felt about losing them, but there was still something there.

"Captain? We're being hailed." Xsit chirped a few times in her native tongue. She mostly did that when startled. "It's Marli."

Vas hit her comm. "How in the hell did you survive that and where are you?"

"You're welcome! I'm in a capsule, got out right before the explosion and almost didn't survive it—luckily there wasn't a lot of firepower left so when it went out the explosion wasn't as big as it could be. Can someone come get me? I'm in a suit but this thing is leaking air and who knows what else."

"Sending a shuttle from the *Victorious Dead*. Sit tight," Vas looked to Gosta who set up a shuttle. The *Victorious Dead* was closer to her and could get her back to her own ship. Vas leaned back in her command chair. The trauma of watching the Fury explode was still making her heart race, but she was glad Marli had survived. Whatever capsule she was in hadn't been in the three Furies Deven had originally gotten from Marli. Vas was going to make sure the current ones had them. Granted, in a full weapons overload—like what Jakiin and Deven had done, it might not make a difference. Yet, those Furies were so touchy any slight chance of survival was better than none.

The *Golaig* was damaged, but it looked to be simple repairs they could do without going back to Home. They were going to take a few hours, so Vas sent them and the

Toin, the ship that had been fighting alongside the *Victorious Dead,* to join the *Scurrilous Monk* and the other hidden ships. The *Victorious Dead* went as well to return Marli.

"I want all of you to stay free of the system. Monitor us, but stay clear." There was a good chance that the Asarlaí ran checks on their worlds and when the station and the two ships around it didn't respond, more ships would likely follow. "We're going to see what we can get from the station."

The suppressant had worked. The fires were gone, but there wasn't much of the structure left. Still, Vas knew if there was anything down there, she needed to find it.

"Captain, permission to join the ground team?" Even though Terel didn't spend a lot of her time on the command deck, she was usually keeping an eye on things from the med labs.

"You're leading the ground team. Take as many as you need. We really can't spend much time down there, but if anything survived, we need to see it. Take decon chambers for anything you can bring back and record the rest."

"Aye, Captain."

Vas turned to Deven. "I assume you want to be part of her team?" Deven was sexy as hell, but he was also incredibly curious and loved scientific inquiry almost as much as he loved sex.

"You read my mind." He flashed his killer smile and ran for the lift.

Vas looked around, most of the rest of her command crew would like to know what was down there, but unless Terel asked for them Vas wasn't going to send them.

When Terel was motivated, she could move very fast. In ten minutes she had a shuttle crew of eight, including stealing Mac for pilot, and was heading for the station.

Vas didn't argue about her taking Mac. Flying through the massive debris of the destroyed ships was going to take a lot of skill. They'd landed a few minutes later and communicated that part of the station was still intact, a sub-basement of some kind. Vas gave the go ahead to enter, but use caution and keep checking in.

"Captain, I'm recording high levels of H-ling," Bathie called up from the planet. "I thought it was just a byproduct of the destruction, but it seems to be coming from within the planet."

"Gosta, can you scan for it?" They hadn't picked it up on the original assessment of the planet, but they'd done a light scan, plus there had been a few enemy cruisers to deal with.

Gosta had moved so he was monitoring both he and Deven's stations and his long arms travelled between the two as if they were one. "Yes, it is there." He looked up to Xsit. "Do you know why your people would build a simple fertility research station on an explosive planet? Any study done would have seen this immediately."

"The selection was driven by the Commonwealth government. They offered it to our people, and since there was controversy when it first started, it was better far from our planets." Xsit shook her head. "I do know there was disagreement when they shut it down as well. It had been up for almost twenty years."

"Are you finding anything intact?" The hairs on the back of Vas's neck were standing up. Why would the Commonwealth offer up a planet for research that wasn't for them as a whole? The Commonwealth didn't offer things to the planets inside it—at least not to any worlds as insignificant as the Xithinals.

"Not much," Terel called back. "The sub-basement had some extra equipment but most of it is destroyed. I've got some pieces in a decon chamber. I'd like to go farther in."

It wasn't Aithnea, but some unspoken feeling told Vas to run.

"No, get back now. Gosta is running scans but you're sitting on an explosive planet. Take what you have and get back to the shuttle."

The moments of silence told her that Terel really wanted some more time. "If you're sure?"

Vas looked to Gosta who nodded. "We're sure. Damn it, those guns might have been aiming at the ground as much as the station. Get to the shuttle immediately."

The only reason to build anything on an H-ling heavy world would be for defense of whatever was being built on it. H-ling was an extremely explosive material, more stable than some of the other powerful explosives, but easily triggered if you knew what to do. This hadn't been set up by the Asarlaí directly, but Vas had a feeling that was who had been indirectly controlling or pushing the Commonwealth. Possibly for the past twenty years or more.

"Captain, there is a reaction starting. It's small...." Gosta's voice drifted off as he processed more data.

"Run! Leave equipment if you have to but all of you get to the shuttle now! Mac, lift off the second everyone is on board." She looked at the deep scan showing bright red creeping toward the surface. "Belay that. Get the shuttle in the air, hover, and only drop to let them in."

They weren't going to make it. The red from below was concentrated right where the station was. Where her people were.

"We're almost to the shuttle, but quakes are making running hard," Deven's voice was out of breath and tight.

"Damn it, you're carrying the decon box, aren't you? I said drop it." Science was good, intel during a war was great, costing lives needlessly wasn't.

"I'm almost to the shuttle." Deven didn't address the box, which meant he was still lugging that thing.

"I'm dropping down. I can get them." Mac switched his outer shuttle cam on. Whether to show the crew was climbing on board or as a recording of the explosions following them, Vas wasn't sure.

There was Deven bringing up the rear—and carrying

a massive decon chamber. She grabbed the arms of her chair as he shoved it into the shuttle then barely got inside before Mac started going up. The ground beneath the shuttle exploded and the outer camera went dead.

CHAPTER THIRTY-NINE

IF DEVEN DIED AGAIN SHE was going to kill him. If he didn't die, she was going to kill him.

None of the personal comms from the shuttle crew that she tried responded. But the charge of the explosion could have blown them out temporarily. "Xsit, can you reach the shuttle?" She was proud of how calm she kept her voice and hoped that no one was close enough to see how she dug even deeper into the arms of her chair.

"Their systems are having trouble. I can almost get a response, and then it vanishes."

Vas watched the planet on the screen as massive waves of explosions came to the surface and ripped it apart. Then she saw the tiny speck flying away from it.

"Gosta, confirm that's our shuttle?" She could have zeroed in on the ship but her hands were shaking too badly.

"It is, Captain," Gosta said. "It looks to have a damaged wing, so it's not flying as straight as possible, but it's our ship."

They weren't that far away. The shuttle would only have to fly a few minutes, but it was starting to go off in the wrong direction and a few minutes could mean life or death if someone was seriously injured.

"Move to intercept, Hrrru." Hrrru was a fine pilot but the pilot sling wasn't designed for someone his size, so he stayed at the secondary pilot station.

"Aye, Captain."

"Xsit, keep trying the shuttle. Let them know we're coming to them." The shuttle was still marginally heading their way, but enough off course to indicate there were some problems with navigation as well as the wing.

"Aye, Captain. I'll keep sending."

"*Deven?*" Vas tried mentally calling, but was met with silence.

"*Is there any way you could tell them? Let Deven know we're coming to them?*" Vas reached out to the voice of Aithnea.

It took a few seconds for a response. "*I can try. He might shut me out.*"

That wasn't good. Deven knew who the voice was. "*Why would he shut you out?*"

"*He's injured. Or upset. Something strong.*"

If Vas squeezed the arms of her chair any harder, they were going to break.

"*Just try.*"

"*Aye, Captain.*" There was the usual Aithnea snark. Two words and she still fit it in there. "*I got through. They're going to slow down so they won't go further off course—they're mostly blind.*" She paused. "*And yes, he knows you're pissed at him.*"

Her fingers cramped as she released the arms of her chair. "*I am seriously…you're sure he's not dying?*"

"*Not dying.*"

"*I'm going to kill him.*"

"*He knows. I have to go now; you're not my only project on this, just my largest.*" Aithnea vanished.

It was odd that Vas couldn't tell for sure when Aithnea was there, but she could usually sense when she'd left. In this case it was just as well she'd gone. She'd helped Vas and the crew on the shuttle and right now the inside of Vas's skull wasn't a good place for anyone. Fear, anger, and a strong feeling of being ill all fought with each other.

Hrrru took a far more cautious approach to the shuttle than Mac or Vas would have, but he got them there safely. The shuttle might be mostly blind, but even it could pick up the *Warrior Wench* right in front of it.

Vas waited until the shuttle was heading toward the shuttle bay, and then ran down to meet them.

The shuttle bay had a shield that kept the air in the operators' side when a ship was going or coming in. Never had waiting for those outer doors to close felt so long. They'd just barely represurized the bay when Vas shoved open the door in the shield and ran toward the shuttle.

The hatch opened and Terel came down first. "I'm thinking you're not here for me. I'm fine by the way; all of us are aside from some scrapes and bruises." She looked back into the shuttle. "And some well-placed shrapnel in a certain ass you're rather fond of. He can walk down on his own, or go down on a med bed—but I need to get a bunch of building and planet parts out of your boyfriend." She climbed down and waved for Marwin to come take the decon box. "Make sure this gets secured in a safe place. No opening without clearance from me or the captain." She gave Vas a nod and strode from the shuttle bay.

Vas would have asked questions, but Terel hadn't seemed too worried about Deven, so he was going to be fine. At least until she got through with him.

The rest of the shuttle crew nodded to her as they climbed out, Terel was right, cuts and scrapes, but nothing big. Even Mac came out silently and quickly followed the others out of the shuttle bay.

"It's just you; you have to come out sometime." Vas glared at the shuttle ramp.

"No help for a wounded man?" He came to the doorway and Vas almost lost her anger. He'd clearly taken more hits from exploding debris than the others. Trickles of blood showed here and there and the left sleeve of his suit was torn off.

Then she narrowed her eyes and folded her arms. "I told you to leave the case behind. It slowed you down."

"We found evidence of what the black suits are in relation to the Asarlaí. And we also found evidence of cloning—non-Asarlaí." He was so calm and matter of fact it was almost possible to ignore the blood dripping down his legs.

Then Vas noticed the blood anyway. She ran forward and hit a non-bloodied part of his chest. "I don't care if it was the lost key to the wonders of Zartin, you were ordered to leave it behind. To not take unnecessary risks. We're at war. How stupid would it be if you had died at a fertility clinic?" She was yelling now and it felt good.

Deven grabbed both her arms and pulled her to him. His kiss shut down her yelling. After a minute, he pulled back. "I am sorry I scared you, but this evidence could be crucial in finding a way to stop the Asarlaí. And also track and destroy any clones they have working for them." That last was said slowly.

Vas's mind was still whirling with anger, fear, and serious lust...but those words caught up to her.

"There were clones? Of other races? Humans?" Damn it. Her brother hadn't been bad enough on his own that the bastard Asarlaí had to clone him? How many of him was she going to have to kill?

"Yes, others, many others. I couldn't leave it behind." He gave a wince at that and an awkward twitch.

Vas turned him slightly. She always enjoyed seeing his behind, but it was chewed up right now. His entire back had some damage, but the ass was the worst.

"If you laugh, I will get you back in your sleep." He was trying to be serious, but the corners of his mouth kept quirking up. It wasn't an idle threat, Vas didn't normally sleep more than six hours at a time, but Deven got by with two or three on a regular basis.

"I will try not to laugh, but no guarantees. We'd better get you down to Terel before she comes looking." Vas walked alongside him as he moved slowly.

"I know I worried you, and I am sorry." He was moving slower; most likely the injuries were stiffening up.

"Just try not to do it again." She shrugged. "Who am I kidding? We're at war against a race who could destroy us all in a blink of an eye if they caught us. I was just pissed that you disobeyed me."

He grinned. "I will obey you in bed, I solemnly swear."

His grin turned into a wince and Vas hit her comm. "Terel, our friend here is slowing down, and it might be a good idea to send a med bed for him. And if he refuses to ride it in, I'll just kick him in his ass."

"I'm sending Pela down. If you do have to kick him, try to avoid the really bloody areas. He was bringing in things I'd asked him to carry; I'd feel bad if you damaged him more."

"Obviously, scientific inquiry held sway over an order from his captain, but I'll try to miss the really bad parts."

Deven said nothing. Which meant his backside was really hurting. He had a high pain tolerance, but while not life threatening, a scatter shot like what he got would be painful.

Vas looked behind him again. "I think you paid a heavy price for disobeying me. And you were doing it for the cause." She reached up to kiss him, careful to keep her hands just on his chest. "Don't do it again, or I'll make that wound seem like a pillow fight."

"Agreed. Thank you for having Aithnea contact me by the way. None of us realized how off the shuttle's systems were."

"Someone has to watch out for you," Vas said. "There might be someone else in this game. When she left she said I wasn't her only project going on. Hopefully I can get more information, but we should keep an eye out."

Pela came up now walking alongside the med bed.

"Is he surrendering, or do I have to tranq him?" She held up a hypo. The fact that Deven helped bring back medical evidence to examine was overshadowed by his reputation of being a horrible patent.

He held up both hands. "I am fully surrendering. This stuff hurts like hell." He didn't even wait for the med bed to stop moving before he climbed on board face down.

Leaving Vas with a good look at the damage. "Try not to leave any scars. It would ruin the aesthetics."

Pela grinned, put the hypo away, and headed back to the med lab. The bed followed her like a well-trained dog.

Vas knew between cleaning up the shuttle crew, pulling the rocks out of Deven, and organizing her own notes, it would be a while before Terel came back with any report on their findings. But it was fascinating and terrifying at the same time. Clones. Perhaps not all of the inner Commonwealth politicians had turned traitor and supported the Asarlaí—they could have been replaced. The clones would need to have been good, and the ones she saw of her brother obviously were. She wasn't sure which one had been a clone. The idea of clones was terrifying, but not more so than a homicidal brother who kept coming back from the dead.

The thoughts chased each other around all the way to the command deck. However unexpected and hopefully helpful this information was, they were still at war.

"Any signs of approaching ships?" she asked Gosta as she went to her chair.

"Not yet, Captain. But that explosion had to have been picked up by long-range sensors. They might even be able to view it from Home."

"Okay, then let's get out of here before they come investigating. Is the *Golaig* ready to travel?"

"They checked in a few minutes ago, Captain," Xsit said. "They have made their repairs."

Vas was going to chastise Xsit for not notifying her immediately, and then shrugged. She'd left the deck in a full steam; she couldn't blame Xsit for not wanting to cut in on that—especially for something that wasn't crucial. Vas wouldn't have ordered the fleet moving until she was sure everything was secure with the shuttle—even if Deven hadn't been injured.

"Then let's move out. Flarik? Did you and Gosta come up with a new target?" The two had been examining the data they'd received about the fall of the Commonwealth. It was patchy, some of the data-gathering satellites had vanished or been destroyed, leaving gaps. But the Asarlaí hadn't been concerned about evidence of their actions existing. Once they had destroyed most of the Commonwealth, at any rate. If what she was seeing was right, the Asarlaí had been hiding in plain sight for a few decades. Slowly building their strength, while they did whatever they'd done in the other dimension they'd been hiding and rebuilding in.

Flarik shared a look with Gosta, and then nodded. "We have an idea. It appears that there are clumps of people hiding in the Solardian system." She shrugged. "Well, there are populations stranded on planets throughout the system. The Solardian system was left mostly unmolested. They are solitary, and very stubborn. But that doesn't explain why they were left mostly alone."

Vas drummed her fingers on the arm of her chair. The Solardians weren't well known to most people. They'd just joined the Commonwealth in the last ten years. They mostly stayed to themselves and traded little with their immediate neighbors. Hell, they might not even know there had been an attack on the rest of the Commonwealth.

"How left alone? Did the Asarlaí go to either of their worlds at all?"

"Not that we can tell, Captain." Gosta said, and then flashed a map on the main screen. "You can see where they hit everything around, but not there."

"Am I the only one who thinks that is more than a little weird?" Vas looked around. An odd feeling had hit her when Flarik mentioned the Solardians. One that she couldn't tell was very good, or very bad.

CHAPTER FORTY

"IS THERE A CLOSER TARGET?" Sometimes giving more time helped the right answer come. Damn,
even when Aithnea wasn't in her head, her teachings were
sneaking in. In this case, it could be the right path. Vas
wasn't sure about the Solardians, the fact they weren't
touched could be good—but was probably bad. There
was a good chance they'd been working with the Asarlaí.
And they needed something quick to hit. Not only was
this campaign hopefully to reduce the Asarlaí ships and
resources, these first steps were to build cohesion within
the fleet. Maneuvering nine warships who had never
worked together was going to take a while. Hell, up until a
few months ago, most of the ships didn't exist.

Gosta bobbed his head and peered through more screens.
Flarik shrugged. If it wasn't something she felt passionate
about—like, say, having an Asarlaí on board her ship—she
didn't get worked up about her suggestions not being followed.

"The Jelias system." She pulled up another world
before Gosta could. "Also two planets, closer to us than
the Solardians, still on the other side of the Commonwealth, and unfortunately we know what happened when
the Asarlaí visited. All ships destroyed, major cities on both
worlds destroyed, half of the remaining population, or
at least that's an estimate, were taken back on the Asarlaí ships." Flarik grinned. "But there is useful information
here, that they had gotten cited numerous times for having non-registered ships. The comment here was that the

Commonwealth could never track them down, as they were not on the planet and were believed to be used for piracy."

Vas hadn't heard of the system, until Flarik mentioned the ships. There had been some pirates that were never caught that were believed to be attached to a planet government. Might be a good place to start.

"Okay, we're going to go see if we can rescue those souls and get them to join us. If they do have hidden ships off world, they might have lost the ability to get to them in the Asarlaí attack. I say we help them with that."Vas didn't really want more ships in her fleet; coordinating nine was already a pain in the ass after just one job. However, if they could get another group up and fighting, then it was worth it.

"Aye, Captain. I can have a full workup on everything we know about them," Gosta said and turned to confer with Hrrru.

Flarik nodded. "A wise choice. I once had to face a Jelias lawyer in court—he was a fierce opponent." She grinned, flashing all of her tiny teeth. "I won of course, but he was one of the closest challengers I'd ever faced. They would give the Asarlaís something to think about should we get them free."

Vas wanted to talk to Deven about it, but being as he was most likely knocked out with Terel operating on his backside, she'd go with her former second-in-command replacements, Flarik and Gosta.

"Xsit, ship wide and ship-to-ship comm, please." Having to tell so many people what they were going to do was going to get old—fast.

"Connected."

Yes, perhaps she should meet with the other captains first and determine the best action. However, she hated meetings with a passion that would outshine the glow of the planet burning below them. Not to mention, this was really a dictatorship—they were her employees as mercs, and this was just a different sort of job. Vas hit the comm button.

"We have found a world in need of some help. The Jelias system has a lot of survivors but no ships on planet. There is speculation that they do have hidden ships. There do not seem to be any Asarlaí vessels in the area. The *Warrior Wench* will take point. I want the rest of you, all of you, to hang back but keep monitoring space and any channels you have access to. Once we've figured things out, I'll call you in. If any of you have crewmembers who have dealt with the Jeliasians, please have them contact Hrrru to relay what information they have. Bathie will be coordinating the travel and will be in contact with your nav officers. Vas out."

Normally Gosta would be running nav, but Vas needed him to keep looking into the Jeliasians. For safety at this point, they needed to stick with the remaining rim worlds. Yet the majority of these worlds took pride in their independence and their people rarely joined in other crews—either the Commonwealth military or a merc crew. She needed as much intel on them as possible. Besides, Bathie would be a bigger hard ass than Gosta if any of the other nine ships gave her trouble.

"Captain? The *Scurrilous Monk* is on the comm. She'd like to speak to you in private."

Vas rolled her eyes. Of course Marli would want to talk. Vas would like to find out if Marli deliberately blew up that Fury, but she *was* going to let it wait until after they got under way.

No such luck.

Vas got out of her chair and headed for her ready room. "Transfer her over in a minute. Flarik, you have the deck."

Flarik gave a vague wave; she was looking at something on her screen.

Vas took her time and settled in her chair with a drink—

in a glass—before she hit the blinking comm. "What is it, Marli?"

"Admiral! Thank you for sending the rescue vessel. I am quite fine by the way. No harm done."

Vas stared at the comm. "What do you want, Marli? We're sort of busy."

"I know, but I do have a few concerns, questions really, not concerns."

Vas waited for her to continue. Usually she couldn't get Marli to shut up; this oddly reluctant version was disturbing. "What. Is. It?"

"To the point, that is what I've always liked about you," Marli said. "I was wondering why we are looking at picking up stragglers instead of taking down more Asarlaí? And also if your lovely doctor found anything in the facility remains?"

Vas finished her drink. "Marli, when you joined us, you agreed to follow my command. My command is that we see if perhaps we can help these poor souls. Poor souls who appear to have some hidden off world ships that they would probably like to go harass the Asarlaí with should we reunite them. We need all the help we can get, or have you forgotten how powerful your people are?"

"They aren't my people." Marli's sweet voice changed immediately.

"I know, you're not like them—"

"They aren't true Asarlaí." Marli cut her off. "I left my Fury because I saw a chance to bring in one of the bodies. It was mostly intact, but I just needed a piece. We've been running studies for the past hour—those *things* are not my people."

Vas wasn't sure what to address first. Wait, yes she was. "You blew up a ship—one we don't have a lot of by the way—so that you could grab some genetic material from a dead Asarlaí? What the hell is your problem?"

"I felt it needed to be done, and I was sure the Fury

would have blown anyway. The capsule protected me."

"That's another thing—I want those capsules in our Furies too."

Marli laughed. "Already done, Captain. I designed them while you were out and about the galaxy. I didn't like losing my favorite Kilesh either. There's no guarantee they will protect in every situation, but they are made of trelliave steel—they can protect against a lot." The sweet Marli had come back into her voice.

Vas shoved that aside, she'd have Mac and Deven go over the Furies and see what else had been added. "Now back to them not being Asarlaí? They seem to think they are, and yes, they don't look exactly like you, but they seem more similar than different."

Marli was silent for a few moments and when she came back all of the theatrics were gone. "They are like my people, yes. But weaker. Even their genetic coding is inferior. But we haven't been able to isolate where the breakdown has occurred. I might have picked up more than one body part while I was out there—there were a lot floating around."

Vas almost asked where she stored them when brought on board the *Victorious Dead*'s shuttle—then thought better of it. She would mention to Ragkor that a thorough cleaning of the shuttle might be in order.

She ran her fingers through her hair; the braid was already coming out again. "Okay, just so we're clear, you will follow my orders from here on out—that includes any implied ones like not sacrificing a ship. You'll be with my away team when we go down to the planet on this one." She paused. "And Savan as well." Especially with Deven down for the count for at least a few hours—having a powerful telepath along would be wise as well.

"When we have any information concerning the remains that were found in the facility, it will be shared with all ships as I determine. Are we clear?"

"Aye, Admiral, very clear." Sweet Marli was back. "I assume that means my ship is up front with yours?"

Vas really didn't like that voice; it made her want to look for hidden traps. "Yes, I'll tell my crew. When we're down on the planet, I want both you and Savan to watch everything—the people, the destruction, everything. I doubt the Asarlaí left traps on these worlds, but we need to be careful. And have Savan scan everyone." It was completely unethical and illegal as hell under Commonwealth law. But Vas knew he'd be doing it anyway—this way Marli would share what he found.

"I will await further orders, my Admiral."

"We'll be in contact; it will take a few hours to get to their system." Vas sighed as she clicked off the comm. If she asked Marli not to call her that, she'd just find a new way to annoy her.

Vas stopped at the command deck to let Flarik, Gosta, and Bathie know about the addition to the plans. Flarik was visibly annoyed but just nodded. The other two shrugged.

That taken care of, Vas made her way down to the med labs. She had no idea how long it would take to remove the debris from Deven, but hopefully it wouldn't be too much longer.

Terel was in the front room looking at some files when Vas walked in.

"I assume our star patient had everything come out in the end?"

"Ignoring your bad puns, yes he did. He's still knocked out; it's getting harder to keep that boy unconscious. But I really couldn't have him moving for this."

Vas wanted to go see him, and she would, soon. But she'd watched Deven sleep before. What she needed were answers. "So, these clones?" She was pleased that she kept her voice calm—especially considering who one of the things was.

"I figured you wanted more than just a crew update,

no matter how important the crewman in question." Terel stood up and walked to the doors that led further into the lab. "I'd rather not talk about this out here." She nodded to Pela who was just outside the recovery room. "Keep an eye on him, but don't disturb us unless there's an emergency."

Vas knew that Pela would be aware of the findings, but she agreed with that information not going out to the general crew just yet. Not until things were more solid, and hopefully they had a plan.

Terel took a seat in one of the smaller rooms and Vas shut the door behind her then sat down. "That bad?"

"That scary. They had been making and experimenting on clones. I don't know that they got far enough for mass production, most of the genetic parts we found weren't viable even before the explosion." She paused. "There was one thing they were mass producing however, but I doubt we were lucky enough to get their only facility." Another pause.

"If you don't tell me, I will hurt you. I swear, first Marli starts being reticent, now you. Knock it off."

"Sorry, Marli is the reason for my hesitation. The thing they were mass-producing—and I say thing, because they seemed not very cohesive—were the black suits. And all of their genetics match Marli. There is positively no doubt where they came from. But something is making them weaker. The ones you faced the first time, on that ambush with Carrix, they were thinking and reacting beings. These new ones are…more like genetic goo in suits. They follow commands, but that's it."

"That explains the explosions." Vas shook her head at Terel's questioning look. "Not the one we just saw. When we initially visited the *Defiant Ruin*, there were some black suits—they exploded once shot." She shivered at the memory of that goo being on her. "But how did Marli get involved?"

Terel called up some screens on the small monitor in the

room. "No idea. But, and I hate to say this, I don't know that she is aware she was involved." She found what screen she was looking for. "This is the earlier data on the black suits that we first encountered then the ones on Mayhira, then the one that crashed on our planet when we were marooned."

Vas wasn't a geneticist, but even she could see the breakdown of the code over time.

"And this is what I got from the ruins in the research facility. They are breaking down because the original material degraded over time and has not been rebuilt with new donor material. If Marli was involved knowingly, she would have been able to provide fresh material easily."

Vas toggled between the samples. "That's not good. Well, neither option is good—her working with them, or the fact that they got her genetic material at all. And probably quite a long time ago." Something about the images made her think of Marli's anger at the rest of the current Asarlaí.

"Marli wants your research, but we need to hold off giving it to her. However, she did some of her own. She blew up her damn Fury so she could gather parts from the dead Asarlaí. She said they are diluted somehow. Like someone is watering down their Asarlaíness."

CHAPTER FORTY-ONE

———◆———

TEREL SCOWLED AND TURNED BACK to her screen. "Like they've been watering down their black suits. The creatures still function, but they're far more fragile than the prior ones. I'd like to know what is behind this impact on the Asarlaí though. It could be breeding with other races, but the Asarlaí of the past were far too xenophobic for that."

"So, they have some genetic material from a single Asarlaí, and they're combining it with....genetic material from other races but not breeding with them? They're all weird, elaborate clones?" Vas was almost more confused than before.

"I'd say there is more than one original Asarlaí as the genetic base of the current ones—the data we'd gathered isn't all the same as it is for the black suits. It was assumed that they all died out a thousand years ago, but what if a small ship escaped the final battle? No one has seen them in this dimension for a thousand years, but we know whoever they are now, they came through from another dimension. That big gate they were trying to build was them trying to come through to here."

This was all pure speculation, but if they got their hands on Marli's stolen Asarlaí body parts, Terel could verify it. At least as well as it could be verified. "Regardless of what they are, or where they came from, they've taken over the Commonwealth. It was never a great government, but it let me live the way I wanted. I'd like it back. How is this going to help us do that?"

"Now, now. I know you want to go kill things. However, there is a chance this cloning and crossing of races can be our way in. The black suits are already breaking down, but it could take years for that to complete. I think we have to assume the current Asarlaí took so many prisoners both as slave labor, but also possibly for genetic harvesting. I need time to find a way to make this work in our favor. I also need those Asarlaí parts of Marli's."

Vas rubbed her face. Terel was right; she'd rather be out killing Asarlaí than studying them. But they'd known when they started that brute power wasn't going to work since they were so outmatched.

"So we have to tell Marli about the black suits."

"I'm afraid so." Terel sounded a bit less upset about it than Vas felt. But she was more excited about the data she'd get from Marli, than concerned about the mercurial Asar-laí's reaction to having been cloned into an entire army of black suits.

Vas was going to have to deal with Marli herself. Ide-ally, she'd wait until they dealt with the Jeliasians, but Terel needed to start work as soon as possible. The research facility had been of more importance to the Asarlaí than Vas originally thought, which meant their time of moving about without being actively hunted was growing shorter.

Vas got to her feet. "I'll go see how my second-in-com-mand is recovering, and then I'll contact Marli and have her come over."

Terel was already back at her scans, but nodded. "Make sure to give me warning before she comes down here."

"I'll try."

Pela was back in the front area, so Vas just let herself into Deven's recovery room. The lights were dim, but bright-ened as she entered.

He was laying on his stomach, one bare arm thrust out from under the covers—even knocked out he still had to be stubborn. She walked over and gently covered it back up, then brushed the black hair free from his face. He was so beautiful in sleep it was hard to remember that he was also an amazing fighter. And someone she knew so little about. Oh, she knew who he'd been since he'd joined her crew—mostly. But who was he before? What was he like as a child? She shook her head—these thoughts were getting way too maudlin again.

"That felt nice." His voice was soft and sleepy and he didn't open his eyes.

Vas brushed his cheek again. "You should be asleep still. I'll come back later."

"No, please stay. I'm waking up." He still hadn't moved.

"Terel really dosed you. Go back to sleep." She brushed his face again and this time his eyes opened.

He studied her face and smiled. "I love you."

Vas knew he felt that way, but he had never said it. "Is that you, or the drugs?"

His eyes focused and he turned slightly. "It's me. I love you and I went into surgery realizing I'd never told you."

She bent over and kissed him. He was still too groggy for anything lustful, but the kiss was the sweetest she'd ever shared. "You know I love you too. Now finish recovering and get that perfect ass back on the deck—we have some Asarlaí to deal with."

His smile was gorgeous, but his eyes closed and Vas watched as he went back to sleep and healing.

Vas left the med lab, with orders for Pela to send Deven up to the deck as soon as he was fully conscious. And she steeled herself for another round with Marli.

"Xsit, get me Marli and send it to my ready room, please." She nodded at the rest of the command crew, but they were all entrenched in their tasks. She had no doubt most of them were going to be as disturbed as she was about the cloning and the reality of the current Asarlaí invasion.

She shut the door to her ready room and almost went for another drink, then changed her mind. If she had one every time she had to deal with Marli, she might start looking forward to her encounters.

"Yes, Admiral?" Marli's voice was somewhere in between super sweet and her normal tone. She also sounded distracted.

"Can you bring your extra Asarlaí parts over? We have a deal to make."

"Is your doctor finished with her research?" There went calculating Marli. Much easier to deal with, in Vas's opinion.

"Not finished, but she's found some things that you might find interesting. However, she does want access to the genetic material in trade." Vas was extremely glad that the current *Scurrilous Monk* apparently didn't have the transfer abilities of the prior one. Marli could have just taken the things she wanted.

"Negotiations, I do love those. Sadly, we don't have time for a prolonged battle, so I will capitulate. I can take a shuttle and come directly over. With the body parts."

"Thank you." Vas cut the comm and leaned back in her chair. First reticent Marli, then sweet Marli, now agreeable Marli. Either the current situation was impacting her more than they'd guessed, or she had changed a lot when they were trapped in that other system.

Vas went back to the deck to see Deven gingerly assuming his chair. She was surprised Terel wasn't right behind him. She'd only left him fifteen minutes ago.

"Terel released you?" she asked as she went to her command chair. She knew damn well Terel wouldn't release him for duty if he were still moving like that. She also knew Deven wouldn't care.

"Pela did. I didn't want to disturb Terel and her studies. I hear we have Marli coming over?"

Vas sighed. "Yes. And you want to be included." It wasn't a question.

"Considering what I sacrificed to get the material that

Terel is working on off that planet, I think I deserve it." His grin was pure Deven. His ass might still be tender, but the rest of him was fine.

"Very well, she's on her way over. Bathie, what's our ETA with the Jelias system?"

"Fifty-three minutes, and still not picking up any other ships—Asarlaí or not."

"Captain, the *Victorious Dead* is calling for you," Xsit said.

Vas hit her comm. "What's up, Ragkor?"

"This is Therlian, Captain. I'd like to go along on your ground trip. My late husband was from the Jelias system and they can be difficult to outsiders."

Vas looked over to Hrrru but he just shrugged. Obviously Therlian hadn't passed that connection along to him.

"Agreed. Shuttle over in thirty minutes. I assume you already told Ragkor?" Granted they were all technically her crew, but borrowing another captain's second-in-command should be cleared first. Especially when they might be going into battle.

"Just finished talking it over with him. He's in agreement if you are."

"We'll see you in a bit then. Vas out." After she cut her comm Vas turned to Hrrru. "Did any crew come forth with connections to the Jeliasians?"

"No, but then again, neither did she. I took the liberty of searching the crew logs—there are two who had known connections to the system, but they are both back on Home."

Vas shook her head. They didn't have the time to go back, nor was she willing to risk exposure of Home by trying to send a communication. "Thank you, Hrrru, we'll make do with who we have."

They would take Flarik, Therlian, Marli, and Savan for sure. Regardless of his coming back on deck, Deven was staying out on this one whether he agreed or not. Besides, if things went bad while they were down on the planet, she wanted him up here to get them out of it. Mac would be along for shuttle flying.

"Captain, Marli's shuttle is approaching the bay."

"I'll go meet them. Have them move the shuttle in to the end; Therlian will be coming over as well." It might have been smart to have both of them bring pilots to take their shuttles back, but it was too late for that now.

Vas got up and noticed that Deven did as well. She almost told him to stay where he was, but she figured she could only win one fight with him today—and his not going to the planet was more important than him not sitting in on the Marli and Terel summit. She waited at the lift for him to catch up.

"You feeling okay?"

"I'm fine, just a little stiff. But Pela assured me that Terel got all of the offending particles out of me."

"Damn," Vas said and hit her comm. "Terel, Marli is docking. We'll be down to your lab after we get her." She'd almost forgotten to warn her.

"Thank you. Do you have Deven? He's escaped."

"He claims he was released."

"He tricked Pela. I assume he is coming back down here with you?"

"I am right here. You can talk to me directly." Deven shook his head.

"Yes, he's coming down. And Marli will have Savan with her as well, so likely she'll be bringing him into the meeting as well." Vas had only intended for him to join on the away mission, but she knew Marli would want him involved completely. Well, this way both sides had a powerful telepath with them.

Terel signed off, most likely to put away anything she didn't want Marli to see just yet.

Vas and Deven got off the lift at the shuttle bay level. Marli's shuttle was coming in so the clear shield was up. The operator was directing it further inside the bay. They better not have anyone else who wanted to come. After Therlian got here, the bay would be full.

"I don't know why you need Savan along. Isn't one telepath enough?"

"It is. You're sitting in on this meeting, but you are not going to the planet." She folded her arms and glared at him. "You just had surgery; I need a telepath who can run if he needs to." It was a low blow, but she didn't want to be arguing with him and dealing with Marli at the same time. And it was true.

Deven opened his mouth to argue, and then shut it with a crooked smile. "Fine, I'm not up to running just yet."

The shuttle bay doors shut, and Marli and Savan came out of their shuttle. Deven was the most handsome man Vas knew, but Savan was a close second. Of course, the fact that she didn't know how much of his fine face and body and long blond hair was real and how much was an esper-powered glamour did put a damper on that.

"Very good to see you, Captain." He took her hand warmly. "And you as well, Deven." Not as warm but he did smile. "I'm glad you didn't have any lasting harm."

Deven paused, and then clapped him on the back. "It's good to see you as well. Keep my crew out of trouble down there?"

Vas narrowed her eyes at both of them. Telepaths were annoying when they chatted only to each other. Clearly, something had gone on between them that they weren't going to share.

"How did you get him to decline joining us?" Marli asked as they went down the corridor to the lift and the med lab. She held the case she'd brought close to her, so Vas presumed it was the Asarlaí genetic material.

"Pointed out he can't run." Vas hooked a finger behind them. Deven was noticeably limping.

"I'm surprised that stopped him. He can be stubborn."

"I am right here, you know," Deven said. "But even I

have to admit when I would be a hindrance to the away mission."

Terel was waiting for them all in the outer office of the med labs. She had all four of the computers in there up and running, and clearly she had no intention of allowing Marli or Savan further in. Vas would bet the computers had been disconnected from the rest of Terel's files and the main system.

She smiled and held out two hypos to Marli and Savan. "If you will both gave me a sample?"

Marli pulled back and glared at Vas. "What is the meaning of this?"

"The captain had no idea," Terel said. "But, considering what we've found is confirmation of cloning, I want to make sure we have originals here."

Even Vas pulled back at that, and gave Terel a what-the-hell-are-you-up-to look while Marli wasn't looking at her.

Deven tilted his head. "You can't scan for clones. There's not enough data on them."

Terel's eyes narrowed a bit, but then her smile came back. "I can now. And if you want to know what I know, I need you to each draw a sample."

Marli turned back to Vas who just shrugged. "I'd do what she says. I've seen what she has."

Savan stepped forward and held out his arm almost as if he was offering to escort Terel somewhere. "I will agree."

"Thank you, Savan." Terel placed the hypo on his arm, then pulled it back and looked to Marli.

"Fine. I am not a clone, however." Not as gracefully or polite as Savan, she still held up her arm.

Terel marked each sample then fed them to an analyzer. There was an awkward few moments while it processed them. Finally a soft ping was heard.

All five moved forward, but Terel held up her hand. "Me first, if you don't mind." She studied the results a bit longer than Vas expected. The scanner would have been concise.

There was no reason for scrutiny unless one of them was a clone. She took a step back to the door, blocking it.

CHAPTER FORTY-TWO

"VERY GOOD, NEITHER OF YOU are clones." She motioned to the chairs and computers. "I've set up one station for each of us. It's better to see what I've found."

Marli nodded but she still watched Terel carefully. "I brought the samples, but also a data chip of what we found." She handed over the case and a small, round, disk.

Terel nodded and inserted the disk to her computer. Vas knew Marli had probably coded the disk to retrieve data as well as download it. The fact that Terel didn't pause at all when she downloaded it confirmed Vas's assumption about these computers being cut off from the rest of the lab.

All of them took chairs and Terel explained what she'd found. She was blunt about the connection to Marli.

Marli kept shaking her head and verifying the information on the computer. Finally, she pulled back. "How did they do this? Who did this?" There was more fury in her face than Vas had ever seen, and she'd seen Marli lose her beloved ship. Savan reached over to take her hand and while she didn't take her eyes off Terel, she did calm down visibly.

"We have no idea. According to Therlian, the black suits invaded her world at least five years ago. There's no way to know how long it took the current Asarlaí to create them from your genetic material though. Nor when and how they got it."

Marli took a few deep breaths, and then nodded to Savan. "They are all from me? Cloning was one of the few atrocities my people never engaged in. It appears that changed when the bastards all died."

"All of the black suits we have found have your genetics," Terel looked at Marli with sympathy. "They are breaking down, however. The sample they had must have been exhausted long ago."

"They might try to get her back," Deven said. "Remember the one who saw her thought she was some kind of savior."

"I will rend them limb from limb, then beat their creations with what remains." Marli clenched her hands tightly and pulled away when Savan tried to reach for her again. "No. I need to keep this anger." She hit a few buttons on her computer. "The Asarlaí facing us are definitely clones as well, but I don't know who they are of, nor why they don't look like the original Asarlaí."

Vas glanced at the data, but it supported Marli's hypothesis. She knew Terel would do her own studies though.

"I know you left them before the end." Deven's voice was gentle. "But do you recall any ships being lost out past the rim? Any interdimensional travels?"

Marli started to shake him off, but Savan nodded. "There was one, right after Marli left." He smiled at her surprised expression. "I've had a lot of time to do research on your people over the last few years. You didn't pay attention to what happened to them after you left—I did. A survey ship left three months before the final war ended their explorations. It was supposed to be looking for lands beyond this system to exploit—in other dimensions."

"But it might have just been lost after the war," Marli said.

"Or it could have been lost in the void and the survivors did whatever they needed to do to survive, and to come back and reclaim their world." Vas shook her head. "We might never know exactly what happened, but somewhere in the last thousand years, the Asarlaí began cloning and found a way to come back."

"And found a way to get people of the Commonwealth to work for them," Terel said.

"The hologram technology." Marli was still looking unfocused. "I never put it in this version of the *Scurrilous Monk*, but it was just starting to be used by our ships at that time."

"The Rillianians were following a hologram of your people." Vas swore as a memory crept in. It was hard to believe it was only a little over a year ago. "Which would have allowed them to work from wherever they were and make sure that they looked like true Asarlaí."

Deven sighed and shook his head. "And it would also give them the chance to appear as anyone they wanted to sway some less than ethical Commonwealth politicians. Damn it, they had the perfect plan. Get people to do their initial work for them, weaken governments for one thing, while they worked on finding a way back to this space."

"People like my brother. I don't recall much of what happened when he sold me to the telepaths, but I know none of them would touch me." Vas really hoped the bastard was alive so she could kill him for good. "Some or all of them could have been holograms. And we're back to how is this going to help us take them down?" Vas shook herself and got up from her seat. "We know the Asarlaí are clones of others mixed with a small pool of original Asarlaí and we know the black suits are clones of Marli and are becoming weaker each time they are created. But we need to find a way to stop them."

"We have the swarm in the Web, not sure if we can bring it out, but if we can, it will cause the Asarlaí to kill themselves—even the diluted ones, as we saw," Deven said. "The dust from the swarm increased the effectiveness of the weapons on the Asarlaí ships—we still need to find a way to replicate that. We need to destroy as many cloning facilities as we can find. And Terel can find a biological weapon that will take down both the black suits and the Asarlaí."

Marli looked confused. "I get the 'destroy facilities' part, but I don't understand the others."

Vas sighed. She still hadn't explained what really happened to Marli inside the Web. It didn't take much time, but Marli looked even more confused. "So these tiny nano things, they took out a full Asarlaí cruiser by convincing the entire crew to kill themselves? Why didn't it happen to me?"

"Mostly, yes. But the black suits were all shot. It looked like they had been trying to stop the Asarlaí from leaving the ship. As for you." Terel shrugged. "Simple. I killed you."

Savan's hand drifted toward the blaster at his hip.

Marli waved him off. "I seem to be alive still."

"You are immortal, makes you a lot harder to kill. But you collapsed and stopped breathing. The swarm backed off at that point." She raised her hand. "Before you ask, I had been examining the black suits' genetic code; from it I was able to create a vaccine against you. But I can't make it go after any other cells, just yours. That's why I wanted the dead Asarlaí parts. If I can make something to use as a bio-weapon, only against the Asarlaí…we might be able to take them down."

Marli went from confused to furious to curious all within less than a minute. "Might not work against the current Asarlaí, but what you have right now could work against the black suits, yes? Infect them all?"

They all looked to Terel, but she shook her head. "It wouldn't work on them; they're too…changing, for want of a better word. Something like a bio-weapon would only work on a more genetically stable being. That's why I need more of both to work on."

Marli deflated. "We have to find something. I'd like to stay on this ship and help you. I think you might be our best chance."

"I can help as well," Savan said with a wan smile. "I was a

geneticist on my home world before joining Marli. I might find something you missed."

Terel shrugged. "I'd welcome the help, as long as you two don't mind working in the office here. I can send you any files you need."

"Still don't trust me, do you? Even after you found a way to kill me?" Marli laughed. "I agree, I wouldn't trust me either. Actually, I don't trust me, since I thought becoming immortal all those years ago was a good idea. We're fine with staying out here."

Deven got to his feet. "Since I won't be going down to the planet, I will do what searching I can from the command deck. I'll have Gosta and Hrrru help me look at the swarm and the interactions with the Web." He turned and left.

"I think he's miffed about not going. But maybe next time he'll listen to me." Vas said. "I'm going to go get ready for our mission. I'll call down here when we're in orbit." She nodded and left them to their gene studies. If anyone could find a way to hurt or destroy their enemies with genes, it would be those three. She just hoped they had enough time.

Vas went up to the command deck, but the second shift crew was on. She'd lost track of time, but usually she went to bed about now. She wasn't tired. After nodding hello to the second shift, she went into her ready room.

And stared at her monitor for a full five minutes. One of the worst feelings in the world was having a large number of things that needed to be done, but not having the ability to do them. Having a bunch of things to get done and having to *wait* to do them was second.

She mindlessly dug through her files until she found the only image of her family she had. Taken a few months before Borlan sold her to the telepaths, it showed her the unforgiving desert of her homeland, her parents, Lon and Dalia Tor Dain, Borlan, and herself. She couldn't recall the last time she'd looked at it.

She was near her parents, her father's hand rested on her shoulder and her wild, red hair flew around. He looked down at the top of her head. Her mother looked directly ahead with that same exhausted and sad look she'd always had while Vas was growing up. Her brother wasn't touching any of them and sneered at the photographer. He'd fought being in the photo and only a bribe from their father had gotten him to agree. His hair was the same color as hers but cut in a short chop popular at the time.

In the background was Bhotia.

Vas jerked up right so quickly she smacked her knee on her desk. The swearing that followed was a combination of both anger at the sharp pain and the image of the Rillianian monk who had tried to take her ship a year ago in a long ago family photo.

He was standing far enough away that she almost didn't pick up who he was. The community they lived in had houses fairly close, so most likely they would have just thought he was a neighbor.

He wasn't looking at the family but was talking to someone with their back squarely to the camera, which left him facing it. Someone who looked almost exactly like Savan. Tall, male, well built, with long blond hair. And standing between them, mostly hidden, so Vas could only see a section of her face and the top of her head, was a familiar-looking brunette—Marli.

CHAPTER FORTY-THREE

"SON OF A BITCH," VAS swore and hit her comm. "Marli? I need you in my ready room—now."

"Can it wait, Captain? We're right in the middle—"

"Now." Vas cut off the comm and blew up the image. Definitely Bhotia, and the same for Marli but she couldn't be sure about Savan. Vas knew he'd been with Marli for a long time; it well could be him. Or Marli just had a thing for tall, good-looking, blond men.

A light rapping at her door startled Vas as she was still examining the picture.

"Come," she yelled but didn't get up.

As expected, an annoyed-looking Marli entered. That she'd come up without giving too much grief told Vas how unsettled she was about the current situation. Vas was going to unsettle her for good if she didn't answer the next few questions right.

"Sit." Vas motioned to one of the two chairs that faced her desk.

"What is this about?" Marli closed the door behind her but she didn't sit.

"Sit." Vas rocked back and folded her arms. Marli had been on her home world on the last day of normalcy in Vas's life. That couldn't be a coincidence.

Marli held her stance for another few seconds, and then nodded at something she saw in Vas's face and took a seat.

Vas spun the monitor toward Marli. It was zeroed in, so only the trio could be seen, not Vas or her family. "Do you want to explain this photo?"

Marli pulled back at first then nodded and turned it back. "Myself, Savan, and Creadlin on some backwater planet. Creadlin used to find us jobs, but he'd lied about something being on that crap water. We stopped working with him after this. Why do you care?"

Vas spun the monitor back to her, widened the photo, but didn't spin it back immediately. "Creadlin was the Rillianian monk pirate who almost took over my ship. He'd been working with my brother. That crap water planet was my home world." She spun the monitor. "And this is my family."

Marli's face actually paled as she took in the image. "We only knew him as Creadlin. He claimed to have found an artifact that Savan and I were looking for on this world. But after two days of him stringing us along, he said it was gone." She looked up. "I swear I never noticed you or your family."

Vas held her gaze, but Marli was unflinching. Of course, the Asarlaí woman had lied more times than Vas had drawn breath.

"You're telling me that it was just a coincidence that you, Savan, and a puppet of the current Asarlaí, were on my home world? Right before my brother sold me to a bunch of rogue telepaths who might have been actually holograms of the new Asarlaí?" That hurt even Vas's head but it was what she needed to say.

"Yes," Marli said. She tapped on the photo. "Why does your brother have an Asarlaí tattoo?" Her voice was too level; she was furious or scared—or both.

Vas spun it back to face her. "That mark on his hand? It was a birthmark." At least that was what her family had always said. It was an odd half circle, with a jagged line going through it. She'd figured he'd started a tattoo but then chickened out so it was only partly finished.

"No, it's an ancient Asarlaí design." Marli flicked her fingers, and then just started drawing in the air. The image hung there in a disturbing blue glow. "Here's your brother's tattoo. Here's the Asarlaí sign for vengeance." She made another drawing next to the first. The second one was cleaner, and smoother, but it was clearly the same.

"Wouldn't someone have recognized it? Your people died, but many of their designs and images lived on. I've never seen that one."

Marli shook her head. "You wouldn't have. No one would unless they were there a thousand years ago."

"My brother was less than twenty-five in that picture."

"And we have no idea how long the current Asarlaí had been infiltrating this system. One of them got to him. The tattoo looks fresh in that picture."

Vas stared at it. She distinctly recalled her parents telling her it was a birthmark and that he'd always had it. She dropped her head in her hands. As much as solving this mystery about her family would help her psyche—or not, depending on the answers—she needed to find a way to stop the flesh and blood creatures who'd now claimed the Commonwealth for themselves.

"Your parents knew." Marli's voice was soft as she continued to look at the photo. "They might not have known what, but they knew something was wrong with their son. They are pulling you away from him, not the other way around. How long after this did you leave?"

Vas looked up with a sigh. "A few months. He sold me not long after this photo. But when I got free of the telepaths, my parents refused to believe me. A few months after that, after he almost succeeded in killing me with poison, I fled."

Marli nodded and gently touched the photo. "They knew they couldn't protect you, so they made you run away."

"No one made me run away. I did it all on my own. I waited until Borlan was off planet on a trip, then fled and managed to catch a ride on a freighter. My parents wouldn't have wanted me to leave."

"They would have if they had no other way to protect you. The planet blew up not long after this, right? Creadlin even went so far as to accuse me of having destroyed it out of anger."

Vas studied the picture. Looking at it as Marli spoke she could see the body language of her parents—and Borlan. He wasn't standing away from them. They were away from him.

"What was this artifact?"

Marli laughed. "Something I wanted but certainly not worth blowing a planet up over. It was an Asarlaí tool to focus mind waves. Not like you think, I wasn't trying to take over people's minds. It could really only work on animals, or very simple creatures."

"Was it dark green and looked like a dragon head?" Vas was really getting tired of finding out how many things in her life were being drawn into each other.

"Yes, sort of. However, I think that description could be a lot of things. It would have to be kept in a special box, something with reflective properties."

"Like red Gathian rustwood?"

Marli tilted her head and narrowed her eyes. "This item was on your home world?"

"No. Or it might have been at one time, I have no idea. But it came into my possession a number of months ago. A Commonwealth diplomat hired us to retrieve an item on Mayhira. He ended up dying before he could take it." She didn't mention that she'd changed her mind about giving it to him, or the possible connection to the nuns.

"You have it." Marli leaned forward. "Please tell me you have it."

"I thought you said it was a minor piece and not very useful?"

"It is and it wasn't. But it might be useful now." She got to her feet and started pacing. "If we can use it, I can reach the black suits and get them to die."

Vas rocked back in her seat. That wouldn't resolve the Asarlaí problem, but taking away their workers, as well as hindering their ability to make more, would slow them down and give Vas and her people more time to find a way to stop them for good.

"How would you kill them?"

Marli shrugged. "Just command them to stop breathing, I would expect."

"I doubt it would be that easy, but I'm willing to chance it." Vas got up and went for the door. "Come with me."

She didn't run through the command deck but she walked very briskly with Marli right on her heels. They took the lift down to the crew quarters in silence, Marli only coming out of her thoughts when they got to Vas's room.

"So you'd never seen this thing before you liberated it for the Commonwealth politician?"

"Nope. He'd claimed it was a family heirloom, but then he also hadn't said he was working for the Commonwealth." She thought about the final battle. "He might have actually been one of the good guys, but he died."

"And he shouldn't have lied to you." That Marli could chastise someone else for lying with a straight face was nothing short of a miracle.

"Agreed." Vas opened her door then started tapping on the far wall.

"What are you doing?"

"Safes can be broken, but only if they can be found. I've found keeping them unseen and un-scanable goes a long way in keeping my possessions with me." She smiled as she heard the sound she was looking for: a slight creak where her safe was. "Stand back." She pressed on the corners and the front panel flew off, almost taking off Marli's head. "One of my defense mechanisms." She opened the safe. There was more in there than just the box, so she quickly closed and relocked it. She handed the box to Marli.

Marli reverently touched the red box before opening it. Then her smile grew as she pulled back the wrappings. "We need to find some black suits to try this on." She quickly covered it back up and closed the box.

"How does it work?" Vas walked alongside Marli but Marli's eyes were focused on the box she carried.

"I'm not exactly certain, but isn't that wonderful? When you've lived as long as I have, finding something you don't know is amazing. Especially something from your own long dead and soon to be dead again, people." She tucked the box in the crook of her arm and finally looked up. "Theoretically, I or any telepath should be able to use this to control the actions of simpleminded beings. The time will be limited, I would imagine, but especially if they are genetically breaking down, they will be simpleminded. Besides, my people would never design tools that were smarter than they need to be."

They hit the lift and Vas coded it for the med lab level. "But how will you reach them? How focused do you have to be?" She liked the concept, but unlike Marli, not knowing how things were going to work didn't make her happy. She wanted something quick and sure to take the black suits out of the equation.

"That's what I'll be looking into once we visit this world. I will secure this in Terel's medical facility. Then we can reexamine it upon our return." She stopped and spun. "Unless you think there might be black suits on the Jelias planets?"

"No. In fact we're counting on them not being there." They'd arrived at the med labs. Terel and Savan were both working silently, but Savan looked up with an expectant grin.

"You found something?" He nodded.

"I found something. Vas found something too, that her parents didn't abandon her. But my something is more useful."

Terel arched a brow toward Vas, but she shook her off. She wasn't completely ready to rethink how she felt about her parents and their actions, but if they were faced with a son who'd started working with people who made evil look good, and they knew Vas was his target—the safest thing to do was get her far away. It was good enough for now to let that thought simmer. She'd revisit it once they got rid of the Asarlaí, and she got to kill all specimens of Borlan for good.

Marli held up the box and took off the lid. Vas noticed she didn't touch the item, and hadn't when she first took it from Vas. This time she pushed back the wrappings and tilted it for Savan and Terel.

Terel shrugged.

Savan's eyes widened and he moved closer. But like Marli he didn't touch it. "Is that the stone of Cerli? It can't be. How did you…?" He turned to Vas. "Rather how did you find it?"

Vas nodded. "Long story and Marli can explain it on the way down to the planet. I'm thinking we'll be hitting their system very soon now, so get ready." She nodded to Terel. "Keep isolating the Asarlaí genetic components. Our attacks will help throw the Asarlaí off, but they won't win the war."

Terel clearly wanted to know what the rock was—actually Vas had shown it to her months ago when they got it. But they hadn't known what it could do. "I'll explain that later. But for now we need you to hide it here." They could have left it back in Vas's room, but this would be a faster access if they needed it. Not to mention Vas didn't want Marli prowling around her room or her safe.

Even though hiding the in Terel's lab had been Marli's idea, it still took a few minutes for her to agree on a place, then a few more for her to actually let go of it. But they eventually found a place that met Marli's standards and she released it.

"It will be fine."

Marli looked back at the hiding place. Not as secretive as
Vas's hidden wall safe, but harder to get to. Terel had a safe
buried under a huge box labeled medical waste.

"Captain? We're approaching the Jelias system. Still no
signs of any ships. Therlian is waiting in the shuttle bay."
Gosta was calling her when it should have been Deven.
Her second was definitely pissed about not going. He
might understand why, but he was still pissed. Not to mention, he'd always been a quick healer, but that had slowed
down a bit since he came back from the dead.

"Excellent. I want Mac, Bathie, Gon, Marwin, and Flarik
to join Marli, Savan, and myself at the shuttle bay. Heavy
weapons and armor." Vas looked to Marli and Savan. "I'm
thinking you don't have armor. Do you want to borrow
some?"

Marli's laugh was almost a giggle. "Thank you, but neither of us have needed armor in a very long time."

Savan nodded.

Vas shrugged, she wanted armor. She led the way to the
shuttle bay; she kept her armor there out of habit even
though it had been a year since they'd done any merc
work. She would treat this as a job. They would go down,
survey the situation, and then make an appropriate plan of
action. She was hoping the Jeliasians would be willing and
able to fight if given access to their hidden ships. She really
hoped they had hidden ships and it wasn't just a rumor.

But as life had shown her, particularly in the past year,
things didn't always go as planned.

Therlian was waiting and fully armored and armed when
they got down to the shuttles. Of course, her main weapon
was a massive blaster that looked like it had come off a
fighter ship. Knowing Therlian, it might have.

"I'm not sure if you all know each other. Marli and
Savan, this is Therlian. Therlian—Marli, and Savan."

Therlian's eyes widened a bit, but she nodded a greeting. The rest of their ground crew came down within a few minutes. All were in armor and had their weapons. Sometimes her crew did her proud. Mac was in full armor even though he'd be on shuttle duty. Leaving a shuttle unmanned in an unknown area was never a good idea, no matter how much security they had on the shuttle. He jogged inside and started the warm up.

"Are you certain you don't want armor or more weapons?" Vas nodded to Marli and Savan. They both had small blasters at their sides, but that was about it. Granted, as an immortal Asarlaí, Marli was damn hard to kill, but Vas had no idea what Savan was really.

"Thank you, Captain," Savan responded first. "But we will be fine." He stood back to let the women board first.

Vas shook her head at his behavior, but motioned for the rest of the ladies to go up, even Marli. Then she tipped her head to him. "Captain's prerogative, I board last."

Savan gave a half bow and entered the shuttle. Gon and Marwin followed, but both were watching him carefully.

Vas boarded and locked into her seat. She'd reviewed what she could skim about the Jeliasians—mid-level tech, sneaky, independent, and known to be good fighters. She liked them on paper; she just hoped she didn't have to fight them to get them to join.

The shuttle ride was slow and for the most part silent. Marli and Savan were conferring about something softly. The rest of the crew seemed lost in their own thoughts. Vas knew they really hadn't had time to fully process the destruction to the entire Commonwealth. As mercs, they saw a lot of destruction—they often were the cause of it— but there had never been something as huge as this. Many of them lost their home worlds completely and hadn't had any time to even ask about possible survivors, much less go looking for them. She knew her people though—they would hold off the deep thinking until this job was done.

Even knowing that the planet had been attacked wasn't enough to prepare for seeing it as they landed. According to Gosta, most of the remaining population would be found in the ruins of their capital city—it had taken huge hits, but must have underground bunkers of some sort. Vas would have headed out of the cities, so there had to be a viable reason as to why these people didn't.

The landing area was mostly clear, at least enough room for a shuttle. Had they wanted to bring down one of their larger ships, they'd have to go far out of the city to find a smooth enough area to land.

Mac landed and cut the engines. Vas stood and faced the ground crew. "We need to maintain a tight formation. Keep your weapons handy, but try not to look aggressive. We're on a mission of good will, not trying to hunt enemy combatants."

Savan pointed to her armor. "Wouldn't less of that have been more conducive?" He wasn't accusatory. He honestly wanted to know.

"Not when you're not sure how you'll be greeted. We have no idea how they are doing. I know I'd be jumpy as hell in their boots. Better to be safe. We'll stay in an alpha spread." She nodded to Savan, Marli, and Therlian. "Marli and Savan will stay in center near me, Therlian will take left flank." Alpha spread was a standard search formation her crew used on recon missions. Keeping Marli and Savan near her meant she'd be responsible for them and none of her crew would have additional issues.

Once everyone nodded, she motioned for Gon to open the ramp then turned to Mac. "Keep the ramp up and door locked and if I say run, you run." She tipped her head. "I mean it, Mac. No heroics. Get this shuttle out of here if things go sideways."

Mac shrugged. "What if it's that voice again? Aithnea?" He always wanted an excuse to have latitude with her orders.

"She wouldn't do anything to harm this crew. I tell you bug out—you bug. Got it?"

"Yes, Captain." With a sigh, he turned back around in the pilot's seat.

Vas was the last to leave the shuttle, and things looked worse in person. According to Gosta, Jelias had been hit in the first wave, just under four months ago. The buildings had continued crumbling after the initial destruction, but there hadn't been enough time for nature to come in and fill in the gaps.

Vas used her sensors, but the damaged buildings were causing havoc. "It looks like we head that way." She nodded and her two front leads, Gon and Bathie, headed out. The rest followed in formation with Marli and Savan flanking Vas.

"Are we in the right position, Admiral?" Marli grinned and patted her blaster. "I am ready."

"Stop enjoying this, and yes, you two are fine."

They'd gotten about fifty yards from the shuttle when a shot was fired over their heads. "The next ones will go through all of you. Stand down and give us your shuttle and no one gets hurt."

CHAPTER FORTY-FOUR

—————◆—————

VAS SIGHED AND TAPPED HER comm. "Take off, Mac."

Even though he'd been pissy, the shuttle was immediately airborne.

"What else do you want to negotiate about? I'm Captain Vaslisha Tor Dain, merc. I have a nice ship that would love to help you out, but not if you're stupid and kill us. We know about the ground bunkers and can easily destroy them."

"Tor Dain's crew was killed. Try again." That voice wasn't Jeliasian, nor was it the same as the first. It was familiar.

"Carrix? You crazy bastard, what are you doing out here and has your eyesight gone to hell? It's me." Carrix was a merc, one Vas and her crew had saved from the first ground ambush by the black suits. The last she knew, he'd been on his way home.

"Vas? Son of a bitch. They told me the Asarlaí were shapeshifting so I couldn't be sure. Not to mention, it was all over the dark lanes—you're dead." There was a rustle and two shapes came out of a building. Vas knew they probably had many more guns pointed at them right now, but at least they were going to come talk.

"Surprise, not dead, but missing for six months. We get trapped outside of the Commonwealth for a bit, and it all falls to crap. Had to come back and save some asses." She motioned for both Marli and Savan to stand back. The rest of her crew, except Therlian, knew Carrix and held their positions, and nodded as he passed.

He looked far older than he had just a year ago, and there was a heavy limp in his right leg. He still had a good grip when he shook her hand though. "I am damn glad to see you, Vas. When I heard your ships had been destroyed…it was sorrowful news. Then the Asarlaí came and everything went to hell and I missed you anew."

Vas motioned to the Jeliasian standing behind him. He was tall and thin like most of his people and his small, upright ears were constantly moving. His hand also rested on the trigger of the heavy blaster he held across his body.

"How did you get here? And can you ask him to stand down? My shuttle pilot gets an itchy trigger finger, and while he is in the air, he's close enough to fire."

Carrix looked up and waved. "Let me guess: Mac? Where's Deven?" As he spoke, he nodded to the Jeliasian. He took his hand off the trigger and lowered the weapon to his side. But his ears were still swiveling.

"Mac is in the shuttle, good guess. Deven was injured on a recent mission so I kept him up in the ship. How and why are you here? Thought they didn't like us outsiders?"

Carrix gave a sad smile. "Long story. But the short version is, this was an early hit, and no one realized they were going after the entire Commonwealth. Some of the people away from the rim formed groups to go rescue or rebuild what we could." He shrugged and nodded to her. "Odd thing for a merc, but apparently it's a trend. Anyway, we were trying to get through to the Jeliasians—they don't like outsiders as you noted—while that was going on, the Asarlaí did a check back and destroyed our ship. Please tell me your crew is watching for that?"

"They are, and there have been some changes. But we need to get you all off this rock." She turned to the sullen Jeliasian. "Rumors were that your folks were pirates." His hand clenched on his blaster and Vas waved him down. Therlian too. She was behind the Jeliasian and had raised her weapon as he clenched his. "Easy there, everyone. It's a good thing. If you still have ships somewhere, my crew and I can get you to them. As long as your goal is to go after the Asarlaí."

The Jeliasian released his blaster and nodded. "I am called Kamin, the closest thing we have to a leader left. We do have some extra ships that were unknown to the Asarlaí. We believe they are unmolested. They are on the dark side of our second moon."

"Will your people stand down so we can help you get to them? How many do you have? Will you fight the Asarlaí?"

"They will stand down on my orders. We have five warships, bedga class—smaller and better for fast jobs. We would welcome the chance to destroy as many Asarlaí as we can." A frown crossed his face. "But thousands of our people were taken by those bastards; we need to free them first."

Here was where the plan might get tricky, same if they were able to do anything with the other rim worlds. They'd all want to get their people. Vas knew Terel and Gosta were working on a final way of getting rid of the Asarlaí, which would liberate any prisoners they had. But if too many ships started going after the core planets, the Asarlaí would start retaliating before Vas's people were ready. Even liberating a dozen worlds wouldn't give them enough brute strength to take on the full Asarlaí fleet. The attack needed to be planned, orderly, and only when the brains of her operation felt they could destroy the Asarlaí in a single run.

"I know you don't know me, or my people, and this is asking for an awful lot of trust. I have a fleet, a small one, but a damn good one. I also have some of the brightest minds in or out of the Commonwealth looking at ways to destroy the Asarlaí without brute force. But I need room to do it. If every world sends their ships to the core to try and free their people, we can't do what we need to do." She met his gaze. "You need to trust me."

Therlian had quietly watched the entire interaction but

finally stepped forward. "I am a clan member of the Jelias by marriage. My late husband was of the Quian clan, and our daughter is half-Jelias. I offer my life that you can trust this woman to save our clans." She held her hand over her heart, and then pushed back the sleeve of her jacket to reveal a small sword tattoo.

Kamin stood very still, then bowed. "Your husband was an honorable man, and I hope one day I can meet his daughter." He turned to Vas with a nod. "We will do what you ask, and trust you with the lives of our people." He motioned and a few hundred Jeliasians and a few of Carrix's people came out from the rubble.

"Very good," Vas said and nodded to Therlian. "Mac, come back down and prepare to go find us some pirate ships."

An explosion came from behind the row of buildings in front of them, flames shot in the air followed by building debris. It was too far away for anything to hit them, but Vas felt the rumble under her feet. Kamin looked surprised and one of his people came jogging up.

"Commander, they got out and they have a ship coming in, maybe two."

Kamin and Carrix both started swearing.

"I told you to destroy them." Carrix was furious and weapons fire could be heard farther back.

"Get everyone out of there," Kamin said to his man, who ran back to the others. Then he turned back to Carrix. "There might have been a chance to negotiate with the Asarlaí bastards. I had to take that chance. They shouldn't have been able to get free."

Marli and Savan had been standing back, but she moved forward now. "You were holding Asarlaí prisoners? And you thought the rest would negotiate for their freedom? How daft are you, boyo? They don't care about their own."

Kamin stiffened but kept his voice even. "It was a calcu-lated risk, and it wasn't the Asarlaí themselves. We captured a dozen of their black-garbed creatures."

"Oh, they care even less about those." Marli's face lit up. "But this might work out well."

Vas didn't like Marli's smile or the way she was patting the side of her coat. "What did you do?"

"I think this would be a perfect time to test our theory about your finding." Again, she patted the side of her coat.

The blood drained out of Vas's face. The damn artifact from the box. "You were supposed to leave that on the ship. You *did* leave that on the ship. I saw you."

"I left the box on the ship." Even Savan grimaced at her smile. "We don't know what will happen, or how it works. You get these lovely pirate people to their ships, and Savan and I will handle our new friends."

Vas so wished she could just punch Marli again. But they had to get Kamin and his people to those ships before a full Asarlaí force got wind of things and came back to finish them off. She pointed at Marli. "You see what you can do, and we will be talking about this later." She turned to Kamin. His people and hers had forced back the black suits for now. There were far less of them, but she knew that wouldn't last for long. "Gather some of your pilots and essential crew—we can't fit more than a dozen in our shuttle and I'm not bringing another one down here if you were taking black suits as prisoners. Your ships have shuttles?" At his nod she continued. "Then have the rest of your people stand down and stay out of the way. That crazy woman and her second have skills that I'm not up to explaining to you. You need to focus on getting your ships running and your people off this rock, got it?"

Kamin clearly wasn't happy about the situation, but he also saw he didn't have much choice. "Agreed. I'll be back." He nodded to Carrix and ran back to his people.

"I told him it was a bad idea. I'd like to stay with your crew, if I could? Most of my surviving team have managed to fit in better with the Jeliasians than I have."

Vas clasped his arm. "I'd be honored to have you along. You still have those mad weapons skills, right?"

Carrix laughed. "I knew you only wanted me for that." He winked. "Aye, that I do."

Vas hit her comm. Even if Marli's mind trick worked on the black suits, their timeline was shrinking.

"Let's try this again. Mac, come down and get the Jeliasians. Their ships are on that distant moon."

"Aye, Captain, I'm on—" His words were cut off as weapons fire came too damn close to the shuttle. Mac tore to the side in an evasive move.

"Who's firing at you?" It wasn't coming from the planet.

"Captain, we're picking up a pair of Asarlaí shadow fighters just entering airspace," Gosta said. "Looks like they were scouting and saw the shuttle. They haven't reacted to us yet."

"Damn it." Vas didn't know if it was a scouting party, or if the ones Kamin had as prisoner found a way to call their people once they were free—his man had mentioned they'd had ships coming. The shuttle was armed but not against two shadow fighters. That they were communicating with a larger ship or their base was a given and if they hadn't seen the *Warrior Wench* or the other ships holding even further out, she wanted to keep it that way.

"We need to find a way to—" Now Vas was cut off as an explosion happened in the air above them. The explosion was near the shuttle but not the shuttle, Vas could still see Mac using his wild evasive maneuvers. It was one of the shadow fighters bursting into a fireball.

"Could we be of some help?" Captain Zarith was possibly one of the last people Vas had been expecting to hear on her comm. "We thought we'd chase those bastards to their source, and here we've found you instead." As she spoke, the second shadow fighter exploded.

"Perfect timing, but I thought your people didn't have any serious war ships?"

"Eh, we had some prototypes. Not as big and heavy as yours, at least the one I can see, but they will get the job done. Those bastards destroyed two of our three worlds—even the Kilesh didn't do that. We want payback." Zarith's anger was in her voice, but so was the need for vengeance.

"Thank you, Captain Zarith. We're helping the folks of this world, but I think we all have to figure the Asarlaí know someone is out here destroying ships. Can you help keep an eye out?"

Kamin and ten of his people came jogging up as Mac brought the shuttle down.

"Gon and Therlian, go on the shuttle as well. We have to get them to their ships before whoever else from the Asarlaí shows up."

If Kamin questioned her sending additional fighters, he didn't say a thing. Right now, he and she were playing a trusting game—Vas hoped it lasted.

"The other ships up there are friends of ours; they will help keep watch."

Kamin nodded and quickly loaded his people. Gon and Therlian followed and the ramp pulled up behind them and locked in. Mac was back in the air when Vas heard more weapons fire coming their way.

"The black suits are returning," Flarik yelled. "Savan is firing back but he's running and has Marli over his shoulder."

"Damn her," Vas muttered as she motioned for the rest of her crew and Carrix to take positions.

The black suits ran in and Vas could see there were only six left and they looked to be in bad shape. "Aim for their heads." She didn't know what was causing the Asarlaí-made creatures to break down, but the two that exploded before had been shot in the head.

Savan and his cargo had made it safely past them when they killed the last black suit. The thing hadn't even tried to hide or fall back.

"What the hell happened?" Vas asked, and then nodded for the rest of her team to do a recon where the black suits had come from.

"She tried to use the stone. It worked at first. They didn't fire, and then lowered their weapons. Then she commanded them to kill themselves. That didn't work. She collapsed and they resumed firing at us."

Vas looked down at the unmoving woman. "You have the stone?" She held out her hand.

He looked down at Marli, shook his head and then took the wrapped item out from his jacket and handed it to her. "I didn't realize she'd taken it until you did. My loyalty is to her, but in this case, she was wrong."

"Gosta, we need to move the timeline. Send down a second shuttle for us now."

"Aye."

"Grab Marli, we'll be moving out once my team finishes their clean up…which, from the sound of it, is now." There was no more weapons fire and Flarik was leading the others back. The lawyer wasn't big on ground fighting, but she was good at it.

A shuttle made its way down just as Marli started regaining consciousness.

"Well, that was unfortunate." She blinked a few times, and then held her hand up for Savan to help her off the ground. "I take it I collapsed after I got them to kill themselves?"

"No. Savan saved your ass when you failed. My team finished them off."

"Damn. I really felt like I was getting in their heads at the end." She shook her head. "They followed my commands up until the last one. They must have programming against that." She scowled and patted her jacket.

"I have it. I agree we hopefully can use it for something, but it needs to be under my terms, not yours." The team and Carrix were loading into the shuttle. "Let's get out of here and work on it later."

Marli pouted but she followed Savan up the ramp.

"Captain, we have three Asarlaí cruisers coming in," Gosta said. "Do you want me to have the others come through the gate?" The rest of her fleet was a gate jump away, not visible to scanners from here, and Vas wanted to keep it that way.

"No. Hold tight." She hit her comm. "Zarith? Do you see the incoming?"

"I do, Captain. But I don't think we can take on more than one."

"Therlian? How are things coming getting those other ships up?"

"Slow, Captain. They've been dormant for months. We can't engage yet."

"I can do this," Marli said as Vas got on the shuttle. "The black suits would be doing most all of the labor. If you get me up there, and if Deven and Savan boost me and the rock, I can make them leave."

Vas hadn't seen Deven before she spoke, but he waved from the pilot's seat. "I don't have to run if I'm piloting. And Marli's plan might work."

"Plan? What plan? I just missed two minutes."

"I'm fast," Marli said. "Like I said, with these two boosting me, I can take over the black suits and lead them off. They might not follow my command to kill themselves, but they will follow me."

"Follow you where? And what's to stop the Asarlaí from noticing what's happening and blowing this shuttle out of the sky?"

"It has to be a short trip. How about the side of that first moon there? Lead them into it." Deven pulled up the sky on the screen. He'd already given up his pilot seat to Bathie.

"Won't they stop following once we turn away from running into the moon? We are turning away, right?" Vas studied the trajectory he pointed out.

"I should be able to mentally hold onto them for a short time after we move away. I'm not going to kill myself until all of them are dead, Vas. You have my word on that." Marli looked serious and held out her hand as Bathie launched the shuttle.

Vas turned to both Deven and Savan, when they both nodded and took seats on either side of Marli, Vas handed her the wrapped stone. "You better know what you're doing."

She buckled in next to Bathie and tapped her comm to Gosta, Zarith, and Therlian. "We have a plan, a weird one that might or might not work. Keep doing what you are to get the other ships up—Gosta and Zarith stand down unless this shuttle gets blown to hell."

"Captain—"

"No time to explain. Sit tight. Vas out." She hit the comm and nodded to Marli.

"The Asarlaí ships are in orbit and heading our way," Bathie said. There was no fear in her voice even though three full crusiers would soon be on their tail. Crazy was strong with her crew.

"Okay, Marli, you're up." Vas looked at Bathie's nav specs. At least they had a good pilot for this trick. If they weren't shot down immediately, they would fly as close as they could, breaking away from the moon at a distance the cruisers wouldn't be able to pull away from but the smaller shuttle could clear.

"How will we know if this thing of yours works?" Carrix didn't sound concerned, but his people embraced death in battle.

"We won't be shot."

Marli closed her eyes and Savan and Deven each took hold of an arm. She kept her hands together holding the rock.

"*Oh dear, I don't know that this will work, but I'll help. Me connecting with a damn Asarlaí.*" The last was muttered but Vas still smiled. She wasn't sure what Aithnea could or couldn't do, but the more help the better. Deven gave a small smile.

"The ships are following us, Captain." Bathie was still calm, but her posture was stiffer. There was no way you could do something like this without having a little stress.

"Marli is shaking." Flarik was closest to the trio. "Now the others are as well."

"Keep heading for that moon, Bathie."

CHAPTER FORTY-FIVE

V AS LOOKED AT THE RAPIDLY approaching moon. She glanced over, ready to take the pilot station if Bathie showed signs of cracking, but she was holding on. In fact, she even increased speed.

"They're getting closer." Marwin had been silent but he was watching the screen carefully.

The moon was filling up the entire view screen. "Now!" Vas yelled but she hadn't needed to. Bathie was already pulling up. The shuttle shook at the sudden directional change at a dangerously high speed, but it held together.

A quick glance back showed that Marli, Deven, and Savan all looked to be in massive pain, but were hanging on.

One after the other, the three Asarlaí ships slammed into the moon. The shuttle had barely been able to pull up in time; there would have been no way for ships as big as those cruisers to stand a chance.

Marli, Deven, and Savan all collapsed in their seats.

Bathie was controlling the shuttle but Vas didn't want to leave her. "Flarik, make sure they're okay."

Flarik unlatched herself and reached over. She nodded at each one. "They're okay. Well, they're still alive; let me put it that way."

Vas let out a long breath and turned back to Bathie. "Excellent flying. Mac will be mad he missed it. What say we go back to our ship now?"

Bathie gave a weak smile and turned the shuttle toward the *Warrior Wench*'s shuttle bay.

Vas checked on the three herself as they were landing in the bay. Pulses were coming back strong but they were still unconscious. She tapped her comm for Terel.

"We're possibly going to need three med beds in the shuttle bay."

"Understood."

"Captain? The Jeliasian ships are up, they have three and aren't sure where to go. Your Garmainian friends are asking the same thing," Gosta said via the comm.

They needed to get out of the area immediately. There was no way the Asarlaí who had just died hadn't communicated with their base or other ships.

"Change of plans. Give all of them the coordinates where the rest of the fleet is. Then have Mac send us after them as soon as they are gone. Leave some tracking buoys behind. Once we get all the ships together, you and Mac lead everyone on at least five jumps. I don't care where." Everyone was off the shuttle and Terel and her team were pulling the semi-conscious trio onto med beds.

"I get an explanation when this is over," Terel said as she escorted the last one down the ramp.

Vas nodded then ran for the command deck.

The other ships had all gone through the gate by the time she got there and Gosta was just unleashing his buoy army. "They won't last long; all of them are rigged to self-destruct once a scan is attempted. But we might get some information before they go."

"Thank you." Vas went alongside Xsit. "I need to speak to all of the ships, ours, and the new ones."

Xsit's front feathers bobbed a bit, but she nodded and pulled them all in. Since the new ships weren't part of her fleet, Xsit had to hail them instead of using a comm.

"Hello, this is Captain Vas. As you saw, the Asarlaí found us. My original plan for a slower hunt and destroy is probably shot down now. You are all part of my fleet, or Jeliasian or Garmainian. I think our best chance now is to hide for a few days, gather what troops we can, and then hit the Commonwealth core worlds. We might have a way to impact the Asarlaí ships, but we're still working on it. If any ship wants to leave, do so now and good luck. Otherwise, you are all now part of my fleet." She figured Zarith's ships would stay; they came this far with the intention of destroying Asarlaí. She wasn't sure about the Jeliasians. They wanted payback, but the original plan of them going off on their own might have been better for them.

"Captain, the Garmainians would like to speak with you."

Vas clicked over. "Vas here."

"That was truly amazing, whatever it was you did. We were already with you, that hasn't changed," Zarith said.

"Thank you. You don't have a problem with me leading your ships? You'll captain them, but follow me on this."

"Not at all, Captain."

"Excellent. I'll have my nav officer send you links to connect us for information and communication only. Vas out."

She sent Zarith's contacts to Gosta's screen.

"Any word from the Jeliasians? We need to start jumping." Yes, they were on the other side of the gate from the destruction, but they were a close jump from it and not hard to find.

"Not yet…wait, they are hailing. Sending it to your comm."

"Vas here."

"Captain, this is Kamin. If you can assure us that we will be able to destroy some of them ourselves, we will follow you. We had intended to go down fighting to the last. I have no problem following your lead."

"I can promise you can destroy as many as you like as long as it doesn't go against an order from me. And there's a very good chance that none of us will survive, so you might still go down fighting to the last."

"I look forward to it." He cut his comm and Vas sent his contact information to Gosta's screen as well.

"Okay, let's get jumping." Gosta updated all of the ships of their plans, and the order of entering the gate. *Victorious Dead* was first through and *Warrior Wench* was last.

Once they were moving, Vas went over to Gosta's station. "Anything from the buoys yet?"

"Captain, it's been less than an hour. Unless the Asarlaí had ships in the next system, even they would take a while to get there. I will let you know as soon as I see something."

Vas clapped him on the shoulder and went for the lift. "Thank you. I'll be in the med lab if anyone needs me." She knew that Terel would call if there was something wrong, but she still needed to check on them.

"*Are you there?*" Only silence echoed her thoughts. If that trick had been as tough on Aithnea as it had been on the others she might be unconscious. If a disembodied voice could do such a thing.

Vas entered the med labs to find Terel trying to yell down Marli. Deven was out of his bed, Savan was still unconscious, and Marli and Terel were screaming at each other.

Terel spotted her. "Vas! Savan isn't responding and she wants to take him."

"He is part of her crew." She nodded to Deven who was wisely staying out of things.

"But he could die."

"He won't," Marli said. "I can care for him."

"You almost killed him. Deven too. They aren't batteries, you know."

Deven finally held up both hands. "Do you mind?" he asked Vas.

Vas held her arm out in a sweeping motion.

"Terel, Marli did some things up there that I don't even understand. Yes, she was using Savan and I like batteries, but it was freely given. She needs to take him back to her ship."

Terel looked to Vas.

"I agree. We don't have the knowledge to fix whatever happened. After the next gate, get on a shuttle and go back to your ship."

Marli nodded to Vas, and then approached Terel. "Thank you. I know you only meant to help."

Vas was sure her eyes were as big as Terel's at that. Terel couldn't even respond beyond a nod.

Marli led Savan's med bed out of the lab.

"I just…damn it, Vas, they all almost died."

Deven rubbed Terel's shoulder. "But we didn't. And Marli's little trick destroyed three gray cruisers."

Terel sighed. "Agreed. However, how is that going to help in the long run? We can't run all of the ships into planets or moons. Not to mention it only works on the black suits, right? Once the Asarlaí figure that out, they'll just start piloting on their own."

"It can still help in emergencies, hopefully without wiping out Marli, Deven, or Savan. And there could be other applications to use it." Vas turned to Deven. "You and Marli have a few days. I'm hoping we can avoid them that long, and then we have to attack." Vas would have preferred to go after the core worlds now, but she just didn't have enough to go after the Asarlaí with.

Terel nodded reluctantly. "I do have some non-Marli news. Well, it is sort of Marli news. I think we've found a way to attack the Asarlaí with the swarm. But it's Gosta's find so we should have him involved." She looked around as if noticing the mess her med lab was in for the first time. "In your ready room in ten?"

"Deal." Vas and Deven left the good doctor to fixing things.

"What exactly did Marli do, and just between you and I, how viable is it going to be in our plans?" Vas waited until they were near the lift before asking.

Deven hit the lift button. "She was using her genetic connection with them. It's not something I've ever seen before. Then again, I don't think there's been a case of thousands of creatures being cloned from one person. She took over their minds. A simple command—follow. And it worked. Through her, and them, I could sense anger, fear, and frustration from the Asarlaí. They couldn't stop their own black suits. But they could have if that moon hadn't been so close." He shook his head. "As for future use? Unsure. Just those three ships almost did us all in, and I felt Aithnea's presence as well. Like Terel said, we can't bash the entire Asarlaí fleet into random planets."

His last words were said as they walked onto the deck, and Flarik looked up hopefully. "I think that would be a wonderful idea."

"We all do, it's just not workable." Vas headed toward her ready room. "Gosta, you're with us. Terel will be on her way. Flarik, you have the deck."

Gosta got up but nodded to Hrrru. "Hrrru might have some interesting information as well, if this is a strategy meeting."

Vas waved to Hrrru. "By all means join us. Bathie, take nav if you will."

She motioned for them all to get seated around her desk. Terel popped in a moment later.

"Okay, since some of you know what Gosta has, but Deven and I do not, please go first."

"Aye, Captain. This was actually Ragkor's idea, but I expanded on it. He's designed containment fields that can trap and hold the swarm in stasis. In the models they could be taken out of the Web and released near Asarlaí ships and planets they have taken over. Now, the theory, based on the swarm's behavior, is that they would fight to get back to the Web. But there is no evidence that they cannot survive outside of the Web and they would hopefully be distracted in trying to return by the buffet of so many Asarlaí to kill."

He finally paused. "But they might have limited use, and I'm not sure how to get them to the Asarlaí."

Vas really admired her big-brained crew, but sometimes they were too smart for their own good. "How about missiles? Get a bunch of blanks, load the containment fields inside, and shoot the Asarlaí ships. Or planets." She raised an eyebrow as wonder took over Gosta's face.

"Brilliant!"

"Seriously? Okay, as soon as we live through this, you are taking a really long vacation." She turned to Hrrru. "You too for not pointing that out to him. Now what is your great find?"

"I have been watching the dark lanes as you said. There are many more ships out there. Some criminal, some just displaced survivors. They want revenge but they are afraid to endanger their people who were taken. I have found thirty-seven ships to join us in the fight."

Vas nodded and Deven whistled approvingly. "I take back the vacation comment for you. Great work, both of you really. Deven, can you work with Hrrru on organizing these ships? Gosta, work with Ragkor to gather containment pods and missiles for as many ships as you can. I just want the *Victorious Dead* to go on recon—but Gosta and Hrrru go with them." A thought hit her. "Damn it, they'll go after Marli again as soon as we release them. We can't kill her, not if we need her mumbo to take out at least some of the black suits."

Gosta beamed. "That we did think of, Captain. A modified full decon suit will block her from being picked up by the swarm. She won't be happy, but she'll be safe."

"Deven? Can you still help her if you can't have skin to skin?"

"Yes, now that I know more of what she was doing, just being near her should be enough. Once we figure out what she's going to do."

Vas turned to Terel. "And you? Or was it just the swarm?"

"The swarm isn't a 'just', and that was the bulk of it. Well, except for the fact that I can destabilize some of the cloned Asarlaí. They used the same Asarlaí base for their entire current race—eight original individuals that I've found. There could be more, but I'd venture not too many. Savan said there had been twelve on the missing exploration vessel. Then they blended in genetics from other races. I have been able to create chemical bio-weapons to remove the non-Asarlaí component in any that are based on human, Welischian, or Xithinal stock. Given time I could get more, but these were the ones I could isolate first. If those genetic codes are destroyed—the being would die."

Vas didn't really have room to pace with all the people in her ready room, but she did a few tiny circles behind her desk. "We have a lot of things that can destroy parts of them. This is going to take everything we have to give us even a shot at taking them down. Many of us won't survive. Maybe none of us."

Her people all looked at her expectantly.

Deven grinned. "We're mercs, Vas. Dying is part of the job."

CHAPTER FORTY-SIX

THREE DAYS AND TWO HOURS later those words of Deven's were still bouncing around Vas's head. He was meeting with a collection of ships from the dark lanes—five ships that weren't sure about joining the now massive fleet for the impending attack on the core worlds and the Asarlaí. They knew of Deven and Vas, but only wanted to talk to him.

The vids from the buoys were running through Vas's monitor for the fifth time, but she couldn't stay focused. Gosta had dug out a few more buoys and left them around but aside from some activity in the Jelias system right after the destruction of the cruisers, there hadn't been any Asarlaí sightings.

Marli had a good hour-long rant about how this again evidenced that the current Asarlaí were not her people. Her people would have stayed in the area and made sure no one survived, not slunk back to the core worlds like cowards. Terel finally cut her off by pointing out that she was right. The black suits *were* her people.

Marli shut up and cut the comm.

Vas had only heard back from Aithnea once since she'd helped Marli. Her voice had been weak, and just said make plans without her help. Vas didn't know if helping what Marli did had been too much for her or not, or if it was whatever else she was working on.

Ragkor and his crew had taken as much of the swarm as they could get out of the Web and had finished placing their containment pods in missiles on all of Vas's original nine ships a few hours ago. She would have put them in every ship, but they didn't have enough. The swarm was smart enough that once they realized what was going on, they stayed clear of Ragkor's crew.

And Marli was truly bitchy in her full decon suit. She understood why she needed it, but it didn't improve her mood any.

"Deven's shuttle is back and two of the dark line ships are leaving the meeting place—but they aren't coming here." Gosta called in from the deck. Deven was only giving the coordinates to new ships once they agreed to join the cause.

Vas shut the vid down. "On my way to the deck."

"The other three just left as well, but heading toward a different gate—also not coming here." Gosta sounded as confused as Vas felt. Deven was a champion negotiator. Second only to Flarik, but he didn't scare people as much. It was odd that he'd failed.

Deven's smiling face when he came up didn't look like that of a failure. "What's wrong?"

"The ships you just met with left the area and didn't come to our coordinates. What happened?"

"I told them not to come here. They have different agendas." His grin was an annoying mix of sexy and smug.

"Not the time—tell me."

He sighed and sat at his station. "The Asarlaí have been using some of their conquered victims as manual labor. The captains of those ships just liberated some. They also had some nice details. The new Asarlaí destroyed the rim worlds, and then ignored them because they can't cover the entire area. That cloning facility we destroyed was a major loss for them—they depleted more of their own people fighting us and the rest of the Commonwealth than intended. They still have twice as many ships as us, but they are sticking to the core because they can't spread out."

"So, that's why the other ships aren't joining us?"

"They are going to the far gates. They have a dozen more ships that they hadn't told us about in case we were spies, all super-fast Halpia ships. They can gate faster than any of ours. They'll hit the capital from two other sides when we strike."

Vas wasn't happy about ships going off on their own, but her fleet was too big for her to lead anyway. Fifty ships total, but she really only closely advised her nine and the Garmainians. The Jeliasians had stuck with them but as more ships joined the cause they fell back with the masses. All of the ships had a code embedded in them that should keep them from firing on each other by accident but that was the best she could do.

"Captain, Zarith inquires why we have not started yet." Carrix had joined the Garmainian crew when their gunner was injured. He also often acted as communications because he was nosy and liked chatting with Vas and her people.

"Deven was setting up some more help along the way." Vas looked at her chrono. Technically, they still had two minutes before the time, but the Garmainians liked being early to parties.

"Xsit, call final check-in for us and the Garmainians. Issue time call to the rest."

The plan was for all of these moving parts to work as one whole and at least damage the Asarlaí. The fleet would launch a gate run where they would come out in the core via different gates—originally the two gates that Deven's friends were taking were excluded from the plan due to the timing to get to them.

When all ships came out, those with the swarm bombs were to run as deep into the Commonwealth core as possible with the capital planet as their goal. Once they got to denser Asarlaí populations, the swarm bombs would be fired. Terel's bio-chemical attacks would work best on planets, so the breakdown chemical would be launched on the ground—specifically the capital but they did modify a few missiles to carry the chemical as well. It wouldn't destroy more than twenty or so percent, but that was still something.

Then came Marli's plot and what Vas saw as the biggest risk. Savan had recovered from the prior attempt and he and Deven would again accompany her in a modified shuttle from the *Scurrilous Monk*. Vas had pulled rank and assigned herself as pilot.

They would do a sweep, with Marli mentally calling to all of the black suits once a majority of the Asarlaí were disabled, dying, or dead. They had configured a jump gate to have her lead them all into a system with a nova sun. Vas would pull the shuttle out, and the black suits would go sundiving.

In theory.

There were so many parts to go wrong it made Vas's teeth ache.

"I'd still rather you stayed with the fleet." Deven was standing next to her command chair.

"I'd rather you were back on Home. I'd rather we were all off on a nice, normal job somewhere. But that's not where life is right now." She looked into his eyes. Grabbing him and kissing the hell out of him was what she really wanted to do—but that really wouldn't help much for crew morale. Besides, they'd spent the last three nights together as if each was their last.

"We might die. *I* might be able to come back again."

"You might not. This time if you go, I'm going with you." She looked out at the ships amassed around them. "But at least we're going out in something larger than just a job. Feels kind of good." Regardless of what the old stories said, there was never a good time to die. But trying to save an entire system of hundreds of worlds and billions of people wasn't a bad way to go.

"Captain, the ships are awaiting your command," Xsit

said.

Vas grinned to Deven. "And we go." A few of the ships were quick on the trigger and got to their gates sooner, but not by much. Within minutes, the attack on the Asarlaí had begun.

They came out of their gate to find the Asarlaí weren't totally unguarded. Two cruisers were on patrol before them. Vas had twelve ships with her through this gate, two of which, the *Aoenyth* and the *Scurrilous Monk*, were easily the size of the Asarlaí grays.

Even though they had the swarm, bio-chem weapons, and Marli, this part was going to all be pure brute force. They didn't have enough of their specialized weapons for use on a few patrol cruisers—they needed to deploy them in the heart of the Asarlaí's conquered territory.

The Asarlaí got off a few shots, more attempts at shield destabilizing. Vas's people expected it, and they only took a few minor hits before they were able to destroy the Asarlaí cruisers. Vas had instructed all of the ships in the fleet that rationing weapons was a must—there wouldn't be time to leave the fight to re-stock. But she couldn't begrudge the overkill on this first engagement.

"Captain, reports coming in. Very minor injuries on the *Defiant Ruin* and the *Golaig*, all other ships clear." Xsit stopped and tilted her head. "The other groups report similar interactions." She grinned and looked up. "Captain Kamin says thank you for the information on the shield modulating."

Vas nodded. She knew the Asarlaí and the black suits could counterattack the shield modulations being used by all of her ships if given enough time. She meant to never give them enough time.

"Continue moving in."

More ships tried to block them, but nothing concentrated until they got within striking distance of the five core Commonwealth worlds.

Here was the Asarlaí armada.

"Captain, two ships have been lost; one each from groups three and five. Two are disabled from group four," Xsit called out as one by one ships fell. But Gosta was keeping track of the Asarlaí ships destroyed and Vas and her fleet were still ahead.

The *Warrior Wench*, the *Aoenyth*, and the *Scurrilous Monk* were in the front formation heading toward the core with the rest of her fleet hanging close.

"Captain! They got through our shield modulating, we're hit!" The *Golaig*'s yell went across all of the comms, an emergency override.

"Damn it, get out of here. You can't stay if they've shattered your shields. Go!" Vas yelled, but it was too late.

The *Golaig* exploded on screen. It happened too fast for any emergency pods to get free. Vas took a deep breath and closed her eyes as the ship burst into a fireball. Those were her people. She would grieve them properly if they survived this.

"Move faster, everyone, and keep changing those shields. Break your regular patterns."

"Captain, Marli's shuttle is on its way."

Vas took a second to mentally send on her lost crew on the *Golaig*, and then nodded to Gosta. "Deven and I are on our way down. Stick to the plan, *no matter what*. Flarik, you have the command deck."

She and Deven ran to the lift and the shuttle bay. Marli had been insistent on using her shuttle. It was much larger and heavier than any of the ones on Vas's ships, but it also seemed she liked the idea of using a modified Asarlaí ship as the tool of their destruction.

Savan was in a full suit and motioned for Vas and Deven to do the same.

Vas held hers up. "Are we planning on space walking the black suits into the sun?" These were full containment suits. Not as bulky as Marli's decon suit, but used mostly for repairs on the outside of a ship.

"No," Marli said. "I just don't know how well we're going to do with this. It won't matter to what the three of us are doing if we're in suits or not. The stone is with me in mine so we're good. But it would suck if we took a hit and something happened to the pilot before we got to our destination."

Vas put on the suit. It wasn't the best way to fly, but if that was what Marli wanted, that's what she got at this point.

Deven and Savan took up similar positions as before, one on each side of Marli. But they couldn't touch directly, because of the suits. It must have worked though, as Marli's grin was clear through the helmet of her suit.

"We are ready. Now let's go destroy some of my off-spring. All of them, if we can."

Vas had a trajectory mapped out. She would stay close to the *Warrior Wench, Defiant Ruin,* and the *Aoenyth* that would break away from the rest of her fleet and run inter-ference from the Asarlaí cruisers. Once the swarm had been released and started creating suicidal Asarlaí at any rate.

"We're in position; begin firing swarm missiles and dropping bombs." Vas ordered as she watched the massive firefights going on around her.

"*I know you might not be around at this point, but thank you for what you've done. You might want to pray for us right now.*" Vas sent the thought out into the void.

"*I've never stopped. I can't help this time, but my thoughts are with you.*" The voice was still very faint, so faint, that Vas might have imagined it. It brought some comfort, so she was good with it.

At first, there was little reaction by the ships hit with the swarm weapons. Some actually had a shot strike them; oth-ers had the swarm disburse against their shields. It looked like the swarm might be too displaced by being out of the Web to work; they initially milled about aimlessly but now appeared to be grouping together.

Then a group of the swarm broke off and passed right through the nearest Asarlaí ship. Then the next and the next. At first, Vas thought the tiny things could fly through metal, and then she realized they were boring through the hulls.

"Asarlaí life signs are dropping on that closest ship, Captain," Gosta said.

That was what they were hoping for. She watched as the swarm went through, literally, through, all of the ships she could see. Then they vanished. Gosta continued to report dropping life signs. So far, no attempted space walks by Asarlaí that she could see, but there were other ways to kill yourself. And those tiny holes couldn't have been good for their ability to breathe.

Vas punched the engines on the shuttle. "Hope you're ready, Marli, we're on now. Flarik, get Terel and her bio-weapons to those planets."

The other ships continued toward the core as Vas aimed the shuttle for the distant gate. A line of ships started trailing behind.

"It's working." She turned but all three of her passengers were locked in their own mental hell. Hopefully, the pain would be worth it.

The Asarlaí ships weren't moving fast, as if someone inside many of them were still fighting back against following the shuttle.

Vas slowed a bit, but not too much. She needed them to move quickly, and while the swarm would make the Asarlaí want to kill themselves, she didn't want them stopping their ships to do it. They were counting on the black suits being at the controls of those ships and being drawn to follow Marli.

They went through the gate with at least thirty Asarlaí ships behind them. The huge sun was about the only thing Vas could see. She turned away at the correct spot; the black suits and the Asarlaí should keep going as they were and slam into the sun.

One or two did, but the rest followed the shuttle as she pulled it away from the massive sun.

"Crap." Vas pulled the shuttle around and made another run, a bit closer; close enough that the shield warnings on the shuttle went off. Still only lost two more Asarlaí ships.

"Let me." Marli was suddenly standing right next to her. "We can't get close enough to draw them all in without destroying the shuttle—I'm taking it in. Get in the pods." Her voice was flat, but her eyes almost glowed with fervor.

"I'm not leaving it to you. We can do one more pass."

Marli sighed and smiled. "Savan, drug them both."

Vas couldn't respond before a hypo pierced her suit and her arm. She froze immediately. She was still conscious but couldn't move as Savan carried her to an escape pod that already had an immobile Deven in it and placed her down next to him. "We thought you both might fight if it came to this." He looked toward Marli. "I'm staying with her. You might not survive even this way, but we wanted you to have a chance."

"I'll finally be free," Marli said from the pilot station. "Good luck, Admiral."

Vas really wished her mouth would work so all the swear words she was thinking could come out. But the panel on the pod slammed shut and moments later they were floating in space.

CHAPTER FORTY-SEVEN

———◆———

V AS WATCHED AS THE POD tumbled. The shuttle heading for the nova sun. The Asarlaí ships all following it in. She imagined the blips as the ships hit—the sun was too large for the impacts to have shown to the naked eye. But imagining worked.

She knew Marli wanted to die, and Savan was as connected to her as she was to Deven. But it was still hard to take—especially when all she could do was watch. She wouldn't have called Marli a friend—but she had been a companion at arms.

Not that it mattered. It might be days before anyone came looking for the shuttle—never, if none of her ships survived their current battles.

"*We have got to break you of this depressing habit.*" Deven's mental voice was weak, but there.

"*We have to break you of jumping in my head all the time.*"

"*Guilty. But if we are going to die, I'd rather be here than anywhere else.*"

"*Agreed.*" Vas mentally snuggled into the warmth of his presence. It had been a good life. Still a lot of questions she would have liked to have answered—but a good life on the whole.

"*Warrior Wench* to pod, are you in there, Captain?"

Crap, Vas still couldn't make her voice work. Gosta might pick them up anyway, or might not.

"*Hang on. I'm about to give Flarik the shock of her life,*" Deven thought. "*Flarik, this is Vas and Deven. We're in the pod but can't communicate. Pick us up.*"

"What in the hell?" Flarik was using the comm, but clearly she heard Deven. "Gosta, pick up that pod."

Vas would have laughed if she could; the lawyer was definitely freaked out at having Deven in her head.

The *Warrior Wench* picked up the pod as whatever Savan had used on them began to wear off.

Vas worked her jaw as she was helped out of the pod. "Marli led the black suits and Asarlaí into the sun. Thank you for picking us up. How did you know to come so quickly?"

"Marli hit the distress for the shuttle." Gosta rarely came down to the shuttle bay but he was a welcome sight. He looked sad, then nodded. "Her sacrifice destroyed all of the ships following you, and removed a very large portion of the Asarlaí fleet. Terel's bio-chem is weakening the ground troops, but there is still fighting on the capital world."

Vas hobbled to the screen in the shuttle bay, shoved off her helmet, and looked at the specs. There were still some Asarlaí ships, but not many. It might take weeks or months to get rid of them when they went to ground.

"How many ships have we lost?" Deven came up behind her.

Gosta shook his head. "Ten more are seriously damaged. The Garmainians lost one of their ships, not Captain Zarith's but the smaller one. Five more of the outer rim ships exploded with all hands on deck. The *Aoenyth* and the *Defiant Ruin* took heavy damage but both are still flying."

There was something odd about the pattern of ships that had been seriously hit. All were on one side of the core worlds. "We need to get back on deck," Vas said as she started stripping out of the suit.

"Not until I've cleared you both," Terel said as she came into the shuttle bay. "I have no idea what they dosed you both with. You're still moving stiffly." She took Vas's arm. "We've won."

Vas shook her head and dumped her suit. She couldn't explain it, but a feeling of terror, of something horrible they'd missed, clawed at her gut. "No, we haven't." She tapped the screen but the one down here was too small. "There is something else out there—waiting. I need a bigger screen. We haven't won, and if I'm right there is something else coming for us."

Her legs were still stiff, but she forced them to move as quickly as possible. Deven had removed his suit and was right behind her.

"Do you want to tell me what you think you see? Saw?" He tilted his head as he met her eyes while they waited for the lift. "Felt? This is more than seeing, you're sensing something."

Gosta and Terel came up behind them. Gosta was silent, but Terel looked ready to explode with questions or comments. She said nothing though.

Vas wished she could explain this feeling—Deven was right, strategy pointed out that a seemingly harmless area of space shouldn't have destroyed so many ships—but it was far more than that.

It felt like the storms of her dreams were tearing at her soul.

The command deck was less hectic than when they'd left, but far too relaxed for the creeping feeling going down her back.

"Get all ships on full alert. There is something else coming for us." Saying that with absolutely no proof to back it up was tricky with her own ships—saying it to the rest of the ones who had joined in was possibly suicidal.

She knew they were seeing what she saw. The Asarlaí losing more battles, their ships going down in balls of flame. But there was something they were missing.

Vas ran to her command chair and pulled up the section where the *Aoenyth* and the *Defiant Ruin* had been damaged. Both ships were leaving the area slowly. She magnified the area on the screen.

Space looked normal there. Completely normal. Yet the Asarlaí had fought back the fiercest there. Not the core worlds where most of their troops and prisoners were—but there.

"Do another scan of that area—what the hell is that planet?"

"Captain, the rim ships are calling in asking for clarification," Xsit said.

"Hold them off," Vas said. "Gosta? Hrrru? Deven? What the hell is that planet? Why weren't we looking at it before?"

"No life signs?" Gosta sounded confused. "I don't know why we didn't notice the planet before. But there are no signs of tech or life."

"Because they had a shield on it, and it wasn't there before the Asarlaí took over." Deven swore as he called up as many scans as he could, finally setting on a pair of images to join the one Vas put up. "This is the Commonwealth core planets five years ago—no extra planet. Here is what we saw when we arrived here—no extra planet. Here's where that planet belongs." He dropped in one more screen, a space map. "That's why the Soldairian system wasn't harassed by the Asarlaí—their home world was turned into a massive bomb and brought here. Everything under the crust is explosive—it will make the Mayhira explosion seem like a shuttle gun." He looked up. "And the sequence has already begun."

Vas hit the all comm override. "Attention all ships. I'm sending over intel, everyone needs to get their ships the hell out of this area now. If you have fighters out, tell them to run. There is no way to explain this—but if you heard of what happened at Mayhira, this will be a hundred times worse. All ships abandon the system." Vas nodded and Deven and Gosta sent their intel to all of the ships. Yes, the actual bulk of the destruction to the Mayhiran system had been due to Marli's exploding ship, but it got the point across. Right now everyone needed to get out of here.

"Captain, the Jeliasians are hailing you." Xsit sounded far calmer than Vas felt.

Vas wasn't going to stop and chat with each ship. She'd warned them and aside from the ones directly reporting to her, there was nothing more she could do. However, she'd deal with this one directly.

"What part of get the hell out of here didn't you get, Kamin?"

"Kamin was killed in the last attack; this is his second in command, Calo. I just wanted to verify that you'd seen the ship hiding behind the planet. It wasn't in your intel, but we are at the edge of the system." An image appeared on the smaller screen and Vas moved it to the main. An Asarlaí warship, perhaps the largest she'd seen, hung in the electronic shadow of the bomb planet.

"Thank you Calo, my condolences on the loss of your captain, he was a good man. Now, unless you have more intel, get the hell out of here."

"Aye, Captain Tor Dain. It has been an honor." The Jeliasian ship tore for the nearest gate and vanished.

"Gosta? Deven? What can you get on that ship?"

Gosta shook his head. "I still can't see it, Captain. It's there, but we're not…wait. Mac can you move us to these coordinates?"

Mac looked to Vas but she nodded. He moved the ship. Vas watched the screens as all of the ships left. The ones that could, anyway. There were many dead Asarlaí in space, but some of her fleet as well. She wasn't going to let all those lives be lost in vain.

One ship wasn't moving toward the gate, it was following the *Warrior Wench*. Vas hit the comm. "Ragkor, what the hell are you doing?"

"Not leaving you behind?"

"Wrong answer." Vas was staying to make sure everyone

else got out, captain's prerogative. But she also was hanging onto a slim thread that there was a way to stop that world from exploding. Why would the Asarlaí go through all of this, conquer the Commonwealth, and then just blow it up? Something else was going on and watching Deven and Flarik frantically running screens told her she wasn't the only one on the ship to think that.

But she wasn't going to endanger anyone else beyond her own ship.

"Turn tail and run. If this thing is as massive as they are saying, it's going to damage gates a few jumps back. Get as far out as you can."

"Respectfully, no. You can court martial me, or whatever happens with mercs, if we survive. But the crew and I talked—we're staying." He paused. "I have a *feeling*."

The emphasis on the last word caught Vas's attention. Ragkor was a weak pre-cog. One who didn't admit to it often and told everyone it wasn't trustworthy. But it had picked up a few things before. The fact that he was sensing something was enough to want him with them.

"Damn it, okay. But we will have a long talk about insubordination if we survive." She shook her head. "I need intel people. Ragkor? What are you feeling? Deven? Gosta? I'm assuming there are Asarlaí and black suits on that ship?"

"I know there are people on the planet—or there will be. There is something more than just them deciding to destroy the worlds they lost. I can't be more specific, but this was planned and probably had nothing to do with our attack," Ragkor said.

"I'm still trying to get a good reading," Gosta said. "The ship is far better shielded than any of their others."

Vas drummed her fingers on her chair as the last ships of her fleet fled. Almost last. Damn it, did no one understand when she told them to flee?

"Zarith? Why am I not seeing your ass?"

"Sorry Captain Tor Dain, but I'm not leaving. My crew

and I want to stay. We don't have a lot to go back to in our system, and this could be a ploy."

Vas looked at the same data she'd sent all the ships, the scans of the Solardian home planet weren't a ruse, it was going to blow up.

"Not to mention there's a trigger on that planet, and along with being former mercs, my people were also former explosive experts."

Vas muted the comm. "A trigger? Someone put a trigger on an exploding planet? Who does this crap?"

Gosta responded. "There is a trigger…of a sort. I wouldn't call it that but it is going to be the fuse. There is a slim chance we can stop this."

"Less than two percent, Vas." Deven was somber.

"Are all of our other ships confirmed out of the system?" Vas finally asked.

"Aye, Captain," Xsit said. "Only the three of us remain."

Vas reopened her comm to the other two ships. "I want intel on that bomb, who the hell is on that ship, and anything pertinent known about the Solardian world in my ready room in…" Vas paused and turned back to Deven, "How long before the sequence finishes?"

"Five hours, more or less." He shrugged. "I can't calculate closer than that."

Vas nodded. "I want all intel in my ready room in two and a half hours."

Once her two non-compliant ships agreed, Vas went to her ready room. She didn't say anything to him, but a look to Deven and he followed her. She paused and faced her crew. "Contact me if anything happens—and I mean anything."

Deven shut the door as they got inside. "What's the plan?"

Vas laughed and went to her chair. "I was hoping you had an idea. I just can't get over the feeling that we're missing something. If Ragkor's feeling is also right—we're missing something that was in place to happen before the Asarlaí got their asses handed to them."

"And they are still carrying it out because losing three-quarters of their ships and people doesn't matter." Deven shook his head. "Which means they have more ships coming."

"Like Mayhira? Damn it, we lost Marli too soon. If they had more than one modified world, they could be opening a portal—like they tried to do with Mayhira. They have more ships, fighters, weapons—everything in another dimension waiting to come to this side."

Vas looked at the screen before her. She wasn't accepting this. Too many people had died for them to lose.

"So then even though it looks massive, the explosion is not going to take out the Commonwealth worlds." She held up her hand and ticked off a finger as the ideas came forward. "They need the planet to do its controlled implosion to open a portal." Another finger. "They will have a ton of ships coming through that portal. Especially now. Our being here might not have started this process, but it will make them modify it. They'll want to get everything here quickly."

"Then we just need to destroy that ship, modify the implosion, and have it go back into the portal destroying their armada and anything else nearby on that end." Deven shook his head. "We're going to need Gosta."

CHAPTER FORTY-EIGHT

VAS LAUGHED. ONLY HER PEOPLE would even think it was possible, let alone be able to come up with a plan. "Gosta, we need you in here. No, belay that, we need everyone out there—we're coming out." She and Deven got up and went back to the command deck. This situation was too insane not to include the entire command deck in on. Besides, they needed more brains working on it.

Vas outlined the situation, and then looked at her command crew. "So? Can we do that?"

There was a full thirty seconds of silence—then eight people all started with ideas at once. All of them quite earnest. If it could be done, these people would do it.

"Okay, that's a yes. I want three teams, work with the brains on the other two ships, but each team has to come up with a workable plan—one with immediate use. Same time as before, two hours."

Terel had stayed quiet during the original outburst, but her face was thoughtful. "This does tie in to what I was coming up to tell you in private." At Vas's nod she continued. "We've been able to scan the ship. It's not just Asarlaí and black suits; there are representatives from at least thirty worlds there. Including humans."

Vas's first thought was they had hostages on there—but Terel's look on the last line changed that. "Clones. They have clones. Only these aren't reading as Asarlaí." She took a deep breath and unclenched her hands. "My brother is on that ship."

Terel nodded. "Unless you have more relatives working with those bastards that I don't know about. I scanned for our missing Wilthuny on a hunch as well—she's there too. Or in both cases—their clones are there."

"Same thing," Vas said. "One way or another we're ending this today."

Vas put herself on the reverse the implosion team—she knew her brother, clones, or whatever, would be part of the actual explosion that opened the portal. The bastard had been exactly the same as she recalled every time she'd seen him. Clone or not, she knew his behavior pattern. She intended to be the one to stop him.

Her people had managed to stop the first Asarlaí dimensional incursion by exploding a massive super gate the Asarlaí wannabes had built on the far edge of this system. Then they'd reversed the explosion of the planet Mayhira, causing it to blow up before it could act as a conduit for the Asarlaí ships to cross out of their current dimension. This was bigger. The amount of explosive material building in it would take out the entire Commonwealth core, destroying at least ten planets, if they tried to detonate it as they had Mayhira.

Vas wasn't a slouch on the science end, but she was far surpassed by most of her crew. Her participation was mostly to keep them on track and bounce ideas off. Then do the heavy work when they got down to the planet.

Terel was leading the ship team—she was hoping they could find a way to go after the genetics in a similar way they'd gone after the Asarlaí clones.

Deven was leading the 'try and get the reversed implosion to feed back into the portal' group. All three were damn near impossible, but his team was facing a serious balancing act. Unlike Mayhira, they had to let the transformation process start so the portal would open and ships would start to come through. Then they had to find a way to detonate the portal and reverse the implosion back into the other dimension before any Asarlaí ships actually made it completely through.

Even though Vas was technically on one team, she walked around the groups—all of which were conferencing with the crews on the other two ships.

They were an hour in when two ships came through the closest gate. Walvento had switched on the missile tracking, but Vas called him off when she saw it was the *Aoenyth* and the *Defiant Ruin*.

"What in the hell are you two doing?" Vas called to both ships at once.

"We realized you might need back up, there are more Asarlaí ships in the outer rim than before. They're waiting for something." Lytton was an experienced captain, that's why Vas had trusted him with the *Aoenyth*. Apparently, insubordination was a big thing with her crew now.

"You could have just told us."

"And you would have told us to stay away," Clasia responded from the *Defiant Ruin*. She was also an old campaigner.

Vas looked at the teams still trying to find a way to do the impossible. Truth was, with all three ships focusing on the problem, their response to an attack—beyond the ship and planet before them—would be delayed.

"Fine. Both of you are on patrol—but stay back. The Asarlaí ship hasn't reacted to us yet, we want to keep it that way.

The lack of response from her brother's ship was concerning, or it was until Bathie pointed out that while the *Warrior Wench* could see the ship, the other two ships couldn't—they were out of range for standard scanners. She just needed to keep it that way until they made their move.

"Good. You will need back up. Your brother is looking for you with his mind, I've shielded you and your ships—but I won't be able to do much more."

Vas smiled at Aithnea's mental voice. "*Thank you. That helps.*"

An hour later, they had a plan. It wasn't a great one, and Deven wasn't re-estimating his perceived slim chance of their pulling it off, but it was something.

Clasia had checked in regularly with the rest of their ships keeping watch around the rim. There were still Asarlaí ships out there, but they were still waiting. Terel had a way to use a modified bio-agent on the crew of the Asarlaí ship, but their shielding was too high. They needed to take out the ship and get the clones down to the planet for it to work.

Turning the explosion was going to be tougher—they were going to have to fly a ship full of explosives into the portal as it opened. If everything worked perfectly, the ship would trigger the implosion to fall back on itself. Providing the Asarlaí ships coming through didn't destroy it before it crossed the dimensional threshold.

The ship Vas sent would be destroyed, obviously.

The debate went around for a few minutes, and then finally Mac stepped up. "The *Defiant Ruin* can be completely run by two people. I was trying to make it automatic, but hadn't gotten that far. I'm volunteering to pilot it in."

"Then we have our ship." Vas gave him a smile. "Thank you. But you won't be going in." As much as she would love to have a face-to-face fight with her brother—she knew she had to be the one who saw this through.

"Vas and I will," Deven said. At Vas's nod he hit the comm. "*Defiant Ruin*, get your people into shuttles. *Aoenyth*, help them get to your ship. Sorry Clasia, you're losing your ship."

Of course everyone from all of the ships had to chime in at once until Vas overrode them all.

"Everyone. We have lost too many people. Good people who died trying to save this damn Commonwealth from those Asarlaí bastards. There is a slim chance that we can end that here. But Deven and I have to go ram the *Defiant Ruin* down their throats. None of us will probably survive this—so our situation isn't different from any of yours. Keep prepping for our attack, and do as Deven has said. Ragkor has command of the fleet once Deven and I are on the *Defiant Ruin*."

She closed the comm.

"Captain? There might be a chance to survive the implosion. Slim, very slim," Hrrru muttered a few words to himself that she missed. "But a plan. We still have the pod Marli came here in, yes? Load that into the *Defiant Ruin*, climb in, and send yourselves as a missile when you enter the collapsing portal."

Deven opened his mouth to argue, and then shrugged. "That's a better chance than we have without it. Marli's pods were pretty damn tough."

"I'm game for any chance, no matter how slim. Make it happen." Vas looked up to see Terel standing in front of her.

"There's no way I can talk you out of this, is there?"

"No, but thank you for thinking about it. And no you can't come with us."

"I didn't say that," Terel said.

"Your eyes did." Vas hugged her friend. Terel had been the closest thing she'd had to family—before she realized her entire crew was her family. When she pulled back, both of them had suspiciously wet eyes. "I need you to keep working on destroying those bastards."

"Understood. Good luck, Vas." Terel quickly left the command deck.

"Captain? Ragkor is trying to reach you." Xsit called out.

"Vas here. Yes, you are in charge of the fleet, and no you cannot order Deven and I not to do this, nor can you order yourself or anyone to join us."

The silence on the other end said at least one of those things were his plan of topic. "Aye, Captain. We'll do what we can to bring you both back safe."

"After those bastards are destroyed."

Ragkor laughed. "Aye, after they are all destroyed. Good luck to both of you."

Vas shook her head. This was going to be hard enough, but even worse if everyone was going to be maudlin about it. She overrode the comm to full ship for all five vessels.

"Some of you have been part of this crew for most of your lives, others are new. To all of you—we have a chance to destroy the biggest abomination that has ever been created. In some ways more than the original Asarlaí. We may not succeed. We might succeed but at the loss of all of our lives. I for one think that is a damn good cause to die for. This is a time to show these bastards that they picked on the wrong system. We do this for a chance of a free Commonwealth—with or without us in it."

Her people were mercs, Zarith's too. They accepted death—but this had been different. She needed them to be focused on the job—not Vas and Deven dying.

One by one the captains checked in, there was a fierceness in their voices she'd hoped to hear.

"Okay all, you heard the captain, let's do this." Deven nodded and went back to his prep.

Claisa quickly moved all but herself, a pilot, and a gunner off to the *Aoenyth*. Those three would take one of the shuttles that Vas and Deven would be bringing over. There would be two-both filled with as many explosive items as could be found but without leaving the *Warrior Wench* defenseless.

"I wish we still had some of the swarm missiles," Walvento said as he helped load up one of the shuttles.

"Agreed. But they might find another way to break down the shielding and get some of Terel's bio-weapons on the ship, that would be almost as good." Vas clasped the large man's shoulder. "I know you'll take them out one way or another."

Walvento nodded.

"Captain, the Asarlaí ship is moving closer to the planet." Gosta called down.

Vas smiled to Walvento and got on a flight suit. "Show time."

Deven came down as Vas started the checks on her shuttle. He already had his suit on but came to her shuttle. "I could do this myself you know."

"You could go to hell too, but I'm not letting either happen." She grabbed him in a fierce kiss. "Things will happen fast once this starts rolling—in case I forget, I love you. We live or die together this time."

"From the moment I saw you; I think I've loved you. I can't think of anyone else I want to spend my last moments with. Let's take these bastards with us." He gave her a quick kiss, and then jogged to his shuttle.

"Gosta, we are ready to take off. Tell Ragkor to not break my fleet."

The *Defiant Ruin* would stay out of communication with the rest of the ships—except for a tight private line to Gosta directly from Vas and Deven's comms. Out of all of their ships, keeping the *Defiant Ruin* hidden until the last moment was the most crucial.

Vas led the two shuttles over to the *Defiant Ruin*, the thing was still ugly as hell, but had a beauty now. It was fitting this ship would be the one to shove oblivion down the Asarlaís' throat. She hoped the clone of her brother recognized it before he died.

They got both shuttles secured in the *Defiant Ruin's* shuttle bay. It didn't take long to move the cart with the extra explosives and the pod out of the first shuttle; they left the explosives in the second. The pod being shot out of the missile bay was a long shot; a shuttle would never make it back out of the explosion. Deven set up the pod outside of the last missile bay—he'd already moved the missiles to the second bay. If all went according to plan, they'd set this ship on its path, get into the pod, and remotely fire themselves out of the vortex.

It sounded even more insane each time Vas thought about it.

"I think we're ready," Deven said and took a final look around the shuttle bay.

Vas nodded and they went to the command deck.

"Are you sure you don't want us to stay?" Clasia said as soon as Vas stepped on the deck, and then shrugged before Vas could respond. "Didn't think so, you're not always the most rational." The taller woman hugged Vas fiercely, nodded to Deven, and then led her people off the command deck.

"I think this entire crew is getting soft," Vas said as she settled into the captain's seat.

"Agreed, but it's not a bad thing." Deven took over weapons. While the shuttle bay was packed with explosives, they needed regular weapons as well. Vas would pilot from the command chair.

"You know, if we survive this, we'll need to have Mac see if he can update more of our ships to run with just two people—never know when that could come in handy." Vas ran through all commands at her station, everything worked perfectly. There was a side to Mac she'd missed before.

"Agreed. Damn it!"

Vas looked on the main screen at Deven's yell. Three ships were coming in from the gate. Asarlaí ships.

CHAPTER FORTY-NINE

————•————

"GOSTA?" VAS HIT HER COMM, but there was no way her ships could have missed them. "We are out of time." Not only were her ships now trapped between an exploding planet and three heavy cruisers, but also the time of the Asarlaí force not knowing she and her crew were out here was over.

"Aye, Captain."

The three cruisers were moving forward to engage the other ships, but Vas needed the *Warrior Wench* to face the Asarlaí guarding the planet. "Tell the other three ships to hold them off; Terel needs to engage her bio-weapons now."

The Asarlaí had to be pushed into triggering their explosion before the new ships could take out either the *Warrior Wench* or the *Defiant Ruin.*

"I don't know if it can get through the shields."

"We don't have a choice." Vas swore as the *Aoenyth* maneuvered to face two of the cruisers, and Zarith's ship followed suit. Three against three might work if all three were the size of the *Aoenyth,* but she had little hope her three ships could keep the cruisers at bay for long. "I have an idea, move forward, fire everything you have at their shields, and then send the bio-missiles. But stay clear of us. We're going to play dead."

Vas turned her conversation internal. "*Is there a way you can block Deven and my life signs?*" Aithnea had been masking them from telepaths on the first Asarlaí ship—but with the new arrivals, that was pointless. However if she cut power, played dead as she had before with the shuttle, it might get the ships to leave them alone.

Until it was hopefully too late for the Asarlaí.

"*I can try.*"

Vas shut down most of the power. It said so much that Deven didn't even ask what she was doing, but followed suit. In seconds, the *Defiant Ruin* was drifting in space like an abandoned derelict. A few sensors, basic life-support, and minimal communication with the *Warrior Wench* were all that stayed on.

The *Warrior Wench* moved away and closed in on the first Asarlaí ship. Walvento was firing everything he had, but their shields were holding. The *Victorious Dead* cut in and started firing as well. Vas wasn't happy about him leaving the other two ships, but she saw the shields flicker.

"There." She pointed to an area near the Asarlaí ship's engines. The shield flickered again and one of the missiles got in a partial hit. "Gosta, fire Terel's bio-weapons where that last missile hit."

The first one bounced off the shielding, but the second one exploded the side of the ship. The damage from the missile itself wasn't enough to bring the ship down, but the bio-weapons it carried should do a good job of that.

"It's almost our time," Deven said. His hands hovered on the controls, ready to punch everything back to life the moment she gave the command.

They needed the first Asarlaí ship to trigger the implosion. The sequence was at its end, but they needed to set off the trigger on the planet for the final step.

Even though Vas knew what to expect, seeing the red lines racing around the planet before them was startling.

"Do we know how long it will take?" She knew that even though the Asarlaí ship was battling internal attacks from the bio-weapons, and starting to drift lower to the planet, they'd still track the *Defiant Ruin* as soon as she came back to life. They needed to wait until the full process had started and ships began coming through.

"Not long at all." Deven kept his eyes on the main screen.

The planet below them started to explode, and then pulled back on itself. But the first explosion was enough to engulf the Asarlaí ship hovering near it.

Part of Vas was upset that she hadn't killed her brother's clone—but most of her was just glad he was dead.

The imploding planet transformed into a giant vortex, one large enough for five of the *Aoenyth* to travel side by side. "I hope we have enough explosives to stop that." Vas said as she hit the controls. The *Defiant Ruin* flared back to life.

"I'm picking up ships in that vortex, it's now or never." Deven brought his side of the controls to life as well.

"I'm not sure what you've got planned, sister, but I'm not going to let you do it." Borlan's voice came from behind them.

Borlan stood there. Not a hologram and not looking good. But he was there and had blasters aimed at Vas and Deven.

"You could have shot us before we knew you were on board," Vas slowly rose out of her chair. "You wanted to face me." She took a step forward. "I have no idea how you got on board, but you're not looking well."

He coughed and blood trailed from his mouth. "I should have killed you when you were born. But you're right; I do want to face you. Him not so much." He fired at Deven and Vas jumped him.

She couldn't take the chance to look back and see if Deven had been hit, she'd knocked the blasters out of Borlan's hands, but he'd managed to disarm her as well.

They tumbled to the floor, both trying to choke the other. Vas glanced at the main screen. They were still charging the vortex.

"You should have stayed dead when Flarik killed you the first time." She turned so he couldn't see the screen and started bashing his head against the floor. Her adrenalin was too high, so it was only when he pulled the knife out of her gut that she realized she'd been stabbed.

Pain was hitting as she grabbed his neck and twisted. The snap was almost as satisfying as the sound of weapons fire as they entered the vortex.

Vas was losing a lot of blood as Deven came to her side. But so was he. Borlan had gotten in a chest shot, but missed Deven's heart.

"We have to get to the pod." Deven pulled her up.

"I think this is it." Vas hugged him but more to pull him close than get up. The explosions around them were intense—no pod was getting through that.

"No." Deven grabbed her and forced her to look at him. "You are not giving up. I will make you crawl if I have to but we are getting to that pod."

The intensity in his eyes gave Vas hope. If anyone could survive this, it would be the man who came back from the dead. If she could get him to go in the pod, at least one of them would survive.

"*He is right, you are too melancholy. Move it.*" Aithnea's voice wasn't as welcome as Vas would have liked. But it did reinforce her moving it.

Together, both leaning on each other, they made their way to the pod. Deven pushed Vas in, and she pulled him in after her. "Don't trust you." She murmured in his ear. The pod wasn't designed for two people, but Vas was starting to lose consciousness.

"*Don't let go,*" Deven said in her head. Then everything went black.

<hr />

"If you two ever pull something like that again, I will personally kill you both," Terel's voice broke through the echoing silence in Vas's head.

Vas slowly opened one eye. Even that hurt. Her entire

body was one giant wall of pain. But she was alive. "Deven?" Her voice was little more than a croak, but Terel had been berating her from very close by.

"He's in the same state as you." Terel's eyes were red. "Stop trying to die, damn it!"

"Did we win?" Vas was fighting to keep her eye open, but sleep was calling.

"*You won. The Defiant Ruin reversed the vortex, the Asarlaí got their ships thrown back at them, and the Asarlaí on this side are being hunted down. You and Deven almost died and have been in medical comas for three months. Now rest, or the good doctor will dose you some more.*"

Vas let her eye close. They'd lost many people and ships.

But they'd won.

EPILOGUE

SIX MONTHS LATER, VAS WAS relaxing. Enjoying the sun as it beat down on her back.

"They're fading, you know," Deven's voice cut into her doze.

She rolled over and accepted a nice frothy drink from him. Sunbathing and frothy drinks weren't normal for her, but she might get used to them. "What's fading?"

"Your scars, soon you won't see them." Deven smiled and took his chair in the sand.

It seemed so long ago that she'd said those words to him. Both of their scars were fading. As she found out, Borlan had managed to stab her clean through. Terel was going to do a medical symposium on the techniques she'd used to save Vas's life.

"That's a good thing." She sat up and took a long sip. They'd spent the past three months—once Terel released them—testing out all of the beaches on Home. So far this was her favorite.

"I think we should build a nice house here."

"Captain? It's the Commonwealth again." Xsit cutting in through the comm lying next to Deven's chair was not what Vas wanted to hear.

Deven tossed her the comm. "You can't keep avoiding them."

"Yes, yes I can." Vas hit the comm. "Xsit, tell them I'm still incommunicado. Injured in the line of saving their asses and all of that." The Commonwealth had recovered with surprising swiftness—well, the politicians had. They'd decided that having the great Captain Tor Dain lead the flagship for the Commonwealth military was a good idea. Vas strongly disagreed.

Xsit sighed. "Aye, Captain." She and the rest of her crew were running interference on this one since Vas wasn't up to the full attack response that she was going to have to give. Not yet.

Vas leaned forward to kiss Deven when the comm buzzed again. "Captain? Sorry to bother you." Gosta this time.

"Gosta, I'm just not up to dealing with politicians, yet. Asarlaí were easier to deal with than them."

"It's not the Commonwealth this time. It's an unidentified source—they are looking for someone called the Pirate of Boagada? And they have enough tech to bust through every electronic shield we have."

———◆———

The Asarlaí wars have ended.
But come back in 2020 for a new Vaslisha Tor Dain adventure!

Dear Reader,

Thank you for joining Vaslisha and her crew on the final Asarlaí adventure. It was difficult seeing this trilogy come to a close, but Vas and her folks did what needed to be done. After some R&R, the entire crew will return in 2020 for a brand new set of adventures—join us!

I really appreciate each and every one of you so please keep in touch. You can find me at *www.marieandreas.com*.

And please feel free to email me directly at *Marie@marie-andreas.com* as well, I love to hear from readers!

If you enjoyed this book—or any book for that matter—please spread the word! Positive reviews on Amazon, Goodreads, and blogs are like emotional gold to any writer and mean more than you know.

ABOUT THE AUTHOR

Marie is a fantasy and science fiction reader with a serious writing addiction. If she wasn't writing about all of the people in her head, she'd be lurking about coffee shops annoying innocent passer-by with her stories. So really, writing is a way of saving the masses. She lives in Southern California and is currently owned by two very faery-minded cats. And yes, sometimes they race.

When not saving the general populace from coffee shop shenanigans, Marie likes to visit the UK and keeps hoping someone will give her a nice summer home in the Forest of Dean.

——◆——

www.marieandreas.com.

www.ingramcontent.com/pod-product-compliance
Lightning Source LLC
Chambersburg PA
CBHW030647120726
47905CB00001B/104